THE WORLD'S #1 STORYTELLER

The first of Arthur Hailey's international best sellers bears the hallmark of his fascinating storytelling: the human conflict seething behind the facade of a great institution. The young, ambitious Dr. Kent O'Donnell fights for the latest medical breakthroughs resisted by the older, entrenched power block of doctors led by Dr. Joe Pearson, Head of Pathology, who must make the final diagnosis on every patient—and eventually on himself.

At stake are the lives of a pretty student nurse facing the agony of cancer; of an unborn baby desperately wanted by a couple who had already lost their first child; and of an entire hospital staff who risk exposure to virulent disease unless the carrier can be found in time.

At stake, too, are the hearts of two women, one a successful physician feeling the ecstasy of passion for the first time; the other, a rich, sensual divorcée determined to find the perfect husband . . . and both in love with the same man in Arthur Hailey's powerful and moving medical drama.

THE FINAL DIAGNOSIS

"A FAST-PACED, POLISHED NOVEL THAT READS EASILY, ENTERTAINS AND INFORMS."
—*Chicago Sunday Tribune*

NOVELS BY ARTHUR HAILEY

STRONG MEDICINE OVERLOAD
THE MONEYCHANGERS
WHEELS
AIRPORT
HOTEL
IN HIGH PLACES
THE FINAL DIAGNOSIS
RUNWAY ZERO EIGHT
(*with John Castle*)

Collected Plays

CLOSE-UP ON WRITING FOR TELEVISION

THE
FINAL
DIAGNOSIS
·
ARTHUR
HAILEY

A DELL BOOK

Published by
Dell Publishing Co., Inc.
1 Dag Hammarskjold Plaza
New York, New York 10017

Dell ® TM 681510, Dell Publishing Co., Inc.

ISBN: 0-440-12508-1

Reprinted by arrangement with Doubleday & Company, Inc.
Printed in the United States of America
First Dell printing— January 1986

One

At midmorning of a broiling summer day the life of Three Counties Hospital ebbed and flowed like tide currents around an offshore island. Outside the hospital the citizens of Burlington, Pennsylvania, perspired under a ninety-degree shade temperature with 78 per cent humidity. Down by the steel mills and the rail yards, where there was little shade and no thermometers, the reading—if anyone had bothered to take it—would have been a good deal higher. Within the hospital it was cooler than outside, but not much. Among patients and staff only the fortunate or influential escaped the worst of the heat in air-conditioned rooms.

There was no air conditioning in the admitting department on the main floor, and Madge Reynolds, reaching into her desk for her fifteenth Kleenex that morning, dabbed her face and decided it was time she slipped out to make another application of deodorant. Miss Reynolds, at thirty-eight, was chief clerk in Admitting and also an assiduous reader of feminine-hygiene advertising. As a result she had acquired a horror of being less than completely sanitary and in hot weather maintained a shuttle service between her desk and the women's toilet down the corridor. First, though, she decided, she must locate four patients for admission that afternoon.

A few minutes earlier the day's discharge slips had come down from the wards, showing that twenty-six patients were being sent home instead of the twenty-four Miss Reynolds had expected. That, added to two deaths which had occurred during the night, meant that four new names could be plucked from the hospital's long waiting list for immediate admission. Somewhere, in four homes in and around Burlington, a quartet of patients who had been waiting for this call either hopefully or in fear would now pack a few essential belongings and put their trust in medicine as practiced at

1

Three Counties. Holding now her sixteenth Kleenex, Miss Reynolds opened a file folder, picked up the telephone on her desk, and began to dial.

More fortunate than the Admitting clerks in the heat were those awaiting treatment in the outpatient clinics, now in full session over in the opposite wing of the main floor. They at least would enjoy air conditioning when their turn came to enter one of the six offices leading off the general waiting room. Within the offices six specialists were making their exclusive talents available free to those who couldn't, or wouldn't, afford the private-patient fees charged on the specialists' home ground in the Medical Arts Building downtown.

Old Rudy Hermant, who worked periodically at laboring when his family bullied him into it, sat back and relaxed in cool comfort as Dr. McEwan, the ear, nose, and throat specialist, probed in search of the cause of Rudy's growing deafness. Actually Rudy didn't mind the deafness too much; at times, when foremen wanted him to do something else or work faster, he found it an advantage. But Rudy's eldest son had decided the old man should get his ears looked at, and here he was.

Dr. McEwan fretted irritably as he withdrew the otoscope from old Rudy's ear. "It might help a little if you washed some of the dirt out," he remarked acidly.

Such ill humor was unusual in McEwan. This morning, however, his wife had carried to the breakfast table a running fight about household expenses which they had started the night before, causing him, afterward, to back his new Olds out of the garage in such a temper that he had crumpled the right rear fender.

Now Rudy looked up blandly. "What was that?" he inquired.

"I said it might help . . . oh, never mind." McEwan was debating whether the old man's condition might be due to senility or a small tumor. It was an intriguing case, and already his professional interest was outweighing his irritability.

"I didn't hear you," the old man was saying again.

McEwan raised his voice. "It was nothing! I said forget it!" At this moment he was glad of old Rudy's deafness and slightly ashamed of his own outburst.

In the general medical clinic fat Dr. Toynbee, an internist, lighting a fresh cigarette from the stub of the last, looked over at the patient on the other side of his desk. As he considered the case he felt a slight biliousness and decided he'd have to lay off Chinese food for a week or two; anyway, with two dinner parties coming off this week, and the Gourmet's Club next Tuesday, it shouldn't be too hard to endure. Deciding his diagnosis, he fixed his eye on the patient and said sternly, "You're overweight and I'm going to put you on a diet. You'd better cut out smoking too."

A hundred yards or so from where the specialists held court Miss Mildred, senior records clerk at Three Counties, perspired profusely as she hurried along a busy main-floor corridor. But, ignoring the discomfort, she moved even faster after a quarry she had just seen disappear around the next corner.

"Dr. Pearson! Dr. Pearson!"

As she caught up with him the hospital's elderly staff pathologist paused. He moved the big cigar he was smoking over to the corner of his mouth. Then he said irritably, "What is it? What is it?"

Little Miss Mildred, fifty-two, spinsterish, and five foot nothing in her highest heels, quailed before Dr. Pearson's scowl. But records, forms, files were her life. She summoned up courage. "These autopsy protocols have to be signed, Dr. Pearson. The Health Board has asked for extra copies."

"Some other time. I'm in a hurry." Joe Pearson was at his imperious worst.

Miss Mildred stood her ground. "Please, Doctor. It'll only take a moment. I've been trying to get you for three days."

Grudgingly Pearson gave in. Taking the forms and the ball-point pen Miss Mildred offered him, he moved over to a desk, grumbling as he scribbled signatures. "I don't know what I'm signing. What is it?"

"It's the Howden case, Dr. Pearson."

Pearson was fretting still. "There are so many cases. I don't remember."

Patiently Miss Mildred reminded him. "It's the workman who was killed when he fell from a high catwalk. If you remember, the employers said the fall must have been caused by a heart attack because otherwise their safety precautions would have prevented it."

Pearson grunted. "Yeah."

As he went on signing Miss Mildred continued her summation. When she started something she liked to finish it and leave it tidy. "The autopsy, however, showed that the man had a healthy heart and no other physical condition which might have caused him to fall."

"I know all that." Pearson cut her short.

"I'm sorry, Doctor. I thought . . ."

"It was an accident. They'll have to give the widow a pension." Pearson tossed out the observation, then adjusted his cigar and scrawled another signature, half shredding the paper. He has rather more egg than usual on his tie, Miss Mildred thought, and she wondered how many days it was since the pathologist had brushed his gray, unruly hair. Joe Pearson's personal appearance verged somewhere between a joke and a scandal at Three Counties Hospital. Since his wife had died some ten years earlier and he had begun to live alone, his dress had got progressively worse. Now, at sixty-six, his appearance sometimes suggested a vagrant rather than the head of a major hospital department. Under the white lab coat Miss Mildred could see a knitted woolen vest with frayed buttonholes and two other holes which were probably acid burns. And gray, uncreased slacks drooped over scuffed shoes that sadly needed shining.

Joe Pearson signed the last paper and thrust the batch, almost savagely, at little Miss Mildred. "Maybe I can get on with some real work now, eh?" His cigar bobbed up and down, discharging ash partly on himself, partly on the polished linoleum floor. Pearson had been at Three Counties long enough to get away with rudeness that would never be tolerated in a younger man and also to ignore the "No Smoking" signs posted conspicuously at intervals in the hospital corridors.

"Thank you, Doctor. Thank you very much."

He nodded curtly, then made for the main lobby, intending to take an elevator to the basement. But both elevators were on floors above. With an exclamation of annoyance he ducked down the stairway which led to his own department.

On the surgical floor three stories above the atmosphere was more relaxed. With temperature and humidity carefully controlled throughout the whole operating section, staff surgeons, interns, and nurses, stripped down to their underwear beneath green scrub suits, could work in comfort. Some of the surgeons had completed their first cases of the morning and were drifting into the staff room for coffee before going on to subsequent ones. From the operating rooms which lined the corridor, aseptically sealed off from the rest of the hospital, nurses were beginning to wheel patients still under anesthesia into one of the two recovery rooms. There the patients would remain under observation until well enough to go back to their assigned hospital beds.

Between sips of scalding coffee Lucy Grainger, an orthopedic surgeon, was defending the purchase of a Volkswagen she had made the day before.

"I'm sorry, Lucy," Dr. Bartlett was saying. "I'm afraid I may have stepped on it in the parking lot."

"Never mind, Gil," she told him. "You need the exercise you get just walking around that Detroit monster of yours."

Gil Bartlett, one of the hospital's general surgeons, was noted for possession of a cream Cadillac which was seldom seen other than in gleaming spotlessness. It reflected, in fact, the dapperness of its owner, invariably one of the best dressed among the Three Counties attending physicians. Bartlett was also the only member of staff to sport a beard —a Van Dyke, always neatly trimmed—which bobbed up and down when he talked, a process Lucy found fascinating to watch.

Kent O'Donnell strolled over to join them. O'Donnell was chief of surgery and also president of the hospital's medical board. Bartlett hailed him.

"Kent, I've been looking for you. I'm lecturing the nurses next week on adult tonsillectomies. Do you have some Kodachromes showing aspiration tracheitis and pneumonia?"

O'Donnell ran his mind over some of the color photographs in his teaching collection. He knew what Bartlett was referring to—it was one of the lesser known effects which sometimes followed removal of tonsils from an adult. Like most surgeons, O'Donnell was aware that even with extreme operative care a tiny portion of tonsil sometimes escaped the surgeon's forceps and was drawn into the lung where it formed an abscess. Now he recalled a group of pictures he had of the trachea and lung, portraying this condition; they had been taken during an autopsy. He told Bartlett, "I think so. I'll look them out tonight."

Lucy Grainger said, "If you don't have one of the trachea, give him the rectum. He'll never know the difference." A laugh ran round the surgeons' room.

O'Donnell smiled too. He and Lucy were old friends; in fact, he sometimes wondered if, given more time and opportunity, they might not become something more. He liked her for many things, not least the way she could hold her own in what was sometimes thought of as a man's world. At the same time, though, she never lost her essential femininity. The scrub suit she was wearing now made her shapeless, almost anonymous, like the rest of them. But he knew that beneath was a trim, slim figure, usually dressed conservatively but in fashion.

His thoughts were interrupted by a nurse who had knocked, then entered discreetly.

"Dr. O'Donnell, your patient's family are outside."

"Tell them I'll be right out." He moved into the locker room and began to slip out of his scrub suit. With only one operation scheduled for the day he was through with surgery now. When he had reassured the family outside—he had just operated successfully for removal of gallstones—his next call would be in the administrator's office.

One floor above surgical, in private patient's room 48, George Andrew Dunton had lost the capacity to be affected by heat or coolness and was fifteen seconds away from death. As Dr. MacMahon held his patient's wrist, waiting for the pulse to stop, Nurse Penfield turned the window fan to "high" because the presence of the family had made the room uncomfortably stuffy. This was a good family, she reflected—the wife, grown son, and younger daughter. The wife was crying softly, the daughter silent but with tears coursing down her cheeks. The son had turned away but his shoulders were shaking. When I die, Elaine Penfield thought, I hope someone has tears for me; it's the best obituary there is.

Now Dr. MacMahon lowered the wrist and looked across at the others. No words were needed, and methodically Nurse Penfield noted the time of death as 10:52 A.M.

Along the corridor in the other wards and private patients' rooms this was one of the quieter times of day. Morning medications had been given; rounds were over, and there was a lull until lunch time would bring the cycle of activity to a peak once more. Some of the nurses had slipped down to the cafeteria for coffee; others who remained were writing their case notes. "Complains of continued abdominal pains," Nurse Wilding had written on a woman patient's chart and was about to add another line when she paused.

For the second time that morning Wilding, gray-haired and at fifty-six one of the older nurses on staff, reached into her uniform and took out the letter she had read twice already since it had been delivered to her desk along with the patients' mail. A snapshot of a young naval lieutenant, j.g., with a pretty girl on his arm, fell out as she opened it, and for a moment she gazed down at the picture before reading the letter again. "Dear Mother," it started. "This will come as a surprise to you, but I have met a girl here in San Francisco and we were married yesterday. I know in some ways this will be a big disappointment since you always said you wanted to be at my wedding, but I'm sure you'll understand when I tell you . . ."

Nurse Wilding let her eyes wander from the letter and thought of the boy she remembered and of whom she had seen so little. After the divorce she had taken care of Adam until college; then there had been Annapolis, a few weekends and brief holidays, after that the Navy, and now he was a man, belonging to someone else. Later on today she must send them a telegram of love and good wishes. Years ago she had always said that as soon as Adam was on his own and self-supporting she would quit nursing, but she never had, and now retirement would come soon enough without hastening it. She put the letter and photograph back in her uniform pocket and reached for the pen she had laid down. Then in careful script she added to the chart: "Slight vomiting with diarrhea. Dr. Reubens notified."

In Obstetrics, on the fourth floor, there was never any time of day which could be predictably quiet. Babies, Dr. Charles Dornberger thought, as he scrubbed alongside two other obstetricians, had an annoying habit of coming in batches. There would be hours, even days, when things would be orderly, quiet, and babies could be delivered in tidy succession. Then suddenly all hell would break loose, with half a dozen waiting to be born at once. This was one of those moments.

His own patient, a buxom, perpetually cheerful Negress, was about to deliver her tenth child. Because she had arrived at the hospital late, and already advanced in labor, she had been brought up on a stretcher from Emergency. While he was still scrubbing Dornberger could hear part of her duologue outside with the intern who had escorted her to Obstetrics.

Apparently, as was normal for an urgent case, the intern had cleared the passenger elevator down below on the main floor.

"All them nice peopl' movin' out of th' elevator fo' me," she was saying. "Why, ah nevah felt so important befo' in all mah life." At this point Dornberger heard the intern tell the patient to relax and the answer came back, "Relax, sonny? Ah am relaxed. Ah always relaxes when ah has a baby. That th' only time there's no dishes, no washin', no cookin'. Why, ah look forward to comin' in here. This just a holiday fo' me." She paused as pain gripped her. Then, partly through clenched teeth, she muttered, "Nine children ah've got, and this'll be the tenth. Th' oldest one's as big as you, sonny. Now you be lookin' fo' me a year from now. Ah tell you, ah'll be back." Dornberger heard her chuckling as her voice faded, the delivery room nurses taking over, while the intern went back to his post in Emergency.

Now Dornberger, scrubbed, gowned, sterile, and sweating from the heat, followed his patient into the delivery room.

In the hospital kitchens, where the heat was less of a problem because people who worked there were used to it, Hilda Straughan, the chief dietitian, nibbled a piece of raisin pie and nodded approvingly at the senior pastry cook. She suspected that the calories, along with others, would be reflected on her bathroom scales a week from now but quelled her conscience by telling herself it was a dietitian's duty to sample as much as possible of the hospital fare. Besides, it was somewhat late now for Mrs. Straughan to be fretting on the subject of calories and weight. The accumulated result of many earlier samplings caused her nowadays to turn the scales around two hundred pounds, a good deal of which was in her magnificent breasts—twin Gibraltars, famed through the hospital, and which made her progress not unlike the majesty of an aircraft carrier preceded by an escort of twin battleships.

But, as well as food, Mrs. Straughan was in love with her job. Glancing around her with satisfaction, she took in her empire—the shining steel ovens and serving tables, the gleaming utensils, the sparkling white aprons of the cooks and their assistants. Her heart warmed at the sight of all of it.

This was a busy time in the kitchens—lunch was the heaviest meal of the day because, as well as patients, there was the full hospital staff to be fed in the cafeteria. In twenty minutes or so the diet trays would be going up to the wards, and for two hours afterward the service of food would continue. Then, while the kitchen help cleared and stacked dishes, the cooks would begin preparing the evening meal.

The thought of dishes caused Mrs. Straughan to frown thoughtfully, and she propelled herself into the back section of the kitchen where the two big automatic dishwashers were installed. This was a part of her domain less gleaming and modern than the other section, and the chief dietitian reflected, not for the first time, that she would be happy when the equipment here was modernized, as the rest of the kitchens had been. It was understandable, though, that everything could not be done at once, and she had to admit she had browbeaten the administration into a lot of expensive new equipment in the two years she had held her job at Three Counties. All the same, she decided as she moved on to check the steam tables in the cafeteria, she would have another talk with the administrator about those dishwashers soon.

The chief dietitian was not the only one in the hospital whose thoughts were on food. In Radiology, on the second floor, an outpatient—Mr. James Bladwick, vice-president of sales for one of Burlington's big-three automobile dealerships—was, in his own words, "as hungry as hell."

There was reason for this. On his physician's instructions Jim Bladwick had fasted since midnight, and now he was in number one X-ray room, ready for a gastric series. The X-rays would confirm or deny the suspicion that flourishing in the Bladwick interior was a duodenal ulcer. Jim Bladwick hoped the suspicion was unfounded; in fact, he hoped desperately that neither an ulcer nor anything else would conspire to slow him down now that his drive and sacrifice of the past three years, his willingness to work harder and longer than anyone else on sales staff, were at last paying off.

Sure he worried; who wouldn't when they had a dealer sales quota to meet every month. But it just *couldn't* be an ulcer; it had to be something else—something trivial that could be fixed up quickly. He had been vice-president of sales only a matter of six weeks, but despite the high-sounding title he knew better than anyone that retention of it depended on a continued ability to produce. And to produce you had to be on the ball—tough, available, fit. No medical certificate would compensate for a declining sales graph.

Jim Bladwick had put this moment off for some time. It was probably two months ago that he had become aware of distress and a general aching in the stomach region, had noticed, too, he was burping a lot, sometimes at awkward moments with customers around. For a while he had tried to pretend it was nothing out of the ordinary, but finally he had sought medical advice, and this morning's session was the outcome. He hoped, though, it was not going to take too long; that deal of Fowler's for six panel trucks was getting hot, and they needed the sale badly. By God, he was hungry!

For Dr. Ralph Bell, the senior radiologist—"Ding Dong" to most of the hospital staff—this was just another G.I. series, no different from any of a hundred others. But, playing a mental game he sometimes indulged in, he decided to bet "yes" on this one. This patient looked the type for an ulcer. From behind his own thick-lensed, horn-rimmed glasses Bell had been watching the other man covertly. He looked a worrier, Bell decided; he was obviously stewing right now. The radiologist placed Bladwick in position behind the fluoroscope and handed him a tumbler of barium. "When I tell you," he said, "drink this right down."

When he was ready he ordered, "Now!" Bladwick drained the glass.

In the fluoroscope Bell watched the path of the barium as it coursed first through the esophagus, then into the stomach, and from there into the duodenum. Sharpened by the opaque liquid, the outline of each organ was clearly visible, and at various stages Bell thumbed a button recording the results on film. Now he palpated the patient's abdomen to move the barium around. Then he could see it—a crater in the duodenum. An ulcer, clear and unmistakable. He reflected that he had won the bet with himself. Aloud he said, "That's all, Mr. Bladwick, thank you."

"Well, Doc, what's the verdict? Am I going to live?"

"You'll live." Most of them wanted to know what he saw in the fluoroscope. *Magic mirror on the wall, who is healthiest of all?* It wasn't his job to tell though. "Your own physician will get these films tomorrow. I imagine he'll be talking to you." Hard luck, my friend, he thought. I hope you like lots of rest and a diet of milk and poached eggs.

Two hundred yards away from the main hospital block, in a run-down building that had once been a furniture factory and now did duty as a nurses' home, Student Nurse Vivian Loburton was having trouble with a zipper that refused to zip.

"Damn and hellfire!" She addressed the zipper with an expression much favored by her father, who had made a comfortable fortune felling tall trees and saw no reason to have one language for the woods and another at home.

Vivian, at nineteen, sometimes provided an interesting contrast between her father's robustness and her mother's innate New England delicacy which close contact with Oregon lumbering had never changed. Now, in her fourth month of training as a nurse, Vivian had already found something of the traits of both parents in her own reaction to the hospital and nursing. At one and the same time she was awed and fascinated, repulsed and disgusted. She supposed that close contact with sickness and disease was always a shock for anyone new. But knowing that did not help much when your stomach was ready to do flip-flops and it took all the will you possessed not to turn and run away.

It was after moments like this that she felt the need for a change of scene, a cleansing antidote; and to some extent she had found it in an old love—music. Surprisingly, for a city of its size, Burlington had an excellent symphony, and, discovering this, Vivian had become one of its supporters. She found the switch in tempo, the balm of good music, helped to steady and reassure her. She had been sorry when concerts had ended for the summer, and there had been moments recently when she had felt the need of something to replace them.

There was no time now, though, for odd, stray thoughts; the gap between morning classes and reporting to a ward for duty had been short enough. Now this zipper! . . . She tugged again, and suddenly the teeth meshed, the zipper closed. Relieved, she ran for the door, then paused to mop her face. Jeepers, it was hot! And all that effort had made her sweat like crazy.

So it went—that morning as all mornings—through the hospital. In the clinics, the nurseries, laboratories, operating rooms; in Neurology, Psychiatry, Pediatrics, Dermatology; in Orthopedics, Ophthalmology, Gynecology, Urology; in the charity wards and the private patients' pavilion; in the service departments—administration, accounting, purchasing, housekeeping; in the waiting rooms, corridors, halls, elevators; throughout the five floors, basement, and sub-basement of Three Counties Hospital the tides and currents of humanity and medicine ebbed and flowed.

It was eleven o'clock on the fifteenth of July.

Two

Two blocks from Three Counties Hospital the clock-tower bell of the Church of the Redeemer was chiming the hour as Kent O'Donnell made his way from the surgical floor down to Administration. The sound of the bell, off-key as always from a flaw in its long-ago casting, drifted in through an open stairway window. Automatically O'Donnell checked his wrist watch, then moved aside as a group of interns passed him hurriedly on the staff stairway, their feet sounding noisily on the metal treads. The interns quietened a little when they saw the medical-board president and offered a respectful "Good morning, Doctor," as each went by. On the second floor O'Donnell halted to let a nurse with a wheel chair pass. In it was a girl of about ten with a bandage over one eye, a woman, plainly the mother, hovering protectively alongside.

The nurse, whom he smiled at but failed to recognize, appraised him covertly. In his early forties, O'Donnell still rated second glances from women. He had retained the build which had made him an outstanding quarterback in his college years—a tall, erect figure with big, broad shoulders and muscular arms. Even nowadays he had a trick of squaring his shoulders when ready to do something difficult or make a decision—as if readying instinctively to stop the charge of a red-dogging tackle. Yet despite his bulk—mostly bone and muscle with less than a pound of overweight—he still moved lightly; and regular sport—tennis in summer, skiing in winter—had kept him robust and lithe.

O'Donnell had never been handsome in the Adonic sense, but he had a rugged, creased irregularity of face (his nose still carried the scar of an old football injury) which women so often, and perversely, find attractive in men. Only his hair showed the real trace of years; not so long ago jet black, now it was graying swiftly as if the color pigments had suddenly surrendered and were marching out.

Now, from behind, O'Donnell heard his name called. He stopped and saw the caller was Bill Rufus, one of the seniors on surgical staff.

"How are you, Bill?" O'Donnell liked Rufus. He was conscientious, dependable, a good surgeon with a busy practice. His patients trusted him because of a forthright integrity which came through when he talked. He was respected by the house staff—interns and residents—who found Dr. Rufus to have a painless, pleasant way of imparting sound instruction while treating them as equals—a condition not always prevailing with other surgeons.

His only peculiarity, if you could call it that, was a habit of wearing impossibly gaudy neckties. O'Donnell shuddered inwardly as he noticed the creation his colleague was sporting today—turquoise circles and vermilion zigzags on a background of mauve and lemon yellow. Bill Rufus took a good deal of ribbing about his ties. One of the psychiatrists on staff had suggested recently that they represented "a pus crater from an inner seething below a conservative surface." But Rufus had merely laughed good-naturedly. Today, though, he seemed troubled.

"Kent, I want to talk to you," Rufus said.

"Shall we go to my office?" O'Donnell was curious now. Rufus was not the type to come to him unless it were something important.

"No; here's as good as anywhere. Look, Kent, it's about surgical reports from Pathology."

They moved over to a window to avoid the traffic in the corridor, and O'Donnell thought: I was afraid of this. To Rufus he said, "What's on your mind, Bill?"

"The reports are taking too long. Much too long."

O'Donnell was well aware of the problem. Like other surgeons, Rufus would frequently operate on a patient with a tumor. When the tumor was exposed he would remove it for examination by the hospital's pathologist, Dr. Joseph Pearson. The pathologist would then make two studies of the tissue. First, working in a small lab adjoining the operating room, and with the patient still under anesthetic, he would freeze a small portion of tissue and examine it under a microscope. From this procedure could come one of two verdicts—"malignant," meaning the presence of cancer and indicating the need for major surgery on the patient; or "benign," a reprieve which usually meant that nothing more need be done once the tumor was out. If a frozen section produced a "malignant" verdict, surgery would continue at once. On the other hand, the opinion "benign" from the pathologist was a signal for the surgeon to make his closure and send the patient to the recovery room.

"There's no delay in frozen sections, is there?" O'Donnell had not heard of any, but he wanted to be sure.

"No," Rufus said. "You'd hear plenty of howling if there were. But it's the full tissue report that's taking so long."

"I see." O'Donnell was maneuvering for time while he marshaled his thoughts. His mind ran over procedures. After a frozen section any removed tumor went to the pathology lab where a technician prepared several slides, more carefully and working under better conditions. Later the pathologist would study the slides and give his final opinion. Sometimes a tumor which had seemed benign or doubtful at frozen section would prove malignant during this subsequent, more close examination, and it was not considered abnormal for a pathologist to reverse his opinion in this way. If this happened the patient would be returned to the operating room and the necessary surgery done. But obviously it was important for the pathologist's second report to be prompt. O'Donnell had already realized that this was the nub of Rufus' complaint.

"If it were just once," Rufus was saying, "I wouldn't object. I know Pathology's busy, and I'm not trying to get at Joe Pearson. But it isn't just once, Kent. It's all the time."

"Let's get specific, Bill," O'Donnell said crisply. He had no doubt, though, that Rufus would have facts to back up a complaint like this.

"All right. I had a patient in here last week, Mrs. Mason —breast tumor. I removed the tumor, and at frozen section Joe Pearson said benign. Afterward, though, on surgical report he had it down as malignant." Rufus shrugged. "I won't quarrel with that; you can't call them all the first time."

"But?" Now that he knew what it was about, O'Donnell wanted to get this over with.

"Pearson took eight days to make the surgical report. By the time I got it the patient had been discharged."

"I see." This was bad all right, O'Donnell thought. He couldn't duck this one.

"It isn't easy," Rufus was saying quietly, "to call a woman back and tell her you were wrong—that she does have cancer after all, and that you'll have to operate again."

No, it wasn't easy; O'Donnell knew that too well. Once, before he had come to Three Counties, he had had to do the same thing himself. He hoped he never would again.

"Bill, will you let me handle this my way?" O'Donnell was glad it was Rufus. Some of the other surgeons might have made things more difficult.

"Sure. As long as something definite is done." Rufus was within his rights to be emphatic. "This isn't just an isolated case, you know. It just happens to be a bad one."

Again O'Donnell knew this was true. The trouble was, Rufus was not aware of some of the other problems which went with it.

"I'll talk to Joe Pearson this afternoon," he promised. "After the surgical-mortality conference. You'll be there?"

Rufus nodded. "I'll be there."

"See you then, Bill. Thanks for letting me know about this. Something will be done, I promise you."

Something, O'Donnell reflected as he moved down the corridor. But what exactly? He was still thinking about it as he turned into the Administration suite and opened the door to Harry Tomaselli's office.

O'Donnell did not see Tomaselli at first, then the administrator called to him. "Over here, Kent." On the far side of the birch-paneled room, away from the desk at which he spent most of his working hours, Tomaselli was leaning over a table. Unrolled before him were whiteprints and sketches. O'Donnell crossed the thick pile carpet and looked down at them too.

"Daydreaming, Harry?" He touched one of the sketches.

"You know, I'm sure we could put you a fancy penthouse there—on top of the East Wing."

Tomaselli smiled. "I'm agreeable, providing you'll convince the board it's necessary." He took off his rimless glasses and began to polish them. "Well, there it is—the New Jerusalem."

O'Donnell studied the architect's profile of Three Counties Hospital as it would appear with the magnificent new extension, now in the advanced stages of planning. The new buildings were to comprise an entire wing and a new nurses' home. "Any more news?" He turned to Tomaselli.

The administrator had replaced his glasses. "I talked with Orden again this morning." Orden Brown, president of the second largest steel mill in Burlington, was chairman of the hospital's board of directors.

"So?"

"He's sure we can count on half a million dollars in the building fund by January. That means we'll be able to break ground in March."

"And the other half million? Last week Orden told me he thought it would take until December." Even at that, O'Donnell reflected, he had considered the chairman to be erring toward optimism.

"I know," Tomaselli said. "But he asked me to tell you that he's changed his mind. He had another session with the mayor yesterday. They're convinced they can get the second half million by next summer and wind up the campaign by fall."

"That *is* good news." O'Donnell decided to shelve his earlier doubts. If Orden Brown had gone out on a limb like that, he would come through all right.

"Oh, and by the way," Tomaselli said with elaborate casualness, "Orden and the mayor have an appointment with the governor next Wednesday. Looks like we may get that increased state grant after all."

"Anything else?" O'Donnell snapped at the administrator in mock sharpness.

"I thought you'd be pleased," Tomaselli said.

More than pleased, O'Donnell reflected. In a way you might call all of this the first step toward fulfillment of a vision. It was a vision which had had its beginnings at the time of his own arrival at Three Counties three and a half years ago. Funny how you could get used to a place, O'Donnell thought. If someone had told him at Harvard Medical School, or later when he was chief surgical resident at Columbia Presbyterian, that he would wind up in a backwater hospital like Three Counties, he would have scoffed. Even when he had gone to Bart's in London to round out his surgical experience, he had fully intended to come back and join the staff of one of the big-name hospitals like Johns Hopkins or Massachusetts General. With the background he had he could pretty well have taken his choice. But before there was time to decide Orden Brown had come to meet him in New York and persuaded him to visit Burlington and Three Counties.

What he had seen there had appalled him. The hospital was run down physically, its organization slack, its medical standards—with a few exceptions—low. The chiefs of surgery and medicine had held their posts for years; O'Donnell had sensed that their objective in life was to preserve an amiable status quo. The administrator—key man in the relationship between the hospital's lay board of directors and its medical staff—was a doddering incompetent. The hospital's intern and resident training program had fallen into disrepute. There was no budget for research. Conditions under which nurses lived and worked were almost medieval. Orden Brown had shown him everything, concealed nothing. Then they had gone together to the chairman's home. O'Donnell had agreed to remain for dinner but afterward planned to catch a night flight back to New York. Disgusted, he never wanted to see Burlington or Three Counties Hospital again.

Over dinner in the quiet, tapestried dining room of Orden Brown's home on a hillside high above Burlington he had been told the story. It was not an unfamiliar one. Three Counties Hospital, once progressive, modern, and rated high in the state, had fallen prey to complacency and lassitude. The chairman of the board had been an aging industrialist who most of the time had delegated responsibility to someone else, appearing at the hospital only for the occasional social function. The lack of leadership had permeated downward. Heads of divisions had mostly held their posts for many years and were averse to change. Younger men beneath them had at first fretted, then, becoming frustrated, had moved elsewhere. Finally the hospital's reputation became such that young, highly qualified graduates no longer sought to join the staff. Because of this others with lesser qualifications had been allowed in. This was the situation at the time O'Donnell had come on the scene.

The only change had come with the appointment of Orden Brown himself. Three months earlier the aged chairman had died. A group of influential citizens had persuaded Brown to succeed him. The choice had not been unanimous; a section of the old guard on the hospital board had wanted the chair for a nominee of their own—a long-time board member named Eustace Swayne. But Brown had been chosen by a majority, and now he was trying to persuade other board members to adopt some of his own ideas for modernization of Three Counties.

It was proving an uphill fight. There was an alliance between a conservative element on the board, for whom Eustace Swayne was spokesman, and a group among the senior medical staff. Together they resisted change. Brown was having to tread warily and to be diplomatic.

One of the things he wanted was authority to increase the size of the hospital board and bring in new, more active members. He had planned to recruit some of the younger executives and professional men from Burlington's business community. But so far the board had not been unanimous and temporarily the plan was shelved.

If Orden Brown had wanted, he had explained frankly to O'Donnell, he could have forced a showdown and had his own way. He could, if he wished, have used his influence to ease some of the elderly, inactive members out of office. But this would have been shortsighted, because most were wealthy men and women and the hospital needed the legacies which normally came to it when its patrons died. If defeated now, some of the people concerned might well change their wills, cutting the hospital off. Eustace Swayne, who controlled a department-store empire, had already hinted that this might happen. Hence the need by Orden Brown for diplomacy and caution.

Some progress had been made, though, and one step which the chairman had undertaken with approval from a majority of the board members was to negotiate for a new chief of surgery. That was why he had approached O'Donnell.

Over dinner O'Donnell had shaken his head. "I'm afraid it's not for me."

"Perhaps not," Brown had said. "But I'd like you to hear me out."

He was persuasive, this man of industry who, though a scion of a wealthy family, had worked his way from puddler, through the mills, to the administrative office and eventually the president's chair. He had a feeling, too, for people; the years in which he had rubbed shoulders daily with laborers in the mill had given him that. This may have been a reason he had accepted the burden of lifting Three Counties out of the mire into which it had fallen. But for whatever reason, even in the short time they had been together O'Donnell had sensed the older man's dedication.

"If you came here," Brown had said to him near the end, "I couldn't promise you a thing. I'd like to say you'd have a free hand, but I think the chances are you'd have to fight for everything you wanted. You'd meet opposition, entrenchment, politics, resentment. There would be areas in which I couldn't help you and in which you would have to stand alone." Brown had paused, then added quietly, "I suppose the only good thing you could say about this situation—from the point of view of someone like yourself—is that it would be a challenge, in some ways the biggest challenge a man could take on."

That was the last word Orden Brown had said that night about the hospital. Afterward they had talked of other things: Europe, the coming elections, the emergence of Middle East nationalism—Brown was a much-traveled and well-informed man. Later his host had driven O'Donnell to the airport and they had shaken hands at the ramp. "I've enjoyed our meeting," Orden Brown had said, and O'Donnell had returned the compliment, fully meaning it. Then he had boarded the airplane, intending to write off Burlington and to think of his journey there as a learning experience.

On the flight back he had tried to read a magazine—there was an article about championship tennis which interested him. But his mind wouldn't register the words. He kept thinking about Three Counties Hospital, what he had seen there and what was needing to be done. Then suddenly for the first time in many years he began to examine his own approach to medicine. What does it all mean? he had asked himself. What do I want for myself? What kind of achievement am I seeking? What have I got to give? At the end what will I leave behind? He had not married; probably he never would now. There had been love affairs—in bed and out—but nothing of permanence. Where is it leading, he

wondered, this trail from Harvard, Presbyterian, Bart's . . .
to where? Then suddenly he had known the answer, known
that it was Burlington and Three Counties, that the decision
was firm, irrevocable, the direction set. At La Guardia, on
landing, he had sent a wire to Orden Brown. It read simply,
"I accept."

Now, looking down at the plans of what the administrator
had called flippantly "the New Jerusalem," O'Donnell
thought back to the three and a half years which lay behind.
Orden Brown had been right when he had said they would
not be easy. All the obstacles which the board chairman had
predicted had proven to be there. Gradually, though, the
most formidable had been overcome.

After O'Donnell's arrival the former chief of surgery had
slipped quietly out. O'Donnell had rallied some of the surgeons already on staff who were sympathetic to raising the
hospital's standards. Between them they had tightened surgical rules and had formed a strong operating-room committee to enforce them. A tissue committee, almost defunct,
was reactivated—its job, to ensure that mistakes in surgery,
particularly the unnecessary removal of healthy organs, were
not repeated.

The less competent surgeons were gently but firmly urged
to limit themselves to work within their capabilities. A few
of the botchers, the assembly-line appendix removers, the
incompetents, were given the choice of resigning quietly or
being ousted officially. Though to some it meant partial loss
of their livelihood, most chose to leave quietly. Among the
latter was one surgeon who had actually removed a kidney
without ascertaining that the patient had already lost one in
previous surgery. The dreadful mistake had been revealed
at autopsy.

Removal of that surgeon from the hospital's roster had
been easy. Some of the others, though, had proved more
difficult. There had been rows before the County Medical
Committee, and two surgeons, formerly on Three Counties'
staff, now had law suits pending against the hospital. This,
O'Donnell knew, was going to mean some bitter controversy
in court, and he dreaded the publicity which was certain to
surround it.

But despite these problems O'Donnell and those behind
him had had their way and the gaps in staff were painstakingly filled with new, well-qualified men, some of them

graduates from his own alma mater whom O'Donnell had cajoled and persuaded to set up practice in Burlington.

Meanwhile the Division of Medicine had a new head—Dr. Chandler, who had been on staff under the old regime but had been frequently outspoken against it. Chandler was a specialist in internal medicine, and while he and O'Donnell sometimes disagreed on hospital policy, and O'Donnell found the other man at times pompous, at least Chandler was uncompromising when it came to upholding medical standards.

In O'Donnell's three and a half years administration methods had been changed as well. A few months after his own arrival O'Donnell had told Orden Brown about a young assistant administrator, one of the best he had known in his hospital experience. The chairman had flown off and, two days later, come back with a signed contract. A month after that the old administrator, relieved to get out from under a job which had grown beyond him, had been honorably pensioned and Harry Tomaselli installed in his place. Now the whole administrative side of the hospital reflected Tomaselli's brisk but smooth efficiency.

A year ago O'Donnell had been elected president of the hospital's medical board, which made him the senior practitioner at Three Counties. Since then he, Tomaselli, and Dr. Chandler had successfully broadened the hospital's intern and resident training program, and already applications for enrollment were growing in number.

There was still a long way to go. O'Donnell knew that in some ways they were only at the beginning of a long program which would embrace the three basic tenets of medicine: service, training, research. He himself was forty-two now, would be forty-three in a few months. He doubted if, in the active years remaining to him, he would complete in full what he had set out to do. But the start was good; that much was reassuring, and he knew that his decision on the airplane three and a half years earlier had been right.

There were soft spots, of course, in the present setup. There had to be. Nothing this big was achieved easily or quickly. Some of the seniors on medical staff still fought off changes, and their influence was strong among the older members of the board, some of whom still remained—Eustace Swayne, as obstinate as ever, at their head. Perhaps this was a good thing, O'Donnell reflected, and perhaps there was justice sometimes in the assertion that "young men make too many changes too quickly." But because of this group and its influence there were occasions when planning had to be tempered with prudence. O'Donnell accepted this fact himself but sometimes had difficulty in getting it across to the newer staff members.

It was just this situation which had made him thoughtful after talking with Bill Rufus. The pathology department at Three Counties was still a stronghold of the old regime. Dr. Joseph Pearson, who ran it like a personal possession, had been thirty-two years at the hospital. He knew most of the old board members intimately and was a frequent chess companion of Eustace Swayne. More to the point, Joe Pearson was no incompetent; his record was good. In his earlier days he had been recognized as an active researcher, and he was a past president of the State Pathology Association. The real problem was that the work in Pathology had become too much for one man to keep the reins in his own hands. O'Donnell suspected, too, that some of the pathology department's lab procedures were in need of overhauling. But desirable as changes might be, this one was going to be tough.

There was the drive for funds for the hospital extension to be considered. If there were trouble between O'Donnell and Joe Pearson, how would Pearson's influence with Eustace Swayne affect Orden Brown's plans for raising all the money by fall next year? Swayne's own donation would normally be a big one, and loss of that alone could be serious. But equally serious was Swayne's influence with other people in the town; in some ways the old tycoon possessed the power to make or mar their immediate plans.

With so many things pending O'Donnell had hoped the problem of Pathology could be left for a while. Nevertheless he had to take some action, and soon, about Bill Rufus' complaint.

He turned away from the plans. "Harry," he said to the administrator, "I think we may have to go to war with Joe Pearson."

Three

In contrast with the heat and activity of the floors above, in the white-tiled corridor of the hospital's basement it was quiet and cool. Nor was the quietness disturbed by a small procession—Nurse Penfield, and alongside her a stretcher gliding silently on ball-bearing casters and propelled by a male orderly wearing rubber-soled shoes below his hospital whites.

How many times had she made this journey, Nurse Penfield speculated, glancing down at the shrouded figure on the stretcher. Probably fifty times in the past eleven years. Perhaps more, because it was not something you kept score of—this final journey between the ward and the hospital's morgue, between the territory of the living and the dead.

A tradition, this last walk with a patient who had died, discreetly timed and routed through back corridors of the hospital, then downward in the freight elevator, so that the living should take no darkness or depression from death so close at hand. It was the last service from nurse to her charge, an acknowledgment that, though medicine had failed, it would not dismiss the patient summarily; the motions of care, service, healing, would continue for at least a token time beyond the end.

The white corridor forked two ways here. From a passage to the right came the hum of machinery. Down there were the hospital's mechanical departments—heating plant, hot-water systems, electrical shops, emergency generators. Pointing the other way, a single sign read: "Pathology Department. Morgue."

As Weidman, the male orderly, swung the stretcher left, a janitor—either on work break or stolen time—lowered the Coke he had been drinking and moved aside. He wiped his lips on the back of his hand, then gestured to the shroud. "Didn't make it, eh?" The remark was to Weidman; it was an amiable gambit, a game played many times.

Weidman, too, had done this before. "I guess they pulled his number, Jack."

The janitor nodded, then raised his Coke bottle again and drank deeply.

How short a time, Nurse Penfield thought, between life and the autopsy room. Less than an hour ago the body under the shroud had been George Andrew Dunton, living, age fifty-three, civil engineer. She remembered the details from the case history on the clip board under her arm.

The family had behaved as well after the death as they had before—solid, emotional, but no hysterics. It had made it easier for Dr. MacMahon to ask for permission to autopsy. "Mrs. Dunton," he had said quietly, "I know it's hard for you to talk and think about this now, but there is something I have to ask. It's about permission for an autopsy on your husband."

He had gone on, using the routine words, how the hospital sought to safeguard its medical standards for the good of everyone, how a physician's diagnosis could be checked and medical learning advanced, how this was a precaution for the family and others who would use the hospital in time to come. But none of this could be done without permission . . .·

The son had stopped him and said gently, "We understand. If you make out whatever is necessary, my mother will sign it."

So Nurse Penfield had made out the autopsy form, and here now was George Andrew Dunton, dead, age fifty-three, and ready for the pathologist's knife.

The autopsy-room doors swung open.

George Rinne, the pathology department's Negro *diener* —keeper of the morgue—looked up as the stretcher rolled in. He had been swabbing the autopsy table. Now it shone spotlessly white.

Weidman greeted him with the timeworn jest. "Got a patient for you."

Politely, as if he hadn't heard the line a hundred times before, Rinne bared his teeth in a perfunctory smile. He indicated the white enameled table. "Over here."

Weidman maneuvered the stretcher alongside, and Rinne removed the sheet covering the naked corpse of George Andrew Dunton. He folded it neatly and handed it back to Weidman. Death notwithstanding, the sheet would have to be accounted for back in the ward. Now, with a second draw-sheet under the torso, the two men slid the body onto the table.

George Rinne grunted as he took the weight. This had been a heavy man, a six-footer who had run to fat near the end of his life. As he wheeled the stretcher clear Weidman grinned. "You're getting old, George. Be your turn soon."

Rinne shook his head. "I'll still be here to lift *you* on the table."

The scene ran smoothly. It had had many performances. Perhaps in the distant past the two had made their grim little jokes with an instinct to create some barrier between themselves and the death they lived with daily. But if so this was long forgotten. Now it was a patter to be run through, a formality expected, nothing more. They had grown too used to death to feel uneasiness or fear.

On the far side of the autopsy room was the pathology resident, Dr. McNeil. He had been shrugging into a white coat when Nurse Penfield and her charge came in. Now, glancing through the case history and the other papers she had handed him, he was acutely conscious of Nurse Penfield's nearness and warmth. He sensed the crisp starched uniform, a faint breath of perfume, a slight disarrangement of hair beneath her cap; it would be soft to run his fingers through. He snatched his thoughts back to the papers in hand.

"Well, everything seems to be here."

Should he try for Nurse Penfield or not? It had been six weeks now, and at the age of twenty-seven six weeks was a long time to be celibate. Penfield was more than averagely attractive, probably thirty-two, young enough to be interesting, old enough to have long since shed innocency. She was intelligent, friendly; good figure too. He could see a slip beneath the white uniform; in the heat she probably was not wearing much else. Roger McNeil calculated. He would probably have to take her out a couple of times before she came through. Then that settled it; it couldn't be this month— money was too short. Save it for me, la Penfield. You'll be back; other patients will die and bring you here.

"Thank you, Doctor." She smiled and turned away. It could be arranged; he was positive of that.

He called after her. "Keep 'em coming! We need the practice." Again the timeworn jest, the defensive levity in face of death.

Elaine Penfield followed the attendant out. Her journey
was done, tradition honored, the extra, unasked service
given. She had gone the second mile; now her duty lay with
the sick, the living. She had a feeling, though, that Dr. Mc-
Neil had come close to suggesting something. But there
would be another time.

While George Rinne slipped a wooden headrest under
the neck of the body, arranging the arms at the side, McNeil
began to lay out the instruments they would need for the
autopsy. Knives, rib cutters, forceps, power saw for the skull
. . . all of them clean—Rinne was a conscientious worker—
but not sterile, as they would have to be in the operating
room four floors above. No need here to worry about infection of a patient on the table; only the pathologists need
take precautions for themselves.

George Rinne looked at McNeil inquiringly, and the resident nodded. "Better phone the nursing office, George. Tell
them the student nurses can come down now. And let Dr.
Pearson know we're setting up."

"Yes, Doctor." Rinne went out obediently. McNeil, as
pathology resident, had authority even though his hospital
pay was little more than the janitor's own. It would not be
long, though, before the gap between them would widen.
With three and a half years of residency behind him only
another six months separated McNeil from freedom to take a
post as staff pathologist. Then he could start considering
some of the twenty-thousand-dollar-a-year jobs, because
fortunately the demand for pathologists continued to be
greater than the supply. He would not have to worry then
about whether he could afford a pass at Nurse Penfield—
or others.

Roger McNeil smiled inwardly at the thought, though he
did not betray it on his face. People who had to deal with
McNeil thought he was dour, which he often was, and sometimes lacking in a sense of humor, which he was not. Actually
he did not make friends easily with men; but women found
him attractive, a fact he had discovered early and turned
to advantage. When he was an intern his colleagues had
found this puzzling. McNeil, the gloomy, brooding figure of
the common room, had had uncanny success in whisking a
succession of student nurses into bed, frequently where others who fancied their ability as paramours had failed.

The autopsy-room door swung open and Mike Seddons breezed in. Seddons was a surgical resident, temporarily assigned to Pathology, and he always breezed. His red hair stood up in odd places as though a self-created wind would never leave it static. His boyish, open face seemed creased permanently in an amiable grin. McNeil considered Seddons an exhibitionist, though in his favor the kid had taken to pathology a lot more readily than some of the other surgical residents McNeil had seen.

Seddons looked over at the body on the table. "Ah, more business!"

McNeil gestured to the case papers and Seddons picked them up. He asked, "What did he die of?" Then, as he read on, "Coronary, eh?"

McNeil answered, "That's what it says."

"You doing this one?"

The resident shook his head. "Pearson's coming."

Seddons looked up quizzically. "The boss man himself? What's special about this case?"

"Nothing special." McNeil snapped a four-page autopsy form onto a clip board. "Some of the student nurses are coming in to watch. I think he likes to impress them."

"A command performance!" Seddons grinned. "This I must see."

"In that case you may as well work." McNeill passed over the clip board. "Fill in some of this stuff, will you?"

"Sure." Seddons took the clip board and began to make notes on the condition of the body. He talked to himself as he worked. "That's a nice clean appendix scar. Small mole on the left arm." He moved the arm to one side. "Excuse me, old man." He made a note, "Slight rigor mortis." Lifting the eyelids, he wrote, "Pupils round, 0.3 cm. diameter." He pried the already stiff jaw open, "Let's have a look at the teeth."

From the corridor outside there was the sound of feet. Then the autopsy-room door opened, and a nurse, whom McNeil recognized as a member of the nursing school's teaching staff, looked in. She said, "Good morning, Dr. McNeil." Behind her was a group of young student nurses.

"Good morning." The resident beckoned. "You can all come in."

The students filed through the doorway. There were six,

and as they entered all glanced nervously at the body on
the table. Mike Seddons grinned. "Hurry up, girls. You want
the best seats; we have 'em."

Seddons ran his eye appraisingly over the group. There
were a couple of new ones here he had not seen previously,
including the brunette. He took a second look. Yes indeed;
even camouflaged by the spartan student's uniform, it was
obvious that here was something special. With apparent casualness he crossed the autopsy room, then, returning, managed to position himself between the girl he had noticed and
the rest of the group. He gave her a broad smile and said
quietly, "I don't remember seeing you before."

"I've been around as long as the other girls." She looked
at him with a mixture of frankness and curiosity, then
added mockingly, "Besides, I've been told that doctors never
notice first-year nursing students anyway."

He appeared to consider. "Well, it's a general rule. But
sometimes we make exceptions—depending on the student,
of course." His eyes candidly admiring, he added, "By the
way, I'm Mike Seddons."

She said, "I'm Vivian Loburton," and laughed. Then,
catching a disapproving eye from the class instructor, she
stopped abruptly. Vivian had liked the look of this redheaded
young doctor, but it did seem wrong somehow to be talking and joking in here. After all, the man on the table was
dead. He had just died, she had been told upstairs; that
was the reason she and the other student nurses had been
taken from their work to watch the autopsy. The thought of
the word "autopsy" brought her back to what was to happen here. Vivian wondered how she was going to react;
already she felt uneasy. She supposed, as a nurse, she would
grow used to seeing death, but at the moment it was still
new and rather frightening.

There were footsteps coming down the corridor. Seddons
touched her arm and whispered, "We'll talk again—soon."
Then the door was flung open and the student nurses moved
back respectfully as Dr. Joseph Pearson strode inside. He
greeted them with a crisp "Good morning." Then, without
waiting for the murmured acknowledgments, he strode to a
locker, slipped off his white coat, and thrust his arms into a
gown which he had taken from the shelf. Pearson gestured
to Seddons, who stepped over and tied the gown strings at
the back. Then, like a well-drilled team, the two moved over

to a washbasin where Seddons shook powder from a can over Pearson's hands, afterward holding out a pair of rubber gloves into which the older man thrust his fingers. All this had been accomplished in silence. Now Pearson shifted his cigar slightly and grunted a "Thanks."

He crossed to the table and, taking the clip board which McNeil held out to him, began to read it, apparently oblivious of everything else. So far Pearson had not even glanced at the body on the table. Watching the performance covertly, as he, too, moved across, it occurred to Seddons that it was like the entry of a maestro before a symphony. All that was missing was applause.

Now that Pearson had digested the case history he, too, inspected the body, comparing his findings with the notes Seddons had written. Then he put the clip board down and, removing his cigar, faced the nurses across the table. "This is your first experience of an autopsy, I believe."

The girls murmured, "Yes, sir," or, "Yes, Doctor."

Pearson nodded. "Then I will explain that I am Dr. Pearson, the pathologist of this hospital. These gentlemen are Dr. McNeil, the resident in pathology, and Dr. Seddons, a resident in surgery, in his third year . . ." He turned to Seddons. "Am I right?"

Seddons smiled. "Quite right, Dr. Pearson."

Pearson continued, "In his third year of residency, and who is favoring us with a spell of duty in Pathology." He glanced at Seddons. "Dr. Seddons will shortly qualify to practice surgery and be released upon an unsuspecting public."

Two of the girls giggled; the others smiled. Seddons grinned; he enjoyed this. Pearson never missed an opportunity to take a dig at surgeons and surgery, probably with good reason—in forty years of pathology the old man must have uncovered a lot of surgical bloopers. He glanced across at McNeil. The resident was frowning. He doesn't approve, Seddons thought. Mac likes his pathology straight. Now Pearson was talking again.

"The pathologist is often known as the doctor the patient seldom sees. Yet few departments of a hospital have more effect on a patient's welfare."

Here comes the sales pitch, Seddons thought, and Pearson's next words proved him right.

"It is pathology which tests a patient's blood, checks his

excrements, tracks down his diseases, decides whether his
tumor is malignant or benign. It is pathology which advises
the patient's physician on disease and sometimes, when all
else in medicine fails"—Pearson paused, looked down sig-
nificantly at the body of George Andrew Dunton, and the
eyes of the nurses followed him—"it is the pathologist who
makes the final diagnosis."

Pearson paused again. What a superb actor the old man is,
Seddons thought. What an unabashed, natural ham!

Now Pearson was pointing with his cigar. "I draw your attention," he was saying to the nurses, "to some words you
will find on the wall of many autopsy rooms." Their eyes
followed his finger to the framed maxim thoughtfully provided by a scientific supply house—*Mortui Vivos Docent*.
Pearson read the Latin aloud, then translated. "The dead
teach the living." He looked down again at the body. "That
is what will happen now. This man apparently"—he emphasized the word "apparently"—"died of coronary thrombosis.
By autopsy we shall discover if that is true."

At this Pearson took a deep draw on his cigar, and Seddons, knowing what was coming, moved nearer. He himself
might be only a bit player in this scene, but he had no intention of missing a cue. As Pearson exhaled a cloud of
blue smoke, he handed the cigar to Seddons who took it and
placed it down, away from the table. Now Pearson surveyed
the instruments laid out before him and selected a knife.
With his eye he calculated where he would cut, then swiftly,
cleanly, deeply, applied the sharp steel blade.

McNeil was watching the student nurses covertly. An autopsy, he reflected, would never be recommended viewing
for the fainthearted, but even to the experienced the first
incision is sometimes hard to take. Until this point the body
on the table has at least borne physical resemblance to the
living. But after the knife, he thought, no illusions are possible. This was not a man, a woman, a child, but merely
flesh and bone, resembling life, yet not of life. This was the
ultimate truth, the end to which all must come. This was
the fulfillment of the Old Testament, "For dust thou art, and
unto dust shalt thou return."

Using the skill, ease, and speed of long experience, Pearson began the autopsy with a deep "Y" incision. With three
strong knife strokes he brought the top two branches of the
"Y" from each shoulder of the body to meet near the bot-

tom of the chest. Then from this point he cut downward, opening the belly all the way from chest to genitals. There was a hissing, almost a tearing sound, as the knife moved and the flesh parted, revealing a layer of yellow fat beneath the surface.

Still watching the student nurses, McNeil saw that two were deathly white, a third had gasped and turned away; the other three were stoically watching. The resident kept his eye on the pale ones; it was not unusual for a nurse to keel over at her first autopsy. But these six looked as if they were going to be all right; the color was coming back to the two he had noticed, and the other girl had turned back, though with a handkerchief to her mouth. McNeil told them quietly: "If any of you want to go out for a few minutes, that's all right. The first time's always a bit hard." They looked at him gratefully, though no one moved. McNeil knew that some pathologists would never admit nurses to an autopsy until the first incision had been made. Pearson, though, did not believe in shielding anyone. He felt they should see the whole thing from the beginning, and it was something McNeil agreed with. A nurse had to witness a lot of things that were tough to take—sores, mangled limbs, putrefaction, surgery; the sooner she learned to accept the sights and smells of medicine, the better for everyone, including herself.

Now McNeil slipped on his own gloves and went to work with Pearson. By this time, moving swiftly, the older man had peeled back the chest flap and, hacking the flesh loose with a larger knife, exposed the ribs. Next, using the sharp levered rib cutters, he cut his way into the rib cage, exposing pericardium and lungs. The gloves, instruments, and table were now beginning to be covered with blood. Seddons, gloved also, on his side of the table, was cutting back the lower flaps of flesh and opening the abdomen. He crossed the room for a pail and began to remove stomach and intestines, which he put into the pail after studying them briefly. The odor was beginning to be noticeable. Now Pearson and Seddons together tied off and cut the arteries so the undertaker would have no trouble when it came to embalming. Taking a small tube from a rack above the table, Seddons turned on a tap and began to siphon blood that had escaped into the abdomen and, after a nod from Pearson, did the same thing for the chest.

Meanwhile McNeil had applied himself to the head. First he made an incision across the vertex of the skull, starting slightly behind each ear and cutting above the hairline so the mark would not be visible if the body were placed on view by the dead man's family. Then, using all the strength in his fingers, he peeled the scalp forward in one piece, so that all the flesh from the head was bunched over the front of the face, covering the eyes. The entire skull was now exposed, and McNeil picked up the portable electric saw which was already plugged in. Before he switched it on he looked over at the student nurses to find them watching him with a mixture of incredulity and horror. Take it easy, girls, he thought; in a few minutes you'll have seen it all.

Pearson was carefully removing the heart and lungs when McNeil applied the saw to bone. The metallic "scrunch" of the oscillating steel teeth biting into the skull cut grimly across the quiet room. Glancing up, he saw the girl with the handkerchief flinch; if she was going to vomit he hoped it wouldn't be in here. He kept the blade cutting until the top of the skull was severed. He put down the saw. George Rinne would remove the blood from it when he cleaned all the instruments later. Now McNeil carefully pried loose the skull, exposing the soft membrane covering the brain beneath. Again he glanced at the nurses. They were standing up to it well; if they could take this they could take anything.

With the bony portion of the skull removed, McNeil took sharp scissors and opened the large vein—the superior sagittal sinus—which ran from front to rear along the center of the membrane. The blood poured out, spilling over the scissors and his fingers. It was fluid blood, he noted; there was no sign of thrombosis. He inspected the membrane carefully, then cut and lifted it clear to expose the mass of brain beneath. Using a knife, he carefully severed the brain from the spinal cord and eased it out. Seddons joined him, holding a glass jar half full of formalin, and McNeil gently lowered the brain into it.

Watching McNeil, his hands steady and competent, Seddons found himself wondering again what went on in the pathology resident's mind. He had known McNeil for two years, first as a fellow resident, though senior to himself in the hospital's pyramid system, and then more closely during his own few months in Pathology. Pathology had interested Seddons; he was glad, though, it was not his own chosen specialty. He had never had second thoughts about his personal choice of surgery and would be glad when he went back to it in a few weeks' time. In contrast to this domain of the dead the operating room was a territory of the living. It was pulsing and alive; there was a poetry of motion, a sense of achievement he knew he could never find here. Each to his own, he thought, and pathology for the pathologists.

There was something else about pathology. You could lose your sense of reality, your awareness that medicine was of and for human beings. This brain now . . . Seddons found himself acutely aware that just a few hours ago it was the thinking center of a man. It had been co-ordinator of the senses—touch, smell, sight, taste. It had held thoughts, known love, fear, triumph. Yesterday, possibly even today, it could have told the eyes to cry, the mouth to drool. He had noticed the dead man was listed as a civil engineer. This, then, was a brain that had used mathematics, understood stresses, devised construction methods, perhaps had built houses, a highway, a water works, a cathedral—legacies from this brain for other humans to live with and use. But what was the brain now?—just a mass of tissue, beginning to be pickled and destined only to be sliced, examined, then incinerated.

Seddons did not believe in God and he found it hard to understand how educated people could. Knowledge, science, thought—the more these advanced, the more improbable all religions became. But he did believe in what, for lack of better phrases, he thought of as "the spark of humanity, the credo of the individual." As a surgeon, of course, he would not always deal with individuals; nor would he always know his patients, and even when he did he would lose awareness of them in concentrating on problems of technique. But long ago he had resolved never to forget that beneath everything was a patient—an individual. In his own training Seddons had seen the cocoon of personal isolation—a safeguard against close contact with individual patients—grow around others. Sometimes it was a defensive measure, a deliberate insulation of personal emotions and personal involvement. He felt strong enough himself, though, to get along without the insulation. Moreover, to make sure it did not grow, he forced himself sometimes to think and soliloquize as he was doing now. Perhaps it would surprise some of his friends who thought of Mike Seddons only as a buoyant extrovert to know some of the thoughts that went on inside him. Perhaps it wouldn't, though; the mind, brain —or whatever you called it—was an unpredictable machine.

What of McNeil? Did he feel anything, or was there a shell around the pathology resident too? Seddons did not know, but he suspected there was. And Pearson? He had no doubts there. Joe Pearson was cold and clinical all the way through. Despite his showmanship the years of pathology had chilled him. Seddons looked at the old man. He had removed the heart from the body and was scrutinizing it carefully. Now he turned to the student nurses.

"The medical history of this man shows that three years ago he suffered a first coronary attack and then a second attack earlier this week. So first we'll examine the coronary arteries." As the nurses watched intently Pearson delicately opened the heart-muscle arteries.

"Somewhere here we should discover the area of thrombosis . . . yes, there it is." He pointed with the tip of a metal probe. In the main branch of the left coronary artery, an inch beyond its origin, he had exposed a pale, half-inch clot. He held it out for the girls to see.

"Now we'll examine the heart itself." Pearson laid the organ on a dissecting board and sliced down the center with a knife. He turned the two sections side by side, peered at them, then beckoned the nurses closer. Hesitantly they moved in.

"Do you notice this area of scarring in the muscle?" Pearson indicated some streaks of white fibrous tissue in the heart, and the nurses craned over the gaping red body cavity to see more closely. "There's the evidence of the coronary attack three years ago—an old infarct which has healed."

Pearson paused, then went on. "We have the signs of the latest attack here in the left ventricle. Notice the central area of pallor surrounded by a zone of hemorrhage." He pointed to a small dark-red stain with a light center, contrasting with the red-brown texture of the rest of the heart muscle.

Pearson turned to the surgical resident. "Would you agree with me, Dr. Seddons, that the diagnosis of death by coronary thrombosis seems fairly well established?"

"Yes, I would," Seddons answered politely. No doubt about it, he thought. A tiny blood clot, not much thicker than a piece of spaghetti; that was all it took to cut you off for good. He watched the older pathologist put the heart aside.

Vivian was steadier now. She believed she had herself in hand. Near the beginning, and when the saw had cut into the dead man's skull, she had felt the blood drain from her head, her senses swim. She knew then she had been close to fainting and had determined not to. For no reason she had suddenly remembered an incident in her childhood. On a holiday, deep in the Oregon forest, her father had fallen on an open hunting knife and cut his leg badly. Surprisingly in so strong a man, he had quailed at the sight of so much of his own blood, and her mother, usually more at home in the drawing room than the woods, had become suddenly strong. She had fashioned a tourniquet, stemmed the blood, and sent Vivian running for help. Then, with Vivian's father being carried through the woods on an improvised litter of branches, every half-hour she had released the tourniquet to keep circulation going, then tightened it to halt the bleeding again. Afterward the doctors had said she had saved the leg from amputation. Vivian had long since forgotten the incident, but remembering it now had given her strength. After that she knew there would not be any problem about watching an autopsy again.

"Any questions?" It was Dr. Pearson asking.

Vivian had one. "The organs—those that you take out of the body. What happens to them, please?"

"We shall keep them, probably for a week. That is—the heart, lungs, stomach, kidneys, liver, pancreas, spleen, and brain. Then we shall make a gross examination which will be recorded in detail. At that time also we'll be studying organs removed at other autopsies—probably six to a dozen cases all together."

It sounded so cold and impersonal, Vivian thought. But maybe you had to get that way if you did this all the time. Involuntarily she shuddered. Mike Seddons caught her eye and smiled slightly. She wondered if he was amused or being sympathetic. She could not be sure. Now one of the other girls was putting a question. She sounded uneasy, almost afraid to ask. "The body—is it buried then . . . just by itself?"

This was an old one. Pearson answered it. "It varies. Teaching centers such as this usually do more study after autopsies than is done in non-teaching hospitals. In this hos-

pital just the shell of the body goes on to the undertakers."
He added as an afterthought: "They wouldn't thank us for
putting the organs back anyway. Just be a nuisance when
they're embalming."

That was true, McNeil reflected. Maybe not the gentlest
way of putting it, but true all the same. He had sometimes
wondered himself if mourners and others who visited funeral parlors knew how little remained in a body that had
been autopsied. After an autopsy like this one, and depending on how busy a pathology department was, it might be
weeks before the body organs were disposed of finally, and
even then small specimens from each were kept stored
indefinitely.

"Are there never any exceptions?" The student nurse asking the questions seemed persistent. Pearson did not appear
to object though. Maybe this is one of his patient days,
McNeil thought. The old man had them occasionally.

"Yes, there are," he was saying. "Before we can do any
autopsy we must have permission from the family of the
deceased. Sometimes that permission is unrestricted, as in
this case, and then we can examine the entire head and torso.
At other times we may get only limited permission. For
example, a family may ask specifically that the cranial contents be undisturbed. When that happens in this hospital
we respect those wishes."

"Thank you, Doctor." Apparently the girl was satisfied,
whatever her reason had been for asking.

But Pearson had not finished.

"You do run into cases where for reasons of religious
faith the organs are required for burial with the body. In
that case, of course, we comply with the request."

"How about Catholics?" It was one of the other girls this
time. "Do they insist on that?"

"Most of them don't, but there are some Catholic hospitals which do. That makes the pathologist's work difficult.
Usually."

As he added the last word Pearson glanced sardonically
at McNeil. Both of them knew what Pearson was thinking
—one of the larger Catholic hospitals across town had a
standing order that the organs of all bodies autopsied were
to be returned to the body for burial. But sometimes a little
sleight of hand was practiced. The busy pathology department of the other hospital frequently kept a spare set of

organs on hand. Thus, when a new autopsy was done, the organs removed were replaced by the spare ones, so that the body could be released and the latest set of organs examined at leisure. These organs, in turn, were then used for the next body. Thus the pathologists were, in effect, always one ahead of the game.

McNeil knew that Pearson, though not a Catholic, disapproved of this. And whatever else you might say about the old man, he always insisted on following autopsy permissions both to the letter and the spirit. There was one phrase, sometimes used in completing the official form, which read "limited to abdominal incision." Some pathologists he knew did a full autopsy with this single incision. As he had heard one man put it, "With an abdominal incision, if you've a mind to, you can reach up inside and get everything, including the tongue." Pearson—to his credit, McNeil thought—would never permit this, and in Three Counties an "abdominal incision" release meant examination of the abdomen only.

Pearson had turned his attention back to the body.

"We'll go on now to examine . . ." Pearson stopped and peered down. He reached for a knife and probed gingerly. Then he let out a grunt of interest.

"McNeil, Seddons, take a look at this."

Pearson moved aside, and the pathology resident leaned over the area that Pearson had been studying. He nodded. The pleura, normally a transparent, glistening membrane covering the lungs, had a thick coating of scarring—a dense, white fibrous tissue. It was a signal of tuberculosis; whether old or recent they would know in a moment. He moved aside for Seddons.

"Palpate the lungs, Seddons." It was Pearson. "I imagine you'll find some evidence there."

The surgical resident grasped the lungs, probing with his fingers. The cavities beneath the surface were detectable at once. He looked up at Pearson and nodded. McNeil had turned to the case-history papers. He used a clean knife to lift the pages so he would not stain them.

"Was there a chest X-ray on admission?" Pearson asked.

The resident shook his head. "The patient was in shock. There's a note here it wasn't done."

"We'll take a vertical slice to see what's visible." Pearson was talking to the nurses again as he moved back to the table.

He removed the lungs and cut smoothly down the center of one. It was there unmistakably—fibrocaseous tuberculosis, well advanced. The lung had a honeycombed appearance, like ping-pong balls fastened together, then cut through the center—a festering, evil growth that only the heart had beaten to the kill.

"Can you see it?"

Seddons answered Pearson's question. "Yes. Looks like it was a tossup whether this or the heart would get him first."

"It's always a tossup what we die of." Pearson looked across at the nurses. "This man had advanced tuberculosis. As Dr. Seddons observed, it would have killed him very soon. Presumably neither he nor his physician were aware of its presence."

Now Pearson peeled off his gloves and began to remove his gown. The performance is over, Seddons thought. The bit players and stagehands will do the cleaning up. McNeil and the resident would put the essential organs into a pail and label it with the case number. The remainder would be put back into the body, with linen waste added if necessary to fill the cavities out. Then they would stitch up roughly, using a big baseball stitch—over and under—because the area they had been working on would be covered decorously with clothing in the coffin; and when they had finished the body would go in refrigeration to await the undertaker.

Pearson had put on the white lab coat with which he entered the autopsy room and was lighting a new cigar. It was a characteristic that he left behind him through the hospital a trail of half-smoked cigar butts, usually for someone else to deposit in an ash tray. He addressed himself to the nurses.

"There will be times in your careers," he said, "when you will have patients die. It will be necessary then to obtain permission for an autopsy from the next of kin. Sometimes this will fall to the physician, sometimes to you. When that happens you will occasionally meet resistance. It is hard for any person to sanction—even after death—the mutilation of someone they have loved. This is understandable."

Pearson paused. For a moment Seddons found himself having second thoughts about the old man. Was there some warmth, some humanity, in him after all?

"When you need to muster arguments," Pearson said, "to convince some individual of the need for autopsy, I hope you will remember what you have seen today and use it as an example."

He had his cigar going now and waved it at the table. "This man has been tuberculous for many months. It is possible he may have infected others around him—his family, people he worked with, even some in this hospital. If there had been no autopsy, some of these people might have developed tuberculosis and it could have remained undetected, as it did here, until too late."

Two of the student nurses moved back instinctively from the table.

Pearson shook his head. "Within reason there is no danger of infection here. Tuberculosis is a respiratory disease. But because of what we have learned today, those who have been close to this man will be kept under observation and given periodic checks for several years to come."

To his own surprise Seddons found himself stirred by Pearson's words. *He makes it sound good,* he thought; *what's more, he believes in what he is saying.* He discovered that at this moment he was liking the old man.

As if he had read Seddons' mind, Pearson looked over to the surgical resident. With a mocking smile: "Pathology has its victories too, Dr. Seddons."

He nodded at the nurses. Then he was gone, leaving a cloud of cigar smoke behind.

Four

The monthly surgical-mortality conference was scheduled for 2:30 P.M. At three minutes to the half-hour Dr. Lucy Grainger, a little harried as if time were working against her, hurried into the administration reception office. "Am I late?" she asked the secretary at the information desk.

"I don't think they've started, Dr. Grainger. They just went in the board room." The girl had indicated the double oak-paneled doorway down the hall, and now, as she approached, Lucy could hear a hum of conversation from inside.

As she entered the big room with its pile carpet, long walnut table, and carved chairs, she found herself close to Kent O'Donnell and another younger man she did not recognize. Around them was a babel of talk and the air was thick with tobacco smoke. The monthly mortality conferences were usually looked on as command performances, and already most of the hospital's forty-odd staff surgeons had arrived, as well as house staff—interns and residents.

"Lucy!" She smiled a greeting at two of the other surgeons, then turned back as O'Donnell called to her. He was maneuvering the other man with him.

"Lucy, I'd like you to meet Dr. Roger Hilton. He's just joined the staff. You may recall his name came up some time ago."

"Yes, I do remember." She smiled at Hilton, her face crinkling.

"This is Dr. Grainger." O'Donnell was always punctilious about helping new staff members to become known. He added, "Lucy is one of our orthopedic surgeons."

She offered Hilton her hand and he took it. He had a firm grasp, a boyish smile. She guessed his age at twenty-seven. "If you're not tired of hearing it," she said, "welcome!"

"Matter of fact, I'm rather enjoying it." He looked as if he were.

"Is this your first hospital appointment?"

Hilton nodded. "Yes. I was a surgical resident at Michael Reese."

Lucy remembered more clearly now. This was a man whom Kent O'Donnell had been very keen to get to Burlington. And undoubtedly that meant Hilton had good qualifications.

"Come over here a minute, Lucy." Kent O'Donnell had moved back near her and was beckoning.

Excusing herself to Hilton, she followed the chief of surgery to one of the board-room windows, away from the immediate press of people.

"That's a little better; at least we can make ourselves heard." O'Donnell smiled. "How have you been, Lucy? I haven't seen you, except in line of duty, for quite a while."

She appeared to consider. "Well, my pulse has been normal; temperature around ninety-eight point eight. Haven't checked blood pressure recently."

"Why not let me do it?" O'Donnell said. "Over dinner, for example."

"Do you think it's wise? You might drop the sphygmomanometer in the soup."

"Let's settle for dinner then and forget the rest."

"I'd love to, Kent," Lucy said. "But I'll have to look at my book first."

"Do that and I'll phone you. Let's try to make it next week." O'Donnell touched her lightly on the shoulder as he turned away. "I'd better get this show opened."

Watching him ease his way through other groups toward the center table, Lucy thought, not for the first time, how much she admired Kent O'Donnell, both as a colleague and a man. The invitation to dinner was not a new thing. They had had evenings together before, and for a while she had wondered if perhaps they might be drifting into some kind of tacit relationship. Both were unmarried, and Lucy, at thirty-five, was seven years younger than the chief of surgery. But there had been no hint in O'Donnell's manner that he regarded her as anything more than a pleasant companion.

Lucy herself had a feeling that, if she allowed it, her admiration for Kent O'Donnell could grow to something more deep and personal. But she had made no attempt to force the pace, feeling it better to let things develop if they happened to, and if not—well, nothing was lost. That at least was one advantage of maturity over the first flush of youth. You learned not to hurry, and you discovered that the rainbow's end was a good deal further than the next city block.

"Shall we get started, gentlemen?" O'Donnell had reached the head of the table and raised his voice across the heads of the others. He too had savored the brief moment with Lucy and found the thought pleasing that he would be meeting her again shortly. Actually he would have called her a good deal sooner, but there had been a reason for hesitation. The truth was that Kent O'Donnell found himself being drawn more and more toward Lucy Grainger, and he was not at all sure this was a good thing for either of them.

By now he had become fairly set in his own mode of life. Living alone and being independent grew on you after a while, and he doubted sometimes if he could adjust to anything else. He suspected, too, that something of the same

thing might apply to Lucy, and there might be problems as
well about their parallel careers. Nonetheless, he still felt
more comfortable in her presence than that of any other
woman he had known in a long time. She had a warmth of
spirit—he had once described it to himself as a strong kind-
ness—that was at once soothing and restoring. And he knew
there were others, particularly Lucy's patients, on whom she
had the same effect.

It was not as if Lucy were unattractive; she had a mature
beauty that was very real. As he watched her now—she had
stopped to speak with one of the interns—he saw her raise
a hand and push back her hair from the side of her face.
She wore it short, in soft waves which framed her face, and
it was almost golden. He noticed, though, a few graying
strands. Well, that was something medicine seemed to do
for everyone. But it reminded him that the years were moving on. Was he wrong in not pursuing this more actively?
Had he waited long enough? Well, he would see how their
dinner went next week.

The hubbub had not died and, this time more loudly, he
repeated his injunction that they start.

Bill Rufus called out, "I don't think Joe Pearson is here
yet." The gaudy necktie which O'Donnell had observed earlier made Rufus stand out from the others around him.

"Isn't Joe here?" O'Donnell seemed surprised as he
scanned the room.

"Has anyone seen Joe Pearson?" he asked. Some of the
others shook their heads.

Momentarily O'Donnell's face revealed annoyance, then
he covered up. He moved toward the door. "Can't have a
mortality conference without a pathologist. I'll see what's
keeping him." But as he reached the doorway Pearson
walked in.

"We were just going to look for you, Joe." O'Donnell's
greeting was friendly, and Lucy wondered if she had been
wrong about the flash of irritation a moment ago.

"Had an autopsy. Took longer than I figured. Then I
stopped for a sandwich." Pearson's words came out muffled,
principally because he was chewing between sentences. Presumably the sandwich, Lucy thought; then she saw he had
the rest of it folded in a napkin among the pile of papers
and files he was carrying. She smiled; only Joe Pearson

could get away with eating lunch at a mortality conference.

O'Donnell was introducing Pearson to Hilton. As they shook hands Pearson dropped one of his files and a sheaf of papers spilled out on the floor. Grinning, Bill Rufus collected them and replaced the file under Pearson's arm. Pearson nodded his thanks, then said abruptly to Hilton, "A surgeon?"

"That's right, sir," Hilton answered pleasantly. A well-brought-up young man, Lucy thought; he shows deference to his elders.

"So we have another recruit for the mechanics," Pearson said. As he spoke, loudly and sharply, there was a sudden silence in the room. Ordinarily the remark would have passed as banter, but somehow from Pearson it seemed to have an edge, a touch of contempt.

Hilton was laughing. "I guess you could call it that." But Lucy could see he had been surprised by Pearson's tone.

"Take no notice of Joe," O'Donnell was saying good-naturedly. "He has a 'thing' about surgeons. Well, shall we begin?"

They moved to the long table, some of the senior staff members going automatically to the front rectangle of chairs, the others dropping into the row behind. Lucy herself was in front. O'Donnell was at the head of the table, Pearson and his papers on the left. While the others were settling down she saw Pearson tak another bite from his sandwich. He made no effort to be surreptitious about it.

Lower down the table she noticed Charlie Dornberger, one of Three Counties' obstetricians. He was going through the careful process of filling his pipe. Whenever Lucy saw Dr. Dornberger he seemed to be either filling, cleaning, or lighting a pipe; he seldom seemed to smoke it. Next to Dornberger was Gil Bartlett and, opposite, Ding Dong Bell from Radiology and John McEwan. McEwan must be interested in a case today; the ear, nose, and throat specialist did not normally attend surgical-mortality meetings.

"Good afternoon, gentlemen." As O'Donnell looked down the table the remaining conversations died. He glanced at his notes. "First case. Samuel Lobitz, white male, age fifty-three. Dr. Bartlett."

Gil Bartlett, impeccably dressed as ever, opened a ring notebook. Instinctively Lucy watched the trim beard, waiting for it to move. Almost at once it began bobbing up and down. Bartlett began quietly, "The patient was referred to me on May 12."

"A little louder, Gil." The request came from down the table.

Bartlett raised his voice. "I'll try. But maybe you'd better see McEwan afterward." A laugh ran round the group in which the e.n.t. man joined.

Lucy envied those who could be at ease in this meeting. She never was, particularly when a case of her own was being discussed. It was an ordeal for anyone to describe their diagnosis and treatment of a patient who had died, then have others give their opinion, and finally the pathologist report his findings from the autopsy. And Joe Pearson never spared anyone.

There were honest mistakes that anybody in medicine could make—even, sometimes, mistakes which cost patients their lives. Few physicians could escape errors like this in the course of their careers. The important thing was to learn from them and not to make the same mistake again. That was why mortality conferences were held—so that everyone who attended could learn at the same time.

Occasionally the mistakes were not excusable, and you could always sense when something like that came up at a monthly meeting. There was an uncomfortable silence and an avoidance of eyes. There was seldom open criticism; for one thing, it was unnecessary, and for another, you never knew when you yourself might be subject to it.

Lucy recalled one incident which had concerned a distinguished surgeon at another hospital where she had been on staff. The surgeon was operating for suspected cancer in the intestinal tract. When he reached the affected area he had decided the cancer was inoperable and, instead of attempting to remove it, had looped the intestine to bypass it. Three days later the patient had died and was autopsied. The autopsy showed there had, in fact, been no cancer at all. What had really happened was that the patient's appendix had ruptured and had formed an abscess. The surgeon had failed to recognize this and thereby condemned the man to death. Lucy remembered the horrified hush in which the pathologist's report had been received.

In an instance like this, of course, nothing ever came out

publicly. It was a moment for the ranks of medicine to close. But in a good hospital it was not the end. At Three Counties nowadays O'Donnell would always talk privately with an offender and, if it were a bad case, the individual concerned would be watched closely for a while afterward. Lucy had never had to face one of these sessions herself, but she had heard the chief of surgery could be extremely rough behind closed doors.

Gil Bartlett was continuing. "The case was referred to me by Dr. Cymbalist." Lucy knew that Cymbalist was a general practitioner, though not on Three Counties' staff. She herself had had cases referred from him.

"I was called at my home," Bartlett said, "and Dr. Cymbalist told me he suspected a perforated ulcer. The symptoms he described tallied with this diagnosis. By then the patient was on the way to the hospital by ambulance. I called the surgical resident on duty and notified him the case would be coming in."

Bartlett looked over his notes. "I saw the patient myself approximately half an hour later. He had severe upper abdominal pain and was in shock. Blood pressure was seventy over forty. He was ashen gray and in a cold sweat. I ordered a transfusion to combat shock and also morphine. Physically the abdomen was rigid, and there was rebound tenderness."

Bill Rufu asked, "Did you have a chest film made?"

"No. It seemed to me the patient was too sick to go to X-ray. I agreed with the original diagnosis of a perforated ulcer and decided to operate immediately."

"No doubts at all, eh, Doctor?" This time the interjection was Pearson's. Previously the pathologist had been looking down at his papers. Now he turned directly to face Bartlett.

For a moment Bartlett hesitate and Lucy thought: Something is wrong; the diagnosi was in error and Joe Pearson is waiting to spring the trap. Then she remembered that whatever Pearson knew Bartlett knew also by this time, so it would be no surprise to him. In any case Bartlett had probably attended the autopsy. Most conscientious surgeons did when a patient died. But after the momentary pause the younger man went on urbanely.

"One always has doubts in these emergency cases, Dr. Pearson. But I decided all the symptoms justified immediate exploratory surgery." Bartlett paused. "However, there was no perforated ulcer present, and the patient was returned to the ward. I called Dr. Toynbee for consultation, but before he could arrive the patient died."

Gil Bartlett closed his ring binder and surveyed the table. So the diagnosis *had* been wrong, and despite Bartlett's outwardly calm appearance Lucy knew that inside he was probably suffering the torments of self-criticism. On the basis of the symptoms, though, it could certainly be argued that he was justified in operating.

Now O'Donnell was calling on Joe Pearson. He inquired politely, "Would you give us the autopsy findings, please?" Lucy reflected that the head of surgery undoubtedly knew what was coming. Automatically the heads of departments saw autopsy reports affecting their own staff.

Pearson shuffled his papers, then selected one. His gaze shot around the table. "As Dr. Bartlett told you, there was no perforated ulcer. In fact, the abdomen was entirely normal." He paused, as if for dramatic effect, then went on. "What was present, in the chest, was early development of pneumonia. No doubt there was severe pleuritic pain coming from that."

So that was it. Lucy ran her mind over what had been said before. It was true—externally the two sets of symptoms would be identical.

O'Donnell was asking, "Is there any discussion?"

There was an uneasy pause. A mistake had been made, and yet it was not a wanton mistake. Most of those in the room were uncomfortably aware the same thing might have happened to themselves. It was Bill Rufus who spoke out. "With the symptoms described, I would say exploratory surgery was justified."

Pearson was waiting for this. He started ruminatively. "Well, I don't know." Then almost casually, like tossing a grenade without warning: "We're all aware that Dr. Bartlett rarely sees beyond the abdomen." Then in the stunned silence he asked Bartlett directly, "Did you examine the chest at all?"

The remark and the question were outrageous. Even if Bartlett were to be reprimanded, it should come from O'Donnell, not Pearson, and be done in private. It was not as if Bartlett had a reputation for carelessness. Those who had worked with him knew that he was thorough and, if anything, inclined to be ultra-cautious. In this instance, obviously, he had been faced with the need to make a fast decision.

Bartlett was on his feet, his chair flung back, his face flaming red. "Of course I examined the chest!" He barked out the words, the beard moving rapidly. "I already said the patient was in no condition to have a chest film, and even if he had——"

"Gentlemen! Gentlemen!" It was O'Donnell, but Bartlett refused to be stopped.

"It's very easy to have hindsight, as Dr. Pearson loses no chance to remind us."

From across the table Charlie Dornberger motioned with his pipe. "I don't think Dr. Pearson intended——"

Angrily Bartlett cut him off. "Of course you don't think so. You're a friend of his. And he doesn't have a vendetta with obstetricians."

"Really! I will not permit this." O'Donnell was standing himself now, banging with his gavel. His shoulders were squared, his athlete's bulk towering over the table. Lucy thought: He's all man, every inch. "Dr. Bartlett, will you be kind enough to sit down?" He waited, still standing, as Bartlett resumed his seat.

O'Donnell's outward annoyance was matched with an inward seething. Joe Pearson had no right to throw a meeting into a shambles like this. Now, instead of pursuing the discussion quietly and objectively, O'Donnell knew he had no choice but to close it. It was costing him a lot of effort not to sound off at Joe Pearson right here and now. But if he did he knew it would make the situation worse.

O'Donnell had not shared the opinion of Bill Rufus that Gil Bartlett was blameless in the matter of his patient's death. O'Donnell was inclined to be more critical. The key factor in the case was the absence of a chest X-ray. If Bartlett had ordered an upright chest film at the time of admission, he could have looked for indications of gas across the top of the liver and under the diaphragm. This was a clear signpost to any perforated ulcer; therefore the absence of it would certainly have set Bartlett thinking. Also, the X-ray might have shown some clouding at the base of the lung, which would have indicated the pneumonia which Joe Pearson had found later at the autopsy. One or another of these factors might easily have caused Bartlett to change his diagnosis and improved the patient's chances of survival.

Of course, O'Donnell reflected, Bartlett had claimed the patient was too sick for an X-ray to be taken. But if the man had been as sick as that should Bartlett have undertaken surgery anyway? O'Donnell's opinion was that he should not.

O'Donnell knew that when an ulcer perforated surgery should normally be begun within twenty-four hours. After that time the death rate was higher with surgery than without. This was because the first twenty-four hours were the hardest; after that, if a patient had survived that long, the body's own defenses would be at work sealing up the perforations. From the symptoms Bartlett had described it seemed likely that the patient was close to the twenty-four-hour limit or perhaps past it. In that case O'Donnell himself would have worked to improve the man's condition without surgery and with the intention of making a more definitive diagnosis later. On the other hand, O'Donnell was aware that in medicine it was easy to have hindsight, but it was quite another matter to do an emergency on-the-spot diagnosis with a patient's life at stake.

All of this the chief of surgery would have had brought out, in the ordinary way, quietly and objectively, at the mortality conference. Indeed, he would probably have led Gil Bartlett to make some of the points himself; Bartlett was honest and not afraid of self-examination. The point of the discussion would have been evident to everyone. There would have been no need for emphasis or recriminations. Bartlett would not have enjoyed the experience, of course, but at the same time he would not have been humiliated. More important still, O'Donnell's purpose would have been served and a practical lesson in differential diagnosis impressed on all the surgical staff.

Now none of this could happen. If, at this stage, O'Donnell raised the points he had had in mind, he would appear to be supporting Pearson and further condemning Bartlett. For the sake of Bartlett's own morale this must not happen. He would talk to Bartlett in private, of course, but the chance of a useful, open discussion was lost. Confound Joe Pearson!

Now the uproar had quieted. O'Donnell's banging of the gavel—a rare occurrence—had had effect. Bartlett had sat down, his face still angry red. Pearson was turning over some papers, apparently absorbed.

"Gentlemen." O'Donnell paused. He knew what had to

be said; it must be quick and to the point. "I think I need hardly say this is not an incident any of us would wish to see repeated. A mortality conference is for learning, not for personalities or heated argument. Dr. Pearson, Dr. Bartlett, I trust I make myself clear." O'Donnell glanced at both, then, without waiting for acknowledgment, announced, "We'll take the next case, please."

There were four more cases down for discussion, but none of these was out of the ordinary and the talk went ahead quietly. It was just as well, Lucy reflected; controversy like that was no help to staff morale. There were times when it required courage to make an emergency diagnosis; even so, if you were unfortunate and guilty of error, you expected to be called to account. But personal abuse was another matter; no surgeon, unless grossly careless and incompetent, should have to take that.

Lucy wondered, not for the first time, how much of Joe Pearson's censure at times like this was founded on personal feelings. Today, with Gil Bartlett, Pearson had been rougher than she remembered his ever being at any mortality meeting. And yet this was not a flagrant case, nor was Bartlett prone to mistakes. He had done some fine work at Three Counties, notably on types of cancer which not long before were considered inoperable.

Pearson knew this, too, of course, so why his antagonism? Was it because Gil Bartlett represented something in medicine which Pearson envied and had never attained? She glanced down the table at Bartlett. His face was set; he was still smarting. But normally he was relaxed, amiable, friendly —all the things a successful man in his early forties could afford to be. Along with his wife, Gil Bartlett was a prominent figure in Burlington society. Lucy had seen him at ease at cocktail parties and in wealthy patients' homes. His practice was successful. Lucy guessed his annual income from it would be in the region of fifty thousand dollars.

Was this what griped Joe Pearson?—Joe Pearson who could never compete with the glamor of surgery, whose work was essential but undramatic, who had chosen a branch of medicine seldom in the public eye. Lucy herself had heard people ask: What does a pathologist do? No one ever said: What does a surgeon do? She knew there were some who thought of pathologists as a breed of hospital technician, failing to realize that a pathologist had to be first a physi-

cian with a medical degree, then spend years of extra training to become a highly qualified specialist.

Money sometimes was a sore point too. On Three Counties' staff Gil Bartlett ranked as an attending physician, receiving no payment from the hospital, only from his patients. Lucy herself, and all the other attending physicians,
were on staff on the same basis. But, in contrast, Joe Pearson
was an employee of the hospital, receiving a salary of twenty-
five thousand dollars a year, roughly half of what a successful surgeon—many years his junior—could earn. Lucy had
once read a cynical summation of the difference between
surgeons and pathologists: "A surgeon gets $500 for taking
out a tumor. A pathologist gets five dollars for examining it,
making a diagnosis, recommending further treatment, and
predicting the patient's future."

Lucy herself had fared well in her relationship with Joe
Pearson. For some reason she was not sure of, he had
seemed to like her, and there were moments she found herself responding and liking him also. Sometimes this could
prove a help when she needed to talk with him about a
diagnosis.

Now the discussion was ending, O'Donnell winding things
up. Lucy brought her attention back into focus. She had let
it wander during the last case; that was not good—she would
have to watch herself. The others were rising from their
seats. Joe Pearson had collected his papers and was sham-
bling out. But on the way O'Donnell stopped him; she saw
the chief of surgery steer the old man away from the others.

"Let's go in here a minute, Joe." O'Donnell opened the
door to a small office. It adjoined the board room and was
sometimes used for committee meetings. Now it was empty.
Pearson followed the chief of surgery in.

O'Donnell was elaborately casual. "Joe, I think you should
quit riding people at these meetings."

"Why?" Pearson was direct.

All right, O'Donnell thought, if that's the way you want
it. Aloud he said, "Because it gets us nowhere." He allowed
his voice to take on an edge. Ordinarily in dealing with the
old man he deferred a little to the gap of years between
them. But this was a moment to exercise his own authority.
Although, as chief of surgery, O'Donnell had no direct control of Pearson's activities, he did have certain prerogatives
when the work of Pathology cut across his own division.

"I pointed out a wrong diagnosis—that's all." Pearson was aggressive himself now. "Do you suggest we keep quiet about such things?"

"You know better than to ask that." O'Donnell slammed out the answer, this time not bothering at all to keep the ice from his voice. He saw Pearson hesitate and suspected the old man knew he had gone too far.

Grumblingly he conceded, "I didn't mean that; not that way."

Despite himself Kent O'Donnell smiled. Apologizing did not come easily to Joe Pearson. It must have cost him quite a lot to say that. Now O'Donnell went on more reasonably, "I think there are better ways to do it, Joe. If you don't mind, at these meetings I'd like you to give us the autopsy findings, then I'll lead the discussion afterward. I think we can do it without getting tempers frayed."

"I don't see why anybody has to get in a temper." Pearson was still grumbling, but O'Donnell sensed he was backing down.

"All the same, Joe, I'd like to do it my way." I don't want to ram it down his throat, O'Donnell thought, but this is the time to make things clear.

Pearson shrugged. "If that's the way you want it."

"Thanks, Joe." O'Donnell knew he had won; it had been easier than he had expected. Maybe this would be a good time to raise the other thing. "Joe," he said, "while we're here, there's something else."

"I've got a lot to do. Couldn't it wait?" As Pearson spoke, O'Donnell could almost read his mind. The pathologist was making it clear that though he had conceded one point he had not abandoned his independence.

"I don't think it can. It's about surgical reports."

"What about them?" The reaction was aggressively defensive.

O'Donnell went on smoothly. "I've had complaints. Some of the reports have been a long time coming through Pathology."

"Rufus, I suppose." Pearson was openly bitter now. You could almost hear him saying: Another surgeon causing trouble.

O'Donnell determined not to be provoked. He said quietly, "Bill Rufus was one. But there have been others. You know that, Joe."

For a moment Pearson made no answer, and O'Donnell reflected that in a way he felt sorry for the old man. The years were slipping by. Pearson was sixty-six now; at best he had another five or six years of active work ahead of him. Some people reconciled themselves to change like that, to younger men moving into prominence and taking over leadership. Pearson had not, though, and he made his resentment plain. O'Donnell wondered what was back of his attitude. Did he feel himself slipping, unable to keep up with new developments in medicine? If so, he would not be the first. And yet Joe Pearson, for all his disagreeable ways, had a lot to commend him. That was one of the reasons why O'Donnell trod circumspectly now.

"Yes, I know." Pearson's reply held a tone of resignation. He had accepted the fact though. That was typical of him, O'Donnell thought. Right from the beginning at Three Counties he had liked Pearson's directness and at times had made use of it in raising surgical standards.

O'Donnell remembered that one of the problems he had faced in his early months at the hospital had been the elimination of needless surgery. Under this heading had come an unnatural number of hysterectomies, and in too many cases healthy, normal uteri were being removed by a few staff surgeons. These were men who found surgery a convenient and profitable remedy for any female pain, even those which might have responded to internal medication. In such instances euphemisms in diagnosis like "chronic myometritis" or "fibrosis of uterus" were resorted to as a smoke screen to cover up the pathology report on the removed tissue. O'Donnell remembered telling Pearson: "When we're reporting on tissue we'll call a spade a spade and a healthy uterus a healthy uterus." Pearson had grinned and co-operated fully. As a result most of the unnecessary surgery had stopped. Surgeons found it embarrassing to have tissue they had removed from patients listed for all their colleagues to see as normal and uninfected.

"Look, Kent." Pearson was more conciliatory now. "Just lately I've been up to my ears. You've no idea how much work there is."

"I do have an idea, Joe." This was the opening O'Donnell had hoped for. "Some of us think you've too much to do. It isn't fair to you." He was tempted to add "at your age" but thought better of it. Instead he added, "How about getting some help?"

The reaction was immediate, Pearson almost shouting. "You're telling *me* to get more help! Why, man alive, I've been asking for months for more lab technicians! We need three at least, so what am I told I can have? One! And stenographers! I've got reports that have been piling up for weeks, and who's going to type them?" Not waiting for an answer, he went storming on. "Me? If the administration would get off its fanny we might get a few things done—including faster surgicals. By God! When you tell me I should get more help, that's really something to hear."

O'Donnell had listened quietly. Now he said, "Finished, Joe?"

"Yeah." Pearson seemed chastened, half ashamed at his outburst.

"It wasn't technicians or office staff I was thinking about," O'Donnell told him. "When I meant help I meant another pathologist. Someone to help you run the department. Maybe modernize it here and there."

"Now look here!" at the word "modernize" Pearson had bridled, but O'Donnell brushed the objection aside. "I listen to *you*, Joe. Now you hear me out. Please." He paused. "I was thinking of maybe some bright young fellow who could relieve you of some duties."

"I don't need another pathologist." It was a flat statement, vehement and uncompromising.

"Why, Joe?"

"Because there's not enough work for two qualified men. I can handle all the pathology myself—without any help. Besides, I've already got a resident in the department."

O'Donnell was quietly persistent. "A resident is with us for training, Joe, and usually for just a short time. Sure, a resident can carry some of the work. But you can't give him responsibility and we can't use him for administration. That's where you need some help right now."

"Let me be the judge of that. Give me a few days and we'll be caught up in surgicals."

It was obvious that Joe Pearson had no intention of giving way. O'Donnell had expected resistance to bringing in a new pathologist, but he wondered about the other man's forcefulness. Was it because he was unwilling to divide his per-

sonal empire, or was he simply protecting his job—fearful
that a new and younger man might undermine him? Actually the idea of removing Pearson had not occurred to
O'Donnell. In the field of pathological anatomy alone Joe
Pearson's long experience would be hard to replace. O'Donnell's objective was to strengthen the department and thereby
the hospital organization. Perhaps he should make this clear.

"Joe, there's no question of any major change. No one
has suggested it. You'd still be in charge . . ."

"In that case let me run Pathology my own way."

O'Donnell found his patience ebbing. He decided that perhaps he had pressed the point enough for now. He would
let it go for a day or two, then try again. He wanted to
avoid a showdown if he could. He said quietly, "I'd think it
over if I were you."

"There's nothing to think over." Pearson was at the door.
He nodded curtly and went out.

So there it is, O'Donnell thought. We've laid the lines of
battle. He stood there, considering thoughtfully what the
next move should be.

Five

The cafeteria of Three Counties
Hospital was a traditional meeting place for most of the
the hospital grapevine, its stems and branches extending
tenuously to every section and department within Three
Counties' walls. Few events occurred in the hospital—pro-
motions, scandals, firings, and hirings—which were not
known and discussed in the cafeteria long before official
word was ever published.

Medical staff frequently used the cafeteria for "curbstone
consultations" with colleagues whom they seldom saw except
at a meal or coffee break. Indeed, a good deal of serious medical business was transacted over its tables, and weighty
specialist opinions, which at other times would be followed
by a substantial bill, were often tossed out freely, sometimes
to the great advantage of a patient who, recovering later
from some ailment which at first had proven troublesome,

would never suspect the somewhat casual channels through which his eventual course of treatment had come.

There were exceptions. A few staff physicians now and then resented this informal use of their arduously acquired talents and resisted attempts by colleagues to draw them out in the discussion of specific cases. In such instances the usual rejoinder was, "I think we'd better set up a consultation in my office. I'll have the meter running then."

Gil Bartlett was one who disapproved of such approaches and at times could be a good deal blunter in refusing off-the-cuff opinions. One story told about his personal tactics of resistance had its origin not in the cafeteria but at a cock-tail party in a private home. His hostess, a grand dame of Burlington society, had buttonholed Bartlett and bombarded him with questions about her illnesses, real and imagined. Bartlett had listened for a while, then announced in a loud voice which brought a hush to the crowded room, "Madam, I believe from what you say you have a menstrual problem. If you'll strip right now I'll examine you here."

Mostly though, much as they might resist informal con-sultations outside the hospital, the medical staff accepted the cafeteria exchanges on the basis that they had as much to gain as lose; and a good many physicians around the hospi-tal used the mildewed quip on leaving their contact points, "If you want me I'll be in my second office." Normally no further explanation was required or given.

Generally the cafeteria was a democratic area where hos-pital rank, if not forgotten, was at least temporarily ignored. An exception, possibly, was the practice of setting aside a group of tables for the medical staff. Mrs. Straughan, the chief dietitian, hovered over this area periodically, knowing that even minor shortcomings in hygiene or service could bring testy complaints at some future meeting of the hospi-tal's medical board.

With few exceptions the senior attending physicians used the reserved tables. House staff, however, were less consistent, residents and interns sometimes asserting their independ-ence by joining the nurses or other groups. There was noth-ing unusual, therefore, in Mike Seddons dropping into a chair opposite Vivian Loburton who, released from an assignment earlier than some of her fellow student nurses, was eating lunch alone.

Since they had met ten days ago in the autopsy room,

Vivian had encountered Mike Seddons several times in the hospital and on each occasion—seeing his thatch of red hair and wall-to-wall grin—she had increasingly come to like the look of him. Intuitively she had expected that soon he might make a direct approach to her, and now here it was.

"Hi!" Seddons said.

"Hullo." The greeting came out awkwardly, Vivian having just bitten, with healthy appetite, into a chicken leg. She pointed to her mouth and mumbled, "Excuse me."

"That's perfectly all right," Seddons said. "Take your time. I'm here to proposition you."

She finished the mouthful of chicken, then said, "I thought that was supposed to come later."

Mike Seddons grinned. "Haven't you heard?—this is the jet age. No time for formal frills. Here's my proposition: theater the day after tomorrow, preceded by dinner at the Cuban Grill."

Vivian asked curiously, "Can you afford it?" Among house staff and student nurses poverty was a time-honored, rueful joke.

Seddons lowered his voice to a stage whisper. "Don't tell a soul, but I'm on to a side line. Those patients we get in autopsy. A lot of 'em have gold fillings in their teeth. It's a very simple matter . . ."

"Oh, shut up; you'll ruin my lunch." She bit the chicken leg again, and Seddons reached over for two of her french fries.

He savored them. "Um, not bad. I must eat more often. Now here's the story." He produced two tickets from his pocket and a printed voucher. "Take a look at this—compliments of a grateful patient." The tickets were for the road show of a Broadway musical. The voucher covered dinner for two at the Cuban Grill.

"What did you do?" Vivian was frankly curious. "Heart surgery?"

"No. Last week I filled in for half an hour for Frank Worth in emergency. A guy had a bad gash on his hand and I stitched it. Next thing I knew, these were in the mail." He chuckled. "Worth is furious, of course. Says he'll never leave his post again. Well, will you come?"

"I'd love to," Vivian said, and meant it.

"Great! I'll pick you up at the nurses' residence at seven o'clock. Okay?" As he spoke Mike Seddons found himself regarding this girl with even greater interest. He was suddenly aware that she had a good deal more than a pretty face and a good figure. When she looked at him and smiled it conveyed the feeling of something warm and fragrant. He thought: I wish we were meeting today instead of the day after tomorrow; it's a long time to wait. Then a faint warning voice inside him cautioned: Beware entanglements! Remember the Seddons policy: love 'em and leave 'em—happy with their memories; parting is such sweet sorrow but, oh, so very practical for staying unattached.

"Okay," Vivian said. "I might be a little late but not much."

A week and a half had passed since Harry Tomaselli had told O'Donnell that construction of the hospital's extension was planned to begin in the spring. Now, in the administrator's office, he, Kent O'Donnell, and Orden Brown, the board chairman, were meeting to discuss immediate things to be done.

Months before, with an architect at their elbows, the three had worked over the detailed plans for each section which would have its home in the new wing. The wishes of heads of medical departments had had to be balanced against the money likely to be available. Orden Brown had been the arbiter with O'Donnell as medical liaison. As always, the chairman had been crisp and incisive, but with a humor that seasoned his basic toughness. Sometimes they had gone along entirely with what was asked; at other times, when they suspected empire building for its own sake, the inquiries had been more searching.

One section head, the chief pharmacist, had pressed hard to have a private toilet included in his own office design. When the architect had pointed out that more general facilities were available a mere forty feet down the corridor, the pharmacist had gone so far as to observe that forty feet was a long way when he was suffering one of his periodic attacks of diarrhea. Orden Brown had dryly referred him to the department of internal medicine.

A few worth-while projects had had to be vetoed solely on the grounds of cost. Ding Dong Bell, the senior radiologist, had made out a convincing case for creation of a cineradiography unit—its purpose to improve diagnosis and treatment of heart disease. But on learning that the equipment alone would cost fifty thousand dollars the plan had regretfully been ruled out.

But now, with the main planning completed, the focus of attention was on the practical matter of getting the money. Strictly speaking, this was the responsibility of the board of directors, but the medical staff was expected to help.

Orden Brown said, "We're suggesting some quotas for the doctors—six thousand dollars for senior attending physicians, four thousand for associates, two thousand for assistants."

O'Donnell whistled softly. He told the chairman, "I'm afraid there'll be some complaining."

Brown smiled. "We must do our best to endure it."

Harry Tomaselli put in, "The money can be spread over four years, Kent. As long as we have written pledges we can use them to borrow from the bank."

"There's another thing," Brown said. "When word gets around town that this is what the doctors themselves are giving, it will help our general fund raising a good deal."

"And you'll see that word does get around?"

Brown smiled. "Naturally."

O'Donnell reflected that it would be his job to break the news at a medical staff meeting. He could visualize the pained expressions he would face. Most medical men he knew, like the majority of people nowadays, lived right up to their incomes. Of course, there would be no compulsion about the quotas, but it would be hard for an individual to take a stand against them, especially since the medical staff had a lot to gain from the hospital's growth. A good many certainly would give the full amount asked and, human nature being what it was, they would bring pressure on others to suffer equally. A hospital was a breeding ground for politics, and there were many ways in which a nonconformist could have life made difficult for him.

Harry Tomaselli, intuitive as usual, said, "Don't worry, Kent. I'll brief you thoroughly before the staff meeting. We'll have all the selling points lined up. In fact, when you're through some people may even want to exceed quota."

"Don't count on it." O'Donnell smiled. "You're about to touch a number of doctors on their tenderest nerve—the pocketbook."

Tomaselli grinned back. He knew that when the chief of surgery made his appeal to the staff it would be as incisive and thorough as everything else O'Donnell did. He reflect-

ed, not for the first time, how good it was to work with someone of O'Donnell's character. In Tomaselli's last hospital,
where he had been assistant administrator, the president of
the medical board had been a man who courted popularity
and trimmed his sails to every wind of opinion. As a result
there had been no real leadership and hospital standards had
suffered accordingly.

Harry Tomaselli admired forthrightness and swift decisions, mostly because those were methods he used himself as
administrator of Three Counties. With swift decisions you
sometimes made mistakes, but on the whole you got a lot
more done, and your average of hits improved as time went
on. Quickness—of speech and thought, as well as action—
was something Harry Tomaselli had learned in courtrooms
long before he ever thought of finding his destiny behind a
hospital desk.

He had entered law school from college and had begun to
lay the foundations of a good practice when war intervened.
Anticipating the draft, he had enlisted in the U. S. Navy
where he had received a commission and a job in medical
administration. Later, as the navy hospitals filled with
wounded, Lieutenant Tomaselli had proven himself an able
administrator with an instinct for sensing the invisible bor-
der line between the practice of medicine and the business of
hospital management.

After the war, faced with the choice of returning to law
or remaining in hospital work, he had chosen the latter and
enrolled in the School of Hospital Administration at Columbia University. He had graduated from Columbia at a
time when there was growing recognition of hospital administration as a specialized field of endeavor in which a medical degree was neither necessary nor particularly useful. This
had opened up a brisk demand for good administrators, and
after two years as an assistant he had accepted Orden
Brown's offer of the top post at Three Counties.

Now Harry Tomaselli was in love with his work.
He shared Kent O'Donnell's views about the standards of
good medicine and respected the business acumen and cagi-
ness of the board chairman, Orden Brown. As administrator,
it was Tomaselli's business to see that all hospital services—
nursing, housekeeping, engineering, building, accounting,
and their subsidiaries—measured up to the standards the
other two men required.

He did this by delegation—he had a happy faculty of appointing good department heads—and also by an intense personal interest in everything that went on within the hospital. Almost nothing of importance escaped Harry Tomaselli. Each day his short, stocky figure could be seen bustling along the corridors but pausing frequently while he talked with nurses, patients, janitors, clerks, cooks—anyone who could tell him something about the hospital or make a suggestion on how to run it better. New ideas excited him; his own enthusiasm engendered more in others. Sometimes, head thrust forward, eyes gleaming behind his big black-rimmed glasses, he would talk volubly, his thoughts moving at a gallop, his hands underscoring points as he made them.

In all his peregrinations Harry Tomaselli seldom made a written note. His lawyer's training enabled him to carry assorted facts readily in his head. But after each inspection tour he fired off a barrage of staccato memoranda on all points, big and little, where he felt the administration of Three Counties could be improved.

Yet, for all this, he had a diplomat's sense of tone and language that seldom gave offense. Verbally he would hand out a reprimand, then talk cheerfully of something else. And though he never wasted words, his written memos were always gracious. He hated to fire a hospital employee unless the provocation were really strong. He frequently told his department heads, "If anyone has worked here more than a month, we have an investment in their experience. It's to our advantage to mold them if we can, rather than try for someone new who may have other faults we haven't thought of." Because this policy was known and respected, employee morale was high.

There were still things about the organization that worried him. Some departments, he knew, could be made more efficient. There were areas where service to patients could be improved. A good deal of old equipment needed junking and replacement. There was newly developed equipment—the cine-radiography unit was an example—which, under ideal conditions, the hospital should have. The new building program would make good some of these deficiencies but not all. Like O'Donnell, he knew there were years of work ahead and that some objectives perhaps would remain beyond reach. But, after all, that was the road to achievement; you always tried for a little more than you knew you could accomplish.

His thoughts were brought back to the present by Orden Brown. The chairman was telling O'Donnell, "There'll be a good deal of social activity, of course, once the campaign gets going. Oh, and something else. I believe it would be a good thing, Kent, if we put you in as a speaker at the Rotary Club. You could tell them what the new building will do, our plans for the future, and so on."

O'Donnell, who disliked public meetings, especially the regimented bonhomie of service clubs, had been about to grimace but checked himself. Instead he said, "If you think it will help."

"One of my people is on Rotary executive," Orden Brown said. "I'll have him fix it up. That had better be the opening week of the campaign. Then the following week we might do the same thing with Kiwanis."

O'Donnell considered suggesting that the chairman leave him some time for surgery, otherwise he might have trouble meeting his own quota. But he thought better of it.

"By the way," Orden Brown was saying, "are you free for dinner the day after tomorrow?"

"Yes, I am," O'Donnell answered promptly. He always enjoyed the quiet, formal dignity of dinner at the house on the hill.

"I'd like you to come with me to Eustace Swayne's." Seeing O'Donnell's surprise, the chairman added, "It's all right —you're invited. He asked me if I'd tell you."

"Yes, I'll be glad to come." All the same, the invitation to the home of the board of directors' most die-hard member was unexpected. Naturally O'Donnell had met Swayne a few times but had not come to know him well.

"As a matter of fact, it's my suggestion," Brown said. "I'd like you to talk with him about the hospital generally. Let him absorb some of your ideas if you can. Frankly, at times he's a problem on the board, but you know that, of course."

"I'll do what I can." Now that he knew what was involved, O'Donnell did not relish the thought of getting close to board politics. So far he had managed to steer clear of them. But he could not say no to Orden Brown.

The chairman picked up his brief case and prepared to leave. Tomaselli and O'Donnell rose with him.

"It will be just a small party," Orden Brown said. "Probably half a dozen people. Why don't we pick you up on the way across town? I'll phone before we leave."

O'Donnell murmured his thanks as, nodding pleasantly, the chairman went out.

The door had scarcely closed on Orden Brown when tall, slim Kathy Cohen, Tomaselli's secretary, came in. "I'm sorry to interrupt," she said.

"What is it, Kathy?"

She told the administrator, "There's a man on the phone who insists on talking to you. A Mr. Bryan."

"I'm busy with Dr. O'Donnell now. I'll call him back." Tomaselli sounded surprised. Normally he would not have to tell Kathy anything so elementary.

"I told him that, Mr. Tomaselli." She sounded doubtful. "But he's very insistent. He says he's the husband of a patient. I thought you ought to know."

"Maybe you should talk with him, Harry." O'Donnell smiled at the girl. "Take him off Kathy's mind. I don't mind waiting."

"All right." The administrator reached for one of his two telephones.

"It's line four." The girl waited until the connection was made, then went back to the outer office.

"Administrator speaking." Tomaselli's tone was friendly. Then he frowned slightly, listening to what was coming from the other end of the line.

O'Donnell could hear the receiver diaphragm rattling sharply. He caught the words, "Disgraceful situation . . . imposition on a family . . . should be an inquiry."

Tomaselli put his hand over the phone's mouthpiece. He told O'Donnell, "He's really boiling. Something about his wife. I can't quite make out . . ." He listened for a moment more, then said, "Now, Mr. Bryan, supposing you start at the beginning. Tell me what this is all about." He reached for a pad and pencil, then said, "Yes, sir." A pause. "Now tell me, please, when was your wife admitted to hospital?" The phone rattled again and the administrator made a swift note. "And who was your physician?" Again a note. "And the date of discharge?" A pause. "Yes, I see."

O'Donnell heard the words, "Can't get any satisfaction," then Tomaselli was talking again.

"No, Mr. Bryan, I don't remember the particular case.

But I will make some inquiries. I promise you that." He listened, then answered, "Yes, sir, I do know what a hospital bill means to a family. But the hospital doesn't make any profit, you know."

O'Donnell could still hear the voice on the telephone, but it sounded calmer, responding to Tomaselli's conciliatory approach. Now the administrator said, "Well, sir, it's the physician who decides how long a patient remains in hospital. I think you should have another talk with your wife's physician, and what I'll do meanwhile is have our treasurer go over your bill, item by item." He listened briefly, then, "Thank you, Mr. Bryan. Good-by."

He hung up the phone, tore off the page of notes, and put it in a tray marked "Dictation."

"What was the trouble?" O'Donnell asked the question casually. In a busy hospital complaints about service and charges were not unique.

"He claims his wife was kept in too long. Now he has to go into debt to pay the bill."

O'Donnell said sharply, "How does he know she was in too long?"

"He says he's checked around—whatever that means." Tomaselli said thoughtfully, "It may have been necessary, of course, but she *was* here nearly three weeks."

"So?"

"Normally I wouldn't think much about it. But we've had an unusual number of these complaints. They're not always as strong as this—but on the same lines."

Something flashed through O'Donnell's mind: the word Pathology. Aloud he said: "Who was the attending physician?"

Tomaselli glanced at his notes. "Reubens."

"Let's see if we can get him and clear this up now."

Tomaselli touched an intercom set. "Kathy," he said, "see if you can locate Dr. Reubens."

They waited in silence. From the corridor outside they could hear a soft voice on the hospital public-address system. "Dr. Reubens. Dr. Reubens." After a moment the phone buzzed. Tomaselli lifted the receiver and listened. Then he passed it to O'Donnell.

"Reub? It's Kent O'Donnell."

"What can I do for you?" O'Donnell could hear the thin, precise voice of Reubens, one of the senior surgeons, at the other end of the line.

"Do you have a patient"—he looked at Tomaselli's notes which the administrator had pushed toward him—"a Mrs. Bryan?"

"That's right. What's the matter? Has her husband been complaining?"

"You know about it then?"

"Of course I know about it." Reubens sounded annoyed. "Personally I think he has good reason to complain."

"What's the story, Reub?"

"The story is that I admitted Mrs. Bryan for possible carcinoma of the breast. I removed a tumor. It turned out to be benign."

"Then why keep her here for three weeks?" As he asked, O'Donnell remembered that you always had to go through this question-and-answer performance with Reubens. The other man seldom volunteered information.

Now he answered, "You'd better ask Joe Pearson that!"

"Be simpler if you told me, Reub." O'Donnell was quietly insistent. "After all, she's your patient."

There was a silence. Then the thin, clipped voice said, "All right. I told you the tumor was benign. But it was two and a half weeks before I found out. That's how long it took Pearson to get it under his microscope."

"Did you remind him about it?"

"If I called him once I called him half a dozen times. He'd probably have been longer if I hadn't kept after it."

"And that's why you kept Mrs. Bryan in—for three weeks?"

"Naturally." The voice on the phone took on a note of sarcasm. "Or are you suggesting I should have discharged her?"

There was reason for Reubens to be sour on the subject, O'Donnell thought. Unquestionably he had been put in a difficult position. If he had discharged the patient, he might have had to call her back for more surgery, as had happened to Bill Rufus. On the other hand, every additional day in hospital meant an extra financial burden for the family. He answered noncommittally, "I'm not suggesting anything, Reub. Just making some inquiries."

The thing had obviously been on Reubens' mind. "Then you'd better talk to some of the other men," he said. "I'm not the only one this has happened to. You know about Bill Rufus?"

"Yes, I know. Frankly, I thought things had been improving a little."

"If they have, it's not so's you'd notice it. What do you propose to do about Bryan's bill?"

"I doubt if we can do anything. After all, his wife was here for three weeks. Hospital money is tight, you know." O'Donnell wondered what Reubens' reaction would be when he heard he was being asked to give six thousand dollars himself to the hospital building fund.

"It's too bad. Husband's a decent little guy—a carpenter or something like that, works for himself. He didn't have any insurance. This'll set 'em back for a long time." O'Donnell made no answer. His mind was already running ahead, thinking of what came next. Again the thin voice on the phone: "Well, is that all?"

"Yes, Reub; that's all. Thanks." He handed the telephone back to Harry Tomaselli.

"Harry, I want a meeting this afternoon." O'Donnell had made up his mind what had to be done. "Let's try to get half a dozen of the senior people on staff. We'll meet here, if that's convenient, and I'd like you to be here too."

Tomaselli nodded. "Can do."

O'Donnell was checking over names in his mind. "We'll want Harvey Chandler, of course, as chief of medicine. Better have Bill Rufus, and Reubens should be included, I think." He paused. "Oh yes, and Charlie Dornberger. He might be useful. How many is that?"

The administrator checked the names he had written. "Six with you and me. How about Lucy Grainger?"

Briefly O'Donnell hesitated. Then he said, "All right. Let's make it seven then."

"Agenda?" Tomaselli had his pencil poised.

O'Donnell shook his head. "We won't need one. There's just one subject—changes in Pathology."

When the administrator had mentioned Lucy Grainger's name, O'Donnell had hesitated for one reason only: it had reminded him of a meeting between himself and Lucy the night before.

They had met for dinner—the outcome of O'Donnell's invitation to Lucy the day of the mortality conference—and in the Palm Court of the Roosevelt Hotel they had had cocktails, then a leisurely meal. It had been a pleasant, relaxed occasion, and they had talked lightly of themselves, of people they had known, and their own experiences in and out of medicine.

Afterward O'Donnell had driven Lucy home. She had recently moved into Benvenuto Grange, a large, fashionable apartment block on the north side of town. She had said, "You'll come in for a nightcap, of course?"

He had left his car for the uniformed doorman to park and followed her. They rode the gleaming, silent elevator to the fifth floor, then turned down a birch-paneled corridor, their footsteps silenced in deep broadloom. He had raised his eyebrows and Lucy smiled. "It is a little awesome, isn't it? I'm still impressed myself."

She had used her key to open a door and inside touched a switch. Tasteful, subdued lighting sprang up around an elegant interior lounge. He could see the partly opened door of a bedroom directly ahead. "I'll mix us a drink," she said.

Her back was to him. Ice clinked in glasses. O'Donnell said, "Lucy, you've never married?"

"No." She had answered without turning.

He said softly, "I've sometimes wondered why."

"It's very simple really. It's quite some time since I was asked." Lucy turned, carrying the drinks she had mixed. She gave O'Donnell his, then moved to a chair. She said thoughtfully, "Now I think of it, there was only one occasion—at least, only one that mattered. I was a good deal younger then."

O'Donnell sipped his drink. "And your answer was 'no'?"

"I wanted a career in medicine. At the time it seemed terribly important. That and marriage didn't seem to go together."

He asked casually, "Any regrets?"

Lucy considered. "Not really, I suppose. I've achieved what I wanted, and it's been rewarding in many ways. Oh, sometimes one wonders how things would have turned out with a different decision, but after all, that's human, isn't it?"

"I suppose so." O'Donnell was conscious of being strangely moved. There was a sense of depth and tenderness about Lucy, a feeling of peacefulness and coming home. She should have children, he thought. He had asked, "Do you still feel the same way about marriage and medicine—for you, that is?"

"I'm no longer dogmatic about anything." She smiled. "That, at least, I've learned."

O'Donnell wondered what, from his own point of view, marriage to Lucy would be like. Would there be love and mellowness? Or had each of their careers gone parallel too far and too long for change and adjustment now. If married, how might they spend their hours of leisure? Would the talk be intimate and domestic? Or would it be of hospital affairs, with charts on the table at dinner and diagnostic problems for dessert? Would he perhaps, instead of gaining sanctuary, find merely another offshoot of medicine and his daily work. Aloud he said, "I've always thought, you know, that we have a good deal in common."

"Yes, Kent," Lucy answered, "so have I."

O'Donnell had finished his drink, then risen to leave. He realized they had both said a good deal more than had passed in words. Now he wanted time to think and to reason things through. Too much was involved for hasty decisions.

"There's really no need to go, Kent. Stay if you wish." Lucy had said it simply, and he knew if he stayed it would be up to him what happened next.

Part of his mind had told him to remain, but caution and habit won out. He took her hands. "Good night, Lucy. Let's think about all this."

When the elevator doors had closed she was still standing at the open apartment door.

Six

"I asked you here," O'Donnell told the group around the board-room table, "because I'd like your support in something I want to do." The others were listening attentively. Of those they had asked, all had come except Reubens, who had a herniorrhaphy scheduled. O'Donnell went on, "I think we all know there's a problem in Pathology. I believe, too, you'll agree it's a personal problem as well as medical."

"What kind of a problem?" It was Charlie Dornberger. As

the elderly obstetrician talked he filled his pipe. "I'm not sure I know what you're getting at, Kent."

O'Donnell had expected something like this. He knew that Dornberger and Pearson were close friends. Politely he said, "I'd like you to hear me out, Charlie, if you will. I'll try to make it clear."

Methodically he went over the issues involved—the delays in surgical reports, the increasing service the hospital required from its pathology department, his own doubts that Joe Pearson could cope with them alone. He related the incident of Bill Rufus' patient, turning to Rufus for confirmation, and followed it with the report he had had from Reubens that morning. He told them of his own interview with Pearson and the old man's refusal to accept a second pathologist. He concluded: "I'm convinced we do need a new man to help Joe out. I want your support in seeing that one is brought in."

"I've been concerned about Pathology too." Promptly, as if to ensure the observance of protocol, Harvey Chandler, the chief of medicine, followed O'Donnell. His words held the suggestion of a judicial opinion weightily delivered; as usual, his simplest statements contained an air of mild pomposity. He continued, "But the situation may be difficult with Joe Pearson feeling the way he does. After all, he's a department head, and we ought to avoid any suggestion of undermining his authority."

"I agree," O'Donnell responded, "and that's why I want some help." He drummed his fingers on the desk top for emphasis. "Some help in convincing Joe Pearson that changes are necessary."

"I'm not sure I like the way we're doing this," Bill Rufus said.

"Why, Bill?" O'Donnell noticed that Rufus was wearing one of his more subdued neckties today. It had only three colors instead of the usual four.

"I don't think a few of us, meeting like this, have any right to talk about a change in Pathology." Rufus looked around at the others. "Certainly I've had some run-ins with Joe Pearson. I guess most of us have. But that doesn't mean I'm going to join some hole-and-corner conspiracy to boot him out."

O'Donnell was glad this had come up; he was ready for it. "Let me say emphatically," he said, "there is no intention on my part or anybody else's of—as you put it"—he glanced at Rufus—"booting Dr. Pearson out." There was a murmur of assent.

"Look at it this way," O'Donnell said. "There seems to be agreement that changes in Pathology are necessary. Take surgical reports alone. Every day's delay where surgery is needed means danger to the patient. I know I don't need to emphasize that."

Harry Tomaselli interjected, "And don't let us forget that these delays are tying up hospital beds we need badly. Our waiting list for admissions is still very long."

O'Donnell took over again. "Of course, instead of handling things this way I could have called the executive committee together." He paused. "I still will if I have to, but I think you know what might happen. Joe is a member of the executive himself and, knowing Joe as we all do, any discussion will mean a showdown. In that case, assuming we force the issue, what have we gained? We've proven to Joe Pearson that he's no longer in charge of his own department. And medically, and every other way—just as Harvey said—we'll have undermined ourselves and the hospital." O'Donnell thought, too, of what he could not tell the others: that he was also weighing Pearson's influence with the old guard on the hospital board and the political repercussions which a showdown might create.

"I'm not saying I go along with you, but what's your suggestion?" The question came from Charlie Dornberger. He punctuated it with puffs of smoke as his pipe got going.

Rufus sniffed. "We'd better hurry this up. It won't be fit to breathe in here soon. Do you import that camel dung, Charlie?"

As the others smiled, O'Donnell decided to lay it on the line. "My suggestion, Charlie, is that you approach Joe—on behalf of the rest of us."

"Oh no!" The reaction from Dornberger was much what O'Donnell had anticipated. He settled in to be persuasive.

"Charlie, we know you're a close friend of Joe's and I had that in mind when I asked you here. You could persuade him about this."

"In other words, you want me to carry your ax," Dornberger said dryly.

"Charlie, it isn't an ax, believe me."

Dr. Charles Dornberger hesitated. He observed that the

others were watching him, waiting for his answer. He debated: should he do as O'Donnell asked or not? He was torn by two conflicting feelings—his concern for the hospital's good and his own relationship with Joe Pearson.

In a way the news of the state of affairs in Pathology was not entirely unexpected; it was a condition he had suspected for some time. Nevertheless the two incidents concerning Rufus and Reubens, which O'Donnell had revealed, had shocked him inexpressibly. Dornberger knew also that O'Donnell would not have called this meeting unless he had been seriously concerned, and he respected the chief of surgery's judgment.

At the same time Charles Dornberger wanted to help Joe Pearson if he could, and at this moment he found himself resenting the tide of events which seemed to be engulfing the elderly pathologist. And yet O'Donnell had appeared to be sincere when he said there was no intention of booting Pearson out, and the others seemed to share this feeling. He decided that perhaps he could be the intermediary. Possibly this way he could help Joe best.

Dornberger looked around at the others. He asked, "Is this unanimous?"

Lucy Grainger said thoughtfully, "I'm very fond of Joe. I think we all are. But I do believe some changes in Pathology are necessary." It was the first time Lucy had spoken. She too had wondered about this meeting with Kent O'Donnell. What had passed between them in her apartment last night had left her strangely disturbed in a way she had not remembered for years. Afterward she had wondered if she were in love with O'Donnell, then told herself—only half believing—that those kind of phrases were all very well for the young and ardent, but at her age—with maturity, independence, and a professional practice—one reasoned and rationalized, eschewing hastily conceived emotions. At this moment, though, she found herself able to separate personal and professional feelings and to think about the problem in Pathology. In medicine you learned to do that—to push things out of your mind when immediate concerns were more important.

O'Donnell looked at Rufus. "Bill?"

The surgeon nodded. "All right—if Charlie will approach Pearson, I agree."

Harvey Chandler was next. The chief of medicine told

Dornberger ponderously, "In my opinion this is the best way to handle the situation, Charlie. You will be doing all of us, as well as the hospital, a very real service."

"Very well," Dornberger said. "I'll see what I can do."

There was a momentary silence, and O'Donnell sensed a feeling of relief. He knew the problem had been understood and now, at least, something would be done. Then, if this approach failed, he would have to resort to more direct methods. Sometimes, he reflected, it might be simpler if medical protocol were less complicated. In industry, if a man was not doing his job adequately, you fired him. If you wanted him to take an assistant, you told him to do so and usually that was that. But in medicine and in a hospital it was less straightforward. The lines of authority were seldom clear-cut, and a medical-department head, once appointed, was pretty well master in his own domain. What was even more important—you hesitated to do really drastic things because you were dealing with more than just a job. You were questioning the ability of a man who, like yourself, was dependent on his professional reputation. It was a delicate issue in which a single decision could affect the entire future and livelihood of a fellow practitioner. That was why you proceeded warily, keeping things like this under wraps and carefully guarded from outside scrutiny.

Harry Tomaselli said softly, "I take it, then, we're going to look for an available pathologist."

"I think we should begin to look around." O'Donnell answered the administrator, then glanced at the others. "I imagine most of us have contacts where we might pass the word along. If you hear of anyone—a good man who's just finishing his residency perhaps—I'd like you to let me know."

"Pathologists can be pretty choosy nowadays," Bill Rufus said.

"I know. This may not be easy." O'Donnell added, "It's all the more reason for handling Joe carefully."

Harry Tomaselli had reached into one of his desk drawers and removed a file folder. He said, "Something here may interest you."

Harvey Chandler asked him, "What is it you have?"

"I've been receiving the 'open list' on pathologists lately," Tomaselli answered. "Frankly, I anticipated something like this and asked for it. This name came in a week or two ago."

"May I see?" O'Donnell reached for the paper Tomaselli had produced. He knew the so-called "open list" was circulated periodically to hospitals on request. It contained information on pathologists available for appointments, and the men concerned had given permission for their names to be used. There was also a "closed list," but this was retained in confidence by the pathologists' professional society. Mostly the "closed list" comprised men dissatisfied with their present appointments who were seeking discreetly to make a change. In this case a hospital would advise the society of its need for a pathologist and those on the "closed list" had this information passed along to them. If he chose, an individual could then approach a hospital direct. Yet with all this machinery in existence, O'Donnell knew that most pathology appointments were still made on the basis of personal contacts and recommendation.

He glanced over the sheet the administrator had given him. The listing was for a Dr. David Coleman, his age thirty-one. O'Donnell's eyebrows went up as he noted Coleman's record and experience. An N.Y.U. honors graduate. Intern at Bellevue. Two years in the Army, mostly in pathology. A five-year pathology residence spread over three good hospitals. Here was a man who plainly shopped for the best in education.

He passed the paper to Rufus. "I doubt very much if he'd look at us," he told Tomaselli. "Not with those qualifications and what we could pay to begin with." O'Donnell knew, from an earlier talk with the administrator, that salary level would have to be around ten thousand dollars a year.

Rufus glanced up. "I agree. This man can take his pick of the big city hospitals." He passed the sheet to Harvey Chandler.

"Well, as a matter of fact . . ." Tomaselli paused; he sounded unusually diffident, as if weighing his words carefully.

O'Donnell asked curiously, "What is it, Harry?"

"Well, the fact is, Dr. Coleman is interested in this hospital." Tomaselli paused. "I gather he's heard something of our recent changes and plans for the future."

O'Donnell broke the sudden stillness. "How do you know?"

"I know because we've had some correspondence."

Rufus said, "Isn't that a little unusual, Harry?"

"Perhaps I was being premature, but after this came"—

Tomaselli indicated the paper which had now passed to Lucy—"I wrote to Dr. Coleman. I said nothing definite, of course. It was just a tentative approach, sounding him out." He turned to O'Donnell. "It was after our conversation a couple of weeks ago. You may remember, Kent."

"Yes. I do." O'Donnell was wishing that Harry had briefed him about this beforehand. Of course, as administrator Tomaselli had a right to correspond with anyone he chose. He hadn't committed the hospital in any way. The correspondence was presumably confidential. Possibly it might prove to have been a good move. He said to Tomaselli, "You say he's interested?"

"Yes. He'd like to come and see us. If this had not come up today, I'd intended to speak to you about it."

Dornberger had the paper now. He tapped it with a forefinger. "What do you want me to do about this?"

O'Donnell glanced at the others, seeking confirmation. "I think you should take it with you, Charlie," he said. "And I suggest you show it to Joe Pearson."

Seven

In an annex to the autopsy room Roger McNeil, the pathology resident, was almost ready for gross conference. All that was necessary to begin was the presence of Dr. Joseph Pearson.

At Three Counties, as at many hospitals, a gross conference was the second stage after autopsy. Half an hour ago George Rinne, *diener* of the morgue, had brought in the organs removed at three autopsies earlier in the week. Two sets of organs now stood neatly arrayed in white enameled pails, and alongside them, in glass jars, were three brains. Centerpiece of the gross-conference room was a stone table with a large sink let into it and with a water tap above. At present the tap was turned on and beneath it was the third pail of organs, the water washing out the formalin in which the organs had been preserved, as well as some of the more objectionable odor.

McNeil looked around, making a final check. Pearson was

always irascible if everything was not ready at hand. Mc-
Neil reflected that the room in which they did their work was
appropriately macabre—particularly when the organs were
laid out, as they would be in a few minutes, making the
place look somewhat like a butcher's shop. He had been in
hospital dissecting rooms where everything was gleaming
stainless steel; but that was the modern way which had not
touched Three Counties' pathology department yet. Now he
heard the familiar, half-shuffling footsteps, and Pearson came
in, the inevitable cloud of cigar smoke with him.

"Can't waste any time." Pearson seldom bothered with
preliminaries. "It's a week and a half since I had that set-to
with O'Donnell, and we're still behind." The cigar bobbed
up and down. "When this is through I want a check on all
surgicals outstanding. What's the first case?" While he had
been talking he had put on a black rubber apron and rubber
gloves. Now he came to the center table and sat down at it.
McNeil perched himself on a stool opposite and looked over
the case notes.

"Fifty-five-year-old woman. Physician's cause of death,
carcinoma of the breast."

"Let me see." Pearson reached for the file. Sometimes he
would sit patiently while the resident described a case; at
other times he would want to read everything himself. In
this, as in all things, he was unpredictable.

"Hm." He put down the papers and turned off the running water. Then he reached into the pail and groped
around until he found the heart. He opened it, using both
hands.

"Did you cut this?"

The resident shook his head.

"I didn't think so." Pearson peered at the heart again.
"Seddons?"

McNeil nodded a little reluctantly. He had noticed himself that the heart was badly cut.

"He left the mark of Zorro." Pearson grinned. "Looks
like he was dueling with it. By the way, where *is* Seddons?"

"I believe there was something in surgery. A procedure he
wanted to see."

"Tell him from me that while any resident is assigned to
Pathology I expect him at all gross conferences. All right,
let's get on with it."

McNeil balanced a clip board on his knee and prepared to write. Pearson dictated: "Heart shows a slight thickening and rolling of the mitral valve. See it there?" He held it out.

Leaning across, McNeil answered, "Yes, I do."

Pearson continued, "The chordae tendineae are fused, shortened and thickened." He added casually, "Looks as if she had an old rheumatic fever. It was not a cause of death though."

He cut away a small portion of tissue and put it into a labeled jar about the size of an ink bottle. This was for microscopic examination later. Then with the ease of long practice he tossed the remainder of the heart accurately into a hole lower down the table. Beneath the hole was a metal bin. Later in the day this would be cleared and cleaned, the contents being burned to fine ash in a special incinerator.

Now Pearson had the lungs. He opened the first lung like the two big leaves of a book, then dictated to McNeil, "Lungs show multiple metastatic nodules." Again he held out the tissue for the resident to see.

He had turned his attention to the second lung when a door behind him opened.

"You busy, Dr. Pearson?"

Pearson turned around irritably. The voice was that of Carl Bannister, senior lab technician in the pathology department. Bannister had his head around the door tentatively, and there was another figure behind him in the corridor.

"Of course I'm busy. What do you want?" It was the tone, half snarling, half bantering, Pearson habitually used to Bannister. Over the years the two of them had become accustomed to it; anything more cordial would probably have confused both.

Bannister was unperturbed. He beckoned to the figure behind him. "Come inside." Then to Pearson he said, "This is John Alexander. You remember—our new lab technician. You hired him a week ago. He starts work today."

"Oh yes. I'd forgotten this was the day. Come in." Pearson sounded more cordial than he had been with Bannister. McNeil thought: Maybe he doesn't want to scare a new employee first day out.

McNeil looked curiously at the newcomer. Twenty-two, he figured; later he was to learn he was exactly right. He knew from what he had heard that Alexander was fresh from college with a degree in medical technology. Well, they could do with someone like that around the place. Bannister, for sure, wasn't any Louis Pasteur.

McNeil turned his eyes to the senior technician. As usual, Bannister's appearance made him something of a minor-league Pearson. His short, paunchy body was partially covered by a stained lab coat. The coat was not buttoned and the clothes beneath it appeared shabby and unpressed. Bannister was mostly bald, and such hair as was left looked as if it were permanently ignored.

McNeil knew something of Bannister's history. He had come to Three Counties a year or two after Pearson's arrival. He had a high-school education, and Pearson had hired him for odd jobs—stock clerk, messenger, washing glassware. Gradually, as the years passed, Bannister had learned a lot of practical things around the lab, becoming more and more a right hand to Pearson.

Officially Bannister's work was in serology and biochemistry. But he had been in the department so long that he could fill in if necessary, and often did, for technicians in other sections of the lab. Because of this Pearson had pushed a good deal of administrative lab work onto Bannister, leaving him, in effect, in charge of all pathology technicians.

McNeil thought it likely that in Bannister's heyday he had been a good technician who, with more education, might have risen to better things. As it was now, McNeil considered Bannister long on experience and short on theory. From observation the resident knew that much of Bannister's work in the lab was from rote rather than reasoning. He could do serologic and chemical tests but without any real understanding of the science behind them. McNeil had often thought that one day this might prove dangerous.

Alexander, of course, was a different proposition. He had come the way of most lab technicians nowadays, with three years of college behind him, the last year in an approved school for medical technologists. The word "technologist" was sometimes a sore point with people like Bannister who only rated the styling "technician."

Pearson waved his cigar at the remaining stool around the table. "Sit down, John."

"Thank you, Doctor," Alexander answered politely. In his spotless lab coat, with a recent crew cut, pressed pants, and shined shoes, he presented a contrast to Pearson as well as Bannister.

"Do you think you'll like it here?" Pearson looked down at the lungs he was holding, continuing the examination while he talked.

"I'm sure I will, Doctor."

Nice kid, this, McNeil thought. He sounds as if he means it.

"Well, John," Pearson was saying, "you'll discover we have certain ways of doing things. They may not always be the ways you've been used to, but we find they work pretty well for us."

"I understand, Doctor."

Do you? McNeil thought. Do you understand what the old man is really telling you?—that he doesn't want any changes around the place, that there's to be no nonsense with ideas you may have picked up in school, that nothing in the department—no matter how trifling—is to be amended without his blessing.

"Some people might say we're old-fashioned," Pearson continued. He was being friendly enough in his way. "But we believe in tried and tested methods. Eh, Carl?"

Called on for endorsement, Bannister was quick to answer. "That's right, Doctor."

Pearson had finished with the lungs now and, dipping into the pail, somewhat like drawing a lottery, had come up with a stomach. He grunted, then held out an open section to McNeil. "See that?"

The resident nodded. "I saw it before. We have it listed."

"All right." Pearson motioned to the clip board, then he dictated, "There is a peptic ulcer lying just below the pyloric ring in the duodenum."

Alexander had shifted slightly to get a better look. Pearson saw his movement and slid the organ across. "Are you interested in dissection, John?"

Alexander answered respectfully, "I've always been interested in anatomy, Doctor."

"As well as lab work, eh?" McNeil sensed that Pearson was pleased. Pathological anatomy was the old man's first love.

"Yes, sir."

"Well, these are the organs of a fifty-five-year-old woman."

Pearson turned over the case-history pages in front of him.
Alexander was raptly attentive. "Interesting history, this case.
The patient was a widow, and the immediate cause of death
was cancer of the breast. For two years before she died her
children knew she had trouble but they couldn't persuade
her to see a physician. It seems she had a prejudice against
them."

"Some people do." It was Bannister. He gave a high-
pitched giggle which dried up as he caught Pearson's eye.

"Just cut out the snide remarks. I'm giving John here some
information. Might not do you any harm either." Anyone
but Bannister would have been crushed by Pearson's rejoinder. As it was, the technician merely grinned.

"What happened, Doctor?" Alexander asked.

"It says here: 'Daughter states that for the past two years
the family has been noticing drainage from the mother's left
breast area. Fourteen months before admission bleeding was
noticed from the same area. Otherwise she appeared in normal health.' "

Pearson turned a page. "It seems this woman went to a
faith healer." He chuckled grimly. "Guess she didn't have
enough faith, though, because she finally collapsed and they
brought her to this hospital."

"By then, I suppose, it was too late."

This isn't politeness, McNeil thought. This guy Alexander
is really interested.

"Yeah," Pearson answered. "But if she had gone to a doctor at the beginning she could have had a radical mastectomy
—that's removal of the breast."

"Yes, sir. I know."

"If she'd had that she might still be alive." Pearson tossed
the stomach neatly through the hole.

Something was troubling Alexander. He asked, "Didn't
you just say, though, she had a peptic ulcer?"

Good for you, McNeil thought. Pearson, it seemed, had
the same reaction, for he turned to Bannister. "There you
are, Carl. Here's a boy who keeps his ears open. You watch
out or he'll be showing you up."

Bannister was grinning, but McNeil suspected a little
sourness. What had been said might prove uncomfortably
true. "Well, John"—Pearson was really expansive now—"she
might have had trouble with that. Then again she might not."

"You mean she'd never have known about it?"

McNeil thought it was time he said something himself. "It's surprising," he told Alexander, "what people have wrong with them besides the things they die of. Things they never know about. You see a lot of that here."

"That's right." Pearson nodded agreement. "You know, John, the remarkable thing about the human body is not what kills us but what we can have wrong inside and still go on living." He paused, then abruptly changed the subject. "Are you married?"

"Yes, sir. I am."

"Your wife here with you?"

"Not yet. She's coming next week. I thought I'd find us a place to live first."

McNeil remembered that Alexander had been one of the out-of-town applicants for the job at Three Counties. He seemed to recall that Chicago had been mentioned.

Alexander hesitated, then he added, "There was something I wanted to ask you, Dr. Pearson."

"What's that?" The old man sounded wary.

"My wife is pregnant, Doctor, and coming into a new town, we don't know anyone." Alexander paused. "This baby is pretty important to us. You see, we lost our first child. A month after she was born."

"I see." Pearson had stopped work now and was listening carefully.

"I was wondering, Doctor, if you could recommend an obstetrician my wife could go to."

"That's easy." Pearson sounded relieved. Plainly he had wondered what was coming. "Dr. Dornberger's a good man. He has an office right here in the hospital. Would you like me to call him?"

"If it's not too much trouble."

Pearson motioned to Bannister. "See if he's in."

Bannister picked up the telephone behind them and asked for an extension. After a pause he said, "He's in," and offered the instrument to Pearson.

With both hands gloved and wet, the old man motioned his head irritably. "Hold it! Hold it!"

Bannister moved in closer and held the receiver against Pearson's ear.

"That you, Charlie?" The pathologist boomed into the mouthpiece. "I've got a patient for you."

In his office three floors above Dr. Charles Dornberger

smiled and moved the telephone slightly away from his ear. He asked, "What can obstetrics do for your kind of patients?" At the same time he reflected that this call was convenient. Since the meeting which O'Donnell had called yesterday, Charles Dornberger had speculated on the best method of approach to Joe Pearson. Now, it seemed, an opportunity was presenting itself.

Down in Pathology Pearson maneuvered the cigar to a corner of his mouth. He always enjoyed exchanges with Dornberger.

"This isn't a dead patient, you old fool. It's a live one. Wife of one of my lab boys here—Mrs. John Alexander. They're new in town. Don't know anybody."

As Pearson mentioned the name Dornberger opened a file drawer and selected a blank card.

"Just a minute." He cradled the phone in his shoulder and, using his left hand to hold the card, wrote in a fine script with the right, "Alexander, Mrs. John." It was typical of Dornberger's organized approach to his practice that this was the first thing he did. Now he said, "Be glad to oblige, Joe. Will you have them call me for an appointment?"

"All right. Be some time next week. Mrs. Alexander won't be in town till then." He grinned at Alexander, then added, still almost shouting, "And if they want twins, Charlie, it's up to you to see they get them."

Pearson listened to Dornberger's answer and chuckled. A thought struck him. "And hey! Another thing! None of your fancy fees for this job. I don't want the boy coming to me for a raise so he can pay his doctor's bill."

Dornberger smiled. He said, "Don't worry." On the card he made a notation, "Hospital employee." It was a signal to himself that this was a patient he would charge no fee. Into the phone he said, "Joe, there's something I want to talk to you about. When would be a convenient time to come and see you?"

"Can't make it today, Charlie," Pearson said. "Got a full schedule. How about tomorrow?"

Dornberger consulted his own appointment list. "I'm crowded tomorrow myself. Let's make it the day after. How about around ten in the morning? I'll come to your office."

"That'll be all right. Unless you want to tell me now—on the phone." Pearson's voice sounded curious.

"No, Joe," Dornberger said, "I'd rather come and see you."

In Pathology Pearson answered, "All right, Charlie. See you then. So long." Impatiently he motioned the telephone away and Bannister replaced it.

To Alexander, Pearson said, "That's all fixed. Your wife can be admitted to this hospital when she comes to term. Because you're an employee you'll get a twenty per cent discount on your bill."

Alexander was beaming. McNeil thought: Yes, go ahead; enjoy it, my friend. This is one of the old man's good moments. But make no mistake—there'll be others, and those you won't enjoy at all.

"I'll only be a moment." In his office Dornberger smiled at the student nurse who had come in while he was talking with Pearson. He motioned her to the chair alongside his desk.

"Thank you, Doctor." Vivian Loburton had brought a patient's chart that Dornberger had asked to see. Ordinarily physicians didn't get this kind of service; they would have to walk to the ward and look at the chart there. But Dornberger was a favorite with the nurses; they were always doing little things for him, and when he had phoned a few minutes ago the staff nurse had sent Vivian off promptly.

"I like to do one thing at a time when I can." Dornberger was writing in pencil now, noting on the card the new facts Joe Pearson had given him. Later, when he had more information from the patient, he would erase the pencil notes and complete the card in ink. Still writing, he asked the girl, "You're new here, aren't you?"

"Fairly new, Doctor," Vivian said. "This is my fourth month in nursing school."

He noticed she had a soft voice with a lilt. Pretty too. He wondered if she had slept yet with any of the interns or residents. Or had things changed since his own student years? He occasionally suspected that interns and residents nowadays were getting more conservative than they used to be. A pity. If true, they were missing a good deal. Aloud he said, "That was Dr. Pearson, our pathologist. Have you met him yet?"

"Yes," Vivian said. "Our class went to an autopsy."

"Oh dear. How did you . . ." He was going to say "like it" but changed it to, "How did you find it?"

Vivian considered. "At first it was rather a shock. Afterward I didn't mind too much though."

He nodded sympathetically. He had finished writing now and put the card away. This had been a quieter day than usual; it was a luxury to be able to clean up one piece of work before going on to another. He held out his hand for the chart. "Thank you." He added, "I'll only be a moment with this, if you'd like to wait."

"All right, Doctor." Vivian decided a few more minutes' respite from the rush of ward work would be welcome. She settled back in the chair. It was cool in here with the air conditioning. There was no such luxury in the nurses' home.

Vivian watched Dr. Dornberger as he studied the chart. He was probably about the same age as Dr. Pearson, she thought, but certainly a lot different to look at. While the pathologist was round-faced and heavy-jowled, Dr. Dornberger was lean and angular. In other ways, too, his appearance was a contrast, with the thatch of white hair carefully combed and parted. She noticed his hands were manicured, his white hospital jacket pressed and spotless.

Dornberger handed back the chart. "Thank you," he said. "It was good of you to bring it." He has a sparkle to him, Vivian thought. She had heard he was much beloved by his women patients. There was little need to wonder why.

"We'll be seeing each other, I expect." Dornberger had risen and opened the door courteously. "Good luck in your studies."

"Good-by, Doctor." She went out, leaving a trace of fragrance behind her, Dornberger thought. Not for the first time the contact with someone youthful left him wondering about himself. He returned to the swivel chair and leaned back meditatively. Almost absently he took out his pipe and began to fill it.

He had been in medicine now for almost thirty-two years; in a week or two he would being his thirty-third. They had been full years and rewarding ones. Financially he had no problems. His own four children were married, and he and his wife could live comfortably on the careful investments he had made. But would he be content to retire and rusticate? That was the rub.

In all his years in medicine Charles Dornberger had prided himself in keeping up to date. He had made up his mind long ago that no young newcomer was going to surpass him, either in technique or knowledge. As a result he had read avidly and still continued to do so. He subscribed to many of the medical journals which he read thoroughly and occasionally contributed articles himself. He was a regular attender at medical conventions and conscientiously took in most of the business sessions. Early in his career, long before the present boundary lines were drawn in medicine, he had foreseen the need for specialization. His own choice had been obstetrics and gynecology. It was a choice he had never regretted, and he often felt it had helped him to keep young in mind.

Because of this by the mid-thirties, when American specialty boards were coming into being, Dornberger was already established in his own field. As a result, under the so-called "grandfather" clause, he had been given Board certification without examination. It was something he had always been proud of. If anything, it had made him keener still to remain up to date.

And yet he had never resented younger men. When he had felt them to be good and conscientious, he had gone out of his way to offer help and advice. He admired and respected O'Donnell. He considered the youthful chief of surgery one of the best things that had ever happened to Three Counties. His own morale had risen with O'Donnell's changes and progress in the hospital.

He had made many friends, some among his own immediate colleagues, others in unlikely places. Joe Pearson might be called one of the unlikely ones. Professionally the two men looked at a lot of things in different ways. Dornberger knew, for example, that Joe did not read much these days. He suspected that in a few areas of knowledge the elderly pathologist had slipped behind the times, and, administratively, there was the problem which yesterday's meeting had revealed. And yet, over the years, the bond between the two men had grown strong. To his own surprise sometimes he had found himself siding with Pearson at medical conferences and defending him occasionally when Pathology was criticized in private.

Dornberger's interjection ten days ago at the mortality conference had been much like that. He supposed other people recognized the alliance between himself and Joe. What was it Gil Bartlett had said? "You're a friend of his; and besides he doesn't have a vendetta with obstetricians." Until this moment he had forgotten the remark, but he realized now it had had an edge of bitterness and he was sorry about that. Bartlett was a good physician, and Dornberger made a mental note to be especially cordial next time they met.

But there was still his own problem. To quit or not to quit? And if he did quit, when? Just lately, despite his carefully guarded physical fitness, he had found himself tiring. And although he had spent a lifetime answering night calls, lately they had seemed harder to take. Yesterday at lunch he had heard Kersh, the dermatologist, telling a new intern, "You should join us in the skin game, son. Haven't been called out at night in fifteen years." Dornberger had laughed with the rest but harbored a little secret envy.

One thing he was sure of though. He would not hang on if he found himself weakening. Right now he knew he was as good as ever. His mind was clear, his hands steady and eyes sharp. He always watched himself carefully because he knew that at the first sign of failing he would not hesitate. He would clear his desk and go. He had seen too many others try to stay the course too long. That would never be for him.

But as for the present, well, maybe he would let things go another three months, then think it over.

By this time he had packed the tobacco tightly in his pipe and now he reached for a folder of matches. He was about to strike one when the telephone rang. Putting down pipe and matches, he answered it. "Dr. Dornberger speaking."

It was one of his patients. She had begun labor pains an hour ago. Now her membranes had ruptured and she had discharged water. She was a young girl in her early twenties, and it would be her first baby. She sounded breathless, as if nervous but trying not to be.

As he had so many times before, Dornberger gave his instructions quietly. "Is your husband at home?"

"Yes, Doctor."

"Then get your things together and have him drive you to the hospital. I'll see you after you've arrived."

"Very well, Doctor."

"Tell your husband to drive carefully and stop at all the red lights. We've plenty of time. You'll see."

He could sense, even over the phone, that he had helped her to relax. It was something he did often, and he considered it as much a part of his job as any course of treatment.

Nevertheless he felt his own senses quickening. A new case always had that effect. Logically, he thought, he should have lost the feeling long ago. As you grew older in medicine you were supposed to become impervious, mechanical and unsentimental. It had never worked that way for him, though—perhaps because, even now, he was doing what he loved to do most.

He reached for his pipe, then changed his mind and picked up the telephone again. He must let Obstetrics know that his patient was coming in.

Eight

"I'm not even sure that defeating polio was a good or necessary thing."

The speaker was Eustace Swayne—founder of a department-store empire, millionaire philanthropist, and member of the board of directors of Three Counties Hospital. The background was the shadowed, oak-paneled library of Swayne's aging but imposing mansion, set alone in fifty acres of parkland and near the eastern fringes of Burlington.

"Come now, you can't be serious," Orden Brown said lightly. The hospital-board chairman smiled at the two women in the room—his own wife, Amelia, and Swayne's daughter, Denise Quantz.

Kent O'Donnell sipped the cognac which a soft-footed manservant had brought him and leaned back in the deep leather chair he had chosen on entering this room with the others after dinner. It occurred to him that the scene they made was almost medieval. He glanced around the softly lighted room, his eyes ranging over tiers of leather-bound books rising to the high-timbered ceiling, the dark and heavy oaken furniture, the cavernous fireplace laid with great logs —not burning now, this warm July evening, but ready to blaze to life at the touch of a servant's torch; and, across from O'Donnell, Eustace Swayne, seated kinglike in a straight-backed, stuffed wing chair, the other four—almost as courtiers—formed in a semicircle, facing the old tycoon.

"I am serious." Swayne put down his brandy glass and

leaned forward to make his point. "Oh, I admit—show me a child in leg braces and I'll cringe with the rest and reach for my checkbook. But I'm talking of the grand design. The fact is—and I challenge anyone to deny it—we're busily engaged in weakening the human race."

It was a familiar argument. O'Donnell said courteously, "Would you suggest that we should stop medical research, freeze our knowledge and techniques, not try to conquer any more diseases?"

"You couldn't do it," Swayne said. "You couldn't do it any more than you could have stopped the Gadarene swine jumping off their cliff."

O'Donnell laughed. "I'm not sure I like the analogy. But if that is so, then why the argument?"

"Why?" Swayne banged a fist on the arm of his chair. "Because you can still deplore something, even though there's nothing you can do to force a change."

"I see." O'Donnell was not sure he wanted to get deeper into this discussion. Besides, it might not help relations with Swayne, either for himself or Orden Brown, which was really why they had come here. He glanced around at the others in the room. Amelia Brown, whom he had come to know well through his visits to the chairman's home, caught his eye and smiled. As a wife who kept herself posted on all her husband's activities, she was well informed about hospital politics.

Swayne's married daughter, Denise Quantz, was sitting forward, listening intently.

At dinner O'Donnell had several times found his eyes traveling, almost involuntarily, in Mrs. Quantz's direction. He had found it difficult to reconcile her as the daughter of the rugged, hard-bitten man who sat at the table's head. At seventy-eight Eustace Swayne still exhibited much of the toughness he had learned in the competitive malestrom of large-scale retail merchandising. At times he took advantage of his age to toss out barbed remarks to his guests, though O'Donnell suspected that most times their host was merely angling for an argument. O'Donnell had found himself thinking: The old boy still likes a fight, even if it's only in words. In the same way he had an instinct now that Swayne was overstating his feelings about medicine, though perhaps in this case merely for the sake of being ornery. Watching the old man covertly, O'Donnell had suspected gout and rheumatism might be factors here.

But, in contrast, Denise Quantz was gentle and softly spoken. She had a trick of taking the edge from a remark of her father's by adding a word or two to what he had said. She was beautiful too, O'Donnell thought, with the rare mature loveliness which sometimes comes to a woman at forty. He gathered that she was visiting Eustace Swayne and came to Burlington fairly frequently. Probably this was to keep an eye on her father; he knew that Swayne's own wife had died many years before. It was evident from conversation, though, that most of the time Denise Quantz lived in New York. There were a couple of references made to children, but a husband was not mentioned. He gained the impression that she was either separated or divorced. Mentally O'Donnell found himself comparing Denise Quantz with Lucy Grainger. There was a world of difference, he thought, between the two women: Lucy with her professional career, at ease in the environment of medicine and the hospital, able to meet someone like himself on ground familiar to them both; and Denise Quantz, a woman of leisure and independence, a figure in society no doubt, and yet—he had the feeling—someone who would make a home a place of warmth and serenity. O'Donnell wondered which kind of woman was better for a man: one who was close to his working life, or someone separate and detached, with other interests beyond the daily round.

His thoughts were interrupted by Denise. Leaning toward him, she said, "Surely you're not going to give up so easily, Dr. O'Donnell. Please don't let my father get away with that."

The old man snorted. "There's nothing to get away with. It's a perfectly clear situation. For years the natural balance of nature kept populations in check. When the birth rate became too great there were famines to offset it."

Orden Brown put in, "But surely some of that was political. It wasn't always a force of nature."

"I'll grant you that in some cases." Eustace Swayne waved his hand airily. "But there was nothing political in the elimination of the weak."

"Do you mean the weak or the unfortunate?" Very well, O'Donnell thought, if you want an argument I'll give you one.

"I mean what I say—the weak." The old man's voice had a sharper tone, but O'Donnell sensed he was enjoying this. "When there was a plague or an epidemic, it was the weak who were wiped out and the strong survived. Other illnesses did the same thing; there was a level maintained—nature's level. And because of this it was the strong who perpetuated themselves. They were the ones who sired the next generation."

"Do you really think, Eustace, that mankind is so degenerate now?" Amelia Brown had asked the question, and O'Donnell saw she was smiling. *She knows that Swayne's enjoying this,* he thought.

"We're moving toward degeneracy," the old man answered her, "at least in the Western world. We're preserving the cripples, the weaklings, and the disease-ridden. We're accumulating burdens on society, non-producers—the unfit, unable to contribute anything to the common good. Tell me— what purpose does a sanatorium or a home for incurables serve? I tell you, medicine today is preserving people who should be allowed to die. But we're helping them to live, then letting them spawn and multiply, passing along their uselessness to their children and their children's children."

O'Donnell reminded him, "The relationship between disease and heredity is far from clear."

"Strength is of the mind as well as the body," Eustace Swayne snapped back. "Don't children inherit the mental characteristics of their parents—*and* their weaknesses?"

"Not all of the time." This was between the old tycoon and O'Donnell now. The others sat back, listening.

"But a lot of the time they do. Well, don't they?"

O'Donnell smiled. "There's some evidence that way, yes."

Swayne snorted. "It's one of the reasons we've so many mental hospitals. And patients in them. And people running to psychiatrists."

"It could also be that we're more aware of mental health."

Swayne mimicked him. "It could also be that we're breeding people who are weak, weak, weak!"

The old man had almost shouted the last words. Now a bout of coughing seized him. *I'd better go easily,* O'Donnell thought. *He probably has high blood pressure.*

Just as if O'Donnell had spoken, Eustace Swayne glared across at him. The old man took a sip of brandy. Then, almost malevolently, he said, "Don't try to spare me, my young medical friend. I can handle all your arguments and more."

O'Donnell decided he would go on but more moderately. He said, quietly and reasonably, "I think there's one thing you're overlooking, Mr. Swayne. You say that illness and disease are nature's levelers. But many of these things haven't come to us in the natural course of nature. They're the result of man's own environment, conditions he's created himself. Bad sanitation, lack of hygiene, slums, air pollution—those aren't natural things; they're man's creation."

"They're part of evolution and evolution is a part of nature. It all adds up to the balancing process."

Admiringly O'Donnell thought: You can't shake the old son of a gun easily. But he saw the chink in the other's argument. He said, "If you're right, then medicine is a part of the balancing process too."

Swayne snapped back, "How do you reason that?"

"Because medicine is a part of evolution." Despite his good resolution O'Donnell felt his voice grow more intense. "Because every change of environment that man has had produced its problems for medicine to face and to try to solve. We never solve them entirely. Medicine is always a little behind, and as fast as we meet one problem there's a new one appearing ahead."

"But they're problems of medicine, not nature." Swayne's eyes had a malicious gleam. "If nature were left alone it would settle its problems before they arose—by natural selection of the fittest."

"You're wrong and I'll tell you why." O'Donnell had ceased to care about the effect of his words. He felt only that this was something he had to express, to himself as well as to the others. "Medicine has only one real problem. It's always been the same; it always will. It's the problem of individual human survival." He paused. "And survival is the oldest law of nature."

"Bravo!" Impulsively Amelia Brown clapped her palms together. But O'Donnell had not quite finished.

"That's why we fought polio, Mr. Swayne, and the black plague, and smallpox, and typhus, and syphilis. It's why we're still fighting cancer and tuberculosis and all the rest. It's the reason we have those places you talked about—the sanatoria, the homes for incurables. It's why we preserve people—all the people we can, the weak as well as the strong. Because it adds up to one thing—survival. It's the standard of medicine, the only one we can possibly have."

For a moment he expected Swayne to lash back as he had before. But the old man was silent. Then he looked over at his daughter. "Pour Dr. O'Donnell some more brandy, Denise."

O'Donnell held out his glass as she approached with the decanter. There was a soft rustle to her dress, and as she leaned toward him he caught a faint, tantalizing waft of perfume. For a moment he had an absurd, boyish impulse to reach out and touch her soft dark hair. As he checked it she moved over to her father.

Replenishing the old man's glass, she asked, "If you really feel the way you say, Father, what are you doing on a hospital board?"

Eustace Swayne chuckled. "Mostly I'm there because Orden and some others are hoping I won't change my will." He looked over at Orden Brown. "They reckon there can't be long to wait in any case."

"You're doing your friends an injustice, Eustace," Brown said. His tone contained the right mixture of banter and seriousness.

"And you're a liar." The old man was enjoying himself again. He said, "You asked a question, Denise. Well, I'll answer it. I'm on the hospital board because I'm a practical man. The world's the way it is and I can't change it, even though I see what's wrong. But what someone like me can be is a balancing force. Oh, I know what some of you think —that I'm just an obstructionist."

Orden Brown interjected quickly, "Has anyone ever said that?"

"You don't have to." Swayne shot a half-amused, malicious glance at the board chairman. "But every activity needs a brake on it somewhere. That's what I've been—a brake, a steadying force. And when I'm gone perhaps you and your friends will find you need another."

"You're talking nonsense, Eustace. And you're doing your own motives an injustice." Orden Brown had evidently decided to be equally direct. He went on, "You've done as many good things in Burlington as any man I know."

The old man seemed to shrink back into his chair. He grumbled, "How do any of us really know our own motives?"

Then, looking up, "I suppose you'll expect a big donation from me for this new extension."

Orden Brown said smoothly, "Frankly, we hope you'll see fit to make your usual generous contribution."

Softly, unexpectedly, Eustace Swayne said, "I suppose a quarter of a million dollars would be acceptable."

O'Donnell heard Orden Brown's quickly indrawn breath. Such a gift would be munificent—far more than they had expected, even in their most sanguine moments.

Brown said, "I can't pretend, Eustace. Frankly, I'm overwhelmed."

"No need to be." The old man paused, twirling the stem of his brandy glass. "I haven't decided yet, though I've been considering it. I'll tell you in a week or two." Abruptly he turned to O'Donnell. "Do you play chess?"

O'Donnell shook his head. "Not since I was in college."

"Dr. Pearson and I play a lot of chess." He was looking at O'Donnell directly. "You know Joe Pearson, of course."

"Yes. Very well."

"I've known Dr. Pearson for many years," Swayne said, "in Three Counties Hospital and out of it." The words were slow and deliberate. Did they have an undertone of warning? It was hard to be sure.

Swayne went on, "In my opinion Dr. Pearson is one of the best-qualified men on the hospital staff. I hope that he stays in charge of his department for many years to come. I respect his ability and his judgment—completely."

Well, there it is, O'Donnell thought—out in the open and in plain words: an ultimatum to the chairman of the hospital board and the president of the medical board. In as many words Eustace Swayne had said: If you want my quarter million dollars, hands off Joe Pearson!

Later Orden Brown, Amelia, and O'Donnell—seated together in the front seat of the Browns' Lincoln convertible—had driven back across town. They had been silent at first, then Amelia said, "Do you really think—a quarter of a million?"

Her husband answered, "He's quite capable of giving it— if he feels inclined."

O'Donnell asked, "I take it you received the message?"

"Yes." Brown said it calmly, without embellishment and without seeking to pursue the subject. O'Donnell thought:

Thank you for that. He knew this had to be his problem, not the chairman's.

They dropped him at the entrance to his apartment hotel. As they said good night Amelia added, "Oh, by the way, Kent, Denise is separated but not divorced. I think there's a problem there, though we've never discussed it. She has two children in high school. And she's thirty-nine."

Orden Brown asked her, "Why are you telling him all that?"

Amelia smiled. "Because he wanted to know." She touched her husband's arm. "You could never be a woman, dear. Not even with surgery."

Watching the Lincoln move away, O'Donnell wondered how she had known. Perhaps she had overheard him and Denise Quantz saying good night. He had said politely that he hoped he would see her again. She had answered, "I live in New York with my children. Why don't you call me next time you're there?" Now O'Donnell wondered if, after all, he might take in that surgeons' congress in New York next month which a week ago he had decided not to attend.

Abruptly his mind switched to Lucy Grainger and, irrationally, he had a momentary sense of disloyalty. He had gone from the sidewalk to the building entrance when his thoughts were broken by a voice saying, "Good night, Dr. O'Donnell."

He looked around and recognized one of the surgical residents, Seddons. There was a pretty brunette with him, and her face seemed familiar. Probably one of the student nurses, he thought; she appeared about the age. He smiled at them both and said "Good night." Then, using his passkey, he went through the glass doors into the elevator.

Vivian said, "He looked worried."

Seddons answered cheerfully, "I doubt it, bright eyes. When you get to where he is, most of the worrying is behind you."

The theater was over and now they were walking back to Three Counties. It had been a good road show—a broad, noisy musical—at which they had both laughed a good deal and held hands, and a couple of times Mike had draped his arm around the back of Vivian's seat, allowing it to fall lightly, his fingers exploring her shoulders, and she had made no move to object.

Over dinner before the show they had talked of themselves. Vivian had questioned Mike about his intentions to practice surgery, and he had asked her why she had become a student nurse.

"I'm not sure I can explain, Mike," she had said, "except that nursing was something I always wanted to do as far back as I can remember." She had told him that her parents at first had opposed the idea, then, on learning how strongly she felt, had given way. "I guess it's really that I wanted to do something for myself, and nursing was what appealed to me most."

Seddons had asked her, "Do you still feel that way?"

"Yes, I do," she had said. "Oh, now and then—when you're tired sometimes, and you've seen some of the things in the hospital, and you're thinking about home—you wonder if it's worth it, if there aren't easier things to do; but I guess that happens to everybody. Most of the time, though, I'm quite sure." She had smiled, then said, "I'm a very determined person, Mike, and I've made up my mind to be a nurse."

Yes, he had thought, you are determined; I can believe that. Glancing at Vivian covertly while she talked, he could sense an inner strength—a toughness of character behind what seemed at first a façade of gentle femininity. Once more, as he had a day or two ago, Mike Seddons had felt his interest quicken, but again he warned himself: No involvements! Remember, anything you feel is basically biological!

It was close to midnight now, but Vivian had signed the late book and there was no problem about hurrying in. Some of the older nurses, who had done their training under spartan regimes, felt the students were allowed too much freedom nowadays. But in practice it was seldom abused.

Mike touched her arm. "Let's go through the park."

Vivian laughed. "That's an old line I've heard before." But she offered no resistance as he steered her to a gateway and into the park beyond. In the darkness she could make out a line of poplars on either side, and the grass was soft underfoot.

"I've a whole collection of old lines. It's one of my specialties." He reached down and took her hand. "Do you want to hear more?"

"Like what, for example?" Despite her self-assurance her voice held the slightest of tremors.

"Like this." Mike stopped and took both her shoulders, turning her to face him. Then he kissed her fully on the lips.

Vivian felt her heart beat faster, but not so much that her mind could not weigh the situation. Should she stop at once or let this go on? She was well aware that if she took no action now, later it might not be so easy.

Vivian already knew that she liked Mike Seddons and believed she could come to like him a good deal more. He was physically attractive and they were both young. She felt the stirrings of desire within her. They were kissing again and she returned the pressure of his lips. The tip of his tongue came lightly into her mouth; she met it with her own and the contact set up a delicious tingling. Mike tightened his arms around her, and through the thin summer dress she felt his thighs pressing tighter. His hands were moving, caressing her back. The right dropped lower; it passed lightly over the back of her skirt, then more heavily, each caress pulling her closer to him. Against her own body she felt a bulkiness. It stirred, intoxicatingly, heavenly. She knew clearly, as if with a second mind, that if she were going to, this was the moment to break away. Just a moment longer, she thought; just a moment longer!

Then suddenly it seemed as if this were an intermission, a release from other things around. Closing her eyes she savored the seconds of warmth and tenderness; these past months there had been so few. So many times since coming to Three Counties she had had to use control and self-discipline, her emotions pent up and tears unshed. When you were young, inexperienced, and a little frightened, sometimes it was hard to do. There had been so many things—the shocks of ward duty, pain, disease, death, the autopsy—and yet no safety valve to release the pressures building up inside. A nurse, even a student nurse, had to see so much of suffering and give so much in care and sympathy. Was it wrong, then, to grasp a moment of tenderness for herself? For an instant, with Mike holding her, she felt the same solace and relief as when, years before, she had run as a little girl into her mother's arms. Mike had released her a little now and was holding her slightly away. He said, "You're beautiful." Impulsively she buried her face in his shoulder. Then he put a hand under her chin and their lips were together again. She felt the same hand drop and, from outside her dress, move lightly over her breasts. From every part of her body the desire to love and be loved welled up, madly, uncontrollably.

His hand was at the neckline of her dress. It was made to open at the front, and a hook and eye secured the top. He was fumbling for it. She struggled. Breathlessly, "No, Mike! Please! No!" She failed even to convince herself. Her arms were around him tightly. He had the dress open a little way now and she felt his hand move, then gasped at the contact as it cupped her own young, soft flesh. He took the nipple gently between his fingers, and a shudder of ecstasy moved through her in a sensual wave. Now she knew that it was too late to stop. She wanted, craved him desperately. Her lips to his ear, she murmured, "Yes, oh yes."

"Darling, darling Vivian." He was equally excited; she could tell from his whispered, breathless voice.

Womanlike, a moment's common sense came through. "Not here, Mike. There are people."

"Let's go through the trees." He took her hand and they moved closely together. She felt a trembling excitement, a wondering curiosity to know what it would be like. She dismissed any consequence; it seemed unimportant. And Mike was a doctor; he would know how to be careful.

They had reached a small clearing surrounded by trees and shrubs. Mike kissed her again, and passionately she returned his kisses, her tongue darting and fighting his. So this is where it's to be, she thought. The real thing. Vivian was not a virgin; she had ceased to be while in high school, and there had been another incident in her first year of college, but neither experience had been satisfactory. She knew this would be. "Hurry, Mike, please hurry." She felt her own excitement transmit itself to him.

"Over here, darling," he said, and they moved toward the far side of the clearing.

Suddenly she felt a searing pain. It was so intense at first she could not be sure where it was. Then she knew it was her left knee. Involuntarily she cried out.

"What is it? Vivian, what is it?" Mike turned to her. She could see he was puzzled, not knowing what to make of it. She thought: He probably thinks it's a trick. Girls do this sort of thing to get out of these situations.

The first sharpness of pain had subsided a little. But it still returned in waves. She said, "Mike, I'm afraid it's my knee. Is there a seat somewhere?" She flinched again.

"Vivian," he said, "you don't have to put on an act. If you want to go back to the hospital, just say so and I'll take you."

"Please believe me, Mike." She took his arm. "It *is* my knee. It hurts me terribly. I have to sit down."

"This way." She could tell he was still skeptical, but he guided her back through the trees. There was a park bench nearby, and they made for it.

When she had rested, Vivian said, "I'm sorry, I didn't do that on purpose."

He said doubtfully, "Are you sure?"

She reached for his hand. "Mike—in there; I wanted to, as much as you. Then this." Again the pain.

He said, "I'm sorry, Vivian. I thought . . ."

She said, "I know what you thought. But it wasn't that. Honestly."

"All right. Tell me what's wrong." He was the doctor now. Back in there he had forgotten.

"I'ts my knee. All of a sudden—the sharpest pain."

"Let me see." He was down in front of her. "Which one?"

She lifted her skirt and indicated the left knee. He felt it carefully, his hands moving lightly. For the moment Mike Seddons dismissed the thought that this was a girl to whom, a few minutes earlier, he had been about to make love. His behavior now was professional, analytical. As he had been trained tc do, his mind went methodically over the possibilities. He found Vivian's nylons impeded his sense of touch.

"Roll down your stocking, Vivian." She did so, and his probing fingers moved over the knee again. Watching him, she thought: He's good; he'll be a fine doctor; people will come to him for help and he'll be kind and do the utmost that he can. She found herself wondering what it would be like—the two of them together always. As a nurse there would be so much she could do to help him and to understand his work. She told herself: This is ridiculous; we scarcely know each other. Then, momentarily, the pain returned and she winced.

Mike asked, "Has this happened before?"

For a moment the absurdity of the situation struck her and she giggled.

"What is it, Vivian?" Mike sounded puzzled.

"I was just thinking. A minute or two ago . . . And now here you are, just like in a doctor's office."

"Listen, kid." He was serious. "Has this happened before?"

She said, "Just once. It wasn't as bad as this though."

"How long ago?"

She thought. "About a month."

"Have you seen anybody about it?" He was all professional now.

"No. Should I have?"

Noncommittally he said, "Maybe." Then he added, "You will tomorrow anyway. I think Dr. Grainger would be the best one."

"Mike, is something wrong?" Now she felt an undercurrent of alarm.

"Probably not," he reassured her. "But there's a small lump there that shouldn't be. Lucy Grainger will give us the word though. I'll talk with her in the morning. Now we have to get you home."

The earlier mood was gone. It could not be recaptured, not tonight anyway, and both of them knew it.

Mike helped her up. As his arm went around her, he had a sudden feeling of wanting to help and protect her. He asked, "Do you think you can walk?"

Vivian told him, "Yes. The pain's gone now."

"We'll just go to the gate," he said; "we can get a taxi there." Then because she looked glum he added cheerfully, "That patient was a cheap skate. He didn't send any cab fare."

Nine

"Give me the details."

Hunched over the binocular microscope, Dr. Joseph Pearson half grunted the words to Roger McNeil.

The pathology resident looked at his folder of notes. "Case was a forty-year-old man, admitted for appendicitis." McNeil was seated opposite Pearson at the desk of the pathology office.

Pearson took out the slide he had been studying and sub-stituted another. He asked, "What did the tissue look like at gross?"

McNeil, who had made the gross examination when the removed appendix came down from the operating room, said, "Grossly it looked normal enough to me."

"Hm." Pearson moved the slide around. Then he said, "Wait a minute; here's something." After a pause he slipped the second slide out and selected a third. Now he said, "Here it is—an acute appendicitis. It was just beginning in this section. Who was the surgeon?"

McNeil answered, "Dr. Bartlett."

Pearson nodded. "He got it good and early. Take a look." He made way at the microscope for McNeil.

Working with the resident, as the hospital's teaching pro-gram required him to, Pearson was endeavoring to catch up on the pathology department's surgical reports.

Despite his best efforts, though, both men knew they were seriously in arrears with work. The slides being studied now had been sectioned from a patient's appendix removed several weeks earlier. The patient had long since been dis-charged, and in this case the report would merely confirm or deny the surgeon's original diagnosis. In this instance Gil Bartlett had been entirely right, in fact, creditably so, since he had caught the disease in its early stages and before the patient could have had much distress.

"Next." Pearson moved back to the microscope as McNeil returned to the other side of the desk.

The resident pushed over a slide folder and, as Pearson opened it, McNeil consulted a fresh set of notes. As they worked Bannister entered the room quietly. With a glance at the other two he passed behind them and began to file papers into a cabinet.

"This is a current one," McNeil said. "It came down five days ago. They're waiting to hear what we say."

"You'd better give me any like this first," Pearson said sourly, "otherwise there'll be more bleating from upstairs."

McNeil was on the point of saying that several weeks ago he had suggested changing their procedure in just that way, but Pearson had insisted on reviewing all specimens in the order they came into the department. However, the resi-dent checked himself. Why bother? he thought. He told Pearson, "It's a fifty-six-year-old woman. The specimen is a

skin lesion—superficially a mole. Question is: Is it a malignant melanoma?"

Pearson put in the first slide and moved it around. Then
he flipped over the highest-powered lens and adjusted the
binocular eyepiece. "It could be." He took the second slide,
then two more. After that he sat back thoughtfully. "On the
other hand it could be a blue nevus. Let's see what you
think."

McNeil moved in. This one, he knew, was important. A
malignant melanoma was a tumor that was viciously malignant. Its cells could spread rapidly and murderously in the
body. If diagnosed as such from the small portion already
removed, it would mean immediate major surgery for the
woman patient. But a blue nevus tumor was entirely harmless. It could stay where it was in the body, doing no harm,
for the rest of the woman's life.

From his own studies McNeil knew that a malignant melanoma was not common, but he also knew that a blue nevus
was extremely rare. Mathematically the odds were on this
being malignant. But this was not mathematics. It was pathology at its purest.

As he had learned to do, McNeil ran over in his mind the
comparative features of the two types of tumor. They were
distressingly similar. Both were partly scarred, partly cellular, with a good deal of pigmentation in them. Again, in both,
the cellular structure was very pronounced. Something else
McNeil had been taught was to be honest. After looking at
all the slides he said to Pearson, "I don't know." He added,
"What about previous cases? Could we get any out? To
compare them."

"It'd take us a year to find any. I don't remember when I
last had a blue nevus." Pearson was frowning. He said heavily, "One of these days we've got to set up a cross file. Then
when a doubtful case like this comes up we can go back and
compare it."

"You've been saying that for five years." Bannister's dry
voice came from behind, and Pearson wheeled. "What are
you doing here?"

"Filing." The senior lab technician answered laconically.
"Something the clerks should be doing if we had some proper
help."

And probably a lot better, McNeil thought. He knew the
department badly needed more clerical staff and the filing

methods used now were hopelessly archaic. The reference to
a cross file, too, had reminded him of a gaping hole in their
administrative system. There were few good hospitals now
whose pathology departments did not have one. Some called
them organ-lesion files, but, whatever the name, one purpose of the system was to help resolve the kind of problem
they were facing at this moment.

Pearson was studying the slides again. He mumbled, as a
lot of pathologists did when they were mentally crossing off
some factors and confirming others. McNeil heard, "It's a
little small . . . absence of hemorrhage . . . no necrosis of
the tissue . . . negative but no indication . . . yes, I'm satisfied." Pearson straightened up from the microscope, replaced
the last slide, and closed the slide folder. Motioning to the
resident to write, he said, "Diagnosis—a blue nevus." Courtesy of Pathology, the woman patient had been reprieved.

Methodically, for McNeil's benefit, Pearson ran over the
reasons for his decision again. As he passed the slide folder
he added, "You'd better study these. It's a specimen you
won't see often."

McNeil had no doubt that the old man's finding was right.
This was one place where years of experience paid off, and
he had come to respect Pearson's judgment in matters of
pathological anatomy. But when you've gone, he thought,
looking at the old man, that's when this place will need a
cross file—badly.

They studied two more cases, both fairly straightforward,
then Pearson slipped in the first slide from the next series.
He took one look through the microscope eyepiece, straightened up, and told McNeil explosively, "Get Bannister!"

"I'm still here." It was Bannister, calmly, behind them at
the file cabinets.

Pearson wheeled. "Look at this!" He was using his loud-
est, hectoring voice. "How many times do I have to give instructions about the way I want slides made? What's wrong
with the technicians in Histology? Are they deaf or just
plain stupid?"

McNeil had heard the same kind of outburst before. He
sat back and watched as Bannister asked, "What's the
trouble?"

"I'll tell you what's the trouble." Pearson ripped the slide
from his microscope and tossed it across the table. "How

can I give a proper diagnosis with this kind of tissue section?"

The senior lab technician picked up the slide and held it to the light. "Too thick, eh?"

"Of course it's too thick." Pearson picked out a second slide from the same set. "Look at this one. If I had some bread I could scrape off the meat and make a sandwich."

Bannister grinned. "I'll check the microtome. We've been having trouble with it." He pointed to the slide folder. "Do you want me to take these away?"

"No. I'll have to make do with them." The explosiveness had gone now; the old man was merely growling. "Just do a better job in supervising Histology."

Bannister, disagreeable himself by this time, grumbled on his way to the door. "Maybe if I didn't have so much else . . ."

Pearson shouted after him, "All right. I've heard that record before."

As Bannister reached the door, there was a light tap and Dr. Charles Dornberger appeared. He asked, "May I come in, Joe?"

"Sure." Pearson grinned. "You might even learn something, Charlie."

The obstetrician nodded pleasantly to McNeil, then said casually to Pearson, "This was the morning I arranged to come down. Had you forgotten?"

"Yes, I had." Pearson pushed the slide folder away from him. He asked the resident, "How many more in this batch?"

McNeil counted the slide folders remaining. "Eight."

"We'll finish later."

The resident began to gather up the case papers already completed.

Dornberger took out his pipe and leisurely filled it. Looking around the big drab room, he shivered. He said, "This place feels damp, Joe. Every time I come here I feel like I'm going to get a chill."

Pearson gave a deep chuckle. He said, "We spray flu germs around—every morning. It discourages visitors." He watched McNeil cross the room and go out of the door. Then he asked, "What's on your mind?"

Dornberger wasted no time. He said, "I'm a deputation. I'm supposed to handle you tactfully." He put the pipe in his mouth, his tobacco pouch away.

Pearson looked up. "What is this? More trouble?"

Their eyes met. Dornberger said quietly, "That depends." After a pause he added, "But it looks as if you may get a new assistant pathologist."

Dornberger had expected an outburst, but Pearson was strangely quiet. He said thoughtfully, "Whether I want one or not, eh?"

"Yes, Joe." Dornberger made it definite; there was no point in holding back. He had thought a good deal about this since the meeting of several days ago.

"I suppose O'Donnell is back of this." Pearson said it with a touch of bitterness but still quietly. As always, he was being unpredictable.

Dornberger answered, "Partly but not entirely."

Again surprisingly, "What do you think I should do?" It was a question asked by one friend of another.

Dornberger laid his pipe, unlighted, in an ash tray on Pearson's desk. He was thinking: I'm glad he's taking it this way. It means I was right. I can help him accept this, adjust to it. Aloud he said, "I don't believe you've much choice, Joe. You *are* behind with surgical reports, aren't you? And a few other things?"

For a moment he thought he had gone too far. This was a sensitive area. He saw the other man brace up and waited for the storm to break. But again it did not. Instead, more strongly than before, but reasonably, Pearson said, "Sure, a few things need straightening out. I'll admit that to you. But there's nothing I can't handle myself—if I can just get the time to do it."

He *has* accepted it, Dornberger thought. He's sounding off now. But he has accepted it just the same. He said casually, "Well, maybe you'll get the time—with another pathologist." With equal casualness he pulled from his inside pocket the paper which the administrator had given him.

Pearson asked, "What's that?"

"There's nothing definite about this, Joe. It's a name that Harry Tomaselli had—apparently some young fellow who might be interested in coming here."

Pearson took the single sheet. He said, "They sure didn't waste any time."

Dornberger said lightly, "Our administrator is a man of action."

Pearson was scanning the paper. He read aloud, "Dr.

David Coleman." There was a pause. Then with bitterness, frustration, and envy the old man added, "Age thirty-one."

It was twenty minutes after midday, and the hospital cafeteria was at its busiest. Most of the doctors, nurses, and hospital employees usually took their lunch about this time, and a line-up was beginning to form at the point where newcomers collected trays before passing counters and steam tables where the food was served.

Mrs. Straughan, as usual at this period, had her eye on proceedings, ensuring that as fast as one batch of food was used up another was brought from the kitchens to keep the line out front moving briskly. Today there was a choice of Irish stew, lamb chops, and broiled halibut. The chief dietitian noticed that the lamb chops were moving slowly. She decided to try some herself in a few minutes to see if there were any reason. Perhaps the meat was not as succulent as it might be; word of something like that was often passed to those arriving in the cafeteria by others who were leaving. Mrs. Straughan noticed a dish at the top of a pile on the servery that appeared to have a mark on it. She stepped forward and removed it quickly; sure enough, it still bore traces of an earlier meal. The dishwashing machines again! she thought. Their inadequacy was a recurring problem, and she decided to broach the subject with the administrator again very soon.

Over at the tables reserved for the medical staff there was the sound of noisy laughter. It came from a group of which Dr. Ralph Bell, the radiologist, was the center.

Gil Bartlett, who had come from the serving counter with a tray, put it down and went over with extended hand. "Congratulations, Ding Dong," he said. "I just heard."

"Heard what?" It was Lewis Toynbee, the internist, also with a tray, behind him. Then as Bell, beaming, passed a cigar to Bartlett, Toynbee exclaimed, "My God! Not again?"

"Certainly again. Why not?" The radiologist held out another cigar. "Join us, Lewis. It's exactly eight Bells."

"Eight! When was this?"

Bell said calmly, "This morning. Another boy for the ball team."

Bill Rufus put in, "Don't sound critical, Lewis. He's doing his best. After all, he's only been married eight years."

Lewis Toynbee offered his hand. "Don't squeeze it too tight, Ding Dong. I'm afraid some of that fertility might rub off."

"I'm impervious to jealousy," Bell said good-naturedly. He had been through all this before.

Lucy Grainger asked, "How is your wife?"

Bell answered, "She's fine, thanks."

"How does it feel to be a sex fiend?" The question was from Harvey Chandler, the chief of medicine, lower down the table.

Bell said, "I'm not a sex fiend. At our house we have intercourse once a year. I'm just a dead shot."

Lucy Grainger joined in the ensuing laughter, then she said, "Ralph, I'm sending you a patient this afternoon. It's one of our student nurses—Vivian Loburton."

The laughter had simmered down. "What is it you're looking for?" Bell asked.

"I want you to take some films of the left knee," Lucy answered. Then she added, "There's some sort of growth there. I don't like the look of it."

Back in his own office, Dr. Charles Dornberger had telephoned Kent O'Donnell to report the outcome of the talk with Pearson. At the end he had told the chief of surgery, "I've let Joe know about the man you people have been corresponding with."

O'Donnell had asked, "How did he take it?"

"I wouldn't say he was enthusiastic," Dornberger said. "But I think if you want to have this fellow . . . what's his name—Coleman? . . . if you want to have him come here for a talk, Joe won't be difficult. But I'd suggest you keep Joe posted on everything you do from here on in."

"You can be sure of that," O'Donnell had said. Then, "Thanks, Charlie. Thank you very much."

Afterward Dornberger had made another telephone call. It was to Mrs. John Alexander, who had phoned earlier that morning and left a message. Before calling he had looked up his record card and was reminded that this was the wife of the pathology technologist, referred to him by Joe Pearson. Talking with Mrs. Alexander, he learned that she had just arrived in town to join her husband. They made an appointment for her to come to Dornberger's downtown office the following week.

About the same time that Mrs. Alexander was talking with Dornberger her husband was receiving his first tongue-lashing from Dr. Joseph Pearson. It happened this way.

After Pearson's outburst that morning about the poor-quality surgical slides, Bannister had come back to the serology lab where John Alexander was working and had told him the whole story. By this time Bannister was seething, and later he had taken out some of his own bad humor on the two girl technicians and their male helper who worked in the histology lab next door. Alexander had heard what was said through the doorway which Bannister had left open behind him.

Alexander, though, knew that not all the blame for the bad slides lay with the histology technicians. Even in the short time he had been at the hospital he had sensed the real problem, and afterward he had told Bannister, "You know, Carl, I don't believe it's all their fault. I think they have too much to do."

Bannister had answered sourly, "We've all got too much to do." Then with clumsy sarcasm he had added, "Maybe if you know so much about it you can do your own work and part of theirs as well."

Alexander had declined to be provoked. "I don't think so. But I do think they'd be a lot better off with a tissue-processing machine instead of having to do everything by hand—the old-fashioned way."

"Forget it, kid. It isn't your problem." Bannister had been loftily condescending. "And, besides, anything that means spending money around here is a dead duck before it starts."

Alexander had not argued. But he resolved to raise the subject, the first chance he got, with Dr. Pearson.

He had had to go into Pearson's office that afternoon to leave some lab reports for signature, and he had found the pathologist going through a pile of mail with obvious impatience. Glancing up at Alexander, Pearson had motioned him to put the papers on the desk and had gone on with his reading. Alexander had hesitated, and the old man had barked, "What is it? What is it?"

"Dr. Pearson, I was wondering if I could make a suggestion."

"Now?"

A more experienced hand would have known the tone of

voice meant: Leave me alone. Alexander answered, "Yes, sir."

Resignedly Pearson said, "Well?"

A little nervously Alexander began, "It's about speeding up the surgical reports, Doctor." As he mentioned surgical reports, Pearson had put down his letter and looked up sharply. Alexander went on, "I was wondering if you'd ever thought of getting a tissue-processing machine."

"What do *you* know about tissue processors?" There was an ominous note in Pearson's voice. "And anyway, I thought we put you to work in Serology."

Alexander reminded him, "I did a full course in histology at technologists' school, Doctor." There was a pause. Pearson said nothing, so Alexander went on. "I've used a tissue processor and it's a good machine, sir. It would save us at least a day in preparing slides. Instead of processing tissue by hand through all the solutions, you set the machine overnight and automatically by morning——"

Abruptly Pearson cut in. "I know how it works. I've seen them."

Alexander said, "I see, sir. Then don't you think——"

"I said I've seen these so-called tissue processors and I'm not impressed." Pearson's voice was harsh and grating. "There's not the quality in the slides that there is with the old hand method. What's more, the machines are expensive. You see these?" He riffled through a stack of typed yellow forms in a tray on his desk.

"Yes, sir."

"They're purchase requisitions. For things I need in this department. And every time I put a bunch through I have a fight with the administrator. He says we're spending too much money."

Alexander had made his first mistake in broaching the suggestion when Pearson had not wanted to hear. Now he made a second error. He mistook Pearson's statement as an invitation to continue the discussion.

He said placatingly, "But surely, if it would save a whole day, maybe two . . ." He became more earnest. "Dr. Pearson, I've seen slides made with a processor and they're good. Perhaps the one you saw wasn't being used properly."

Now the older man had risen from his chair. Whatever the provocation, Alexander had overstepped the bounds between physician and technologist. Head forward, Pearson shouted, "That'll do! I said I'm not interested in a tissue processor, and that's what I meant, and I don't want any argument about it." He came around the desk until he was directly in front of Alexander, his face close to the younger man's. "And there's something else I want you to remember: I'm the pathologist here and I'm running this department. I don't mind suggestions if they're reasonable. But don't get stepping out of line. Understand?"

"Yes, sir. I understand." Crestfallen and miserable, not really understanding at all, John Alexander went back to his work in the lab.

Mike Seddons had been preoccupied all day; several times he had had to check himself and make a conscious effort to pull back his mind to the work he happened to be doing. Once, during an autopsy, McNeil had been forced to warn him, "There's a piece of your hand under that section you're about to slice. We like people to leave here with all the fingers they came with." Seddons had changed his grip hastily; it would not have been the first time that some inexperienced learner had lopped off a gloved finger with one of the razor-edged knives of pathology.

All the same his attention still kept wandering, the question recurring: What was it about Vivian that disturbed him so? She was attractive and desirable, and he was anxious to take her to bed as quickly as possible—Mike Seddons was under no illusions about that. She seemed amenable, too, assuming the pain in her knee the night before had been genuine, and he now believed it was. He hoped she would still feel the same way, though there was no guarantee she would, of course. Some girls were inconsistent like that—you could have the most exotic intimacies with them one day, then the next time round they would reject even the most basic advance, pretending that the earlier incident had never even happened.

But was there something more to Vivian and himself than merely sex? Mike Seddons was beginning to wonder. Certainly none of the earlier episodes—and there had been several —had caused him to do half so much thinking as he was doing right now. A new thought occurred to him: Perhaps if he could get the sex bit out of his system other things might become clearer. He decided to ask Vivian to meet him again; and tonight—assuming she would be free—was as good a time as any.

Vivian had found the note from Mike Seddons when she finished her last class of the day and went back to the student nurses' residence. It had been delivered by hand and was waiting for her in the mail rack under "L." It asked her to be on the hospital's fourth floor near Pediatrics at 9:45 that night. At first she had not intended to go, knowing she would have no reason officially to be in the hospital and she might be in trouble if she ran into any of the nursing supervisors. But she found herself wanting to go, and at 9:40 she crossed the wooden boardwalk between the nurses' home and the main hospital buildings.

Mike was waiting, strolling in the corridor, apparently preoccupied. But as soon as he saw her he motioned to a door and they went inside. It led to an interior stair well, with a metal stairway leading up and down. At this time of night it was quiet and deserted and there would be plenty of warning of anyone's approach. Mike went down half a flight onto the next landing, leading her by the hand. Then he turned, and it seemed the most natural thing in the world that she should go into his arms.

As they kissed she felt Mike's arms tightening and the magic of the night before came sweeping back. At this moment she knew why she had wanted so much to come here. This man with the wild red hair had suddenly become indispensable to her. She wanted him in every way—to be close to him, talk with him, make love with him. It was an electric, exciting feeling she had never known before. He was kissing her cheeks now, her eyes, her ears. His face in her hair, he whispered, "Vivian darling, I've been thinking about you all day. I haven't been able to stop." With both hands he took her face and looked into it. "Do you know what you're doing?" She shook her head. "You're undermining me."

She reached out for him again. "Oh, Mike darling!"

It was hot on the stairway. Vivian felt the warmth of his body against the fire of her own. Now his hands were questing, seeking. She whispered, trembling, "Mike, isn't there somewhere else?"

She felt his hands pause and knew he was considering.

He said, "I share a room with Frank Worth. But he's out tonight, won't be back till late. Do you want to take a chance and come to the residents' quarters?"

She hesitated. "What would happen? If we got caught."

"We'd both get thrown out of the hospital." He kissed her again. "At this moment I couldn't care." He took her hand. "Come on."

They went down one flight of stairs and along a corridor. They passed another resident who grinned as he saw them but made no comment. Then more stairs, another corridor. This time a white figure turned out of a doorway just ahead. Vivian's heart leaped as she recognized the night nursing supervisor. But the supervisor did not turn around and went in another doorway before they passed. Then they were in a narrower, quieter corridor with closed doors on each side. There were lights beneath some of the doors, and from one she could hear music. She recognized it as Chopin's Prelude in E Minor; the Burlington Symphony had played it a month or two before.

"In here." Mike had opened a door, and quickly they moved inside. It was dark, but she could make out the shape of bunk beds and an armchair. Behind her she heard the lock click as Mike fastened the catch.

They reached for each other demandingly, urgently. His fingers were at the buttons of her uniform. When they hesitated she helped him. Now she was standing in her slip. For a moment he held her tightly, together savoring the torture of delay. Then, his hands moving gently, tenderly, and with exquisite promise, he lifted the slip over her head. As she moved to the bed she kicked off her shoes. There was a swift movement and then he was with her, his hands helping her again. "Vivian, darling Vivian!"

She scarcely heard him. "Mike, don't wait! Please don't wait!" She felt the contours of his body pressing madly, abandonedly, into her. She responded wildly, fought fiercely to bring him tighter, nearer, deeper. Then suddenly there was nothing else in the world, nothing but a peak of tempestuous ecstasy, now sweeping, searing, surging . . . coming closer, closer, closer.

As they lay quietly together afterward, Vivian could hear the music again, coming faintly from down the hall. It was still Chopin, this time the Etude in E Major. It seemed strange, at this moment, to be identifying a musical composition, but the liquid, haunting melody, heard softly in the darkness, fitted her mood of completion.

Mike reached over and kissed her gently. Then he said, "Vivian dearest, I want to marry you."

She asked him softly, "Mike darling, are you sure?"

The impetuousness of his own words had surprised even himself. Mike had spoken them on impulse, but suddenly, deeply, he knew them to be true. His objective in avoiding entanglements seemed pointless and shallow; this was an entanglement he wanted, to the exclusion of all others. He knew now what had troubled him today and earlier; at this moment it troubled him no more. Characteristically he answered Vivian's questions with a touch of humor. "Sure I'm sure. Aren't you?"

As her arms went around him Vivian murmured, "I've never been more sure of anything."

"Hey!" Mike broke away and he propped himself on an elbow, facing her. "All this put it out of my mind. What about your knee?"

Vivian smiled mischievously. "It wasn't any trouble tonight, was it?"

After he had kissed her again he asked, "Tell me what Lucy Grainger said."

"She didn't. She had Dr. Bell take some X-rays this afternoon. She said she'd send for me in a couple of days.

Mike said, "I'll be glad when it's cleared up."

Vivian said, "Don't be silly, darling. How could a little bump like that be anything serious?"

Ten

Boston, Mass.
August 7

Mr. H. N. Tomaselli,
Administrator,
Three Counties Hospital
Burlington, Pa.

Dear Mr. Tomaselli:
Since my visit to Burlington a week ago I have thought a

great deal about the appointment in pathology at Three Counties Hospital.

This letter is to advise you that, subject, of course, to your still feeling the same way about me, I have decided to accept the appointment on the terms we discussed.

You mentioned that you were anxious for whoever accepted the post to begin work as soon as possible. There is really nothing to delay me here, and after clearing up a few minor things I could be in Burlington ready to begin on August 15—that is, in just over a week from now. I trust this will be a convenient arrangement.

In talking with Dr. O'Donnell he mentioned knowing of some bachelor apartments which will be completed soon and are quite near the hospital. I wonder if you have any more information on this subject and, if so, I would be interested to know of it. Meanwhile, perhaps you would be good enough to make a reservation for me at one of the local hotels for arrival August 14.

On the subject of the work I shall be doing at the hospital, there is one point which I felt we did not clear up entirely, and I am mentioning it now in the hope that perhaps you may be able to discuss it with Dr. Pearson sometime before my arrival.

It is my feeling that it would be advantageous, both for the hospital and myself, if there were some clearly defined areas of responsibility where I could have a reasonably free hand, both in general supervision of the day-to-day work and also the carrying-out of any changes of organization and technique which, of course, are always necessary from time to time.

My own wishes in this regard would be to have direct responsibility, within the pathology department, for Serology, Hematology, and Biochemistry, though, of course, assisting Dr. Pearson in pathological anatomy and other matters at any time he might see fit.

As I say, I have raised this point now in the hope that it may be possible for you and Dr. Pearson to consider it before August 15. But please be assured that at all times I will seek to co-operate fully with Dr. Pearson and to serve Three Counties Hospital to the best of my ability.

Yours very truly,
David Coleman, M.D.

Coleman read through the neatly typed letter once more, put
it in an envelope, and sealed it. Then, going back to his portable typewriter, he tapped out a similar but slightly shorter
note to Dr. Joseph Pearson.

David Coleman left the furnished apartment which he had
rented on a short lease for the few months he had been in
Boston and walked to a mailbox with both letters. Thinking
over what he had written, he still was not sure why he had
chosen Three Counties in preference to the seven other posts
he had been offered within recent weeks. Certainly it was not
the most remunerative. Thought of in financial terms, it was
more than halfway down the list. Nor was it a "name" hospital. Two of the other medical centers in which he had
been offered employment had names that were internation-
ally renowned. But Three Counties was scarcely known outside the immediate area it served.

Why then? Was it because he was afraid of being lost,
swallowed up, in a bigger center? Scarcely, because his own
record already showed he could hold his own in that kind
of environment. Was it because he felt he would be freer
for research in a small place? He certainly hoped to do some
research, but if that were what he wanted most he could
have chosen a research institute—there had been one on his
list—and done nothing else. Was it because of the challenge
that he had made his choice? Maybe. There were certainly
a lot of things wrong in pathology at Three Counties Hospital.
He had seen that just in the two brief days he had spent there
last week, following the phone call from the administrator
inviting him to visit the hospital and look the situation over.
And working with Dr. Pearson was not going to be easy. He
had sensed resentment in the older man when they had met,
and the administrator had admitted under Coleman's questioning that Pearson had a reputation for being hard to get
along with.

So was it because of the challenge? Was that why he had
picked Three Counties? Was it? Or was it something else,
something quite different? Was it . . . self-mortification? Was
it that still—the old specter that had haunted him so long?

Of all his traits of character David Coleman had long
suspected pride to be the strongest, and it was a defect he
feared and hated most. In his own opinion he had never
been able to conquer pride; he spurned it, rejected it, yet

always it came back—seemingly strong and indestructible.

Mostly his pride stemmed from an awareness of his own superior intellect. In the company of others he frequently felt himself to be mentally far out front, usually because he was. And, intellectually, everything he had done so far in his life proved this to be true.

As far back as David Coleman could remember, the fruits of scholarship had come to him easily. Learning had proved as simple as breathing. In public school, high school, college, medical school, he had soared above others, taking the highest honors almost as a matter of course. He had a mind which was at once absorbent, analytical, understanding. And proud.

He had first learned about pride in his early years of high school. Like anyone who is naturally brilliant, he was regarded initially by his fellow students with some suspicion. Then, as he made no attempt to conceal his feelings of mental superiority, suspicion turned to dislike and finally to hate.

At the time he had sensed this, but he had not consciously cared until one day the school principal, himself a brilliant scholar and an understanding man, had taken him aside. Even now David Coleman remembered what the other man had said.

"I think you're big enough to take this, so I'm going to spell it out. In these four walls, aside from me, you haven't a single friend."

At first he had not believed it. Then because, above all, he was supremely honest, he had admitted to himself that the fact was true.

Then the principal had said, "You're a brilliant scholar. You know it and there's no reason why you shouldn't. As to what's ahead, you can be anything you choose. You have a remarkably superior mind, Coleman—I may say, unique in my experience. But I warn you: if you want to live with others, sometimes you'll have to seem less superior than you are."

It was a daring thing to say to a young, impressionable man. But the master had not underrated his pupil. Coleman went away with the advice, digested it, analyzed it, and finished up despising himself.

From then on he had worked harder than ever—to rehabilitate himself with a planned program almost of self-mortification. He had begun with games. From as far back

as he could remember David Coleman had disliked sports of
every kind. At school, so far, he had never participated, and
he inclined to the opinion that people who went to sports
events and cheered were rather stupid juveniles. But now he
turned up at practice—football in winter, baseball in summer.
Despite his own first feelings he became expert. At college
he found himself in the first teams. And when not playing,
as a supporter in college and high school he attended every
game, cheering as loudly as the rest.

Yet he was never able to play without a feeling of indifference to games, which he carefully concealed. And he never
cheered without an inward uneasiness that he was behaving
childishly. It was this which made him believe that, though he
had humbled pride, he had never banished it.

His relationship with people had gone much the same way.
In the old days, on meeting someone whom he considered
intellectually inferior, he had never bothered to conceal his
boredom or disinterest. But now, as part of his plan, he
went out of his way to be cordial to such people. As a result,
in college he had taken on the reputation of a friendly sage.
It had become a password among those in academic difficulties
to say, "Let's have a bull session with David Coleman. He'll
straighten us out." And invariably he did.

By all normal thinking the process should have shaped
his feelings for people into a kindlier mold. Time and experience should have made him sympathetic to those less gifted
than himself. But he was never sure that it had. Within himself Coleman found he still had the old contempt for mental
incompetence. He concealed it, fought it with iron discipline
and good acting, but, it seemed, it would never go away.

He had gone into medicine partly because his father, now
dead, had been a country doctor and partly because it was
something he had always wanted to do himself. But in entering a specific field he had chosen pathology because it was
generally considered the least glamorous of the specialties.
It was part of his own deliberate process of beating down
the inevitable pride.

For a while he believed he had succeeded. Pathology is at
times a lonely specialty, cut off as it is from the excitements
and pressures of direct contact with hospital patients. But
later, as interest and knowledge grew, he found the old contempt returning for those who knew less than he of the hid-

den mysteries a high-powered microscope revealed. Not to the same extent, though, because inevitably in medicine he met minds which were a match for his own. And still later he found he could relax, lowering some of the iron self-discipline with which he had clad himself. He still met those whom he considered fools—even in medicine there were some. But he never showed it and found occasionally that contact with such people disturbed him less. With such relaxation he began to wonder if at last he had beaten down his old enemy.

He was still wary though. A program of deliberate self-adjustment which had lasted fifteen years was not easy to shake off suddenly. And at times he found it hard to decide whether his motives came from pure choice or were from the habit of sackcloth he had worn so patiently and for so long.

Thus the question to himself on his choice of Three Counties Hospital. Had he chosen it because this was what he really wanted—a medium-size, second-line hospital, without reputation or glamor? Or had it been an old subconscious feeling that here was where his pride would suffer most?

As he mailed the two letters he knew these were questions that only time could answer.

On the seventh floor of the Burlington Medical Arts Building, Elizabeth Alexander dressed herself in the examining room adjoining Dr. Dornberger's office. In the last half-hour Charles Dornberger had given her his usual thorough physical examination, and now he had gone back to his desk. Through the partly opened door she heard him say, "Come and sit down when you're ready, Mrs. Alexander."

Pulling a slip over her head, she answered cheerfully, "I'll just be a minute, Doctor."

Seated at his desk, Dornberger smiled. He liked to have patients who were obviously enjoying pregnancy, and Elizabeth Alexander was. She'll be a good no-nonsense mother, he thought. She seemed an attractive girl, not pretty in the conventional sense, but with a lively personality which more than compensated for it. He glanced at the notes he had recorded earlier; she was twenty-three. When he was a younger man he always took the precaution of having a nurse present when he did physicals on women patients. He had heard of physicians failing to do this and later having nasty accusations hurled at them by unbalanced women. Nowadays, though, he seldom bothered. That, at least, was one advantage of being old.

He called out, "Well, I'd say you're going to have a normal, healthy baby. There don't seem to be any complications."

"That's what Dr. Crossan said." Fastening the belt of a summer green-print dress, Elizabeth emerged from the other room. She seated herself in a chair alongside the desk.

Dornberger checked his notes again. "He was your doctor in Chicago. Is that right?"

"Yes."

"Did he deliver your first child?"

"Yes." Elizabeth opened her purse and took out a slip of paper. "I have his address here, Doctor."

"Thank you. I'll write him for your medical history." Dornberger clipped the paper to his notes. He said matter-of-factly, "What did your first baby die of, Mrs. Alexander?"

"Bronchitis. When she was a month old." Elizabeth said it normally. A year ago the words would have been hard to bring out and she would have had to fight back tears. Now, with another baby coming, the loss seemed easier to accept. But this time her baby would live—of that she was determined.

Dr. Dornberger asked, "Was the delivery normal?"

"Yes," she answered.

He returned to his notes. As if to counter any distress the questions might have caused, he said conversationally, "I understand you've just arrived in Burlington."

"That's right," she said brightly, then added, "My husband is working at Three Counties."

"Yes, Dr. Pearson was telling me." Still writing, he asked, "How does he like it there?"

Elizabeth considered. "John hasn't said too much. But I think he likes it. He's very keen on his work."

Dornberger blotted what he had written. "That's a help. Particularly in pathology." He looked up and smiled. "The rest of us depend very much on the work of the laboratories."

There was a pause while the obstetrician reached in a drawer of his desk. Then, extracting a pad of forms, he said, "Talking of the lab, we must send you for a blood test."

As he wrote on the top form Elizabeth said, "I meant to

tell you, Doctor. I'm Rh negative and my husband is Rh positive."

He laughed. "I should have remembered you were the wife of a technologist. We'll have to make it a very thorough check." He tore off the form and gave it to her. "You can take this to the outpatients' department at Three Counties any time."

"Thank you, Doctor." She folded the form and put it in her purse.

On the point of ending the interview Dornberger hesitated. He knew, as most physicians did, that patients frequently had incomplete or wrong ideas about medical matters. When that happened with one of his own patients he was usually at pains to set them straight, even if it meant taking time to do so. In this case the girl had lost her first baby; therefore this second pregnancy was doubly important to her. It was Dornberger's business to see that she had no anxieties.

She had mentioned Rh factors, and obviously the subject was on her mind. Yet he doubted if she had any real understanding of what was involved. He decided to take the time to reassure her.

"Mrs. Alexander," he said, "I want you to be quite clear that, even though you and your husband have differing Rh blood types, it doesn't mean there will necessarily be any problem with the baby. You do understand that?"

"I think so, Doctor." He knew he had been right. In her voice there was a trace of doubt.

Patiently he asked, "Do you understand exactly what is meant by the terms Rh positive and Rh negative?"

She hesitated. "Well, I suppose not. Not exactly anyway."

This was what he had expected. He thought for a moment, then said, "Let me put it as simply as I can. All of us have certain factors in our blood. And when you speak of a 'factor' you might say that it's another name for an 'ingredient.' "

Elizabeth nodded. "I see." She found herself concentrating, adjusting mentally to take in what Dr. Dornberger was saying. For a moment she was reminded, almost nostalgically, of days in class. At school she had always taken pride in her capacity to understand things, to focus on a particular problem—absorbing facts quickly by excluding other things from consciousness. It had made her one of the brighter pupils. She was curious to know if she had retained the ability.

Dornberger continued, "Different human beings have different blood factors. The last time anyone counted there were forty-nine of these factors known to medicine. Most people—you and I, for example—have between fifteen and twenty of them in our own blood stream."

Elizabeth's brain clicked: question one. She asked, "What causes people to be born with different factors?"

"Mostly we inherit them, but that isn't important now. What's important is to remember that some factors are compatible and some are not."

"You mean . . ."

"I mean that when these blood factors are mixed together, some will get along quite happily, but some will fight one another and won't get along at all. That's why we are always careful in blood typing when we give a transfusion. We have to be sure it's the right kind of blood for the person receiving it."

Frowning thoughtfully, Elizabeth said, "And it's the factors that fight each other—the incompatible ones—that cause trouble? When people have babies, I mean." Again her own classroom formula: be clear on each point before going on to the next.

Dornberger answered, "Occasionally they do, but more often they don't. Let's take the case of you and your husband. You say he's Rh positive?"

"That's right."

"Well, that means his blood contains a factor called 'big D.' And because you're Rh negative you don't have any 'big D.' "

Elizabeth nodded slowly. Her mind was registering: Rh negative—no "big D." Using an old memory trick, she quickly made up a mnemonic:

> *If you haven't got "big D"*
> *Your blood's a minus quantity.*

She found Dornberger watching her. "You make it so interesting," she said. "No one's ever explained it like this before."

"Good. Now let's talk about your baby." He pointed to the

bulge below her waist. "We don't know yet whether Junior here has Rh-negative blood or Rh-positive. In other words, we don't know if he has any 'big D.' "

For a moment Elizabeth forgot the mental game she was playing. With a trace of anxiety she asked, "What happens if he does? Does it mean that his blood will fight with mine?"

Dornberger said calmly, "There's always that possibility." He told her with a smile, "Now listen very carefully."

She nodded. Her attention was focused again. Briefly, back there, she had let her mind become sidetracked.

He said deliberately, "A baby's blood is always quite separate from the mother's. Nevertheless, in pregnancy, small amounts of the baby's blood often escape into the mother's blood stream. Do you understand that?"

Elizabeth nodded. "Yes."

"Very well then. If the mother is Rh negative and the baby happens to be Rh positive, sometimes that can mean our old friend 'big D' seeps into the mother's blood stream, and he isn't welcome there. Got it?"

Again Elizabeth said, "Yes."

He said slowly, "When that happens, the mother's blood usually creates something we call antibodies, and those antibodies fight the 'big D' and eventually destroy it."

Elizabeth was puzzled. "Then where's the problem?"

"There never is any problem—for the mother. The problem, if there is one, begins when the antibodies—the 'big D' fighters which the mother has created—cross over the placental barrier into the baby's blood stream. You see, although there's no regular movement of blood between mother and baby, the antibodies can, and do, cross over quite freely."

"I see," Elizabeth said slowly. "And you mean the antibodies would start fighting with the baby's blood—and destroying it." She had it now—clearly in her mind.

Dornberger looked at her admiringly. This is one smart girl, he thought. She hadn't missed a thing. Aloud he said, "The antibodies might destroy the baby's blood—or part of it—if we let them. That's a condition we call *Erythroblastosis Foetalis*."

"But how do you stop it happening?"

"If it happens we can't stop it. But we can combat it. In the first place, as soon as there are any antibodies in the mother's blood we get a warning through a blood-sensitization test. That test will be done on your blood—now and later during your pregnancy."

"How is it done?" Elizabeth asked.

"You're quite a girl with the questions." The obstetrician smiled. "I couldn't tell you the lab procedure. Your husband will know more about that than I do."

"But what else is done? For the baby, I mean."

He said patiently, "The most important thing is to give the baby an exchange transfusion of the right kind of blood immediately after birth. It's usually successful." He deliberately avoided mention of the strong danger of an erythroblastotic child being born dead or that physicians often induced labor several weeks early to give the child a better chance of life. In any case he felt the discussion had gone far enough. He decided to sum it up.

"I've told you all this, Mrs. Alexander, because I thought you had something on your mind about Rh. Also, you're an intelligent girl, and I always believe it's better for someone to know all the truth than just a part of it."

She smiled at that. She guessed she really was intelligent. After all, she had proved she still possessed her old classroom ability to understand and memorize. Then she told herself: Don't be smug; besides, it's a baby you're having, not an end-of-semester exam.

Dr. Dornberger was talking again. "But just let me remind you of the important things." He was serious now, leaning toward her. "Point one: you may never have an Rh-positive baby, either now or later. In that case there can't be any problem. Point two: even if your baby happens to be Rh positive, you may not become sensitized. Point three: even if your baby were to have erythroblastosis, the chances of treatment and recovery are favorable." He looked at her directly. "Now—how do you feel about it all?"

Elizabeth was beaming. She had been treated like an adult and it felt good. "Dr. Dornberger," she said, "I think you're wonderful."

Amusedly Dornberger reached for his pipe and began to fill it. "Yes," he said, "sometimes I feel that way too."

"Joe, can I talk to you?"

Lucy Grainger had been on her way to Pathology when

Pearson's bulky figure loomed ahead in the main-floor corridor. As she called to him he stopped.

"Got a problem, Lucy?" It was his usual catarrhal, rumbling voice, but she was glad to notice there was no unfriendliness. She hoped she was still immune from his bad temper.

"Yes, Joe. I'd like you to see a patient of mine."

He was busy lighting one of the inevitable cigars. When he had it going he surveyed the red tip. "What's the trouble?"

"It's one of our own student nurses. A girl named Vivian Loburton. She's nineteen. Do you know her?"

Pearson shook his head. Lucy went on. "The case is worrying me a little. I suspect a bone tumor and I've a biopsy scheduled for the day after tomorrow. The tissue will be coming down to you, of course, but I thought perhaps you'd like to take a look at the girl."

"All right. Where is she?"

"I've had her admitted for observation," Lucy said. "She's on the second floor. Could you see her now?"

Pearson nodded. "Might as well." They moved toward the main vestibule and the passenger elevators.

Lucy's request to Pearson was not unusual. In a case like this, where malignancy was a possibility, it was the pathologist who would give a final opinion on the patient's condition. In the diagnosis of any tumor there were many factors—sometimes conflicting—for a pathologist to weigh in balance. But determination of bone tumors was even more difficult, something of which Lucy was aware. Consequently it was an advantage for the pathologist to be involved with a case at the beginning. In that way he could know the patient, discuss symptoms, and hear the radiologist's opinion, all of which added to his knowledge and aided diagnosis.

As they moved into the elevator Pearson paused and winced. He put a hand to his back.

Lucy pressed the button for the second floor. As the automatic doors slid closed she asked, "Is your back bothering you?"

"Sometimes it does." With an effort he straightened up. "Probably too much hunching over a microscope."

She looked at him concernedly. "Why don't you come to my office? I'll take a look at it."

He puffed his cigar, then grinned. "I'll tell you, Lucy. I can't afford your fees."

The doors opened and they went out on the second floor. Walking down the corridor, she said, "It'll be complimentary. I don't believe in charging my colleagues."

He gave her an amused glance. "You're not like the psychiatrists then?"

"No, I'm not." She laughed. "I hear they send you a bill, even if you work in the same office."

"That's right." She had seldom seen him quite so relaxed as this. "They say it's part of the treatment."

"Here we are." She opened a door and Pearson went first. Then she followed him in, closing the door behind her.

It was a small semi-private room with two patients. Lucy greeted a woman in the bed nearest the door, then moved over to the second bed where Vivian looked up from the magazine she had been reading.

"Vivian, this is Dr. Pearson."

"Hullo, Vivian." Pearson said it absently as he took the chart which Lucy offered him.

She answered politely, "Good afternoon, Doctor."

It was still a puzzle to Vivian why she was here at all. Her knee had been paining her again, it was true, but it seemed such a small thing to be put to bed for. However, she didn't mind very much. In a way the break from nursing-school routine was welcome, and it was pleasant to be reading and resting for a change. Mike had just phoned too. He seemed concerned on hearing what had happened and had promised to come in later, as soon as he could.

Lucy drew the overhead curtain between the two beds, and now Pearson said, "Let me see both knees, please."

Vivian turned back the bedclothes and lifted the hem of her nightgown. Pearson put down the chart and bent over for a close inspection.

Lucy watched the pathologist's short stubby fingers move carefully over the limbs. She thought: For someone who can be so rough with people he's surprisingly gentle. Once Vivian winced as a finger probed. Pearson looked up. "Hurt you there, eh?" Vivian nodded.

"I see from Dr. Grainger's report that you hit your knee about five months ago," he said.

"Yes, Doctor." Vivian was being careful to get her facts straight. "I didn't remember it at first—not until I started thinking back. I hit it on the bottom of a swimming pool though. I guess I dived too deeply."

Pearson asked her, "Did it hurt very much at the time?"

"Yes. But then the pain went away and I didn't think any more about it—not until now."

"All right, Vivian." He gestured to Lucy, who pulled the bedclothes back into place.

He asked Lucy, "Have you got the X-rays?"

"I have them here." She produced a large manila envelope. "There are two sets. The first set didn't show anything. Then we softened them up to see the muscles, and that showed an irregularity in the bone."

Vivian listened interestedly to the exchange. She found herself experiencing a sense of importance that all this should be about her.

Now Pearson and Lucy had moved to the window and the pathologist held the X-ray negatives to the light. As he studied the second one Lucy pointed. "There. You see?" They looked at it together.

"I guess so." Pearson grunted and handed back the negatives. His attitude to X-rays was always that of one specialist groping on the unfamiliar territory of another. He said, "Shadows from shadow land. What does Radiology say?"

"Ralph Bell confirms the irregularity," Lucy answered. "But he can't see enough for a diagnosis. He agrees we should have a biopsy."

Pearson turned back to the bed. "Do you know what a biopsy is, Vivian?"

"I have an idea." The girl hesitated. "But I'm not really sure."

"Haven't taken it in your nursing course yet, eh?"

She shook her head.

Pearson said, "Well, what happens is that Dr. Grainger will take out a small piece of tissue from your knee—just where the trouble seems to be. Then it will come down to me and . . . I'll study it."

Vivian asked, "And can you tell from that . . . what's the matter?"

"Most times I can." He started to leave, then hesitated. "Do you play a lot of sports?"

"Oh yes, Doctor. Tennis, swimming, skiing." She added, "I love horse riding too. I used to do a lot in Oregon."

"Oregon, eh?" He said it thoughtfully; then, turning away, "All right, Vivian; that's all for now."

Lucy smiled. "I'll be back later." She gathered up the chart and X-rays and followed Pearson out.

As the door closed, for the first time Vivian felt an uneasy chill of fear.

When they were well down the corridor Lucy asked, "What's your opinion, Joe?"

"It could be a bone tumor." Pearson said it slowly, thinking.

"Malignant?"

"It's possible."

They came to the elevator and stopped. Lucy said, "Of course, if it's malignant, I'll have to amputate the leg."

Pearson nodded slowly. Suddenly he looked very old. "Yes," he said. "I was thinking of that."

Eleven

The prop-jet Viscount turned evenly into wind and began to lose height. Landing gear and flaps down, it was lined up with number one runway of Burlington's municipal airport, dead ahead. Watching the airplane's approach from the public mezzanine, just below the control tower, Dr. Kent O'Donnell reflected idly that aviation and medicine had a good deal in common. Both were products of science; both were changing the world's life and destroying old concepts; both were moving toward unknown horizons and a future only dimly seen. There was another parallel too. Aviation nowadays was having trouble keeping pace with its own discoveries; an aircraft designer he knew had told him recently, "If an airplane's flying it's already out of date."

The practice of medicine, O'Donnell thought, shading his eyes from the bright afternoon sun of mid-August, was very much the same. Hospitals, clinics, physicians themselves, were never able to be entirely up to date. No matter how they tried, experimentation, development, new techniques were always ahead—sometimes by years. A man might die today when the drug that could save him was already invented and even, perhaps, in limited use. But it took time

for new developments to become known and to gain acceptance. The same was true of surgery. One surgeon, or a group
of surgeons, might develop a new life-saving technique. But
before it could be used generally others must master it and
pass their skill along. Sometimes it was a long process. Heart
surgery, for example, was fairly general now and within
reach of most who needed it badly. But for a long time only
a handful of surgeons were qualified or willing to attempt it.

There was always the question, too, with new things: is
this good; is it a wise development? Not all change meant
progress. Plenty of times in medicine there were false scents,
theories running contrary to fact, individuals with enthusi-
asms and obsessions who would go off half cocked, mislead-
ing others when they did. Sometimes it was hard to steer a
mid-course between open-mindedness and reasonable caution. At Three Counties, with its quota of diehards and
progressives—and with good men in both camps—it was a
continuing problem for someone like O'Donnell to know, at
any given moment, exactly where and with whom his
allegiance lay.

His thoughts were broken by the Viscount taxiing in, the
shrill whine of its motors drowning out the voices of others
around him. O'Donnell waited until the motors stopped and
passengers began to disembark. Then, seeing Dr. Coleman
among them, he went down the stairs to greet the hospital's
new assistant director of pathology in the arrival lobby.

David Coleman was surprised to see the chief of surgery—
tall, bronzed, standing out from the crowd—waiting for him
with outstretched hand. O'Donnell said, "It's good to see you.
Joe Pearson couldn't make it, but we thought that someone
should be around to say 'welcome.'" What O'Donnell failed
to add was that Joe Pearson had flatly refused to go and,
Harry Tomaselli being out of town, O'Donnell had taken
the time to drive out himself.

As they moved through the hot, crowded lobby O'Donnell
saw Coleman glance around him. He got the impression
that the younger man was making a quick assessment of his
surroundings. Perhaps it was a habit—if so, a good one.
Certainly David Coleman would stand up to scrutiny himself. Though he had had a three-hour air journey, his gab-
ardine suit was uncreased, his well-trimmed hair carefully
parted and brushed, his shave recent. He wore no hat, which
made him look younger than his thirty-one years. Though

slighter than O'Donnell in build, his features were clear-cut
and well defined; he had a longish face and an incisive jaw.
The brief case under his arm added a professional touch;
picture of a young scientist, O'Donnell thought. He steered
Coleman toward the baggage counter. A trailerload of bags
was being unloaded, and they joined the scrimmage with
other passengers who had disembarked.

O'Donnell said, "This is the part of air travel I dislike."

Coleman nodded and smiled faintly. It was almost as if he
had said, Let's not waste our talents on small talk, shall we?

This is a cool customer, O'Donnell thought. He noticed,
as he had at their previous meeting, the steel-gray eyes and
wondered what it took to penetrate behind them. Now Coleman was standing, unmoving among the crowd, glancing
around. Almost as if by command, ignoring others, a redcap
gravitated toward him.

Ten minutes later, as O'Donnell threaded his Buick
through the airport traffic and headed toward town, he said,
"We've put you up in the Roosevelt Hotel. It's as comfortable as any and quiet. I believe our administrator wrote you
about the apartment situation."

"Yes, he did," Coleman said. "I'd like to do something
about that quite quickly."

"You won't have any problem," O'Donnell said, then
added, "Perhaps you'd like to take a day or two to fix up an
apartment before you report at the hospital."

"I don't think so, thank you. I plan to start work tomorrow
morning."

Coleman was polite but definite. O'Donnell thought: This
is a man who makes up his mind, then states his opinion
plainly. He sounded, too, as if he were not dissuaded easily.
O'Donnell found himself speculating on how Joe Pearson
and David Coleman were going to get along. Superficially it
looked as if they might clash. But you could never tell.
Sometimes in a hospital the most unlikely people hit it off
like lifetime friends.

Looking around him as they drove through the approaches
to the city, David Coleman found himself close to a sense
of excitement at the prospect ahead. This was unusual because mostly he took whatever came with a matter-of-fact
acceptance. But it was, after all, his first staff appointment to
a hospital. He told himself: a touch of down-to-earth hu-

manity is nothing to be ashamed of, my friend, then smiled inwardly at the silent self-criticism. Old habits of thought, he reflected, were hard to break.

He wondered about O'Donnell, sitting beside him. Everything he had heard about the chief of surgery at Three Counties had been good. How was it, he wondered, that a man with O'Donnell's background and qualifications would choose a place like Burlington? Did he, too, have a mixed-up motivation, or was there some other reason? Maybe he just liked it here. There were some people, Coleman supposed, whose preferences were straightforward and uncomplicated.

O'Donnell pulled out to pass a tractor-trailer. Then he said, "I'd like to tell you a couple of things, if I may."

Coleman said politely, "Please do."

"We've had a number of changes at Three Counties these past few years." O'Donnell was going slowly, choosing his words. "Harry Tomaselli told me you'd heard of some of them—as well as our plans."

Coleman smiled. "Yes, I had."

O'Donnell sounded his horn and a car ahead of them moved over. He said, "The fact of your being here represents a major change, and I imagine that, once installed, there will be other changes you'll want to make yourself."

Coleman thought of the hospital's pathology department as he had seen it during his brief visit. "Yes," he responded, "I'm sure there will."

O'Donnell was silent. Then, more slowly, he said, "Whenever we could, we've tried to make our changes peaceably. Sometimes that hasn't been possible; I'm not one who believes in sacrificing a principle just to keep the peace." He looked sideways at Coleman. "Let's be clear about that."

Coleman nodded but made no answer. O'Donnell went on, "All the same, wherever you can, I'd suggest you move discreetly." He smiled. "Do what you can by persuasion, and save the big guns for things that really matter."

Noncommittally Coleman said, "I see." He was not sure just what he was being told; he would need to know O'Donnell better before deciding that. Had he been wrong in his impression of O'Donnell? Was the chief of surgery, after all, just a pussyfooter? Was Coleman being told here and now, as a newcomer, not to rock the boat? If that were so, they would quickly find they had obtained the wrong man. David Coleman made a mental note not to take a long lease on any apartment he might find in Burlington.

O'Donnell was wondering now if he had been wise in saying what he had. They had been fortunate to get this man Coleman, and he had no wish to put him off, not right at the beginning. But all the time at the back of O'Donnell's mind had been the problem of Joe Pearson and Pearson's admitted influence with Eustace Swayne. As far as he could O'Donnell wanted to be loyal to Orden Brown; in the past the board chairman had done a good deal to support the chief of surgery. O'Donnell knew that Brown wanted Swayne's quarter million dollars and, indeed, the hospital needed it badly. And if that meant placating Joe Pearson a little, O'Donnell was prepared to go along—within reason.

But where did hospital politics end and O'Donnell's responsibility as a medical practitioner begin? It was a question that troubled him; someday he might have to decide just where the line of demarcation lay. Was he himself playing politics now? O'Donnell supposed he was. If he were not, he would not have just said what he had to Dr. Coleman. Power corrupts, he thought; you can't escape it, no matter who you are. He considered expanding the subject a little more with Coleman, perhaps taking the younger man into his confidence, then decided against it. Coleman was, after all, a newcomer; and O'Donnell was acutely aware that he had not penetrated yet behind those cool gray eyes.

Now they were coming into the city center, the streets of Burlington hot and dusty, sidewalks shimmering and the black-top roadways sticky in the heat. He turned the Buick into the forecourt of the Roosevelt Hotel. A porter opened the car doors and began to remove Coleman's bags from the rear seat.

O'Donnell said, "Would you like me to come in? Make sure everything's in order?"

From outside the car Coleman answered, "There's really no need." Once more the quiet but definite statement.

O'Donnell leaned across the seat. "All right. We'll expect you tomorrow then. Good luck."

"Thank you."

The porter slammed the doors, and O'Donnell eased the car into the city traffic. He glanced at his watch. It was 2

P.M. He decided he would go to his own office first, the hospital later.

Seated on the leather-covered bench outside the outpatients' laboratory of Three Counties, Elizabeth Alexander wondered why it was that the corridor walls had been painted two shades of brown instead of something lighter and brighter. It was a dark part of the hospital anyway; a little yellow, or even a light green, would have made the place so much more cheerful.

From as far back as her memory went Elizabeth had liked bright colors. She remembered, as a little girl, the first pair of draperies she had made for her own room at home; they had been powder-blue chintz with shapes of stars and moons woven into them. She suspected now that they had been very badly made, but at the time they had seemed quite wonderful. To hang them she had gone downstairs into her father's store and indulgently he had sought out the things she needed—a rod cut to the right length, metal brackets, screws, a screw driver. She remembered his groping to find what he wanted among the other hardware—always piled high and untidily so that more often than not he had to search for whatever a customer asked for.

That was back in New Richmond, Indiana—two years before her father had died in the accident. Or was it three? It was hard to be sure; time went by so quickly. She knew it was six months before her father's death that she had first met John. In a way that had had to do with color too. He was on vacation from high school and had come into the store to buy some red paint. By then Elizabeth was helping in the store, and she had talked him out of it and sold him green instead. Or was it the other way around? That too was misty now.

She knew, though, she had fallen in love with John right at the first moment. Probably it was just to keep him in the store that she had suggested the switch in colors. And looking back, it seemed from then on there had never been any doubt about their feelings for each other. They had stayed sweethearts through the transition from high school to college and had been married six years after their first meeting. Strangely, though neither had any money and John was still at college on a scholarship, no one had urged them to wait.

Everyone they knew seemed to accept their marriage as natural and inevitable.

To some people their first year together might have seemed difficult. To John and Elizabeth it had been a gloriously happy time. The previous year Elizabeth had gone to night secretarial school. And in Indianapolis, where John was at college, she had worked as a stenographer and supported them both.

That was the year they had discussed seriously the question of John's future—whether he should aim high and try for medical school or settle for the shorter course of a medical technologist. Elizabeth had favored medical school. Though it would mean several more years before John began earning, she had been willing to continue working. But John was less sure. For as long as he could remember he had wanted to enter medicine, and his college grades were good, but he was impatient to contribute something to their marriage. Then they had discovered that Elizabeth was pregnant and, for John, it was the deciding factor. Over his wife's protests he had enrolled in medical-technology school and they had moved to Chicago.

There they had had their baby and had called her Pamela. Four weeks later the child had died of bronchitis, and for a while all of Elizabeth's world seemed to have fallen in about her. For all her stability and common sense, she had gone to pieces and had ceased to care. John had done all he could, had never been kinder or more considerate, but it had not helped.

She had felt she had to get away and had gone home to her mother in New Richmond. But after a week she had longed for John and had gone back to Chicago. From that point on her return to normalcy had been gradual but sure. Six weeks before John's graduation she had learned she was pregnant again; it was the final thing she had needed for readjustment. Now she felt healthy, her old cheerfulness back, and there was a growing excitement at the thought of the unborn child within her.

In Burlington they had found a small but pleasant apartment. The rent was economical. Out of their careful savings they had made a down payment on furniture and could meet the monthly installments out of John's hospital pay. As of this moment everything was fine. Except, Elizabeth thought, that horrible brown on the corridor walls.

The door of the outpatients' lab opened and a woman who had been waiting ahead of Elizabeth came out. A white-coated girl technician was behind her. The technician consulted a clip board. "Mrs. Alexander?"

"That's right." Elizabeth stood up.

"Will you come in, please?"

She followed the girl through the doorway.

"Sit down, Mrs. Alexander. This won't take long."

"Thank you."

At her desk the technician consulted the requisition slip which Dr. Dornberger had written. "Rh typing and sensitivity. All right, just put your hand here, please, and clench your fist." She took Elizabeth's wrist and sponged it with antiseptic, then deftly slipped on a rubber tourniquet. From a tray she selected a hypodermic and broke open a package with a sterile needle which she fitted to the syringe. Quickly selecting a vein on Elizabeth's arm, the girl inserted the needle with a single sharp movement and eased back the plunger. She drew blood until it was level with the 7 cc. mark on the syringe, then whipped the needle out, putting a tuft of cotton batting on the puncture it had made. The whole procedure had taken less than fifteen seconds.

"I think you've done that before," Elizabeth said.

The girl smiled. "A few hundred times."

Elizabeth watched while the technician labeled a test tube and transferred the blood sample to it. When she had finished she put the test tube in a rack. Then she announced, "That's all, Mrs. Alexander."

Elizabeth pointed to the tube. "What happens to it now?"

"It goes to the serology lab. One of the technicians there will do the test."

Elizabeth speculated on whether it might be John.

Mike Seddons, sitting alone in the house-staff lounge, was deeply troubled. If someone had told him a month ago that he could be this concerned about a girl that to all intents and purposes he scarcely knew, he would have adjudged the other person crazy. Yet for forty-eight hours, ever since he had read the chart in the nursing station near Vivian's hospital room, his worry and distress had steadily grown. Last night he had scarcely slept; for hours he had lain awake, his mind turning over the full significance of the words written on the chart in Dr. Lucy Grainger's handwriting, "Vivian

Loburton—suspected osteogenic sarcoma—prepare for biopsy."

On the first occasion he had seen Vivian—the day of the autopsy—she was merely another pretty student nurse. Even at their second meeting—before the incident in the park—he had thought of her principally as an interesting, exciting lay. Mike Seddons never fooled himself either about words or his own intentions.

Nor did he now.

For the first time in his life he was deeply and genuinely in love. And tortured with a haunting, dreadful fear.

The night he had told Vivian that he wanted to marry her he had had no time to think the implications through. Up to that point Mike Seddons had always told himself there would be no question of marriage until he was established in practice, his wild oats sown, his future financially secure. But once the words to Vivian were out he had known them to be true. A hundred times since he had repeated them silently, without a single thought of wanting to turn back.

Then this.

Unlike Vivian, who still thought of her problem as a small bump below the knee—a nuisance, but something which treatment of one kind or another would clear up—Mike Seddons knew the implications of the phrase "suspected osteogenic sarcoma." He knew that if the diagnosis were confirmed it would mean that Vivian had a virulent, malignant tumor which could spread, and perhaps already had, elsewhere in her body. In that event, without swift surgery, her chances of survival beyond a year or so were almost nil. And surgery meant amputation of the limb—with all speed once the diagnosis was confirmed—in the hope of containing the spreading, poisonous cells before they moved too far beyond the original site. And even then, statistically, only 20 per cent of osteogenic patients were free from further trouble after amputation. The rest went steadily downhill, sometimes living only a few more months.

But it didn't *have* to be osteogenic sarcoma. It could be a harmless bone tumor. The chances either way were fifty-fifty—odds even, the same chance you got with the spin of a single coin. Mike Seddons felt himself sweating at the thought of how much—both for himself and Vivian—was riding on the biopsy result. He had considered going to Lucy Grainger and talking the whole thing over; then he had decided no. He could probably find out more by staying on the fringes. If he declared a personal interest some sources of information might be closed off to him. To spare his feelings others might be guarded in what they said. He did not want that. One way or the other he had to know!

Talking with Vivian and, at the same time, trying to keep his thoughts to himself had not been easy. Last night, sitting alone with her in the hospital room—the other woman patient had been discharged, and for the time being the second bed was empty—she had teased him about seeming downcast.

Cheerfully chewing grapes, which he had brought her earlier, she had said, "I know what's wrong. You're scared of being pinned down—not being able to hop from bed to bed."

"I never did hop from bed to bed," he had said, trying to match her mood. "It isn't that easy; you have to work at it."

"You didn't do much work on me."

"You were different. It just sort of happened."

She had stopped at that. "Yes, I know." Then, gaily again, she had said, "Well, anyway, it's no good thinking you're going to get out of this, Dr. Michael Seddons, M.D. I have no intention of letting you loose again—ever."

He had kissed her at that, holding her tightly, feeling more emotion than he had believed he had. She moved her face and nuzzled his ear. Her hair against his cheek was soft and fragrant. Softly she said, "And another thing, Doctor—stay away from those student nurses; they have no morals."

"Really!" Again he responded with a brightness he did not feel. He held her away from him. "Why didn't someone tell me this before?"

She was wearing a thin blue negligee, open at the front. Beneath it was a nylon nightgown of the same transparent blue. All at once he realized, breathlessly, how young and beautiful she was.

Vivian had looked at the door. It was closed. She said, "They're busy at the nursing station tonight. I know because they told me. It'll probably be an hour, at least, before anyone comes around."

For a moment he had been shocked. Then he had laughed and fallen in love all over again with her honesty and simple frankness. He said, "You mean here? Now?"

"Why not?"

"If anyone came I'd be thrown out of the hospital."

Softly she said, "You weren't so worried about that the other night." Her finger tips moved lightly down his face. Impulsively he had bent and kissed her neck. As his lips moved lower he heard her breathing quicken and felt her fingers tighten on his shoulder.

For a moment he had been tempted, then sanity won out. He put his arms around her. Tenderly he murmured, "When all this is over, Vivian darling, then we'll be really alone. What's more, we'll have all the time we want."

That was yesterday. This afternoon, on the operating floor, Lucy Grainger would be performing the biopsy. Mike Seddons looked at his watch. It was 2:30 P.M. According to the O.R. schedule, they should be starting now. If Pathology worked fast the answer might be known by tomorrow. With a fervor at once incongruous and real he found himself praying: *Oh, God! Please, God—let it be benign!*

The anesthetist nodded. "We're ready when you are, Lucy."

Dr. Lucy Grainger came around to the head of the operating-room table. She was already gloved and gowned. Smiling down at Vivian, she said reassuringly, "This won't take long, and you won't feel a thing."

Vivian tried to smile back confidently. She knew, though, she didn't quite succeed. Maybe it was because she was a little drowsy—she was aware that she had been given some kind of sedation as well as the spinal anesthetic which had taken away all feeling from the lower portion of her body.

Lucy nodded to her assisting intern. He lifted Vivian's left leg, and Lucy began to remove the towels which were taped around it. Earlier this morning, before Vivian had been brought to the operating floor, the leg had been shaved, bathed thoroughly, and painted with merthiolate. Now Lucy repeated the antiseptic procedure and draped fresh sterile towels above and below the knee.

On the other side of the operating table the scrub nurse was holding a folded green sheet. With Lucy taking one side, they draped it over the table so that a hole in the sheet was immediately above the exposed knee. The anesthetist reached over, fastening the top of the sheet to a metal bar above Vivian's head, so that her view of the rest of the operating room was cut off. As he looked down at her he said, "Just stay relaxed, Miss Loburton. This is really like having a tooth out—only a lot more comfortable."

"Knife, please." Lucy held out her hand and the scrub nurse put a scalpel into it. Using the belly portion of the blade, she made a quick, firm incision, just below the knee and about four centimeters long. Immediately blood welled up.

"Mosquito clamps." The scrub nurse was ready, and Lucy clamped off two small spurters. "Will you tie off, please?" She moved back to allow the intern to put ligatures around both clamps.

"We'll make our incision through the periosteum." The intern nodded as Lucy applied the knife she had used previously to the thick fibrous tissue above the bone, cutting cleanly down.

"Ready for the saw." The scrub nurse passed Lucy a Stryker oscillating saw. Behind her a circulating nurse held the trailing electric cable clear of the operating table.

Talking again for the intern's benefit, Lucy said, "We shall take a wedge-shaped sample of bone. About half to three-quarters of an inch should be enough." She glanced up at the X-ray films, in place on a lighted screen at the end of the room. "We must be sure, of course, that we are into the tumor and don't take a piece of normal bone that has been forced outward."

Lucy switched on the saw and applied it twice. There was a soft crunching sound each time it bit into bone. Then she switched off and passed the saw back. "There, I think that will do. Tweezers!"

Gingerly she extracted the bone sample, dropping it into a small jar of Zenker's solution which the circulating nurse was holding out. Now the specimen—identified and accompanied by a surgical work requisition—would go to Pathology.

The anesthetist asked Vivian, "Still feel all right?"

She nodded.

He told her, "They won't be long now. The bone sample is out. All they have to do is zip up your knee."

At the table Lucy was already sewing the periosteum, using a running suture. She was thinking: If only this were all, how simple everything would be. But this was merely exploratory. The next move would depend on Joe Pearson's verdict about the bone sample she was sending to him.

The thought of Joe Pearson reminded Lucy of what she had learned earlier from Kent O'Donnell: that this was the day on which the hospital's new assistant pathologist was due to arrive in Burlington. She hoped that things would go smoothly with the new man—for O'Donnell's sake as much as any other reason.

Lucy respected the chief of surgery's efforts to achieve improvement within the hospital without major upheavals, though she knew from observation that O'Donnell would never shun an issue if it really became necessary to meet it head on. There she went again, she reflected: thinking about Kent O'Donnell. It was strange how, just recently, her thoughts had kept returning to him. Perhaps it was the proximity in which they worked; there were few days when the two of them failed to meet sometime during their stint in surgery. Now Lucy found herself wondering how soon it would be before he invited her to dinner once more. Or perhaps she could arrange a small dinner party at her own apartment. There were a few people she had been planning to invite for some time, and Kent O'Donnell could be among them.

Lucy let the intern move in to sew the subcutaneous tissue. She told him, "Use interrupted sutures; three should be sufficient." She watched closely. He was being slow but careful. She knew some of the surgeons at Three Counties gave interns very little to do when they were assisting. But Lucy remembered how many times she herself had stood by an operating table, hoping for at least a little practice in tying knots.

That had been in Montreal—all of thirteen years ago since she had begun her internship at Montreal General, then stayed on to specialize in orthopedic surgery. She had often thought how much chance there was in the specialty which anyone in medicine decided to enter. Often so much depended on the kind of cases you became involved in as an intern. In her own case, in pre-med school at McGill, and later at Toronto University School of Medicine, her interest had switched first to one field, then to another. Even on return to Montreal she had been undecided whether to specialize at all or enter general practice. But then chance had caused her to work for a while under the tutelage of a surgeon known to the hospital generally as "Old Bones," because of his concern with orthopedics.

When Lucy first knew him, Old Bones had been in his mid-sixties. In terms of behavior and personality, he was one of the most objectionable people she had ever met. Most teaching centers have their prima donnas; in Old Bones the worst habits of them all had appeared to be combined. He regularly insulted everyone in the hospital—interns, residents, his own colleagues, patients—with equal impartiality. In the operating room, if crossed at all, he had shouted abuse at nurses and assistants in language borrowed from the bar-room and the water front. If handed a wrong instrument, on his normal days he would throw it back at the offender; in a more tolerant mood he would merely hurl it at the wall.

Yet, for all the performance, Old Bones had been a master surgeon. He had worked mostly on correcting bone deformities in crippled children. His spectacular successes had made his fame world-wide. He never modified his manner, and even the children he dealt with got the same rough treatment as their elders. But, somehow, children seldom seemed to fear him. Lucy had often wondered if childish instinct were not a better barometer than adult reasoning.

But it was the influence of Old Bones that really decided Lucy's future. When she had seen at first hand what orthopedic surgery could accomplish, she had wanted to share the accomplishment herself. She had stayed at Montreal General as a three-year intern, assisting Old Bones whenever it was possible. She had copied everything from him except his manner. Even toward Lucy that had never changed, though near the end of her senior internship she took pride in the fact that he had shouted at her a good deal less than at other people.

Since then, in the time she had been in practice, Lucy had had successes of her own. And in Burlington her referrals from other physicians nowadays made her one of the busiest people on Three Counties' staff. She had gone back to Montreal only once—on an occasion two years earlier, to attend Old Bones' funeral. People said it was one of the biggest funerals of a medical man the city had ever seen. Practically everyone the old man had ever insulted had been present in the church.

Her mind switched back to the present. The biopsy was almost complete. At a nod from Lucy the intern had gone on to sew up the skin, again using interrupted sutures. Now he was putting in the final one. Lucy glanced at the wall clock above her. The whole procedure had taken half an hour. It was 3 P.M.

At seven minutes to five a sixteen-year-old hospital messenger sashayed, whistling, hips swaying, into the serology lab. Usually he came in this way because he knew it infuriated Bannister, with whom he maintained a state of perpetual running warfare. As usual, the senior lab technician looked up and snarled at him. "I'm telling you for the last time to stop making that infernal racket every time you come in here."

"I'm glad it's the last time." The youth was unperturbed. "Tell you the truth, all that complainin' o' yours was get'n on my nerves a bit." He went on whistling and held up the tray of blood samples he had collected from the outpatients' lab. "Where you want this blood, Mr. Dracula?"

John Alexander grinned. Bannister, however, was not amused. "You know where it goes, wise guy." He indicated a space on one of the lab benches. "Put it over there."

"Yessir, captain, sir." Elaborately the youth put down the tray and gave a mock salute. Then he essayed a pelvic gyration and moved toward the door singing:

> *"Oh, give me a home where the viruses roam,*
> *Where the bugs and the microbes all play,*
> *When often is heard an old bloodsucker's word,*
> *And the test tubes stand stinkin' all day."*

The door swung closed and his voice faded down the corridor.

Alexander laughed. Bannister said, "Don't laugh at him. It just makes him worse." He crossed to the bench and picked up the blood specimens, glancing casually at the work sheet with them. Halfway across the lab he stopped.

"Hey, there's a blood sample here from a Mrs. Alexander. Is that your wife?"

Alexander put down the pipette he had been using and moved across. "It probably is. Dr. Dornberger sent her in for a sensitivity test." He took the work sheet and looked down it. "Yes, it's Elizabeth all right."

"It says typing and sensitivity both," Bannister said.

"I expect Dr. Dornberger wanted to be sure. Actually Elizabeth is Rh negative." As an afterthought he added, "I'm Rh positive."

Expansively, and with a fatherly air of great knowledge, Bannister said, "Oh well, most of the time that doesn't cause any trouble."

"Yes, I know. All the same, you like to be sure."

"Well, here's the specimen." Bannister picked out the test tube labeled "Alexander, Mrs. E." and held it up. "Do you want to do the test yourself?"

"Yes, I would. If you don't mind."

Bannister never objected to someone else doing work which might otherwise fall to himself. He said, "It's all right with me." Then, glancing at the clock, he added, "You can't do it tonight though. It's quitting time." He replaced the test tube and handed the tray to Alexander. "Better put this lot away until the morning."

Alexander took the blood samples and put them in the lab refrigerator. Then, closing the refrigerator door, he paused thoughtfully.

"Carl, there's something I've been meaning to ask you."

Bannister was busily clearing up. He always liked to leave right on the dot of five. Without turning his head he asked, "What is it?"

"The blood-sensitization tests we're doing here—I've been wondering about them."

"Wondering what?"

Alexander chose his words carefully. Right from the beginning, because of his own college training, he had realized the possibility of arousing resentment in people like Bannister. He tried now, as he had before, to avoid giving offense. "I noticed we're only doing two sensitization tests—one in saline, the other in high protein."

"So?"

"Well," Alexander said diffidently, "isn't just doing the two tests alone . . . a bit out of date?"

Bannister had finished clearing up. He came around the center table, wiping his hands on a paper towel. He said sharply, "Suppose you tell me why."

Alexander ignored the sharpness. This was important. He said, "Most labs nowadays are doing a third test—an indirect Coombs—after the test in saline."

"A 'what' test?"

"An indirect Coombs."

"What's that?"

"Are you kidding?" The moment the words were out Alexander knew he had made a tactical mistake. But he had spoken impulsively, reasoning that no serology technician could fail to know of an indirect Coombs test.

The senior technician bridled. "You don't have to get smart."

Hastily trying to repair the damage, Alexander replied, "I'm sorry, Carl. I didn't mean it to sound like that."

Bannister crumpled the paper towel and threw it into a waste bin. "Well, that's the way it did sound." He leaned forward aggressively, his bald head reflecting a light bulb above. "Look, fella, I'll tell you something for your own good. You're fresh out of school, and one thing you haven't found out is that some things they teach you there just don't work out in practice."

"This isn't just theory, Carl." Alexander was in earnest now, his blunder of a moment ago seeming unimportant. "It's been proven that some antibodies in the blood of pregnant women can't be detected either in a saline solution or high protein."

"And how often does it happen?" Bannister put the question smugly, as if knowing the answer in advance.

"Very seldom."

"Well, there you are."

"But it's enough to make the third test important." John Alexander was insistent, trying to penetrate Bannister's unwillingness to know. "Actually it's very simple. After you've finished the saline test you take the same test tube——"

Bannister cut him off. "Save the lecture for some other time." Slipping off his lab coat, he reached for the jacket of his suit behind the door.

Knowing it to be a losing argument, Alexander still went on. "It isn't much more work. I'd be glad to do it myself. All that's needed is Coombs serum. It's true it makes the testing a little more expensive . . ."

This was familiar ground. Now Bannister could understand better what the two of them were talking about. "Oh, yeah!" he said sarcastically. "That would go great with Pearson. Anything that's more expensive is sure to be a big hit."

"But don't you understand?—the other way isn't foolproof." Alexander spoke tensely; without realizing it he had raised his voice. "With the two tests we're doing here you can get a negative test result, and yet a mother's blood may still be sensitized and dangerous to the baby. You could kill a newborn child that way."

"Well, it isn't your job to worry about it." This was Bannister at his crudest, the words almost snarled.

"But——"

"But nothing! Pearson isn't keen on new ways of doing things—especially when they cost more money." Bannister hesitated, and his manner became less aggressive. He was aware that it was one minute to five and he was anxious to wind this up and get away. "Look, kid, I'll give you some advice. We're not doctors, and you'd be smart to quit trying to sound like one. We're lab assistants and we work in here the way we're told."

"That doesn't mean to say I can't think, does it?" It was Alexander's turn to be aroused. "All I know is, I'd like to see my wife's test done in saline, *and* in protein, *and* in Coombs serum. You may not be interested, but this baby happens to be important to us."

At the door the older man surveyed Alexander. He could see clearly now what he had not realized before—this kid was a troublemaker. What was more, troublemakers had a habit of involving other people in uncomfortable situations. Maybe this smart-aleck college graduate should be allowed to hang himself right now. Bannister said, "I've told you what I think. If you don't like it you'd better go see Pearson. Tell him you're not satisfied with the way things are being run around here."

Alexander looked directly at the senior technician. Then he said quietly, "Maybe I will."

Bannister's lip curled. "Suit yourself. But remember—I warned you."

With a final glance at the clock he went out, leaving John Alexander in the laboratory alone.

Twelve

Outside the main entrance to Three Counties Hospital Dr. David Coleman paused to look around him. It was a few minutes after eight on a warm, mid-August morning, with promise already of a hot and sultry day ahead. At this moment there was little activity outside the hospital. Beside himself, the only other people in sight were a janitor, hosing some of yesterday's dust from a section of the forecourt, and a middle-aged nurse who had just alighted from a bus on the opposite side of the street. The main stream of hospital business, he supposed, would not begin to flow for another hour or so.

David Coleman surveyed the block of buildings which comprised Three Counties. Certainly, he decided, the hospital's builders could never be accused of having wasted money on aesthetic frills. The architecture was strictly utilitarian, the facings of plain brick unadorned by any other masonry. The effect was a succession of conventional rectangles: walls, doors, and windows. Only near the main doorway did the pattern vary, and here a single foundation stone announced, "Laid by His Honor Mayor Hugo Stouting, April 1918." As he walked up the entry steps David Coleman found himself wondering what kind of a man that long-forgotten dignitary had been.

Carl Bannister was sorting papers on Dr. Pearson's desk when Coleman knocked and entered the pathologist's office.

"Good morning."

Surprised, the senior lab technician looked up. It was unusual to have visitors this early. Most people around the hospital knew that Joe Pearson seldom arrived before ten o'clock, sometimes later.

"Good morning." He returned the greeting, not too affably. Bannister was never at his best in the early morning. He asked, "Are you looking for Dr. Pearson?"

"In a way, yes. I'm starting work here today." Seeing the other start, he added, "I'm Dr. Coleman."

The effect, Coleman thought, was somewhat like letting off

142

firecrackers under a hen. Bannister put down his papers hurriedly and came around the desk, almost at a run, his bald head gleaming. "Oh, excuse me, Doctor. I didn't realize. I'd heard you were coming, but we had no idea it would be this soon."

Coleman said calmly, "Dr. Pearson is expecting me. Is he in, by the way?"

Bannister seemed shocked. "You're too early for him. He won't be here for another two hours." His face creased in a confidential man-to-man smile. It seemed to say: I expect you'll keep the same kind of hours yourself as soon as the newness wears off.

"I see."

As Coleman glanced around him Bannister remembered an omission. He said, "Oh, by the way, Doctor, I'm Carl Bannister—senior lab technician." With careful geniality he added, "I expect we'll be seeing a lot of each other." Bannister made a habit of taking no chances with anybody senior to himself.

"Yes, I expect we will." Coleman was not sure how much the idea appealed to him. But he shook hands with Bannister, then looked around for a place to hang the light raincoat he had brought; the morning forecast predicted thunder showers later in the day. Once again Bannister was alert to serve and please.

"Let me take your coat." He found a wire hanger and carefully put coat and hanger on a rack near the door.

"Thank you," Coleman said.

"That's perfectly all right, Doctor. Now, would you like me to show you around the labs?"

Coleman hesitated. Perhaps he ought to wait for Dr. Pearson. On the other hand, two hours was a long time to sit around and he might as well be doing something in the meantime. The labs would be his domain anyway. What was the difference? He said, "I saw part of the labs with Dr. Pearson when I was here a few weeks ago. But I'll take another look if you're not too busy."

"Well, of course, we're always busy around here, Doctor. But I'll be glad to take the time for you. In fact, it'll be a pleasure." The working of Bannister's mind was incredibly transparent.

"This way, please." Bannister had opened the door of the serology lab and stood back for Coleman to enter. John

Alexander, who had not seen Bannister since their argument
the night before, looked up from the centrifuge in which he
had just placed a blood sample.

"Doctor, this is John Alexander. He just started work
here." Carl Bannister was warming to his role of showman.
He added facetiously, "Still wet behind the ears from technology school, eh, John?"

"If you say so." Alexander answered uncomfortably, resenting the condescension but not wanting to be rude.

Coleman moved forward, offering his hand. "I'm Dr.
Coleman."

As they shook hands Alexander said interestedly, "You
mean you're the new pathologist, Doctor?"

"That's right." Coleman glanced around him. As he had
on the previous visit, he could see that a lot of changes
would need to be made in here.

Bannister said expansively, "You just look around, Doctor—at anything you want."

"Thank you." Turning back to Alexander, Coleman asked,
"What are you working on now?"

"It's a blood sensitization." He indicated the centrifuge.
"This specimen happens to be from my wife."

"Really." Coleman found himself thinking this young lab
assistant was a good deal more impressive than Bannister.
In appearance anyway. "When is your wife having her
child?" he asked.

"In just over four months, Doctor." Alexander balanced
the centrifuge and switched it on, then reached over to set
a timing dial. Coleman noticed that all the movements were
economical and quick. There was a sense of fluidity in the
way this man used his hands. Politely Alexander asked, "Are
you married, Doctor?"

"No." Coleman shook his head.

Alexander seemed on the point of asking another question, then appeared to change his mind.

"Did you want to ask me something?"

For a moment there was a pause. Then John Alexander
made up his mind. "Yes, Doctor," he said. "I do."

Whether this meant trouble or not, Alexander thought, at
least he would bring his doubts out into the open. Last
night, after the dispute with Bannister, he had been tempted
to drop the whole subject of the extra test on blood samples

coming to the lab. He remembered only too clearly the
dressing down he had received from Dr. Pearson on the last
occasion he had chosen to make a suggestion. This new doctor, though, certainly seemed easier to deal with. And even
if he considered Alexander wrong, it didn't seem likely there
would be any big scene. He took the plunge. "It's about the
blood tests we're doing—for sensitization."

As they had been speaking he had become aware of Ban-
ister in the background, the older technician moving his
bald head from side to side, intent on missing nothing that
was said. Now he moved forward, annoyed and aggressive,
to put Alexander in his place. "Now listen! If that's what you
were talking about last night, you leave it alone!"

Coleman asked curiously, "What was it you were talking
about last night?"

Ignoring the question, Bannister continued to lecture Alexander. "I don't want Dr. Coleman bothered with stuff like
that five minutes after he gets here. Forget it! Understand?"
He turned to Coleman, the automatic smile switched on.
"It's just some bee he's got in his bonnet, Doctor. Now, if
you'll come with me, I'll show you our histology setup." He
put a hand on Coleman's arm to steer him away.

For the space of several seconds Coleman did nothing.
Then, deliberately, he reached down and removed the hand
from his sleeve. "Just a moment," he said quietly. Then to
Alexander, "Is this something medical? To do with the
laboratory?"

Deliberately avoiding Bannister's scowl, Alexander answered, "Yes, it is."

"All right, let's hear it."

"It came up, really, because of this blood-sensitization
test—the one for my wife," Alexander said. "She's Rh negative; I'm Rh positive."

Coleman smiled. "Well, that applies to plenty of people.
There's no problem—that is, as long as the sensitization test
shows a negative result."

"But that's the point, Doctor—the test."

"What about it?" Coleman was puzzled. He was not at all
clear about what this young lab assistant was getting at.

Alexander said, "I think we should be doing an indirect
Coombs test on all these samples, *after* the tests in saline
and high protein."

"Of course."

There was a silence which Alexander broke. "Would you mind saying that again, Doctor?"

"I said 'of course.' Naturally there should be an indirect Coombs." Coleman still could see no point in this discussion. For a serology lab this sort of thing was elementary, basic.

"But we're not doing an indirect Coombs." Alexander shot a triumphal glance at Bannister. "Doctor, the Rh-sensitivity tests here are all being done just in a saline solution and in high protein. There's no Coombs serum being used at all."

At first Coleman was sure Alexander must be wrong. Apparently the young technologist had been working here only a short time; no doubt he had become confused. Then Coleman remembered the tone of conviction in which the statement had been made. He asked Bannister, "Is this true?"

"The way we do all our tests are according to Dr. Pearson's instructions." The elderly technician made it plain that in his opinion the entire discussion was a waste of time.

"Perhaps Dr. Pearson doesn't know you're doing the Rh tests that way."

"He knows all right." This time Bannister let his surliness come through. It was always the same with new people. They weren't inside a place five minutes before they started making trouble. He had tried to be pleasant with this new doctor, and look what you got for it. Well, one thing was for sure—Joe Pearson would soon put this fellow in his place. Bannister just hoped he was around to see it happen.

Coleman decided to ignore the senior technician's tone. Whether he liked it or not he was going to have to work with this man for a while. All the same, this thing had to be cleared up now. He said, "I'm afraid I don't quite understand. Surely you know that some antibodies in the blood of pregnant women will get past a saline test and a high-protein test, whereas they won't if you go on and do a further test in Coombs serum."

Alexander interjected, "That's what I've been saying."

Bannister made no answer. Coleman went on, "Anyway, I'll mention it to Dr. Pearson sometime. I'm sure he wasn't aware of it."

"What shall we do about this test?" Alexander asked. "And the others from here on?"

Coleman answered, "Do them in all three mediums, of course—saline, high protein, *and* Coombs serum."

"We haven't any Coombs serum in the lab, Doctor." Alexander was very glad now that he had brought this up. He liked the look of this new pathologist. Maybe he'd change some other things around the place. Goodness knows, he thought, there's plenty that can stand it.

"Then let's get some." Coleman was deliberately brisk. "There's no shortage anywhere."

"We can't just go out and get lab supplies," Bannister said. "There has to be a purchase requisition." He wore a superior smile. There were some things, after all, these Johnny-come-latelys didn't know.

Coleman carefully kept his feelings in check. Sometime soon it might be necessary to have a showdown with this man Bannister; he certainly had no intention of taking this kind of behavior permanently. But the first day of arrival was obviously not the time. He said pleasantly enough, but firmly, "Let me have the form then. I imagine I can sign it. That's one of the reasons I'm here."

Briefly the older technician hesitated. Then he opened a drawer and produced a pad of forms which he handed to Coleman.

"A pencil, please?"

With the same reluctance Bannister produced one. Handing it over, he said pettishly, "Dr. Pearson likes to order all lab supplies himself."

Coleman scribbled the order and signed it. With a tight, cool smile, "I expect to have a good deal more responsibility here than just ordering fifteen dollars' worth of rabbit serum," he said. "There you are." As he handed back the pad and pencil the phone rang on the other side of the lab.

It was an excuse for Bannister to turn his back. His face red with anger and frustration, he crossed to the wall phone to answer it. After listening briefly he gave a curt answer and replaced the instrument. "Gotta go down to Outpatients." The words, almost mumbled, were addressed to Coleman.

He answered icily, "You can go ahead."

With the incident closed Coleman found himself more angry than he had realized. What kind of discipline existed which allowed insolence like this from a lab technician? The inadequate procedure was serious enough. But having to correct it over the objections of someone like this man Bannister was intolerable. If this were the general order of things, it seemed probable that the entire pathology department was even more run-down than he had believed at first.

With Bannister gone he began to take a more careful look at the rest of the lab. The worn equipment, some of it inadequate, had already been evident. Now he saw how deplorably sloppy and disorganized the whole place was. The tables and benches were cluttered untidily with an assortment of apparatus and supplies. He noticed a heap of dirty glassware, a pile of yellowed papers. Moving across the lab, he observed a section of a worktable with fungus growing from it. From the other side of the room Alexander was uncomfortably watching the inspection.

"Is this the way the lab is usually kept?" Coleman asked.

"It isn't very tidy, is it?" Alexander felt a surge of shame that anyone should see this place the way it was. What he could not say was that he had already offered to reorganize it but Bannister had emphatically told him to leave things the way they were.

"I'd put it a little stronger than that." Coleman ran one of his fingers over a shelf. It came away grimed with dust. He thought disgustedly: All this is something to be changed. On second thought, though, it might have to wait awhile. He knew he was going to have to be cautious in his dealings with people here, and his own experience had already taught him that there were limits to what you could accomplish quickly. All the same, he knew it would be hard to curb his own natural impatience, especially with this sort of mess visible right under his nose.

For the past few moments John Alexander had been watching Coleman closely. Ever since this new doctor had first come in with Bannister there had been something vaguely familiar about him. He was young—probably not much older than Alexander himself. But it was not that alone. Now Alexander said, "Doctor, excuse my mentioning it, but I have a feeling we've met somewhere before."

"It's possible." Coleman was elaborately casual. Because he had supported this man in one incident, he did not want him to get any impression there was some sort of alliance between them. Then it occurred to him that perhaps he had been a little too curt. He added, "I interned at Bellevue, then I was at Walter Reed and Massachusetts General."

"No." Alexander shook his head. "It must have been before then. Have you ever been in Indiana? New Richmond?"

"Yes," Coleman said, startled, "I was born there."

John Alexander beamed. "I should have remembered the name, of course. Your father would be . . . Dr. Byron Coleman?"

"How do you know that?" It had been a long time since someone other than himself had recalled his father's name.

"I'm from New Richmond too," Alexander said. "So is my wife."

"Really?" Coleman asked. "Did I know you there?"

"I don't think so, though I remember seeing you a couple of times." In the social life of New Richmond, John Alexander had been several stages removed from the orbit of the doctor's son. As the thought occurred to him, there was a "ping" from the centrifuge timer. He paused to remove the blood sample which had been spun down, then went on, "My father was a truck farmer. We lived a few miles outside town. You may remember my wife though. Her family had the hardware store. She was Elizabeth Johnson."

Coleman said thoughtfully, "Yes, I believe I do." Memory stirred. "Wasn't there something about her . . . she was in an accident of some sort?"

"That's right; she was," John Alexander said. "Her father was killed in his car at the rail crossing. Elizabeth was with him."

"I remember hearing about it." David Coleman's mind flew back over the years—to the country doctor's office in which his father had healed so many bodies until in the end his own had failed him. He said, "I was away at college at the time, but my father told me afterward."

"Elizabeth almost died. But they gave her blood transfusions and she made it. I think that was the first time I was ever in a hospital. I almost lived there for a week." Alexander paused. Then, still pleased at his discovery, "If you happen to be free one evening, Dr. Coleman, I'm sure my wife would enjoy meeting you. We have a small apartment . . ." He hesitated, sensing the truth: though both had moved on from New Richmond, there was still a social gulf between them.

Coleman was aware of it too. His brain clicked out a warning: be cautious of alliances with subordinates—even one like this. He rationalized: It isn't snobbery; it's just a matter of hospital discipline and common sense. Aloud he said, "Well, I'm going to be working quite hard for a while. Let's leave it, shall we, and see how things go?"

Even as he spoke them the words sounded hollow and false. He thought: You could have let him down more lightly than that. Mentally he added a footnote to himself: You haven't changed, my friend; you haven't changed at all.

Momentarily Harry Tomaselli found himself wishing that Mrs. Straughan would go back to her kitchens and stay there. Then he checked himself: a good chief dietitian was a pearl to be prized. And Mrs. Straughan was good; of that fact the administrator was well aware.

But there were times when he wondered if Hilda Straughan ever thought of Three Counties Hospital as a unified whole. Most times when talking with her he gained the impression that the hospital's heart consisted of kitchens, from which other and less important facilities radiated outward. He reflected, though—Harry Tomaselli was, above all, a fair-minded man—that this sort of attitude was often found in people who took their jobs seriously. And, if it were a failing, he certainly preferred it to slackness and indifference. Another thing: a good department head was always willing to fight and argue for something which he or she believed in, and Mrs. Straughan was a fighter and arguer in every ample cubic inch of her.

At this moment, her big bulk overflowing a chair in the administrator's office, she was fighting hard.

"I wonder if you realize, Mr. T., how serious this is." Mrs. Straughan invarably used the surname initial when addressing people she knew; she had a habit of referring to her own husband as "Mr. S."

"I think so," Harry Tomaselli said.

"The dishwashers I have now were obsolete at least five years ago. Every year since I've been here I've been told: Next year we'll give you your new ones. And when next year comes, where are my dishwashers? I find they're put off for another twelve months. It won't do, Mr. T. It just won't do."

Mrs. Straughan always used the personal pronoun "my" when referring to equipment in her charge. Tomaselli had no objection to this. What he did object to was Hilda Straughan's unwillingness to consider any problems other than her own. He prepared to cover, once more, the ground they had gone over just a week or two before.

"There's no question, Mrs. Straughan, that the dishwashers are going to be replaced eventually. I know the problem you have down there in the kitchens, but those are big, expensive machines. If you remember, the last estimate we had ran a little under eleven thousand dollars, allowing for changes in the hot-water system."

Mrs. Straughan leaned over the desk, her massive bosom brushing a file tray aside. "And the longer you leave it the more the cost will go up."

"Unfortunately I'm aware of that too." The rising cost of everything the hospital bought was a problem Tomaselli lived with daily. He added, "But right at this moment hospital money for capital expenditures is extremely tight. The building extension, of course, is partly responsible. It's simply a question of allocating priorities, and some of the medical equipment has had to come first."

"What good is medical equipment if your patients don't have clean plates to eat their food from?"

"Mrs. Straughan," he said firmly, "the situation is not as bad as that, and both of us know it."

"It's not very far removed from it." The chief dietitian leaned forward and the file tray took another shove; Harry Tomaselli found himself wishing she would keep her breasts off his desk. She went on, "Several times lately whole loads of dishes going through my machines have still been dirty when they came out. We try to check as much as we can, but when there's a rush it isn't always possible."

"Yes," he said. "I can understand that."

"It's the danger of infection I'm worried about, Mr. T. There's been a lot of intestinal flu among the hospital staff lately. Of course, when that happens everyone blames the food. But it wouldn't surprise me if this was the cause of it."

"We'd need considerably more evidence to be sure of that." Harry Tomaselli's patience was beginning to wear thin. Mrs. Straughan had come to him on an exceptionally busy morning. There was a board meeting this afternoon, and right now he had several pressing problems to consider in advance of it. Hoping to wind up the interview, he asked, "When did Pathology last run a bacteria test on the dishwashers?"

Hilda Straughan considered. "I could check, but I think it's about six months ago."

"We'd better have them do another. Then we'll know exactly where we stand."

"Very well, Mr. T." Mrs. Straughan resigned herself to

accomplishing nothing more today. "Shall I speak to Dr. Pearson?"

"No, I'll do it." The administrator made a penciled note. At least, he thought, I can save Joe Pearson a similar session to this.

"Thank you, Mr. T." The chief dietitian eased herself upward and out of the chair. He waited until she had gone, then carefully moved the file tray back to its original position.

David Coleman was returning to Pathology from lunch in the cafeteria. Making his way through the corridors and down the basement stairway, he pondered over the time he had spent so far with Dr. Joseph Pearson. Up to this moment, he decided, it had been unsatisfactory and inconclusive.

Pearson had been cordial enough—later, if not at the beginning. On finding Coleman waiting in his office his first remark had been, "So you really meant what you said about starting right away."

"There didn't seem much point in waiting." He had added politely, "I've been looking around the labs. I hope you don't mind."

"That's your privilege." Pearson had said it with a half-growl, as if it were an invasion he did not like but had to put up with. Then, as if realizing his own ungraciousness, he had added, "Well, I guess I should welcome you."

When they had shaken hands the older man had said, "First thing I have to do is get some of this work cleared away." He gestured at the untidy pile of slide folders, dockets, and loose memoranda on his desk. "After that maybe we can figure out what you'll be doing around here."

Coleman had sat, with nothing else to do but read a medical journal, while Pearson had plowed through some of the papers. Then a girl had come in to take dictation, and after that he had accompanied Pearson to a gross conference in the autopsy-room annex. Sitting beside Pearson with two residents—McNeil and Seddons—on the opposite side of the dissecting table, he had felt very much like a junior resident himself. There had been almost nothing for him to contribute; Pearson had conducted the gross conference with Coleman merely a spectator. Nor had the older man made any acknowledgment of Coleman's status as the new assistant director of the entire department.

Later he and Pearson had gone to lunch together and, in

the course of it, Pearson had introduced him to a few people on the medical staff. Then the older pathologist had excused himself and left the table, saying there was some urgent work he had to attend to. Now Coleman was returning to Pathology alone, weighing in his mind the problem which seemed to face him.

He had anticipated some slight resistance from Dr. Pearson, of course. From odd pieces of information which had come to him he had pieced together the fact that Pearson had not wanted a second pathologist, but he had certainly not expected anything quite like this.

He had assumed, at the very least, that there would be an office ready for him on arrival and a few clearly defined duties. Certainly David Coleman had not expected to take over a great number of major responsibilities at once. He had no objection to the senior pathologist checking on him for a while; in fact, in Pearson's position, he himself would take the same precaution with a newcomer. But this situation went far beyond that. Apparently, despite his letter, no thought whatever had been given to what Coleman's duties were to include. The idea seemed to be that he should sit around until Dr. Pearson could take enough time away from his mail and various other chores to hand out a few tasks. Well, if that were the case, some of the thinking would have to be changed—and soon.

David Coleman had long been aware of defects in his own character, but he was equally aware of a number of important qualities. Among the most significant was his own record and ability as physician and pathologist. Kent O'Donnell had stated nothing more than truth when he had referred to Coleman as highly qualified. Despite his youthfulness he already had qualifications and experience which many practicing pathologists would find it hard to match. Certainly there was no reason for him to stand in awe of Dr. Joseph Pearson and, while he was prepared to defer a little to the other man's age and seniority, he had no intention of being treated, himself, like a raw and inexperienced hand.

There was another strength, too: a feeling which overrode all other considerations, whether of character, attempts at tolerance, or anything else. It was a determination to practice medicine uncompromisingly, cleanly, honestly—even exactly, as far as exactness was possible in medical affairs. For any who did less—and even in his own few years he had seen and known them—the compromisers, the politicians, the lazy, the at-any-cost ambitious—David Coleman had only anger and disgust.

If he had been asked from whence this feeling sprang, he would have found it hard to answer. Certainly he was no sentimentalist; nor had he entered medicine because of some overt urge to aid humanity. The influence of his own father might have had some effect but, David Coleman suspected, not too much. His father, he realized now, had been an averagely good physician, within the limits of general practice, but there had always been a striking difference between their two natures. The elder Coleman had been a warm, outgoing personality with many friends; his son was cool, hard to know, often aloof. The father had joked with his patients and casually given them his best. The son—as an intern, before pathology cut him off from patients—had never joked but carefully, exactly, skillfully, had given a little better than the best of many others. And even though, as a pathologist, his relationship with patients had changed, this attitude had not.

Sometimes, in his moments of honest self-examination, David Coleman suspected his approach would have been the same, whether his occupation had been medicine or something else. Basically, he supposed, it was a quality of exactitude combined with intolerance of mistake or failure—the feeling, too, that whoever and whatever you set out to serve was entitled, by right, to the utmost you had to give. In a way, perhaps, the two feelings were contradictory. Or possibly they had been summed up accurately by a medical classmate who had once drunk an ironic toast to "David Coleman—the guy with the antiseptic heart."

Passing now through the basement corridor, his mind returned to the present and instinct told him that conflict lay very close ahead.

He entered the pathology office to find Pearson hunched over a microscope, a slide folder open in front of him. The older man looked up. "Come and take a look at these. See what you make of them." He moved away from the microscope, waving Coleman toward it.

"What's the clinical story?" Coleman slipped the first slide under the retaining clips and adjusted the binocular eyepiece.

"It's a patient of Lucy Grainger's. Lucy is one of the surgeons here; you'll meet her." Pearson consulted some notes.

"The case is a nineteen-year-old girl, Vivian Loburton—one of our own student nurses. Got a lump below her left knee. Persistent pain. X-rays show some bone irregularity. These slides are from the biopsy."

There were eight slides, and Coleman studied each in turn. He knew at once why Pearson had asked him for an opinion. This was a hairline case, as difficult as any came. At the end he said, "My opinion is 'benign.' "

"I think it's malignant," Pearson said quietly. "Osteogenic sarcoma."

Without speaking Coleman took the first slide again. He went over it once more, patiently and carefully, then repeated the process with the other seven. The first time around he had considered the possibility of osteogenic sarcoma; now he did so again. Studying the red- and blue-stained transparencies which could reveal so much to the trained pathologist, his mind ticked off the pros and cons . . . All the slides showed a good deal of new bone formation—osteoblastic activity with islands of cartilage within them . . . Trauma had to be considered. Had trauma caused a fracture? Was the new bone formation a result of regeneration—the body's own attempt to heal? If so, the growth was certainly benign. . . . Was there evidence of osteomyelitis? Under a microscope it was easy to mistake it for the more deadly osteogenic sarcoma. But no, there were no polymorphonuclear leukocytes, characteristically found in the marrow spaces between the bone spicules . . . There was no blood-vessel invasion . . . So it came back basically to examination of the osteoblasts—the new bone formation. It was the perennial question which all pathologists had to face: was a lesion poliferating, as a natural process to fill a gap in the body's defenses? Or was it proliferating because it was a neoplasm and therefore malignant? Malignant or benign? It was so easy to be wrong, but all one could do was to weigh the evidence and judge accordingly.

"I'm afraid I disagree with you," he told Pearson politely. "I'd still say this tissue was benign."

The older pathologist stood silent and thoughtful, plainly assessing his own opinion against that of the younger man. After a moment he said, "You'd agree there's room for doubt, I suppose. Both ways."

"Yes, there is." Coleman knew there was often room for doubt in situations like this. Pathology was no exact science;

there were no mathematical formulas by which you could prove your answer right or wrong. All you could give sometimes was a considered estimate; some might call it just an educated guess. He could understand Pearson's hesitation; the old man had the responsibility of making a final decision. But decisions like this were part of a pathologist's job —something you had to face up to and accept. Now Coleman added, "Of course, if you're right and it is osteogenic sarcoma, it means amputation."

"I know that!" It was said vehemently but without antagonism. Coleman sensed that however slipshod other things might be in the department, Pearson was too experienced a pathologist to object to an honest difference of opinion. Besides, both of them knew how delicate were the premises in any diagnosis. Now Pearson had crossed the room. Turning, he said fiercely, "Blast these borderline cases! I hate them every time they come up! You have to make a decision, and yet you know you may be wrong."

Coleman said quietly, "Isn't that true of a lot of pathology?"

"But who else knows it? That's the point!" The response was forceful, almost passionate, as if the younger man had touched a sensitive nerve. "The public doesn't know—nothing's surer than that! They see a pathologist in the movies, on television! He's the man of science in the white coat. He steps up to a microscope, looks once, and then says 'benign' or 'malignant'—just like that. People think when you look in there"—he gestured to the microscope they had both been using—"there's some sort of pattern that falls into place like building bricks. What they don't know is that some of the time we're not even close to being sure."

David Coleman had often thought much the same thing himself, though without expressing it as strongly. The thought occurred to him that perhaps this outburst was something the old man had bottled up for a long time. After all, it was a point of view that only another pathologist could really understand. He interjected mildly, "Wouldn't you say that most of the time we're right?"

"All right, so we are." Pearson had been moving around the room as he talked; now they were close together. "But what about the times we're not right? What about this case, eh? If I say it's malignant, Lucy Grainger will amputate; she won't have any choice. And if I'm wrong, a nineteen-year-old girl has lost a leg for nothing. And yet if it *is* malignant, and there's no amputation, she'll probably die within two years." He paused, then added bitterly, "Maybe she'll die anyway. Amputation doesn't always save them."

This was a facet of Pearson's make-up that Coleman had not suspected—the deep mental involvement in a particular case. There was nothing wrong in it, of course. In Pathology it was a good thing to remind yourself that a lot of the time you were dealing not merely with bits of tissue but with people's lives which your own decisions could change for good or ill. Remembering that fact kept you on your toes and conscientious; that is—provided you were careful not to allow feelings to affect scientific judgment. Coleman, though so much younger, had already experienced some of the doubts which Pearson was expressing. His own habit was to keep them to himself, but that was not to say they troubled him less. Trying to help the older man's thinking, he said, "If it is malignant, there isn't any time to spare."

"I know." Again Pearson was thinking deeply.

"May I suggest we check some past cases," Coleman said, "cases with the same symptoms?"

The old man shook his head. "No good. It would take too long."

Trying to be discreet, Coleman persisted, "But surely if we checked the cross file . . ." He paused.

"We haven't got one." It was said softly, and at first Coleman wondered if he had heard aright. Then, almost as if to anticipate the other's incredulity, Pearson went on, "It's something I've been meaning to set up for a long time. Just never got around to it."

Hardly believing what he had heard, "You mean . . . we can't study any previous cases?"

"It would take a week to find them." This time there was no mistaking Pearson's embarrassment. "There aren't too many just like this. And we haven't that much time."

Nothing that Pearson might have said could have shocked David Coleman quite so much as this. To him, and to all pathologists whom he had trained and worked with until now, the cross file was an essential professional tool. It was a source of reference, a means of teaching, a supplement to a pathologist's own knowledge and experience, a detective which could assimilate clues and offer solutions, a means of reassurance, and a staff to lean on in moments of doubt.

It was all of this and more. It was an indication that a pathology department was doing its work efficiently; that, as well as giving service for the present, it was storing up knowledge for the future. It was a warranty that tomorrow's hospital patients would benefit from what was learned today. Pathology departments in new hospitals considered establishment of a cross file a priority task. In older, established centers the type of cross file varied. Some were straightforward and simple, others elaborate and complex, providing research and statistical data as well as information for day-to-day work. But, simple or elaborate, all had one thing in common: their usefulness in comparing a present case against others in the past. To David Coleman the absence of a cross file at Three Counties could be described with only one word: criminal.

Until this moment, despite his outward impression that the pathology department of Three Counties was seriously in need of changes, he had tried to withhold any personal opinion on Dr. Joseph Pearson. The old man had, after all, been operating alone for a long time, and the amount of work involved in a hospital this size could not have been easy for one pathologist to handle. That kind of pressure could account for the inadequate procedure which Coleman had already discovered in the lab, and, while the fault was not excusable, at least it was understandable.

It was possible, too, that Pearson might have been strong in other ways. In David Coleman's opinion good administration and good medicine usually went together. But, of the two, medicine—in this case pathology—was the more important. He knew of too many whited sepulchers where gleaming chrome and efficient paper work ranked first, with medicine coming in a poor second. He had considered it possible that the situation here might be the reverse—with administration poor and pathology good. This was the reason he had curbed his natural tendency to judge the older pathologist on the basis of what had been evident so far. But now he found it impossible to pretend any longer to himself. Dr. Joseph Pearson was a procrastinator and incompetent.

Trying to keep the contempt out of his voice, Coleman asked, "What do you propose?"

"There's one thing I can do."

Pearson had gone back to his desk and picked up the

telephone. He pressed a button labeled "Intercom." After a pause, "Tell Bannister to come in."

He replaced the phone, then turned to Coleman. "There are two men who are experts in this field—Chollingham in Boston and Earnhart in New York."

Coleman nodded. "Yes, I've heard of their work."

Bannister entered. "Do you want me?" He glanced at Coleman, then pointedly ignored him.

"Take these slides." Pearson closed the folder and passed it across the desk. "Get two sets off tonight—air mail, special delivery, and put on an urgent tag. One set is to go to Dr. Chollingham at Boston, the other to Dr. Earnhart in New York. Get the usual covering notes typed; enclose a copy of the case history, and ask both of them to telegraph their findings as quickly as possible."

"Okay." The slide folder under his arm, Bannister went out.

At least, Coleman reflected, the old man had handled that part of it efficiently. Getting the two expert opinions in this case was a good idea, cross file or not.

Pearson said, "We ought to get an answer within two or three days. Meanwhile I'd better talk to Lucy Grainger." He mused. "I won't tell her much. Just that there's a slight doubt and we're getting"—he looked sharply at Coleman—"some outside confirmation."

Thirteen

Vivian kept very still—bewildered, uncomprehending. This thing could not be happening to her; it must be someone else Dr. Grainger was speaking about. Her thoughts raced. That was it! Somehow the charts of two patients had become mixed. It had happened before in hospitals. Dr. Grainger was busy; she could easily be confused. Perhaps some other patient was even now being told . . .

Abruptly she stopped her thoughts, made them stand still, tried to clear her mind. There was no mistake. She knew it, clearly and definitely, from the expressions of Dr. Grainger and Mike Seddons. They were watching her now, seated on either side of the hospital bed where Vivian half lay, half sat, propped up by pillows behind her.

She turned to Lucy Grainger. "When will you know . . . for sure?"

"In two days. Dr. Pearson will tell us then. One way or the other."

"And he doesn't know . . ."

Lucy said, "Not at this moment, Vivian. He doesn't know. He doesn't know anything for sure."

"Oh, Mike!" She reached for his hand.

He took it gently. Then she said, "I'm sorry . . . but I think . . . I'm going to cry."

As Seddons put his arms around Vivian, Lucy rose to her feet. "I'll come back later." She asked Seddons, "You'll stay for a while?"

"Yes."

Lucy said, "Make sure that Vivian is quite clear in her mind that nothing is definite. It's just that I want her to be prepared . . . in case."

He nodded, the untidy red hair moving slowly. "I understand."

As she went out into the corridor Lucy thought: Yes, I'm quite sure you do."

Yesterday afternoon, when Joe Pearson had reported to her by telephone, Lucy had been undecided whether to tell Vivian at this stage what the possibilities were or to wait until later. If she waited, and Pathology's report on the biopsy was "benign," all would be well and Vivian would never know of the shadow which, for a while, had drifted darkly over her. But, on the other hand, if, two days from now, the pathology report said "malignant," amputation would become vitally urgent. In that case, could Vivian be prepared in time, or would the psychological impact be too great? The shock, suddenly thrust upon a young girl who had not suspected that anything serious was wrong, could be tremendous. It might be days before Vivian was ready mentally to accept major surgery—days they could ill afford to lose.

There was something else Lucy had also weighed in balance. The fact that Joe Pearson was seeking outside opinion was significant in itself. If it had been a clear-cut case of benign tissue, he would have said so at once. The fact that he had not, despite his unwillingness to commit himself either way when they had talked, meant that malignancy was at least a strong possibility.

Deliberating all these things, Lucy had decided that Vivian must be told the situation now. If, later, the verdict was "benign," it was true she would have suffered fear unneedfully. But better that than a sudden explosive impact for which she was completely unprepared.

The immediate problem had also been simplified by the appearance of Dr. Seddons. Last evening the young resident had come to Lucy and told her of his own and Vivian's plans for marriage. He had admitted that at first his own intention had been to remain in the background, but now he had changed his mind. Lucy was glad he had. At least it meant that Vivian was no longer alone and there was someone whom she could turn to for support and comfort.

Without question, the girl would need plenty of both. Lucy had broken the news that she suspected osteogenic sarcoma—with all its tragic possibilities—as gently as she could. But no matter how one put it, there was no real way of softening the blow. Now Lucy remembered the next thing she had to do: apprise the girl's parents of the situation as it stood. She glanced down at a slip of paper in her hand. It contained an address in Salem, Oregon, which she had copied earlier from the "next-of-kin" entry on Vivian's admitting form. She already had the girl's agreement that her parents could be told. Now Lucy must do the best job she could of breaking the news by long-distance telephone.

Already her mind was anticipating what might happen next. Vivian was a minor. Under state law a parent's consent was required before any amputation could be performed. If the parents planned to fly here immediately from Oregon, the written consent could be obtained on arrival. If not, she must do her best to persuade them to telegraph the authority, giving Lucy the discretion to use it if necessary.

Lucy glanced at her watch. She had a full schedule of appointments this morning in her office downtown. Perhaps she had better make the call now, before leaving Three Counties. On the second floor she turned into the tiny hospital office she shared with Gil Bartlett. It was little more than a cubicle —so small that they rarely used it at the same time. Now it was very much occupied—by Bartlett and Kent O'Donnell.

As he saw her O'Donnell said, "Sorry, Lucy. I'll get out. This place was never built for three."

"There's no need." She squeezed past the two men and sat down at the tiny desk. "I have a couple of things to do, then I'm leaving."

"You'd be wise to stay." Gil Bartlett's beard followed its usual bobbing course. His voice was bantering. "Kent and I are being extremely profound this morning. We're discussing the entire future of surgery."

"Some people will tell you it doesn't have a future." Lucy's tone matched Bartlett's. She had opened a desk drawer and was extracting some clinical notes she needed for one of her downtown appointments. "They say all surgeons are on the way to becoming extinct, that in a few years we'll be as out-of-date as the dodo and the witch doctor."

Nothing pleased Bartlett more than this kind of exchange. He said, "And who, I ask you, will do the cutting and plumbing on the bloomin' bleeding bodies?"

"There won't be any cutting." Lucy had found the notes and reached for a brief case. "Everything will be diagnostic. Medicine will employ the forces of nature against nature's own malfunctioning. Our mental health will have been proven as the root of organic disease. You'll prevent cancer by psychiatry and gout by applied psychology." She zippered the brief case, then added lightly, "As you may guess, I'm quoting."

"I can hardly wait for it to happen." Kent O'Donnell smiled. As always, nearness to Lucy gave him a feeling of pleasure. Was he being foolish, even ridiculous, in holding back from allowing their relationship to become more intimate? What was he afraid of, after all? Perhaps they should spend another evening together, then let whatever happened take its course. But here and now—with Gil Bartlett present—was obviously no time to make arrangements.

"I doubt if any of us will live that long." As Lucy spoke the phone on the desk rang softly. She picked it up and answered, then passed the instrument to Gil Bartlett. "It's for you."

"Yes?" Bartlett said.

"Dr. Bartlett?" They could hear a woman's voice at the other end of the line.

"Speaking."

"This is Miss Rawson in Emergency. I have a message from Dr. Clifford." Clifford was the hospital's senior surgical resident.

"Go ahead."

"He would like you to come down and scrub, if you can. There's been a traffic accident on the turnpike. We've several seriously injured people, including a bad chest case. That's the one Dr. Clifford would like your help with."

"Tell him I'll be right there." Bartlett replaced the phone. "Sorry, Lucy. Have to finish some other time." He moved to the doorway, then paused. "I'll tell you one thing, though—I don't think I'll worry about unemployment. As long as they go on building bigger and faster motorcars there'll always be a place for surgeons."

He went out and, with a friendly nod to Lucy, O'Donnell followed him. Alone, Lucy paused a moment, then picked up the telephone again. When the operator answered, "I want a long-distance call, please," she said, reaching for the slip of paper. "It's person-to-person—Salem, Oregon."

Threading the corridor traffic with the skill of long practice, Kent O'Donnell headed briskly for his own office in the hospital. He too had a full schedule ahead. In less than half an hour he was due on the operating floor; later there was a meeting of the medical executive committee, and after that he had several patients to see downtown, a program which would take him well into the evening.

As he walked he found himself thinking once more of Lucy Grainger. Seeing her, being as close as they were a few moments ago, had set him wondering again about Lucy and himself. But now the old familiar doubts—the feeling that perhaps their interests had too much in common for any permanent relationship—came crowding back.

He wondered why he had thought so much about Lucy lately—or any woman for that matter. Perhaps it was because the early forties were traditionally a restive time for men. Then he smiled inwardly, recollecting that there had seldom been a period when occasional love affairs—of one kind or another—had not come naturally to him. Nowadays they were merely spaced more widely apart. Also, of necessity, he was obliged to be considerably more discreet than in his younger years.

From Lucy his thoughts switched to Denise Quantz. Since the invitation to call her, which she had given him the night they had met at Eustace Swayne's house, O'Donnell had confirmed his attendance at a surgeons' congress in New

York. It occurred to him that the date was next week; if he were to meet Mrs. Quantz, he had better make the arrangements soon.

As he turned into his office the clock over his desk showed twenty minutes before his first operation was scheduled. He picked up the telephone, telling himself it was always a good idea to do things when you thought of them.

He heard the operator trace the number through New York Information, then there was a ringing tone and a click. A voice said, "This's Mrs. Quantz's apartment."

"I have a long-distance call for Mrs. Denise Quantz," the Burlington operator said.

"Mrs. Quantz's not here now."

"Do you know where she can be reached?" The telephone company's ritual was in motion.

"Mrs. Quantz's in Burlington, Pennsylvania. Do you wish the number there?"

"If you please." It was the Burlington operator again.

"The number is Hunter 6-5735."

"Thank you, New York." There was a click, then the operator said, "Did you get that number, caller?"

"Yes, thank you," O'Donnell said, and hung up.

With his other hand he had already reached for the Burlington phone directory. He thumbed through it until he came to "Swayne, Eustace R." As he had expected, the number listed was the one he had just been given.

Lifting the phone, he dialed again.

A male voice said, "Mr. Eustace Swayne's residence."

"I'd like to speak with Mrs. Quantz."

"One moment, please."

There was a pause. Then, "This is Mrs. Quantz."

Until this moment O'Donnell had forgotten how much her voice had attracted him before. It had a soft huskiness, seeming to lend grace to the simplest words.

"I wonder if you remember," he said. "This is Kent O'Donnell."

"Of course! Dr. O'Donnell, how nice to hear from you!"

He had a sudden vision of her beside the telephone, the soft dark hair tumbled about her shoulders. Then he said, "I just called you in New York. They gave me the number here."

"I flew down last night," Denise Quantz said. "Father had

a touch of bronchitis. I thought I'd stay with him for a day or two."

He asked courteously, "It's not too serious, I hope?"

"Not really." She laughed. "My father has the constitution of a mule—as well as the obstinacy."

He thought: I can believe that. Aloud he said, "I was going to ask you to have dinner with me in New York. I expect to be there next week."

"You can still ask me." The reply was prompt and definite. "I'll be back by then."

On impulse he said, "Possibly I could anticipate. Do you have a free evening in Burlington?"

After a moment's pause she said, "Tonight would be the only time."

O'Donnell calculated quickly. His office appointments would go on until seven. But if nothing else came up . . .

His thoughts were interrupted. "Oh, wait!" It was Denise Quantz again. "I'd forgotten. Dr. Pearson is having dinner with my father; I think I ought to stay." She added, "Unless you'd care to join us?"

Mentally he chuckled. Joe Pearson might be surprised to find him there. Instinct, though, told him it was not a good idea. He said, "Thank you, but I think perhaps we'd better postpone it."

"Oh dear." Her voice sounded disappointed; then she brightened. "I could meet you after dinner if you like. Father and Dr. Pearson are sure to get into one of their chess games, and when they do that anyone else might just as well not be there."

He found himself suddenly delighted. "That would be wonderful. What time will you be free?"

"About nine-thirty, I imagine."

"Shall I call for you?"

"It would probably save time if we met downtown. You tell me where."

He thought for a moment, then said, "The Regency Room?"

"All right; at half-past nine. Good-by now."

As O'Donnell replaced the phone he had a pleasant sense of anticipation. Then he glanced at the clock again. He would have to hurry if he were to be in the O.R. on time.

The after-dinner chess game between Eustace Swayne and

Dr. Joseph Pearson had been in progress for forty minutes. The two old men faced each other across a low rosewood games table in the same paneled library where, three weeks earlier, O'Donnell and Swayne had had their verbal joust. Only two lights were burning in the room—one from a single pendant shade immediately above the table, the other a dimly glowing rococo lamp by the hallway door.

Both men's faces were in shadow, the light between them playing directly on the inlaid chessboard in the table's center. Only when one or the other leaned forward to make a move in the game were their features defined momentarily by the lamplight's outer edges.

At this moment both were still, the room's deep silence hovering like a padded mantle over the pair of Louis XV beechwood wing chairs in which they sat. Eustace Swayne had leaned back. Holding a brandy glass of ruby crystal lightly between his fingers, he surveyed the game as it had progressed so far.

The previous move had been Dr. Joseph Pearson's. A minute or two ago, gently cradling the white queen from the exquisitely carved Indian-ivory chess set, he had moved the piece a single square ahead.

Now, putting down the brandy glass, Eustace Swayne selected a pawn from his far right wing and transferred it two squares forward. Then gruffly, breaking the silence, he said, "There have been changes at the hospital, I hear."

Beyond the lamplight, Joe Pearson studied the chessboard. When he was ready he leaned forward and moved a pawn on his left wing one square forward, countering the other's advance. Only then did he grunt the one word, "Some."

Again the silence, peace, the sense of time halted. Then the old tycoon stirred in his chair. "Do you approve these changes?" He reached forward and slid his bishop diagonally two squares to the right. Half humorously he glanced across the table in the semi-darkness. His expression said: Beat that line-up if you can.

This time Joe Pearson answered before he made his move. "Not entirely." He remained in shadow, studying the other's gambit, pondering the alternatives ahead. Then, slowly, still handling the pieces tenderly, he moved his rook one square to the left, dominating an open line.

Eustace Swayne waited. A minute passed, two minutes, then three. Finally his hand reached out for his rook and made a similar move to the same open line, meeting his opponent's challenge. Then he said, "You have a means of veto for the future if you choose to exercise it."

"Oh? What kind of veto?" The question was casual but the action which accompanied it swift. Pearson picked up his queen's knight and swung it over the pieces, lodging it on a central square.

Studying the board, assessing the strength of his own position, Swayne said, "I've told Orden Brown—and your chief of surgery—I'm willing to give a quarter million dollars to the building fund." With the last word he made a corresponding move to Pearson's, sending his king's knight forward until it reached the square beside the strongly lodged knight of his opponent.

A long silence this time. At the end of it the pathologist took his bishop and, swooping down the board, removed an opposing pawn. He said quietly, "Check." Then, "That's a lot of money."

"I've attached a condition." Swayne, on the defensive now, moved his king one square to the right. "The money will only be given if you remain free to run your own department in the hospital the way you want for as long as you choose."

This time Joe Pearson made no move. He seemed to be musing, looking away into the darkness over the other man's head. Then he said simply, "I'm touched." His eyes returned to the chessboard. After a while he lifted his knight to a square so that the piece attacked Swayne's now cramped king.

Eustace Swayne had watched the action carefully. But before making his own move he reached for a brandy decanter, filled Pearson's glass and then his own. Putting the decanter down, "It's a young man's world," he said, "and I suppose it always has been. Except that sometimes old men still have power . . . and the sense to use it." Then, his eyes glinting, he reached down, picked up the pawn in front of his king, and with it captured the troublesome knight.

Thoughtfully Pearson stroked his chin with thumb and forefinger. Then he selected his queen, moved it six squares down the open file, and captured the black king's pawn. "You say . . . Orden Brown, O'Donnell . . . they know this?"

"I made it plain." The old tycoon took his king's bishop and captured his opponent's bishop on king's knight five.

Suddenly Joe Pearson chuckled. There was nothing to show whether the game or the conversation had caused his amusement. But swiftly he reached out. He moved his queen beside the black king. Then, softly, "Checkmate!"

Though defeated, caught unawares, Eustace Swayne had watched admiringly. He nodded, as if to confirm his own judgment.

"Joe," he said, "there's no doubt of it—you're as good a man as ever!"

The music stopped, and the couples on the dance floor of the small but fashionable supper club—one of the few which existed in Burlington—began drifting back to their tables.

"Tell me what you were thinking then," Denise Quantz said. She smiled at Kent O'Donnell across the small black-topped table which divided them.

"Frankly, I was thinking how pleasant it would be to do this again."

Very slightly she raised the glass she was holding. It held the last of her second old-fashioned. "To more thoughts of the same kind."

"I'll drink to that." He finished his own scotch and soda, then signaled a waiter to repeat their order. "Shall we dance?" The music had begun again.

"I'd love to." She rose, turning half toward him as he followed her to the small, dimly lighted dance floor. He held out his arms and she moved into them. They danced close together. O'Donnell had never been an expert dancer; medicine had left him too little time to become accomplished. But Denise Quantz matched every movement to his own. As the minutes went by he could feel her body—tall, willowy—moving obediently, anticipating the music and his own motion. Once her hair brushed lightly against his face; it brought with it a breath of the same perfume he had noticed at their first meeting.

The five-piece orchestra, unobtrusive, its arrangements carefully attuned to the intimate setting, was playing a popular ballad of several years before.

> *See the Pyramids along the Nile,*
> *Watch the sunrise on a tropic isle,*
> *Just remember, darling—all the while*
> *You belong to me.*

For a moment he had a sense of borrowed time, of existing in a vacuum, insulated, away from medicine, Three Counties, all the other things he lived with daily. Then the music changed to a faster tempo, and he smiled at himself for sentimentality.

As they danced he asked, "Do you come here often—to Burlington, I mean?"

"Not really," she answered. "Occasionally, to see my father, but that's all. Frankly it's a city I dislike." Then laughingly, "I hope I'm not offending your civic pride."

"No," he said. "I've no strong views one way or the other. But weren't you born here?" He added, "Denise—if I may."

"Of course. Don't let's be formal." She looked at him directly and flashed a smile. Answering his question, "Yes, I was born here," she said. "I went to school and lived at home. My mother was alive then."

"Then why New York—now?"

"I think I'm a New Yorker by instinct. Besides, my husband lived there; he still does." It was the first time she had mentioned her marriage. She did it now, easily and unselfconsciously. "After we separated I found I'd never want to leave. There's no other city quite like it."

"Yes," he said, "I suppose that's true." He was thinking again how beautiful this woman was. She had a composure, a lack of artifice, that younger women could rarely attain. But nothing of her suggested a retreat from femininity; rather the reverse. To Kent O'Donnell, holding her now, her body moving evenly against his own, she seemed infinitely desirable. He suspected she could be extremely sensual.

Deliberately he switched his thoughts away. This was premature. He noticed again, as he had earlier, the gown she had on tonight. Worn off-shoulder, it was a brilliant scarlet, of rich *peau de soie,* curved closely around her figure and falling into fullness only below the hips. At one and the same time the effect was dramatic, discreet, expensive.

It was a reminder of another thought that had occurred to him this evening for the first time—the fact that Densie was obviously a rich woman. They had arrived at the Regency Room almost together. He had parked his own car and walked to the night club's street entrance when a gleaming Cadillac had pulled up, a uniformed chauffeur hurrying around to open the door for Denise to alight. They had greeted each other, then she had turned to the chauffeur, now standing discreetly in the background. "Thank you, Tom. I don't think you need come back. I expect Dr. O'Donnell will drive me home."

The man had answered courteously, "Thank you, madam," then to O'Donnell, "Good night, sir," and had driven off.

Of course, if he had thought about it, O'Donnell would have realized that the daughter of Eustace Swayne was obviously an heiress. Not that the realization concerned him greatly; his own income nowadays was ample for a comfortable life and more besides. Nevertheless, a really rich woman was something new in his personal experience. Again he found his mind framing the comparison between Denise and Lucy Grainger.

With a modest crescendo the orchestra ended the group of selections. O'Donnell and Denise applauded briefly, then moved from the dance floor. Taking her arm lightly, he steered her to their table. A waiter was hovering; he held out their chairs and served the drinks O'Donnell had ordered.

Sipping the fresh old-fashioned, Denise said, "We talked about me. Now tell me about you."

He poured more soda into his scotch. He liked the liquor well diluted—a practice most waiters seemed to abhor. "It's pretty routine stuff."

"I'm a pretty good listener, Kent." Denise was speaking with half her mind. The other half was thinking: This is a man—all man! Her eyes took in the big frame, broad shoulders, the strong face. She wondered if he would kiss her tonight and what it might lead to later. She decided there were interesting possibilities in Dr. Kent O'Donnell.

O'Donnell told her about Three Counties, his work there, and what he hoped to do. She asked him questions about the past, his experiences, people he had known—admiring all the while the depth of thought and feeling which came through everything he said.

They danced again; the waiter replaced their drinks; they talked; they danced; the waiter returned; the sequence was repeated. Denise told him about her marriage; it had taken place eighteen years ago, had lasted ten. Her husband was a corporation lawyer with a busy practice in New York. There were two children—twins, Alex and Philippa—who had remained in Denise's custody; in a few weeks the children would be seventeen.

"My husband is a perfectly rational being," she said. "It's

simply that we were quite incompatible and wasted a lot of time coming to an obvious conclusion."

"Do you ever see him now?"

"Oh, often. At parties and around town. Occasionally we meet for lunch. In some ways Geoffrey is quite delightful. I'm sure you'd like him."

Both of them were talking more freely now. Without waiting to be told, the waiter put fresh drinks in front of them. O'Donnell asked her about divorce; was there some barrier to it?

"Not really." She answered frankly. "Geoffrey is quite willing to divorce me but insists that I supply the evidence. In the state of New York, you know, it has to be adultery. So far I haven't got around to it."

"Has your husband never wanted to remarry?"

She seemed surprised. "Geoffrey? I don't imagine so. In any case, he's married to the law."

"I see."

Denise twirled the stem of her glass. "Geoffrey always considered that bed was a good place in which to read his legal briefs." She said it softly, almost with intimacy. O'Donnell sensed a hint of why the marriage had failed. He found the thought exciting.

The waiter was at his elbow. "Excuse me, sir, the bar is closing in a few minutes. Do you wish to order now?"

Surprised, O'Donnell glanced at his watch. It was almost one o'clock in the morning. Though it seemed much less, they had been together for three and a half hours. He glanced at Denise; she shook her head.

He told the waiter, "No, thank you," and paid the check the man presented. They finished their drinks and prepared to go. The waiter offered a friendly "Good night"; the tip had been generous. O'Donnell had a sense of comfort and well-being.

In the foyer he waited for Denise while an attendant went to the parking lot for his car. When she came she took his arm. "It's such a shame to go. I almost wish we'd had that last drink after all."

He had hesitated, then said lightly, tentatively, "We could stop at my apartment if you like. I have a well-stocked bar, and it's on the way."

For an instant he feared he had been unwise. He thought he detected a sudden coolness, a hint of pained surprise.

Then it was gone. She said simply, "Why don't we do that?"

Outside the Buick was waiting, the doors held open, the motor running. Going across town, he drove carefully, more slowly then usual, aware he had had a good deal to drink. It was a warm night and the car windows were down. From the other side of the front seat he caught a subtle breath of perfume once again. At his apartment he parked the car on the street and they went up in the elevator.

When he had mixed drinks he took them across and gave the old-fashioned to Denise. She was standing by an open window in the living room, looking out at the lights of Burlington below. The river which ran through the city cut a deep swath of darkness between both its banks.

Standing beside her, he said quietly, "It's been a while since I mixed an old-fashioned. I hope it isn't too sweet."

She sipped from the glass. Then softly, huskily, "Like so much else about you, Kent, it's absolutely right."

Their eyes met and he reached out for her glass. When he had put it down she came gently, effortlessly, to him. As they kissed his arms tightened around her.

Then stridently, imperiously, in the room behind them a phone bell clamored out. There was no ignoring it.

Gently Denise disengaged herself. "Darling, I think you'd better answer it." She touched his forehead gently with her lips.

As he crossed the room he saw her gather up her purse, stole, and gloves. It was obvious the evening was over. Almost angrily he picked up the phone, answered curtly, and listened. Then the anger dissolved. It was the hospital—the night-duty intern. One of O'Donnell's own patients had developed symptoms which appeared to be serious. He asked two swift questions, then, "Very well, I'll come at once. Meanwhile, alert the blood bank and prepare for a transfusion." He broke the connection, then called the night porter to get a taxi for Denise.

Fourteen

Most nights of the week Dr. Joseph Pearson made a practice of going to bed early. Necessarily, though, on the evenings he played chess with Eustace Swayne he was much later—an occurrence which left him tired and more irritable than usual next morning. This effect, from last night's session, was with him now.

Working his way through purchase requisitions for lab supplies—a task he detested ordinarily and more than ever at this moment—he snorted and put one of the vouchers aside. He scribbled a few more signatures, then paused again and snatched a second voucher from the pile. This time there was a scowl as well as the snort. An intimate would have known the danger signs—Dr. Pearson was ready to blow his top.

The moment came when he hesitated over a third voucher. Then, explosively, he threw his pencil down, grabbed up all the papers in an untidy heap, and made for the door. Storming into the serology lab, he looked around for Bannister. He found the senior technician in a corner preparing a stool culture.

"Drop whatever you're doing and come over here!" Pearson dumped the pile of papers on a center table. Several fell to the floor, and John Alexander bent down to retrieve them. He felt an instinctive relief that Bannister, and not himself, was the object of Dr. Pearson's anger.

"What's the trouble?" Bannister strolled across. He was so used to these outbursts that sometimes they had the effect of making him calmer.

"I'll tell you what's the trouble—it's all these purchase orders." Pearson himself was more subdued now, as if his ill temper was simmering instead of being on the boil. "Sometimes you seem to think we're running the Mayo Clinic."

"We gotta have lab supplies, haven't we?"

Ignoring the question, "There are times I wonder if you eat the stuff. And besides, didn't I tell you to put a note on anything out of the ordinary, explaining what it was for?"

"I guess I forgot." Bannister's tone was resigned.

"All right, you can start remembering." Pearson picked a form from the top of the pile. "What's the calcium oxide for? We never use that here."

Bannister's face creased in a malicious grin. "*You* asked me to get that. Isn't it for your garden?" The senior technician was referring to a fact which both of them knew but seldom spoke of. As one of the county horticultural society's leading rose growers, Joe Pearson absorbed a good-

ly quantity of hospital lab supplies in improving the growing
power of his soil.

He had the grace to appear embarrassed. "Oh . . . yeah . . .
okay, let that one go." He put down the voucher and picked
up a second. "What about this one? Why do we want Coombs
serum all of a sudden? Who ordered that?"

"It was Dr. Coleman." Bannister answered readily; this
was a subject he had hoped would come up. Alongside him
John Alexander had a sense of foreboding.

"When?" Pearson's question was sharp.

"Yesterday. Dr. Coleman signed the requisition anyway."
Bannister pointed to the voucher, then added maliciously,
"In the place where you usually sign."

Pearson glanced down at the form. Until now he had not
noticed there was a signature on it. He asked Bannister,
"What does he want it for? Do you know?"

The senior technician relaxed. He had set the wheels of
retribution in motion and now he could enjoy this scene as a
spectator. He told John Alexander, "Go ahead. Tell him."

A shade uneasily John Alexander said, "It's for a blood-
sensitization test, Dr. Pearson. For my wife. Dr. Dornberger
ordered it."

"Why Coombs serum?"

"It's for an indirect Coombs test, Doctor."

"Tell me—is there something special about your wife?"
Pearson's voice had an edge of sarcasm. "What's wrong with
the saline and high-protein tests? The same as we use for
everybody else?"

Alexander swallowed nervously. There was a silence.
Pearson said, "I'm waiting for an answer."

"Well, sir." Alexander hesitated, then blurted out, "I suggested to Dr. Coleman—and he agreed—it would be more
reliable if, after the other tests, we did a——"

"*You* suggested to Dr. Coleman, eh?" The tone of the
question left no doubt of what was about to happen. Sensing
it, Alexander blundered on.

"Yes, sir. We felt that since some antibodies can't be detected in saline and high protein, running the extra test——"

"Cut it out!" The words were loud, harsh, brutal. As he
said them Pearson slammed his hand hard down on the
pile of forms and the table beneath. There was silence in the
laboratory.

Breathing hard, the old man waited, eying Alexander.

When he was ready he said grimly, "There's one big trouble with you—you're just a bit too free with some of that stuff you picked up in technician's school."

As Pearson spoke his bitterness came through—the bitterness against all who were younger, who were interfering, trying to deprive him of authority—absolute and unquestioned—which until now had been his. In a different mood, and at another time, he might have handled this more tolerantly. Now, coming as it did, he had plainly decided, once and for all, to put this upstart lab assistant in his place.

"Listen to me and get this straight! I told you this once before and I don't aim to do it again." This was Authority speaking, the head of a department, heavy-handed, making it clear to a minor employee that there would be no more warnings, merely action, from this point on. His face close to Alexander's, Pearson said, "I'm the one in charge of this department, and if you or anybody else have any queries, they come to me. Do you understand?"

"Yes, sir." At this instant all Alexander wanted was for this to end. He already knew he had made his last suggestion. If this was what you got for thinking, from here on he would do his work and keep his thoughts to himself. Let other people do the worrying—and let them have the responsibility too.

But Pearson had not finished. "Don't go running around behind my back," he said, "and taking advantage of Dr. Coleman because he's new."

Briefly Alexander's spirit flared. "I didn't take advantage . . ."

"And I say you did! And I'm telling you to cut it out!" The old man shouted angrily, his face muscles working, his eyes fiery.

Alexander stood, crushed and silent.

For a moment or two Pearson surveyed the younger man grimly. Then, as if satisfied that his point was made, he went on to speak again. "Now I'll tell you something else." His tone this time, if not cordial, was at least less harsh. "As far as that blood test is concerned, a test in saline and high protein will give us all the information we need. And let me remind you I happen to be a pathologist and I know what I'm talking about. Have you got that?"

Dully Alexander answered, "Yes, sir."

"All right. I'll tell you what I'll do." Pearson's voice became more moderate; it was almost as if he were offering a truce. "Since you're so keen on this test being right, I'll do it myself. Here and now. Where's the blood specimen?"

"In the refrigerator," Bannister said.

"Get it."

Crossing the lab, Bannister decided this scene had not turned out exactly the way he would have liked. It was true the Alexander kid had needed to be taken down a peg, but, all the same, the old man had laid it on the kid a bit hard. Bannister would have liked to see some of the storm move in the direction of that snide young doctor. But maybe the old man was saving that for later. He selected the blood specimen marked "Alexander, Mrs. E." and closed the refrigerator door.

Pearson took the blood sample, which already had the clot removed. As he did, Bannister noticed the purchase order which had been the cause of the trouble; it had fallen to the floor. He bent down and picked it up.

He asked Pearson, "What shall I do with this?"

The old pathologist had taken two clean test tubes. Now he was aspirating a portion of the blood serum into each. Without looking up he said irritably, "What is it?"

"It's the purchase requisition—for Coombs serum."

"We won't need it now. Tear it up." Pearson was scrutinizing the label of a small bottle containing Rh-positive cells. Prepared by a drug house, the solution was used as a reagent in testing Rh-negative blood.

Bannister hesitated. Much as he objected to Coleman, he knew there was a question of medical protocol involved. "You ought to let Dr. Coleman know," he said doubtfully. "Do you want me to tell him?"

Pearson was having trouble with the cork of the bottle. He said impatiently, "No, I'll tell him myself."

Bannister shrugged. He had pointed something out; if there were any trouble now, it would not be his responsibility. He took the purchase requisition and tore it up, allowing the pieces to flutter down into a wastebasket below.

Roger McNeil, the pathology resident, suspected that no matter how many years he stayed in medicine he would never become hardened to performing autopsies on children. He had just completed one, and now, in the autopsy room, the red-gaping body of the four-year-old boy lay open, pathetically, before him. The sight disturbed NcNeil as much as ever. He knew, as always, there would be little sleep for him tonight. This scene would keep recurring in his mind—particularly when he remembered, as inevitably he would, how unnecessary and futile this particular death had been.

Looking up, he saw Mike Seddons watching him. The surgical resident said, "Poor little bastard." Then, bitterly, "How stupid can people get!"

McNeil asked, "Are the police still waiting?"

Seddons nodded. "Yes—and the others."

"You'd better call Pearson."

"All right." There was a telephone in the autopsy-room annex, and Seddons went to it.

McNeil wondered if he were being cowardly in avoiding this responsibility. But this was a case the old man should be told of anyway. Then he could make the decision on who would break the news outside this room.

Seddons had returned from the phone. "Pearson was in Serology," he said. "He's coming across now."

The two men waited silently. Then they heard Pearson's shuffling footsteps, and the old man came in. He glanced at the body as McNeil recited the details of the case. An hour or two earlier the child had been struck by an automobile outside his own home. He had been brought to the hospital by ambulance but was dead on arrival. Notified, the coroner had ordered an autopsy. McNeil told Pearson what they had discovered.

The old man said, "You mean that's all?" He seemed incredulous.

McNeil answered, "That's all that killed him. Nothing else."

Pearson moved toward the body, then stopped. He knew McNeil well enough to be aware that the resident would have made no mistake. He said, "Then they must have just stood there . . . and watched."

Seddons put in, "Most likely nobody knew what was happening."

Pearson nodded slowly. Seddons wondered what the old man was thinking. Then Pearson asked, "How old was the child?"

"Four," McNeil answered. "Nice-looking kid too."

All of them glanced at the autopsy table and the still, small figure. The eyes were closed, the fair, tousled hair pulled back in place now that the brain had been removed. Pearson shook his head, then turned toward the door. Over his shoulder he said, "All right; I'll go up and tell them."

The three occupants of the hospital anteroom looked up as Pearson entered. One was a uniformed patrolman of the city police, and near him was a tall man whose eyes were red-rimmed. The third occupant—dejected and sitting alone in the far corner—was a mousy little man with a straggling mustache.

Pearson introduced himself. The patrolman said, "I'm Stevens, sir. Fifth Precinct." He produced a notebook and pencil.

Pearson asked him, "Were you at the scene of the accident?"

"I arrived just after it happened." He indicated the tall man. "This is the father of the boy. The other gentleman was the driver of the car."

The mousy man looked up. Appealing to Pearson, he said, "He ran straight out—straight out from the side of the house. I'm not a careless driver. I've got kids of my own. I wasn't going fast. I was almost stopped when it happened."

"And I say you're a lousy liar." It was the father, his voice choked with emotion and bitterness. "You killed him, and I hope you go to jail for it."

Pearson said quietly, "Just a moment, please." There was silence, the others watching him. He motioned to the police-man's notebook. "There'll be a full report for the coroner, but I can tell you the preliminary findings now." He paused. "The autopsy has shown it was not the car that killed the boy."

The patrolman looked puzzled. The father said, "But I was there! I tell you . . ."

"I wish there were some other way to tell you this," Pearson said, "but I'm afraid there isn't." He addressed the father. "The blow your boy received knocked him to the road, and there was a mild concussion which rendered him unconscious. He also sustained a small fracture of the nose —quite minor, but unfortunately it caused his nose to bleed profusely." Pearson turned to the patrolman. "The boy was left lying on his back, I believe—where he fell."

The officer said, "Yes, sir, that's right. We didn't want to move him until the ambulance came."

"And how long was that?"

"I'd say about ten minutes."

Pearson nodded slowly. It was more than enough time; five minutes would have been sufficient. He said, "I'm afraid that that was the cause of death. The blood from the nose-bleed ran back into the boy's throat. He was unable to breathe and he aspirated blood into the lungs. He died of asphyxiation."

The father's face revealed horror, incredulity. He said, "You mean . . . if we'd only turned him over . . ."

Pearson raised his hands expressively. "I meant what I said—I wish there were some other way to tell you this. But I can only report the truth: the original injuries to your boy were minor."

The patrolman said, "Then the blow from the car . . . ?"

"One can't be sure, of course, but my own opinion is that it was glancing and comparatively light." Pearson gestured to the mousy man, now standing close beside them. "I imagine this man is telling the truth when he says the car was moving slowly."

"Mother of God!" It came from the father—a despairing, tortured wail. He was sobbing, his hands to his face. After a moment the mousy man led him to a settee, his arm around the other's shoulders, his own eyes glistening.

The patrolman's face was white. He said, "Doctor, I was there all the time. I could have moved the boy . . . but I didn't know."

"I don't think you should blame yourself."

The man appeared not to have heard. He went on as if in a daze. "I took a first-aid course. I got a badge for it. All the time they taught us—don't move anybody; whatever you do, don't move them!"

"I know." Pearson touched the patrolman's arm gently. He said slowly, "Unfortunately there are some exceptions to the rule—one of them is when someone is bleeding in the mouth."

In the main-floor corridor on his way to lunch David Coleman saw Pearson emerge from the anteroom. At first Coleman wondered if the senior pathologist were ill. He seemed distracted, unaware of his surroundings. Then he caught sight of Coleman and moved toward him. The younger man halted.

"Oh yes . . . Dr. Coleman . . . There was something I had to tell you." Coleman sensed that for some reason Pearson was having trouble marshaling his thoughts. Now he reached out absently and grasped the lapel of Coleman's white lab coat. Coleman noticed that the old man's hands were nervous and fumbling. He disengaged his coat.

"What was it, Dr. Pearson?"

"There was . . . something to do with the lab." Pearson shook his head. "Well, it's gone now . . . I'll remember later." He seemed about to turn away when another thought came to him. "I think you'd better take over the autopsy room. Starting tomorrow. Keep your eye on things. See they do a good job."

"Very well. I'll be glad to do that." David Coleman had some clear-cut ideas about the performance of autopsies, and this would be an opportunity to put them into effect. It occurred to him that while they were talking he might as well bring up something else. He said, "I wonder if I could speak to you—about the laboratories."

"The laboratories?" The old man's mind still seemed to be elsewhere.

"You'll remember in my letter I suggested you might consider giving me charge of some part of the laboratories." It seemed a little odd to be discussing this here and now, but Coleman sensed the opportunity might not occur again.

"Yes . . . yes, I remember something being said." Pearson appeared to be watching a group of three moving down the corridor away from them—a policeman and a little man, supporting a bigger man in the middle.

"I wonder if I might start in Serology," Coleman said. "I'd like to do some checks on the procedures—standard lab checks, that is."

"Um? What was that?"

It was annoying to have to keep repeating things. "I said I would like to make some lab checks in Serology."

"Oh yes, yes . . . that's all right." Pearson said it absently. He was still looking away, down the corridor, when Coleman left.

Elizabeth Alexander was feeling good. About to begin lunch in Three Counties Hospital cafeteria, she realized she had been feeling that way for days, but especially so this morning. The child inside her was alive and stirring; even at this moment she could detect its movements faintly. She had just come from a department-store sale where, amid the melee of women, she had victoriously acquired some bright fabrics for the apartment, including one length for the tiny extra bedroom which was to be the baby's. And now she had met John.

It was the first time they had had a meal together in the hospital. Use of the cafeteria by employees' families was an unwritten privilege the hospital allowed, and John had learned about it a few days earlier. A few minutes ago they had lined up to select their food and Elizabeth had chosen a salad, soup, a roll, roast lamb with potatoes and cabbage, pie with cheese, and milk. John had asked good-humoredly, "Are you sure you have enough?"

Elizabeth selected a stick of celery. Biting into it, she said, "This is a hungry baby."

John smiled. A few minutes earlier, on the way to lunch, he had felt defeated and depressed, this morning's tongue-lashing by Dr. Pearson still fresh in mind. But Elizabeth's infectious spirits had caused him to shrug it off, at least for the time being. After all, he reflected, there would be no more trouble in the lab because from now on he intended to watch his step carefully. In any case, Dr. Pearson had now done the sensitization tests himself—in saline and high protein—and had pronounced both test results negative. "So far as your wife's blood is concerned," he had said, "there is nothing for anyone to worry about." In fact, he had been almost kindly about it—at least it seemed that way after the earlier outburst.

There was another thing to remember: Dr. Pearson was a pathologist and John was not. Maybe Dr. Pearson was right; perhaps John had placed too much importance on some of the things that were taught at technology school. Wasn't it a well-known fact that schools always pumped a lot of theory into you that you had no use for in the practical world outside? Goodness knows, he thought, there are plenty of subjects in high school and college that you never work at again once final exams are over. Couldn't this be the same thing? Couldn't John himself have taken too seriously the school theory about the need for a third sensitization test, whereas Dr. Pearson, with all his practical knowledge, knew it was unnecessary?

What was it Dr. Pearson had said while he was doing the

tests this morning? "If we changed our laboratory methods every time something new came up, there'd never be any end to it. In medicine there are new ideas coming out every day. But in a hospital we have to make sure they're proven and valuable before we start to use them. Here we're dealing with people's lives and we can't afford to take chances."

John had not quite been able to see how an extra blood test would imperil anybody's life, but, all the same, Dr. Pearson did have a point about the new ideas. John knew from his own reading that there were lots of them around and not all good. Of course, Dr. Coleman had been pretty definite about the need for a third sensitization test. But then he was a lot younger than Dr. Pearson; certainly he had not had as much experience . . .

"Your soup's getting cold." Elizabeth broke in on his thoughts. "What are you so pensive about?"

"Nothing, honey." He decided to put the whole thing out of his mind. Elizabeth, at times, had a disconcerting habit of worming out his thoughts. "I meant to ask you last week," he said. "How was your weight?"

"It's about right," Elizabeth answered cheerfully. "But Dr. Dornberger said I have to eat well." She had finished her soup and was attacking the roast lamb hungrily.

Glancing up, John Alexander noticed Dr. Coleman approaching. The new pathologist was on his way to the tables where the medical staff usually sat. On impulse Alexander rose from his chair. "Dr. Coleman!"

David Coleman glanced across. "Yes?"

"Doctor, I'd like to have you meet my wife." Then, as Coleman came toward them, "Elizabeth, honey, this is Dr. Coleman."

"How do you do, Mrs. Alexander?" Coleman paused, holding the tray he had collected from the counter.

A trifle awkwardly John Alexander said, "You remember, honey?—I told you the doctor came from New Richmond too."

"Yes, of course," Elizabeth said. Then directly to Coleman, smiling, "Hullo, Dr. Coleman—I remember you very well. Didn't you used to come into my father's store sometimes?"

"That's right." He recalled her clearly now: a cheerful, long-legged girl who used to clamber obligingly around that cluttered, old-fashioned store, finding things that had got lost in the confusion. She didn't seem to have changed much.

He said, "I think you once sold me some clothesline."

She answered brightly, "I believe I remember that. Was it all right?"

He appeared to ponder. "Now you mention it, I think it broke."

Elizabeth laughed. "If you take it back, I'm sure my mother will exchange it. She still runs the store. It's more of a mess than ever." Her good humor was infectious. Coleman smiled.

John Alexander had pulled back a chair. "Won't you join us, Doctor?"

For a moment Coleman hesitated. Then, realizing it would be churlish to refuse, "All right," he said. He put down his tray—it contained a Spartan lunch—a small fruit salad and a glass of milk—and sat at the table. Looking at Elizabeth, he said, "If I remember, didn't you have pigtails when I knew you?"

"Yes," she answered promptly, "and bands on my teeth as well. I grew out of them."

David Coleman found himself liking this girl. And seeing her here today had been like suddenly turning a page from the past. She reminded him of earlier years; Indiana had been a good place to live. He remembered the summers home from school, driving on rounds with his father in the doctor's old and battered Chevrolet. He said reflectively, "It's a long time since I was in New Richmond. My father died, you know, and Mother moved to the West Coast. There's nothing to take me back there now." Then drawing his thoughts away, "Tell me," he said to Elizabeth, "how do you like being married to a medical man?"

Swiftly John Alexander put in, "Not a medical man—just a technologist." When he had said it he wondered why. Perhaps it was a reflex action from what had happened this morning. A few minutes ago, when Coleman had joined them, John had considered telling him about the incident in the lab. But immediately afterward he had decided not to. Talking freely with Dr. Coleman had got him into enough trouble already. He decided to leave well enough alone.

"Don't sell technology short," Coleman said. "It's pretty important."

Elizabeth said, "He doesn't. But sometimes he wishes he had become a doctor instead."

Coleman turned to him. "Is that right?"

Alexander wished Elizabeth had not brought this up. He said reluctantly, "I did have ideas that way. For a time."

Coleman speared some fruit salad with his fork. "Why didn't you go to medical school?"

"The usual reasons—money mostly. I didn't have any, and I wanted to start earning."

Between mouthfuls Coleman said, "You could still do it. How old are you?"

Elizabeth answered for him. "John will be twenty-three. In two months' time."

"That's pretty old, of course." They laughed, then Coleman added, "You've still got time."

"Oh, I know." John Alexander said it slowly, thoughtfully, as if knowing in advance that his own argument was unconvincing. "The trouble is, it would mean a big financial struggle just when we're beginning to get settled. And besides, with a baby coming . . ." He left the sentence hanging.

Coleman took the glass of milk and drank deeply. Then he said, "Plenty of people have gone through medical school with a baby. And financial problems."

"That's exactly what I've been saying!" Elizabeth said it intensely, leaning forward across the table. "I'm so glad to hear it from someone else."

Coleman wiped his mouth with a napkin, then put it down. He looked directly at Alexander. He had a feeling that he had been right in his first impression of this young technologist. He seemed intelligent and conscientious; certainly he was interested in his work—that had been evident the other day. Coleman said, "You know what I think, John? I think if you feel like this, and don't go to medical school while you have the chance, it may be something you'll regret the rest of your life."

Alexander was looking down, absently moving his knife and fork.

Elizabeth asked, "There's still a need for a lot of doctors in pathology, isn't there?"

"Oh yes." Coleman nodded emphatically. "Perhaps more in pathology than anywhere else."

"Why is that?"

"There's a need of research for one thing—to keep medicine moving ahead; to fill in the gaps behind."

She asked, "What do you mean—the gaps behind?"

Momentarily the thought occurred to David Coleman that he was talking more freely than usual. He found himself about to express ideas which most of the time he kept locked in his own mind. But the company of these two had seemed refreshing, possibly because it was a change to be with someone younger after being around Dr. Pearson. Answering Elizabeth's question, he said, "In a way medicine is like a war. And, just as in a war, sometimes there's a spectacular advance. When that happens, people—doctors—rush to the new front. And they leave a lot of pockets of knowledge to be filled in behind."

Elizabeth said, "And that's the pathologist's job—to fill them?"

"It's the job of every branch of medicine. But sometimes in pathology there are more opportunities." Coleman thought a moment, then continued, "There's another thing too. All research in medicine is very much like building a wall. Someone adds a piece of knowledge—puts one brick on another; someone else adds one more, and gradually the wall grows. Finally someone comes along and puts the last brick on top." He smiled. "It isn't given to many to do spectacular things—to be a Fleming or a Salk. The best a pathologist can do, usually, is to make some modest contribution to medical knowledge—something within his own reach, within his own time. But at least he should do that."

John Alexander had been listening intently. Now he asked eagerly, "Will you be doing research here?"

"I hope so."

"On what?"

Coleman hesitated. This was something he had not spoken of before. But he had said so much now, he supposed one more thing would not make any difference. "Well, for one thing, on lipomas—benign tumors of fat tissue. We know very little about them." Unconsciously, as he had warmed to his subject, his normal coolness and reserve had fallen away. "Do you know there have been cases of men starving to death, yet having tumors thriving inside them? What I hope to do is——" He stopped abruptly. "Mrs. Alexander, is something wrong?"

Elizabeth had gasped suddenly and put her face in her hands. Now she took her hands away. She shook her head, as if to clear it.

"Elizabeth! What is it?" Alarmed, John Alexander jumped

up from his chair. He moved to go around the table.

"It's . . . it's all right." Elizabeth motioned him back. She closed her eyes momentarily, then opened them. "It was just . . . for a moment—a pain, then dizziness. It's gone now."

She drank some water. Yes, it was true it had gone. But for a moment it had been like sharp hot needles—inside where the baby moved—then her head swimming, the cafeteria spinning around her.

"Has this happened before?" Coleman asked.

She shook her head. "No."

"Are you sure, honey?" It was John, his voice anxious.

Elizabeth reached across the table and put a hand on his. "Now don't begin worrying. It's too early for the baby. There's at least another four months to go."

"All the same," Coleman said seriously, "I suggest you call your obstetrician and tell him what happened. He might want to see you."

"I will." She gave him a warm smile. "I promise."

At the time Elizabeth had meant what she said. But afterward, away from the hospital, it seemed silly to bother Dr. Dornberger about a single pain that had come and gone so quickly. If it happened again, surely then would be the time to tell him—not now. She decided to wait.

Fifteen

"Is there any news?"

From the wheel chair Vivian looked up as Dr. Lucy Grainger came into the hospital room. It was four days since the biopsy, three since Pearson had sent the slides to New York and Boston.

Lucy shook her head. "I'll tell you, Vivian—just as soon as I know."

"When . . . when will you know . . . for sure?"

"Probably today." Lucy answered matter-of-factly. She did not want to reveal that she, too, was troubled by the waiting. She had spoken to Joe Pearson again last night; at that time he had said that if the second opinions were not forthcoming by midday today he would phone the two consultants to hurry them along. Waiting was hard on everyone—including Vivian's parents, who had arrived in Burlington from Oregon the previous day.

Lucy removed the dressing from Vivian's knee; the biopsy scar appeared to be healing well. Replacing the dressing, she said, "It's hard to do, I know, but try to think of other things as much as you can."

The girl smiled faintly. "It isn't easy."

Lucy was at the door now. She said, "Perhaps a visitor will help. You have an early one." She opened the door and beckoned. Mike Seddons came in as Lucy left.

Seddons was wearing his hospital whites. He said, "I stole ten minutes. You can have them all."

He crossed to the chair and kissed her. For a moment she closed her eyes and held on to him tightly. He ran his hands through her hair. His voice in her ear was gentle. "It's been hard, hasn't it?—just waiting."

"Oh, Mike, if only I knew what was going to happen! I don't think I'd mind so much. It's . . . wondering . . . not knowing."

He drew slightly away, looking into her face. "Vivian darling, I wish there were something, just something I could do."

"You've done a lot already." Vivian was smiling now. "Just being you—and being here. I don't know what it would have been like without . . ." She stopped as he reached out and put a finger across her lips.

"Don't say it! I had to be here. It was preordained—all worked out by cosmic coincidence." He gave her his bright, broad grin. Only he knew there was a sense of hollowness behind it. Mike Seddons, like Lucy, was aware of the implications of the delayed report from Pathology.

He had succeeded in making Vivian laugh though. "Rubbish!" she said. "If I hadn't gone to that old autopsy, and if some other student nurse had got to you first . . ."

"Uh, uh!" He shook his head. "It might look that way, but you can't escape predestination. Ever since our great-great ancestors were swinging from trees, scratching their underarms, our genes have been moving together across the dusty sands of Time, Life, and Fortune." He was talking now for the sake of it, using the first words which came into his head, but it was having the effect he wanted.

Vivian said, "Oh, Mike, you talk such wonderful nonsense. And I do love you very much."

"I can understand that." He kissed her again, lightly. "I think your mother likes me too."

She put a hand to her mouth. "You see what you do to me! I should have asked first. Was everything all right —after you all left here last night?"

"Sure it was. I went back with them to the hotel. We sat around and talked for a bit. Your mother didn't say much, but I could see your father summing me up, thinking to himself: What kind of a man is this who presumes to marry my beautiful daughter?"

Vivian said, "I'll tell him today."

"What will you say?"

"Oh, I don't know." She reached out and held Seddons by the ears, turning his head from side to side, inspecting it. "I might say, 'He has the nicest red hair which is always untidy, but you can put your fingers through it and it's very soft.'" She matched the action to her words.

"Well, that should be a big help. No marriage is complete without it. What else?"

"I'll say, 'Of course, he isn't much to look at. But he has a heart of gold and he's going to be a brilliant surgeon.'"

Seddons frowned. "Couldn't you make it 'exceptionally brilliant'?"

"I might, if . . ."

"If what?"

"If you kiss me again—now."

On the second floor of the hospital Lucy Grainger knocked lightly on the chief of surgery's office door and went inside.

Looking up from a sheaf of reports, Kent O'Donnell said, "Hullo, Lucy—rest your weary bones."

"Now you mention it, they are a little weary." She dropped into the big leather chair which faced O'Donnell's desk.

"I had Mr. Loburton in to see me first thing this morning." O'Donnell came around the desk and perched informally on the corner nearest Lucy. "Cigarette?" He held out an embossed gold case.

"Thank you." She took a cigarette. "Yes—Vivian's father." Lucy accepted the light which O'Donnell offered and inhaled deeply; the smoke was cool, relaxing. She said, "Both parents got here yesterday. Naturally they're very concerned,

and they know nothing about me, of course. I suggested
Mr. Loburton have a talk with you."

"He did." O'Donnell spoke quietly. "I told him that in my
opinion his daughter couldn't possibly be in better hands,
that there was no one on the hospital's staff in whom I would
have greater confidence. I may tell you he seemed quite reassured."

"Thank you." Lucy found herself intensely gratified by
O'Donnell's words.

The chief of surgery smiled. "Don't thank me; it's an
honest appraisal." He paused. "What about the girl, Lucy?
What's the story so far?"

In a few words she summed up the case history, her tentative diagnosis, and the biopsy.

O'Donnell nodded. He asked, "Is there any problem with
Pathology? Has Joe Pearson come through promptly?"

Lucy told him of the delay and the reasons for it. He
thought briefly, then said, "Well, I guess that's reasonable.
I don't believe we can complain about that. But keep after
Joe; I don't think you should let it go beyond today."

"I won't." Lucy glanced at her watch. "I plan to see Joe
again after lunch. He expected to know something definite
by then."

O'Donnell made a wry face. "As definite as anything like
that can ever be." He mused. "Poor kid. How old did you
say she is?"

"Nineteen." Lucy was watching Kent O'Donnell's face. To
her eyes it seemed to mirror thought, character, and understanding. She reflected: He has greatness and he wears it
easily because it belongs to him. It made what he had said
a few moments ago about her own ability seem warmer and
more significant. Then suddenly, explosively, as if in a burst of
revelation, Lucy knew what she had denied herself knowing
these past months: that she loved this man—profoundly and
ardently. She became aware, with startling clarity, that she
had shielded herself from the knowledge, perhaps from an
instinctive fear of being hurt. But now, whatever happened,
she could shield herself no longer. For a moment the
thought made her weak; she wondered if she had betrayed
it on her face.

O'Donnell said apologetically, "I'll have to leave you,
Lucy. It's another full day." He smiled. "Aren't they all?"

Her heartbeat faster, her emotions surging, she had risen

and gone to the door. As he opened it O'Donnell put an arm
around her shoulders. It was a casual, friendly gesture that
any other of her colleagues might have made. But at this
moment the effect seemed electric; it left her breathless and
confused.

O'Donnell said, "Let me know, Lucy, if there's any problem. And if you don't mind, I might drop in today and see
your patient."

Collecting her thoughts, she told him, "I'm sure she'd like
it, and so would I." Then, as the door closed behind her,
Lucy shut her eyes for a moment to control her racing
mind.

The ordeal of waiting for the diagnosis concerning Vivian
had had a profound effect on Mike Seddons. By nature a
genial and outgoing personality, in normal times he was
noted for being one of the livelier spirits on Three Counties'
house staff, and it was not unusual to find him the focus of
a noisy, boisterous group in the residents' quarters. For the
past several days, however, most of the time he had avoided
the company of others, his spirits dampened by the knowledge of what an adverse verdict from Pathology could mean
to Vivian and himself.

His feelings about Vivian had not wavered; if anything,
they had become more intense. He hoped he had conveyed
this in the time he had spent last evening with Vivian's
parents after their initial meeting at the hospital. At first, as
was to be expected, all of them—Mr. and Mrs. Loburton,
Vivian, and himself—had been constrained, their talk awkward and at times formal. Even afterward it had seemed
that the Loburtons' meeting with a prospective son-in-law,
which in other circumstances might have been an important
occasion, had taken second place to their concern with the
immediate problem of Vivian's health. In a sense Mike Seddons felt he had become accepted because there was no time
for anything else.

Back at the Loburtons' hotel, though, they had talked
briefly about himself and Vivian. Henry Loburton, his big
frame spilling from an overstuffed chair in the sitting room
of their hotel suite, had asked Mike Seddons about his future,
more, Seddons suspected, from courtesy than from any real
concern. He had responded by telling them briefly of his
own intention to practice surgery in Philadelphia when

his residency at Three Counties ended. The Loburtons had nodded politely and had left the matter there.

Certainly, it seemed, there would be no opposition to a marriage. "Vivian has always seemed to know what she wanted," Henry Loburton had observed at one point. "It was the same way when she wanted to be a nurse. We were doubtful about it, but she had already made up her mind. There wasn't much else to say after that."

Mike Seddons had expressed the hope that they would not consider Vivian too young to marry. It was then that Angela Loburton had smiled. "I imagine it would be rather difficult to object on that account," she had said. "You see, I was married at seventeen. I ran away from home to do it." She smiled at her husband. "We didn't have any money, but we managed to get by."

Seddons had said with a grin, "Well, that much we'll have in common—anyway, until my practice gets going."

That had been last night. This morning, after the visit with Vivian, he had felt for some reason a sense of lightness and relief. Perhaps he had been depressed unnaturally long and brighter spirits were seeking an outlet. But, whatever the cause, he felt himself seized by a cheerful conviction that everything would turn out well. The feeling was with him now—in the autopsy room where he was assisting Roger McNeil with the autopsy of an elderly woman patient who had died last night in the hospital. It had prompted him to begin telling humorous stories to McNeil; Mike Seddons had a fund of them—another reason for his reputation as a joker.

Pausing in the middle of the latest, he asked McNeil, "Have you any cigarettes?"

The pathology resident motioned with his head. He was sectioning the heart he had just removed from the body.

Seddons crossed the room, found the cigarettes in McNeil's suit coat, and lighted one. Returning, he continued, "So she said to the undertaker, 'Thank you for doing that, even though it must have been a lot of trouble.' And the undertaker said, 'Oh, it wasn't any trouble really. All I did was change their heads.'"

Grim as the jest was in these surroundings, McNeil laughed aloud. He was still laughing as the autopsy-room door opened and David Coleman stepped inside.

"Dr. Seddons, will you put out that cigarette, please?" Coleman's voice cut quietly across the room.

Mike Seddons looked around. He said amiably, "Oh, good morning, Dr. Coleman. Didn't see you there for a minute."

"The cigarette, Dr. Seddons!" There was ice in Coleman's tone, his eyes steely.

Not quite understanding, Seddons said, "Oh . . . oh yes." none, moved his hand toward the autopsy table with the body upon it.

"Not there!" Coleman rapped out the words, stopping the surgical resident short. After a moment Seddons moved across the room, found an ash tray, and deposited the cigarette.

"Dr. McNeil."

"Yes, Dr. Coleman," Roger McNeil answered quietly.

"Will you . . . drape the face, please?"

Uncomfortably, knowing what was going through Coleman's mind, McNeil reached out for a towel. It was one they had used earlier; it had several big bloodstains. Still with the same soft intensity, Coleman said, "A *clean* towel, please. And do the same for the genitals."

McNeil nodded to Seddons, who brought over two clean towels. McNeil placed one carefully across the face of the dead woman; the other he used to cover the external genitalia.

Now the two residents stood facing Coleman. Both showed traces of embarrassment. Both sensed what was coming next.

"Gentlemen, I think there is something I should remind you of." David Coleman still spoke quietly—at no time since entering the room had he raised his voice—but there was no mistaking the underlying purpose and authority. Now he said deliberately, "When we perform an autopsy we do so with permission from the family of the one who has died. Without that permission there would be no autopsy. That *is* quite clear to you, I presume?"

"Quite clear," Seddons said. McNeil nodded.

"Very well." Coleman glanced at the autopsy table, then at the others. "Our own objective is to advance medical learning. The family of the deceased, for its part, gives us the body in trust, expecting that it will be treated with care, respect, and dignity." As he paused there was silence in the room. McNeil and Seddons were standing very still.

"And that is the way we *will* treat it, gentlemen." Coleman emphasized the words again, "With care, respect, and dignity." He went on, "At all autopsies the face and genitals will be draped and there will be no smoking in the room at any time. As for your own demeanor, and particularly the use of humor"—at the word Mike Seddons flushed a deep red—"I think I can leave that to your imagination."

Momentarily Coleman looked directly at each man in turn. Then, "Thank you, gentlemen. Will you carry on, please?" He nodded and went out.

For several seconds after the door had closed neither spoke. Then, softly, Seddons observed, "We appear to have been skillfully taken apart."

Ruefully McNeil said, "With some reason, I think. Don't you?"

As soon as they could afford it, Elizabeth Alexander decided, she would buy a vacuum cleaner. The old-fashioned carpet sweeper she was using now collected the superficial dirt, but that was about all. She pushed it back and forth a few more times over the rug and inspected the result critically. Not very good, but it would have to do. She must remember to have a talk with John tonight. Vacuum cleaners were not terribly expensive, and one extra monthly payment shouldn't make all that difference. The trouble was, though, there were so many things they needed. It was a problem, deciding which should come first.

In a way, she supposed, John was right. It was all very well to talk of making sacrifices and doing without things so that John could go to medical school. But when you came right down to it, it was hard to manage on any reduced income once you became accustomed to a certain standard. Take John's salary at the hospital, for example. It certainly did not put them in the big brackets, but it had made their life together comfortable and they were able to enjoy small luxuries which a few months ago had been out of reach. Could they surrender those things now? Elizabeth supposed so, but it would be difficult all the same. Medical school would mean another four years of struggling, and even after that there would be internship and perhaps residency, if John decided to specialize. Would it be worth it? Weren't they perhaps better off taking their happiness as they found it at this moment, accepting a role—even if a modest one —in the here and now?

That made sense, didn't it? And yet, somehow, Elizabeth was still unsure. Should she still continue to urge John to aim higher, to enter medical school, at whatever cost? Dr. Coleman obviously believed he should. What was it he had said to John?—*If you feel like this, and don't go to medical school while you have the chance, it may be something you'll regret the rest of your life.* At the time the words had made a deep impression on Elizabeth and, she suspected, on John too. Now, remembering, they seemed more significant than ever. She frowned; perhaps they had better talk over the whole subject again tonight. If she were convinced of what John really wanted, maybe she could force him into a decision. It would not be the first time Elizabeth had had her own way about things that concerned them both.

Elizabeth put the sweeper away and began to move around the apartment, tidying and dusting. Now, dismissing more serious thoughts for the time being, she sang as she worked. It was a beautiful morning. The warm August sun, shining brightly into the small but comfortable living room, showed off to advantage the new draperies she had made and had hung last night. Elizabeth stopped at the center table to rearrange a vase of flowers. She had removed two blooms which had faded and was about to cross to the tiny kitchen when the pain struck her. It came suddenly, without warning, like a blazing, searing fire and worse, much worse, than the day before in the hospital cafeteria. Drawing in her breath, biting her lip, trying not to scream aloud, Elizabeth sank into a chair behind her. Briefly the pain went away, then it returned, even—it seemed—more intensely. It was as if it were a cycle. Then the significance dawned uoon her. Involuntarily she said, "Oh no! No!"

Dimly, through the enveloping anguish, Elizabeth knew she had to act quickly. The hospital number was on a pad by the telephone. Suddenly the instrument on the other side of the room became an objective. Biding her time between each onset of pain, grasping the table for support, Elizabeth eased out of the chair and moved across. When she had dialed and a voice answered, she said, gasping, "Dr. Dornberger . . . it's urgent."

There was a pause and he came on the line. "It's . . . Mrs. Alexander," Elizabeth said. "I've started . . . to have . . . my baby."

David Coleman knocked once on the door of Dr. Pearson's

office, then went in. He found the senior pathologist seated behind the desk, Carl Bannister standing alongside. The lab technician's face had a taut expression; after a first glance he studiously avoided looking Coleman's way.

"You wanted to see me, I believe." Coleman had been returning from doing a frozen section on the surgical floor when his name had been called on the public-address system.

"Yes, I did." Pearson's manner was cool and formal. "Dr. Coleman, I have received a complaint concerning you from a member of the staff. Carl Bannister here."

"Oh?" Coleman raised his eyebrows. Bannister was still looking straight ahead.

Pearson went on, "I understand you two had a little brush this morning."

"I wouldn't call it exactly that." Coleman kept his voice casual and unperturbed.

"What would you call it then?" There was no mistaking the acidity in the old man's tone.

Coleman said levelly, "Frankly, I hadn't planned to bring the matter to your attention. But, since Mr. Bannister has chosen to, I think you had better hear the whole story."

"If you're sure it's not too much trouble."

Ignoring the sarcasm, Coleman said, "Yesterday afternoon I told both serology technicians that I planned to make occasional spot checks of laboratory work. Early this morning I did make one such check." Coleman glanced at Bannister. "I intercepted a patient's specimen before delivery to the serology lab and divided the specimen into two. I then added the extra sample to the listing on the requisition sheet, showing it as an extra test. Later, when I checked, I found that Mr. Bannister had recorded two different test results when, of course, they should have been identical." He added, "If you wish, we can get the details from the lab record now."

Pearson shook his head. He had risen from his chair and was half turned away; he appeared to be thinking. Coleman wondered curiously what would happen next. He knew that he himself was on perfectly secure ground. The procedure he had followed was standard in most well-run hospital labs. It provided a protection for patients and was a safeguard against carelessness. Conscientious technicians accepted lab checks without resentment and as a part of their job. Moreover, Coleman had followed protocol in telling both Bannister and John Alexander yesterday that the checks would be made.

Abruptly Pearson wheeled on Bannister. "All right, what have you got to say?"

"I don't like being spied on." The answer was resentful and aggressive. "I've never had to work that way before and I don't figure I should start now."

"And I tell you you're a fool!" Pearson shouted the words. "You're a fool for making a damn silly mistake, and you're an even bigger fool for coming to me when you get caught out." He paused, his lips tight, his breathing heavy. Coleman sensed that part of the old man's anger stemmed from his frustration at having no choice but to support what the younger pathologist had done, much as he might dislike it. Now, standing directly in front of Bannister, he snarled, "What did you expect me to do—pat you on the back and give you a medal?"

Bannister's face muscles were working. For once he appeared to have no answer. Surveying him grimly, Pearson seemed about to go on, then abruptly he stopped. Turning partly away, he gestured with his hand. "Get out! Get out!"

Without a word, his face set, looking neither to right nor left, Bannister went out of the room and closed the door behind him.

Now Pearson turned sharply to Coleman. "What the devil do you mean by this?"

David Coleman could see the burning anger in the old man's eyes. He realized that the affair with Bannister was merely a preliminary skirmish. Determined not to lose his own temper, he answered mildly, "What do I mean by what, Dr. Pearson?"

"You know damn well what I mean! I mean by making lab checks—without my authority."

Coleman said coldly, "Do I really need your authority? For something routine like that?"

Pearson slammed his fist on the desk. "Any time I want lab checks I'll order them!"

"If it's of any interest," Coleman said, still quietly, "I happen to have had your authority. As a matter of courtesy I mentioned to you yesterday that I would like to do standard lab checks in Serology, and you agreed."

Suspiciously Pearson said, "I don't remember."

"I assure you the conversation took place. In any case, I'm not in the habit of making that kind of invention." David Coleman felt his own anger rising; it was hard to conceal his contempt for this aged incompetent. He added, "I may say you seemed rather preoccupied at the time."

He appeared to have checked Pearson, at least partially. Grumblingly the old man said, "If you say so, I'll believe you. But it'll be the last time you do something like that on your own. Understand?"

Coleman sensed that this was a critical moment, both for Pearson and himself. Icily he asked, "Do you mind telling me what kind of responsibility I'm to have in this department?"

"You'll get whatever I choose to give you."

"I'm afraid I don't find that at all satisfactory."

"You don't, eh?" Pearson was directly in front of the younger man now, his head jutted forward. "Well, there happen to be a few things I don't find satisfactory either."

"For instance?" David Coleman had no intention of being intimidated. And if the old man wanted a showdown, he himself was quite willing to have it, here and now.

"For instance, I hear you've been laying down the law in the autopsy room," Pearson said.

"You asked me to take charge of it."

"I told you to supervise autopsies, not to set up a lot of fancy rules. No smoking, I understand. Is that supposed to include me?"

"I imagine that will be up to you, Dr. Pearson."

"I'll say it'll be up to me!" The other's calmness seemed to make Pearson angrier. "Now you listen to me, and listen good. You may have some pretty fancy qualifications, mister, but you've still got a lot to learn and I'm still in charge of this department. What's more, there are good reasons I'm going to be around here for a long time yet. So now's the time to decide—if you don't like the way I run things, you know what you can do."

Before Coleman could answer there was a knock on the door. Impatiently Pearson called out, "Yes?"

A girl secretary came in, glancing curiously from one to the other. It occurred to Coleman that Pearson's voice, at least, must have been clearly audible in the corridor outside. The girl said, "Excuse me, Dr. Pearson. There are two telegrams for you. They just came." Pearson took the two buff envelopes the girl held out.

When she had gone Coleman was about to reply. But Pearson stopped him with a gesture. Beginning to thumb open the first envelope, he said, "These will be the answers about the girl—Lucy Grainger's patient." His tone was quite different from that of a few moments before. He added, "They took long enough about it."

Automatically David Coleman felt a quickening of interest. Tacitly he accepted Pearson's view that their argument could be postponed; this was more important. As Pearson had the first flap open the telephone jangled sharply. With an exclamation of annoyance he put the two envelopes down to answer it.

"Yes?"

"Dr. Pearson, this is Obstetrics," a voice said. "Dr. Dornberger is calling you. One moment, please."

There was a pause, then Dornberger came on the line. He said urgently, "Joe, what's wrong with you people in Pathology?" Without waiting for an answer, "Your technician's wife—Mrs. Alexander—is in labor and the baby will be premature. She's on the way here in an ambulance, and I haven't got a blood-sensitivity report. Now get it up here fast!"

"Right, Charlie." Pearson slammed the receiver down and reached for a pile of forms in a tray marked "Signature." As he did, the two telegraph envelopes caught his eye. Quickly he passed them to Coleman. "Take these. See what they say."

Pearson riffled through the forms. The first time, in his haste, he missed the one he wanted; the second time through he found it. He lifted the telephone again, listened, then said brusquely, "Send Bannister in." Replacing the phone, he scribbled a signature on the form he had removed.

"You want me?" Bannister's tone and expression made it plain that he was still smarting from the reprimand earlier.

"Of course I want you!" Pearson held out the form he had signed. "Get this up to Dr. Dornberger—fast. He's in Obstetrics. John Alexander's wife is in trouble. She's going to have a premie."

Bannister's expression changed. "Does the kid know? He's down in———"

Impatiently Pearson cut him off. "Get going, will you! Get going!" Hastily Bannister went out with the form.

Dimly David Coleman had been aware of what was going on around him. His mind, however, had not yet grasped the details. For the moment he was too concerned with the awesome significance of the two telegrams which he held, opened, in his hand.

Now Pearson turned to him. The old man said, "Well, does the girl lose her leg or not? Are they both definite?"

Coleman thought: This is where pathology begins and ends; these are the borderlands where we must face the truth of how little we really know; this is the limit of learning, the rim of the dark, swirling waters of the still unknown. He said quietly, "Yes, they're both definite. Dr. Chollingham in Boston says, 'Specimen definitely malignant.' Dr. Earnhart in New York says, 'The tissue is benign. No sign of malignancy.'"

There was a silence. Then Pearson said slowly, softly, "The two best men in the country, and one votes 'for,' the other 'against.'" He looked at Coleman, and when he spoke there was irony but no antagonism. "Well, my young pathologist friend, Lucy Grainger expects an answer today. She will have to be given one, and it will have to be definite." With a twisted smile, "Do you feel like playing God?"

Sixteen

A police patrolman on duty at Main and Liberty heard the ambulance's siren six blocks away. Moving out from the sidewalk, and with the skill of long practice, he began to expedite the traffic flow so as to leave the intersection clear. As the siren grew louder and the flashing warning light became visible, threading its way toward him, the patrolman inflated his cheeks and blew two sharp whistle blasts. Then, signaling a halt to all traffic in the side roads, he authoritatively waved the ambulance driver through a red light. Pedestrians at the intersection, turning their heads curiously, caught a blurred glimpse of a young woman's white face as the ambulance swept by.

Inside, Elizabeth was only dimly conscious of their progress through the busy city streets. She sensed they were moving fast, but the buildings and people outside were a confused pattern racing past the window near her head. Momentarily, between each onset of pain, she could see the driver
up ahead, his two big hands nursing the wheel, turning quickly, first right, then left, taking advantage of every opening
as it occurred. Then the pain came back and all she could
think of was to cry out and to hold on.

"Hold my wrists! And hang on all you want." It was the
ambulance attendant, leaning over her. He had a stubble of
beard and a cleft chin, and for a moment Elizabeth believed
it was her father come here now to comfort her. But her father was dead; hadn't he been killed at the railroad? Or perhaps he had not and he was in this ambulance along with
her, being taken to some place they could be cared for together. Then her head cleared and she saw it was not her
father but a stranger whose wrists were red with the gouge
marks her nails had made.

She had time to touch the marks before the next pain
came. It was a gesture, all she could do. The man shook his
head. "Don't worry. Just you hold on all you want. We'll be
there soon. Old Joe up front is the best wagon driver in the
city." Then the pain again, worse than before, the intervals
between growing shorter, the sensation as if all her bones
were being twisted beyond endurance with the agony cen-
tered in her back, the torture of it overflowing into a flame
of red, yellow, purple in front of her eyes. Her nails dug
deeper and she screamed.

"Can you feel the baby coming?" It was the attendant
again; he had waited until the last pain subsided, then leaned
close.

She managed to nod her head and gasp. "I . . . I think so."

"All right." He eased his hands gently away. "Hang on to
this for a minute." He gave her a towel he had rolled tight,
then turned back the blanket over the stretcher and began
to loosen her clothing. He talked softly while he worked.
"We'll do the best we can if we have to. It wouldn't be the
first one I've delivered in here. I'm a grandfather, you see,
so I know what it's all about." His last words were drowned
out by her cry; once more, at her back, flooding around her,
blinding, overpowering, the crescendo of agony, crushing,
unrelenting. "Please!" She grasped for his wrists again, and

he gave them, faint lines of blood appearing as her nails ripped flesh. Turning his head, he called forward, "How are we doing, Joe?"

"Just went through Main and Liberty." The big hands turned the wheel sharply right. "There was a cop there; he had it sorted. Saved us a good minute." A swing to the left, then the head leaned back. "You a godfather yet?"

"Not quite, Joe. It's getting pretty close though, I reckon."

Again the wheel spinning; a sharp turn to the right. Afterward: "We're on the home stretch, boy. Try to keep the cork in a minute more."

All Elizabeth could think, through the miasma that engulfed her, was: My baby—he'll be born too soon! He'll die! Oh God, don't let him die! Not this time! Not again!

In Obstetrics, Dr. Dornberger was scrubbed and gowned. Emerging from the scrub room into the busy interior hallway which separated the labor rooms from the delivery areas, he looked around him. Seeing him through the glass partitions of her office, Mrs. Yeo, the head nurse, got up and came toward him, holding a clip board.

"Here's the blood-sensitivity report on your patient, Dr. Dornberger. It just came in from Pathology." She held out the board so he could read without touching it.

"About time!" Unusual for him, it was almost a growl. Scanning the form on top of the clip board, he said, "Sensitivity negative, eh? Well, there's no problem there. Is everything else ready?"

"Yes, Doctor." Mrs. Yeo smiled. She was a tolerant woman who felt that every man, including her own husband, was entitled to be grouchy now and then.

"How about an incubator?"

"It's here now."

As Dornberger glanced around, a nurse held the outer doorway wide while a woman orderly wheeled in an Isolette incubator. Holding the trailing cord clear of the floor, the orderly glanced inquiringly at Mrs. Yeo.

"In number two, please."

The orderly nodded and wheeled the incubator through a second swing door immediately ahead. As it closed behind her a girl clerk came toward them from the nursing office.

"Excuse me, Mrs. Yeo."

"Yes?"

"Emergency just phoned." The girl turned to Dornberger. "Your patient just arrived, Doctor, and she's on the way up. They say she's well advanced in labor."

Ahead of the hospital stretcher, to which she had been transferred from the ambulance, Elizabeth could see the young intern who had received her on arrival. Moving forward at a steady but unhurried pace, he was clearing a way, calmly and methodically, through the groups of people in the busy main-floor corridor. "Emergency . . . emergency, please." The words were quiet, almost casual, but their effect was immediate. Passers-by halted, groups moved back against the wall, to allow the small procession—intern, stretcher, and nurse propelling it—to go by. At the corridor's end an elevator operator had seen them and was clearing the car.

"Next car, please. This car for an emergency." Obediently the occupants moved out and the stretcher rolled in. The smooth, established drill of hospital procedure was functioning effortlessly to admit another supplicant.

Something of the calm seemed to transfer itself to Elizabeth. Though the pain was continuous now, and a new pressure in her uterus was building up, she found herself able to endure both better than before. She discovered that by biting her lower lip, and by gripping the edge of the sheet which covered her, it was possible not to cry out. She knew, though, that the final stage of birth had begun; involuntarily she began to bear down and, between her thighs, felt the first beginning of emergence.

Now they were in the elevator with the doors gliding closed and the nurse behind reaching down and holding her hand. "Just a minute or two more; that's all it will be." Then the doors were opened again and she saw Dr. Dornberger, gowned and waiting for her.

As if there were a hope that he had misread them earlier, Dr. Pearson picked up the two telegrams again. Looking at them, he put them down one at a time. "Malignant! Benign! And no doubt in either one. We're back where we started."

"Not quite," David Coleman said quietly. "We've lost almost three days."

"I know! I know!" Joe Pearson was beating a bulky fist into his palm, uncertainty around him like a mantle. "If it *is* malignant, the leg has to be amputated quickly; otherwise we'll be too late." He turned to face Coleman directly. "But the girl's nineteen. If she were fifty I'd say malignant and never turn a hair. But nineteen!—and maybe have your leg off when you didn't need to."

Despite his feelings about Pearson, despite his own conviction that the tissue they were speaking of was benign and not malignant, Coleman felt his sympathy for Pearson grow. The old man did have the final responsibility in the case; it was understandable that he should be troubled; the decision was extremely tough. He said tentatively, "It takes a lot of courage to make this kind of diagnosis."

As if he had touched a match to open flame, Pearson flared up. "Don't give me any of your high-school clichés! I've been doing this for thirty years!" He glared at Coleman, eyes blazing, the earlier antagonism returning. At that moment the telephone rang.

"Yes?" Though Pearson had answered the phone brusquely, as he listened his expression softened. Then he said, "All right, Lucy. I think you'd better come down. I'll wait for you here." Replacing the phone, he stood looking down at a point in the center of his desk. Then, without raising his head, he said to Coleman, "Lucy Grainger's on her way. You can stay if you want."

Almost as if he had not heard, Coleman said thoughtfully, "You know, there's one other thing might work, might give us a better pointer."

"What?" Pearson raised his head abruptly.

"That X-ray that was done." Coleman was still going slowly, the words keeping pace with his thoughts. "It was taken two weeks ago. If there *is* a tumor, and it's developing, another X-ray might show it."

Without a word Pearson reached down and once more picked up the telephone. There was a click and then he said, "Get me Dr. Bell in Radiology." Waiting, the old man eyed Coleman strangely. Then, covering the mouthpiece, he said with grudging admiration, "I'll say this for you: you're thinking—all the time."

In the room which the hospital staff jestingly referred to as "the expectant father's sweatbox" John Alexander butted a half-smoked cigarette into an ash stand. Then he got up from the padded leather chair where he had sat for the last hour and a half, looking up each time the door opened and someone had come in from the corridor outside. On each occasion, though, the news had been for someone else, and now, of the five men who had occupied the room ninety minutes ago, only he and one other remained.

Crossing to the big windows which looked down on the hospital forecourt and across other buildings to the industrial heart of Burlington, he saw that the streets and roofs were wet. It must have rained since he had come here without his noticing it. Now the area surrounding the hospital looked its worst—squalid and depressing, the roofs of mean houses and tenements stretching away toward the factories and grimy smokestacks lining both banks of the river. Glancing down at the street on which the hospital fronted, he saw a group of children run from an alley, nimbly dodging the pools of water left by the rain or broken sidewalks. Watching them, he saw one of the bigger boys in the group halt and put out a foot to trip a child behind. It was a small girl, probably four or five, and she fell face forward into one of the larger puddles, dirty water splashing up around her. She arose crying, wiping streaks of mud from her face and attempting pathetically to wring the water from her soiled, soaked dress. By now the others had stopped and they formed a ring around her, dancing and, from their expressions, chanting derision.

"Kids!" The disgusted voice came from alongside, and John was aware for the first time that the other occupant of the room had joined him at the window. Glancing sideways, he saw that the man was tall and pencil thin; hollow cheeks made him appear gaunt, and he was in need of a shave. Probably twenty years older than John, he wore a stained corduroy jacket with soiled coveralls beneath. With him across the room he brought an odor of grease and stale beer.

"Kids! They're all alike!" The man turned away from the window and began fumbling in his pockets. After a moment he produced paper and tobacco and began to roll a cigarette. Looking sharply at John, he asked, "This your first?"

"Not really. It's our second, but the first baby died."

"We lost one like that—in between the fourth and the fifth. A good thing too." The other man was searching his pockets. He asked, "You got a light?"

John produced a lighter and held it out. He asked, "You mean this is your sixth?"

"No—eighth." The thin man had his cigarette going now. "Sometimes I reckon that's eight too many." Then he said sharply, "I suppose you wanted yours."

"The baby, you mean?"

"Yeah."

"Yes, of course." John sounded surprised.

"We never did.. Not after the first—that was more than enough for me."

"Why did you have eight then?" John felt impelled to ask; the conversation had taken on an almost hypnotic quality.

"My wife could tell you better'n me—she's the one with the hot pants. Give her a couple of beers, let her wiggle her behind at a dance, and she's got to have it right there and then, and no messing around waiting to get home." The thin man blew out smoke, then went on calmly, "I reckon all our kids have been started in queer places. Once we was shopping in Macy's and we had it in a broom closet in the basement. That's where our fourth came from, I reckon— Macy's basement, but no bargain."

For a moment John was ready to laugh aloud, then he remembered his own reason for being there and stopped. Instead he said, "I hope everything's all right for you—this time, I mean."

The gaunt man said gloomily, "It's always all right; that's our trouble." He returned to the other side of the room and picked up a newspaper.

Left alone, John glanced at his watch again. He saw that it was an hour and three quarters since he had come here; surely there must be something soon in the way of news. He wished he had seen Elizabeth before she had gone into the delivery room, but everything had happened so quickly that there had not been time. He had been in the hospital kitchens when Carl Bannister had come to bring him the news. John had gone to the kitchens on Dr. Pearson's instructions. Pearson had told him to take cultures from plates which had passed through the kitchen dishwashers; John gathered that the machines were suspected of being unhygienic. But he had left the work as soon as Bannister had told him about Elizabeth and had gone to Emergency, hoping to intercept her there. But by that time she had already arrived by ambulance and had gone upstairs to Obstetrics. It was after that that he had come straight here to wait.

Now the door from the corridor opened, and this time it

was Dr. Dornberger. From his face John tried to read the news, but without success. He asked, "You *are* John Alexander?"

"Yes, sir." Though he had seen the elderly obstetrician several times in the hospital, this was the first time they had spoken to each other.

"Your wife is going to be all right." Dornberger knew better than to waste time on preliminaries.

John's first impression was of overwhelming relief. Then he asked, "The baby?"

Dornberger said quietly, "You have a boy. He was premature, of course, and I have to tell you, John—he's very frail."

"Will he live?" Only when he had asked the question did it occur to him how much depended on the answer.

Dornberger had taken out his pipe and was filling it. He said evenly, "Let's say the chances are not as good as if he had gone to full term."

John nodded dully. There seemed nothing to say, nothing that would matter now.

The older man paused to put away his tobacco pouch. Then in the same quiet, careful tone he said, "As near as I can tell, you have a thirty-two-week baby; that means he was born eight weeks early." Compassionately he added, "He wasn't ready for the world, John; none of us are that soon."

"No, I suppose not." John was scarcely conscious of speaking. His mind was on Elizabeth and what this baby was to have meant to them both.

Dr. Dornberger had produced matches and was lighting his pipe. When he had it going he said, "Your baby's birth weight was three pounds eight ounces. Perhaps that will mean more if I tell you that nowadays we consider any baby less than five pounds eight ounces at birth to be premature."

"I see."

"We have the baby in an incubator, of course. Naturally we'll do everything we can."

John looked at the obstetrician directly. "Then there *is* hope."

"There's always hope, son," Dornberger said quietly. "When we haven't much else, I guess there's always hope."

There was a pause, then John asked, "May I see my wife now?"

"Yes," Dornberger said. "I'll come to the nursing station with you."

As they went out John saw the tall, gaunt man watching him curiously.

Vivian was not quite sure what was happening. All she knew was that one of the staff nurses had come into her room and told her they were going to Radiology immediately. With help from another student nurse she had been put on a stretcher and now was being wheeled along the corridors where so short a time ago she had walked herself. Her movement through the hospital had a dream-like quality; it complemented the unrealness of everything else that had happened so far. Momentarily Vivian found herself abandoning fear, as if whatever followed could not matter to her in the end because it was inevitable and would not be changed. She found herself wondering if this feeling were a form of depression, of abandoning hope. She had known already that this was the day which might bring the verdict she had dreaded, a verdict which would make her a cripple, depriving her of freedom of movement, removing from her in one swift stroke so many things she had taken for granted until this time. With this latest thought the moment of passivity left her and fear came crowding back. She wished desperately that Mike were with her at this moment.

Lucy Grainger met the stretcher at the entrace to Radiology. "We've decided to do another X-ray, Vivian," she said. "It won't take long." She turned to a white-coated man beside her. "This is Dr. Bell."

"Hullo, Vivian." He smiled at her through thick horn-rimmed glasses, then, to the nurse, "May I have the chart, please?" As he studied it, turning the pages quickly, Vivian moved her head to look around her. They were in a small reception room with a glass-enclosed nursing station in one corner. Against one wall other patients were seated—two men in wheel chairs wearing pajamas and hospital robes, and a woman and a man in street clothes, the latter with a cast around his wrist. The last two, she knew, would have come here either from Outpatients or Emergency. The man with the cast looked uncomfortable and out of place. In his good hand was clasped a printed form; he seemed to be clutching it as if it were a passport he would need to come and go from these alien surroundings.

Bell finished reading the chart and handed it back. He
said to Lucy, "Joe Pearson phoned me. I gather that you'd
like to re-X-ray, so we can see if there's any change in the
bone appearance."

"Yes." Lucy nodded. "It's Joe's idea that something"—she
hesitated, aware that Vivian would hear her words—"might
have become visible in the meantime."

"It's possible." Bell had crossed to the nursing station and
was scribbling an X-ray requisition. He asked a girl clerk behind the desk, "Which technicians are free?"

She consulted a list. "There's Jane or Mr. Firban."

"I think we'll have Firban do this one. Will you find him,
please?" He turned to Lucy as they moved back toward the
stretcher. "Firban's one of our best technicians, and we want
good films." He smiled at Vivian. "Dr. Pearson asked me to
take a personal interest in this case, so that's what I'm doing.
Now let's go in this room over here."

With help from Bell the nurse guided the stretcher out of
the reception area and into a larger room opening from it.
Most of the room was taken up by an X-ray table, with the
machine's picture tube above and suspended on overhead
rollers. In an adjoining smaller section, behind thick glass,
Vivian could see an electric control panel. Almost at once
they were followed into the room by a short, youngish man
with crew-cut hair and wearing a white lab coat. His movements were jerky and hurried, as though he wished to
achieve whatever he was doing quickly but with a minimum
of energy expended. He glanced at Vivian, then turned to Bell.

"Yes, Dr. Bell?"

"Oh, Karl, I'd like you to handle this case for me. By the
way, do you know Dr. Grainger?" To Lucy, "This is Karl
Firban."

"I don't think we've met." Lucy offered her hand and the
technician took it.

"How do you do, Doctor."

"And our patient is Vivian Loburton." Bell smiled down
at the stretcher. "She's a student nurse. That's why we're
making such a fuss over her."

"Hullo, Vivian." Firban's greeting was as taut as his
other actions. Now, swinging the X-ray table from a vertical
position to horizontal, he talked on with brisk brightness.
"For special customers we offer a choice of VistaVision or
CinemaScope—all in glorious gray and black." He glanced

at the requisition which Bell had put down. "The left knee, eh? Anything special, Doctor?"

"We'll want some good A.P., lateral and oblique views, and then I think a coned-down view of the knee area." Bell paused and considered. "I'd say about five or six films, and then duplicates of the opposite extremity."

"Do you want any views on a fourteen by seventeen, to include the anterior tibia and fibula?"

Bell considered, then nodded. "That might be a good idea." To Lucy he said, "If it's osteomyelitis there could be periosteal reaction further down the bone."

"All right, Doctor. I'll have something for you in half an hour." It was a polite hint from Firban that he preferred to work alone, and the radiologist accepted it.

"We'll have a coffee and come back." Bell smiled in Vivian's direction. "You're in good hands." Then, with Lucy ahead of him, he went ouside.

"All righty. Let's get to work." The technician motioned to the nurse, and together they eased Vivian from the stretcher to the X-ray table. After the stretcher's comparative softness the black ebonite table felt hard and unyielding.

"Not so comfortable, eh?" Firban was moving Vivian carefully into the position he wanted, leaving her left knee exposed. As she shook her head he went on, "You get used to it. I've slept on this table plenty of times when I've been on night duty and things have been quiet." He nodded to the nurse, and the girl went to wait behind the glassed-in section.

With Vivian watching, the technician went through the routine movements of an X-ray series. Still with the same swift jerkiness, he took a film casette from an upright container built into the wall, inserting it deftly in a tray beneath the X-ray table. Next he positioned the tray below the area of Vivian's knee. Then, using press-button controls suspended from the ceiling by a heavy electrical cord, he maneuvered the heavy X-ray tube along its rollers and downward, until it was immediately above the knee, the arrow on the machine's calibrated height scale pointing to forty inches.

In contrast to so much else in the hospital, Vivian thought, this room appeared almost unearthlike and remote. The shining black and chrome machinery seemed monstrous as it slid slowly and in massive murmur. There was an aura of science and neutrality in this place, in a way as remote from medicine as a great ship's engine room might seem from a sunlit bridge deck far above. And yet here, with these ominous, ponderous instruments, so much of medicine's real detective work was done. The thought for a moment frightened her. There was a dreadful impersonality in it all, so little of people in these machines. Whatever they might discover was relayed and reported without warmth or pleasure, without sadness or regret. Good, bad—it was all the same. For a moment she fancied the picture tube suspended above her to be an eye of judgment, inflexible, dispassionate. What was its judgment now? Would there be hope, or even reprieve . . . or a solemn sentence from which there could be no appeal? Again she found herself wishing for Mike; she would call him as soon as she returned to the hospital room.

The technician had finished his preparation. "I think that will do." He took a final look around. "I'll tell you when to keep perfectly still. This is the only place in the hospital, you know, where we can say you won't feel a thing and really mean it."

Now he moved behind the inch-thick glass screen which protected the X-ray operator from radiation. Out of the periphery of her vision Vivian could see him moving, holding a check list, setting switches.

At the master control panel Firban was thinking: A pretty kid. Wonder what's wrong. Must be something serious for Bell to take all that interest; usually the chief doesn't pay attention to patients until after the films are made. He double-checked the panel controls; in this work you acquired the habit of taking no chances. Settings were okay—84 kilovolts, 200 milliamps, exposure time fifteen hundredths of a second. He pressed a button which set the rotating anode of the picture tube in motion. Then calling out the familiar formula, "Don't move! Keep still!" he thumbed the second button and knew that whatever was to be seen by the osmotic eye of X-ray was recorded now for others to evaluate.

In the X-O-Mat room of Radiology, the venetian blinds lowered to cut off the light from outside, Drs. Bell and Lucy Grainger were waiting. In a few minutes the films which Firban had taken would be ready for comparison with those of two weeks before. The technician had already fed his undeveloped negatives into the autodeveloping machine, and at this moment, looking somewhat like an oversized oil furnace, its interior was humming. Now, one by one, the developed films began to fall into a slot at the front of the machine.

As each film appeared Bell placed it under the clip of a viewing box, lighted by fluorescent tubes behind. On a second viewing box, immediately above, he had already put in position the earlier films.

"Did we get good pictures?" There was a touch of pride in the technician's question.

"Very good indeed." It was a reflex answer; Bell was already studying the new negatives intently, then comparing the corresponding areas in the two sets of films. He used a pencil point to aid his own thought process and so that Lucy could follow him.

When they had gone over both sets completely, Lucy asked, "Do you see any difference? I can't, I'm afraid."

The radiologist shook his head. "There's a little periosteal reaction here." He pointed with the pencil to a slight difference in gray shading at two points. "But that's probably the result of your own biopsy. Otherwise there's been no conclusive change." Bell removed his heavy glasses and rubbed his right eye. He said, almost apologetically, "I'm sorry, Lucy; I guess I have to throw the ball back at Pathology. Will you tell Joe Pearson, or shall I?" He began to take down the two sets of films.

"I'll tell him," Lucy said thoughtfully. "I'll go and tell Joe now."

Seventeen

Staff Nurse Mrs. Wilding pushed back a wisp of gray hair that seemed forever to be falling out from under her starched cap and walked briskly down the fourth-floor corridor of Obstetrics a little ahead of John Alexander. At the fifth door they came to she stopped and looked inside. Then she announced cheerfully, "A visitor for you, Mrs. Alexander," and ushered John into the small semiprivate room.

"Johnny darling!" Elizabeth held out her arms, wincing

slightly as the movement caused her to change position in the bed, and he went to her, kissing her tenderly. For a moment she held him tightly. He felt her warmth and under his hand the crisp, clean coarseness of the hospital nightgown she had on. There was a smell in her hair that resembled a combination of sweat and ether; it seemed a reminder of something he had been unable to share, as if she had been to a distant place and was now returned, a touch of strangeness with her. For a moment he sensed a constraint between them, as if, after separation, there was the need to find and to know each other again. Then gently Elizabeth drew back.

"I must look a mess."

"You look beautiful," he told her.

"There wasn't time to bring anything." She looked down at the shapeless hospital garment. "Not even a nightgown or a lipstick."

He said sympathetically, "I know."

"I'll make a list. Then you can bring the things in."

Behind them Mrs. Wilding had drawn the overhead curtain that separated them from the other bed in the tiny room.

"There you are. Now you're as private as can be." She took a tumbler that was on a bed table beside Elizabeth and refilled it from a jug of ice water. "I'll come back in a little while, Mr. Alexander; then you can see your baby."

"Thank you." They both smiled gratefully as the nurse went out.

As the door closed Elizabeth turned to face John again. Her expression was strained, her eyes searching.

"Johnny dear, I want to know. What are the baby's chances?"

"Well, honey . . ." He hesitated.

She reached out and covered his hand. "Johnny, I want the truth. The nurses won't tell me. I've got to hear it from you." Her voice wavered. He sensed that tears were not far distant.

He answered softly, "It could go either way." He went on, choosing the words carefully. "I saw Dr. Dornberger. He said the chances are just fair. The baby might live, or . . ." John stopped, the sentence unfinished.

Elizabeth had let her head fall back into the pillows behind her. Looking at the ceiling, the words little more than a whisper, she asked, "There really isn't much hope, is there?"

John weighed the impact of what he might say next. Perhaps, if the baby were going to die, it was better for them both to face it now, better than to buoy up Elizabeth's hopes and then in a day or two have them cruelly destroyed. Gently he said, "He's . . . awfully small, you see. He was born two months too soon. If there's any kind of infection . . . even the smallest thing . . . He doesn't have much strength."

"Thank you." Elizabeth was quite still, not looking at him, but holding his hand tightly. There were tears on her cheeks, and John found his own eyes moist.

Trying to keep his voice even, he said, "Elizabeth darling . . . Whatever happens . . . We're still young. We've a lot ahead of us."

"I know." The words were scarcely audible, and his arms went around her again. Her head close against him, he heard her, muffled through sobs. "But . . . two babies . . . this way . . ." She lifted her head, her cry despairing. "It isn't fair!"

He felt his own tears coursing. Softly he whispered, "It's hard to figure . . . We've still got each other."

For a minute longer he held her; she was sobbing quietly, then he felt her stir. She murmured, "Handkerchief," and, taking one from his own pocket, he passed it to her.

"I'm all right now." She was wiping her eyes. "It's just . . . sometimes."

He told her softly, "If it helps, honey . . . you cry. Any time you want."

She smiled wanly and returned the handkerchief. "I'm afraid I've messed it all up." Then her voice changed. "Johnny . . . lying here . . . I've been thinking."

"What about?"

"I want you to go to medical school."

He protested gently. "Now, honey, we've been over all this . . ."

"No." Elizabeth stopped him. Her voice was still weak, but it had an edge of determination. "I've always wanted you to, and now Dr. Coleman says you should."

"Do you have any idea what it would cost?"

"Yes, I do. But I can get a job."

Gently he said, "With a baby?"

There was a moment's silence. Then Elizabeth said softly, "We may not have a baby."

The door opened noiselessly and Nurse Wilding came in. She glanced at Elizabeth's red-rimmed eyes, then discreetly avoided them. To John she said, "If you like, Mr. Alexander, I'll take you to see your baby now."

After he had left John Alexander at the nursing station Dr. Dornberger had headed for the hospital nursery.

The nursery lay at one end of a long, bright corridor, decorated cheerfully in pastel shades. It was in a section of the building which had been remodeled two years earlier and reflected the newer trend to spaciousness and light. Approaching, Dornberger could hear, as always, the cries of infants, ranging in pitch and volume from full-lunged, anguished howls to tentative falsettos. More out of habit than thought, he stopped to glance through the thick glass paneling which screened the nursery's main area on three sides. Business, he reflected, noting the preponderance of occupied bassinets, appeared as brisk as ever. His glance ranged over the orderly rows.

These, he thought, were the normal, healthy animals who had won, for the moment, their battle for existence and in a few days more would go outward and onward into the waiting world. Their destinations were the home, the school, the strife of living, the competition for fame and possessions. Among these were some who would taste success and suffer failure; who, barring casualty, would enjoy youth, accept middle age, and grow old sadly. These were those for whom more powerful and glossier automobiles would be designed, in whose service aircraft would wing faster and farther, whose every whim and appetite would be wooed by others of their kind with wares to market. These were some who would face the unknown future, most with misgiving, many bravely, a few craven. Some here, perhaps, might breach the barriers of outer space; others with the gift of tongues might move their fellow men to anger or despair. Most, within twenty years, would fulfill their physical maturity, obeying, but never understanding, the same primeval craving to copulate which had sown their seed and brought them, mewling, puking, here. But for now these were the victors—the born and urgent. Their first and greatest barrier was down, the other battles yet to come.

Across the hallway was another area with a smaller nursery beyond. In it, quiet and separate, each in an incubator, were the premature babies; these—the doubtful starters, their existence insecure, their first encounter not yet won.

Turning away from the main nursery, it was this section that Dornberger entered now.

When he had viewed his newest patient—a tiny fragment of insecure humanity—he pursed his lips and shook his head doubtfully. Then, methodical as always, he wrote careful instructions on the treatment to be followed.

Later, as Dornberger left by one door, Nurse Wilding and John Alexander came in by another.

Like everyone who approached the premature nursery, they had put on sterile gowns and face masks, even though plate glass separated them from the air-conditioned, humidity-controlled interior. Now, as they stopped, Mrs. Wilding leaned forward and tapped lightly on the glass. A younger nurse inside looked up and moved toward them, her eyes above the mask inquiring.

"Baby Alexander!" Wilding raised her voice enough to carry through to the other nurse, then pointed to John. The girl inside nodded and motioned for them to move. They followed her the length of the plate-glass window and stopped. Now she pointed to an incubator—one of the dozen the nursery contained—and turned it slightly so they could see inside.

"My God! Is that *all?*" The exclamation was torn from John even as it framed itself in mind.

Nurse Wilding's glance was sympathetic. "He's not very big, is he?"

John was staring as if in unbelief. "I've never seen anything so . . . so incredibly small."

He stood looking down into the Isolette cabinet. Could this be human?—this tiny, shriveled, monkeylike figure, little larger than his own two hands.

The baby lay perfectly still, its eyes closed, only a slight regular movement of the tiny chest testifying to its breathing. Even in the incubator, designed for the smallest infants, the little helpless body appeared forlorn and lost. It seemed incredible that in such fragility life could exist at all.

The younger nurse had come outside to join them. Wilding asked, "What was the birth weight?"

"Three pounds eight ounces." The young nurse turned to John. "Do you understand what's happening, Mr. Alexander —how your baby is being cared for?"

He shook his head. He found it hard to tear his eyes away, even for a moment, from the tiny child.

The young nurse said practically, "Some people like to know. They seem to think it helps."

John nodded. "Yes; if you'd tell me. Please."

The nurse pointed to the incubator. "The temperature inside is always ninety-eight degrees. There's oxygen added to the air—about 40 per cent. The oxygen makes it easier for the baby to breathe. His lungs are so small, you see. They weren't really developed when he was born."

"Yes. I understand." His eyes were back on the faint pulsing movement in the chest. While it continued it meant there was life, that the tiny burdened heart was beating, the thread of survival still unbroken.

The nurse went on. "Your baby isn't strong enough to suck, so we have to use intubation. You see the little tube?" She pointed to a plastic cord with a hollow center which ran from the top of the incubator into the infant's mouth. "It goes directly into the stomach. He'll be having dextrose and water through the tube every hour and a half."

John hesitated. Then he asked, "You've seen a lot of these cases?"

"Yes." The nurse nodded gravely, as if sensing the question which would follow. He noticed she was petite and pretty, with red hair tucked under her cap. She was surprisingly young, too; perhaps twenty, certainly no more. But she carried an air of professional competence.

"Do you think he'll live?" He glanced down again through the paneled glass.

"You can never tell." The younger nurse's forehead was creased in a frown. He could sense that she was trying to be honest, not to destroy his hopes and yet not to raise them. "Some do; some don't. Sometimes it seems as if some babies have a will to live. They fight for life."

He asked her, "This one—is he fighting?"

She said carefully, "It's too early to know. But those extra eight weeks would have made a lot of difference." She added quietly, "This will be a hard fight."

Once more he let his eyes stray back to the tiny figure. For the first time the thought occurred to him: This is my son, my own, a part of my life. Suddenly he was consumed by a sense of overwhelming love for this fragile morsel, fighting his lonely battle inside the warm little box below. He had an absurd impulse to shout through the glass: *You're not alone, son; I've come to help.* He wanted to run to the in-

cubator and say: *These are my hands; take them for your
strength. Here are my lungs; use them and let me breathe
for you. Only don't give up, son; don't give up! There's so
much ahead, so much we can do together—if only you'll
live! Listen to me, and hold on! This is your father and I
love you.*

He felt Nurse Wilding's hand on his arm. Her voice said
gently, "We'd better go now."

He nodded, unable to speak. Then with a last glance back-
ward they moved away.

Lucy Grainger knocked and went into the pathology office.
Joe Pearson was behind his desk, David Coleman on the far
side of the room, studying a file. He turned as Lucy entered.

"I have the new X-rays," Lucy said, "on Vivian Loburton."

"What do they show?" Pearson was interested at once. He
pushed some papers aside and got up.

"Very little, I'm afraid." Lucy had moved to the X-ray
viewer which hung on the office wall, and the two men followed her. Coleman reached out and snapped a switch; after
a second or two the fluorescent lights in the viewer flickered
on.

Two at a time, they studied the comparative films. Lucy
pointed out, as Dr. Bell had done in Radiology, the area of
periosteal reaction created by the biopsy. Otherwise, she reported, there had been no change.

At the end Pearson thoughtfully rubbed his chin with
thumb and forefinger. Glancing at Coleman, he said, "I
guess your idea didn't work."

"Apparently not." Coleman kept his voice noncommittal.
In spite of everything they were still left with a question—a
division of opinion. He wondered what the older man would
do.

"It was worth trying anyway." Pearson had a way of making the most ordinary acknowledgment sound grudging, but
Coleman guessed he was talking to gain time and to cover up
his indecision.

Now the old man turned to Lucy. Almost sardonically, he
said, "So Radiology bows out."

She answered levelly, "I suppose you could say that."

"And it leaves it up to me—to Pathology?"

"Yes, Joe," she said quietly, waiting.

There was a ten-second silence before Pearson spoke again. Then he said clearly and confidently, "My diagnosis is that your patient has a malignant tumor—osteogenic sarcoma."

Lucy met his eyes. She asked, "That's quite definite?"

"Quite definite." In the pathologist's voice there was no hint of doubt or hesitation. He went on, "In any case, I've been sure from the beginning. I thought this"—he indicated the X-ray films—"would give some extra confirmation."

"All right." Lucy nodded her acceptance. Her mind was working now on immediate things to do.

Pearson asked matter-of-factly, "When shall you amputate?"

"Tomorrow morning, I expect." Lucy gathered up the X-rays and went to the door. Her glance taking in Coleman, she said, "I suppose I'd better go and break the news." She made a small grimace. "This is one of the hard ones."

When the door had closed behind her, Pearson turned to Coleman. He said with surprising courtesy, "Someone had to decide. I didn't ask your opinion then because I couldn't take the chance of letting it be known that there was doubt. If Lucy Grainger knew, she would have no choice but to tell the girl and her parents. And once they heard, they would want to delay. People always do; you can't blame them." He paused, then added, "I don't have to tell you what delay can do with osteogenic sarcoma."

Coleman nodded. He had no quarrel with Pearson's having made the decision. As the old man had said, someone had to do it. All the same, he wondered if the amputation to be performed tomorrow was necessary or not. Eventually, of course, they would know for sure. When the severed limb came down to the lab, dissection would show if the diagnosis of malignancy was right or wrong. Unfortunately, though, an error discovered then would be too late to do the patient any good. Surgery had learned many ways to amputate limbs effectively, but it had no procedures for putting them back.

The afternoon flight from Burlington landed at La Guardia Airport a little after four o'clock, and from the airport Kent O'Donnell took a taxi to Manhattan. On the way into town he leaned back, relaxing for the first time in several days. He always tried to relax in New York taxis, mainly because any attempt to watch the traffic, or his own progress through it, usually left him in a state of nervous tension. He had long ago decided that the correct attitude to adopt was one of fatalism; you resigned yourself to disaster, then, if it failed to happen, you congratulated yourself on abundant good luck.

Another reason for relaxing was that for the past week he had worked at full pressure, both in the hospital and outside. He had extended his office appointments and scheduled extra surgery to make possible the four-day absence from Three Counties he had now embarked on. As well, two days ago, he had presided at a special meeting of the hospital's medical staff at which—aided by data prepared by Harry Tomaselli—he had revealed the suggested scale of donations to the hospital building fund for attending physicians and others. As he had expected, there had been plenty of grumbling, but he had no doubt that the pledges, and eventually the money, would be forthcoming.

Despite his mental withdrawal, O'Donnell was conscious of the activity of New York outside and of the familiar angled sky line of mid-town Manhattan, now growing closer. They were passing over Queensborough Bridge, the warm afternoon sun slanting lancelike through drab green girders, and down below he could see Welfare Island, its city hospitals squatting somberly and institutional midway in the gray East River. He reflected that on each occasion he saw New York its ugliness seemed greater, its disorder and grime more strikingly apparent. And yet, even to the non-New Yorker, after a while these things became comfortable and familiar, seeming to hold a welcome for the traveler, as though an old, worn garment were good enough between friends. He smiled, then chided himself for unmedical thinking—the kind that held back air-pollution control and slum removal. Sentimentality, he reflected, was an aid and comfort to the opponents of progress.

They moved off the bridge and along Sixtieth Street to Madison, then jogged a block, turning west on Fifty-ninth. At Seventh Avenue and Central Park they went left in the traffic and stopped four blocks down at the Park Sheraton Hotel.

He checked into the hotel and later, in his room, showered and changed. From his bag he took the program of the surgeons' congress—ostensible reason for his presence in

New York. He noted that there were three papers he wanted
to hear—two on open heart surgery and a third on replacement of diseased arteries by grafts. But the first was not
until eleven next morning, which gave him plenty of time
tomorrow. He glanced at his watch. It was a little before
seven—more than an hour before he was due to meet Denise.
He took an elevator downstairs and strolled through the
foyer to the Pyramid Lounge.

It was the cocktail hour and the place was beginning to
fill with pre-dinner-and-theater groups, mostly, he guessed,
like himself, from out of town. A headwaiter showed him
to a table, and as they moved across he saw an attractive
woman, sitting alone, glance at him interestedly. It was not a
new experience, and in the past similar incidents had occasionally led to interesting results. But tonight he thought:
Sorry, I have other plans. A waiter took his order for scotch
and soda, and when the drink came he sipped it slowly, his
mind coasting leisurely over random thoughts.

Moments like this, he reflected, were all too rare in
Burlington. That was why it was good to get away for a
while; it sharpened your sense of perspective, made you
realize that some of the things you deemed important on
your own home ground were a good deal less so when
looked at from a distance. Just lately he had suspected
that his own closeness to hospital business had thrown some
of his thinking out of balance. He looked around him. Since
he had come in the lounge had filled; waiters were hurrying
to bring the drinks which three bartenders were dispensing;
one or two of the earlier groups were moving out. How
many of these people, he wondered—the man and the girl
at the next table, the waiter by the door, the foursome just
leaving—had ever heard of Three Counties Hospital and, if
they had, would care what went on there? And yet, to himself just lately, the hospital's affairs seemed almost to have
become the breath of life. Was this a healthy symptom? Was
it a good thing professionally? O'Donnell had always mis-
trusted dedicated people; they tended to become obsessed,
their judgment undermined by enthusiasm for a cause. Was
he in danger now of becoming one such himself?

The question of Joe Pearson, for example. Had O'Donnell's
own closeness to the scene misled him there? It had been
necessary for the hospital to hire a second pathologist; he
was convinced of that. But had he himself tended to criticize

the old man unduly, to magnify organizational weaknesses
—and every hospital department had a few—out of true
proportion? For a time O'Donnell had even considered asking Pearson to retire; was that in itself a symptom of unbalanced judgment, a hasty condemnation of an older man
by one his junior in years? Of course, that was before
Eustace Swayne had made it clear that his quarter-million-
dollar donation was contingent on Joe Pearson's remaining
at the helm of Pathology; Swayne, incidentally, had still not
confirmed the gift. But O'Donnell felt his judgment was superior to considerations like that, however important they
might seem. In all probability Joe Pearson had a lot to give
Three Counties still; his accumulated experience should
surely count for something. It *was* true, he decided; your
thinking did improve when you were away—even if you had
to find a cocktail bar to do some reasoning quietly.

A waiter had stopped at the table. "A refill, sir?"

O'Donnell shook his head. "No, thanks."

The man produced a check. O'Donnell added a tip and
signed it.

It was seven-thirty when he left the hotel. There was still
plenty of time to spare, and he walked cross-town on Fifty-
fifth as far as Fifth Avenue. Then, hailing a cab, he continued
uptown to the address Denise had given him. The driver
stopped near Eighty-sixth, outside a gray stone apartment
building. O'Donnell paid off the cab and went in.

He was greeted respectfully by a uniformed hall porter.
The man asked his name, then consulted a list. He said,
"Mrs. Quantz left a message to say would you please go up,
sir?" He motioned to the elevator, an identically uniformed
operator beside it. "It's the penthouse floor, sir—the twentieth. I'll tell Mrs. Quantz you're on the way."

At the twentieth floor the elevator doors opened silently
onto a spacious carpeted hallway. Occupying most of one
wall was a large Gobelin tapestry depicting a hunting scene.
Opposite were double carved oak doors which now opened,
and a manservant appeared. He said, "Good evening, sir. Mrs.
Quantz asked me to show you into the lounge. She'll be with
you in a moment."

He followed the man down a second hallway and into a
living room almost as large as his own entire apartment at
Burlington. It was decorated in shades of beige, brown,
and coral, a sweep of sectional settees offset by walnut end

tables, their rich darkness in simple, striking contrast to the deep broadloom of pale beige. The living room opened onto a flagstoned terrace, and he could see the last rays of evening sunshine beyond.

"May I get you something to drink, sir?" the manservant said.

"No, thanks," he answered. "I'll wait for Mrs. Quantz."

"You won't have to," a voice said, and it was Denise. She came toward him, her hands held out. "Kent dear, I'm so glad to see you."

For a moment he looked at her. Then he said slowly, "I am too," and added truthfully, "Until this moment I hadn't realized how much."

Denise smiled and leaned forward to kiss his cheek lightly. O'Donnell had a sudden impulse to take her into his arms, but restrained it.

She was even more beautiful than he remembered, with a smiling radiance that left him breathless. She had on a short, full-skirted evening gown of jet-black lace over a strapless sheath of black silk, the lace about her shoulders accenting the filmy vision of white flesh beneath. At her waist was a single red rose.

She released one of his hands and with the other led him to the terrace. The manservant had preceded them, carrying a silver tray with glasses and a cocktail shaker. Now he withdrew discreetly.

"The martinis are already mixed." Denise looked at O'Donnell inquiringly. "Or if you like I can get you something else."

"Martini is fine."

Denise poured two drinks and handed him one. She was smiling, her eyes warm. Her lips said softly, "Welcome to New York from a committee of one."

He sipped the martini; it was cool and dry. He said lightly, "Please thank the committee."

For a brief moment her eyes caught his. Then, taking his arm, she moved across the terrace toward the low, pillared balustrade which marked its end.

O'Donnell asked, "How is your father, Denise?"

"He's well, thank you. Entrenched like a true die-hard, of course, but in good health. Sometimes I think he'll outlive us all." She added, "I'm very fond of him."

They had stopped and stood looking down. It was dusk

now, the warm, mellow dusk of late summer, and the lights of New York were flickering on. From the streets below the throb of evening traffic was steady and insistent, punctuated by the peaklike whine of diesel buses and the full points of impatient horns. Across the way, its outline blurring into shadow, was Central Park, only scattered street lamps marking the roadways through. Beyond, the west-side streets dimmed darkly into the Hudson River; and on the river the pin-point lamps of shipping were a link between the blackness and the distant glimmering New Jersey shore. Uptown, O'Donnell could see the George Washington Bridge, its highstrung floodlights a chain of white, bright beads, and, below, the headlights of cars, multi-laned, streaming across the bridge, away from the city. O'Donnell thought: People going home.

A warm, soft breeze stirred around them, and he was conscious of Denise's closeness. Her voice said softly, "It's beautiful, isn't it? Even though you know that under the lights there are things that are wrong and hateful, it's still beautiful. I love it all, especially at this time of evening."

He said, "Have you ever considered going back—to Burlington, I mean?"

"To live?"

"Yes."

"You can never go back," Denise said quietly. "It's one of the few things I've learned. Oh, I don't mean just Burlington, but everything else—time, people, places. You can revisit, or renew acquaintance, but it's never really the same; you're detached; you're passing through; you don't belong because you've moved on." She paused. "I belong here now. I don't believe I could ever leave New York. Do I sound terribly unrealistic?"

"No," he said. "You sound terribly wise."

He felt her hand on his arm. "Let's have one more cocktail," she said, "then you may take me to dinner."

Afterward they had gone to the Maisonette, a discreet and pleasantly appointed night club on Fifth Avenue. They had dined and danced, and now they had come back to their table. "How long have you in New York?" Denise asked.

"I go back in three more days," he answered.

She inclined her head. "Why so soon?"

"I'm a workingman." He smiled. "My patients expect me to be around and there's a lot of hospital business too."

Denise said, "I rather think I shall miss you."

He thought for a moment, then turned to face her. Without preliminary he said, "You know that I've never been married."

"Yes." She nodded gravely.

"I'm forty-two," he said. "In that time, living alone, one forms habits and patterns of life that might be hard to change or for someone else to accept." He paused. "What I'm trying to say, I suppose, is that I might be difficult to live with."

Denise reached out and covered his hand with her own. "Kent, darling, may I be clear about something?" She had the slightest of smiles. "Is this by any chance a proposal of marriage?"

O'Donnell was grinning broadly; he felt absurdly, exuberantly, boyish. "Now that you mention it," he said, "I rather think it is."

There was a moment's silence before Denise answered, and when she spoke he sensed that she was maneuvering for time. "I'm very flattered, but aren't you being a little rash? After all, we scarcely know one another."

"I love you, Denise," he said simply.

He felt her regarding him searchingly. "I could love you too," she said. Then she added, speaking slowly and choosing her words, "At this moment everything in me tells me to say yes and to grab you, dearest, with two eager hands. But there's a whisper of caution. When you've made one mistake you feel the need to be careful about committing yourself again."

"Yes," he said, "I can understand that."

"I've never fallen in," she said, "with the popular idea that one can shed partners quickly and afterward get over it, rather like taking an indigestion tablet. That's one of the reasons, I suppose, why I've never got a divorce."

"The divorce wouldn't be difficult?"

"Not really. I imagine I could go to Nevada to arrange it, or some such place. But there's the other thing—you're in Burlington; I'm in New York."

He said carefully, "You really meant what you said, Denise—about not living in Burlington?"

She thought before answering. "Yes. I'm afraid I do. I couldn't live there—ever. There's no use pretending, Kent; I know myself too well."

A waiter appeared with coffee and replenished their cups. O'Donnell said, "I feel a sudden compulsion for the two of us to be alone."

Denise said softly, "Why don't we go?"

He called for the check and paid it, helping Denise on with her wrap. Outside a doorman summoned a cab and O'Donnell gave the address of the Fifth Avenue apartment. When they had settled back, Denise said, "This is a very selfish question, but have you ever considered moving your practice to New York?"

"Yes," he answered, "I'm thinking about it now."

He was still thinking when they entered the apartment block and rode up in the elevator. Ever since Denise's question he had been asking himself: Why shouldn't I go to New York? There are fine hospitals; this is a medical city. It would not be difficult to get on staff somewhere. Setting up practice would be comparatively easy; his own record, as well as the friends he had in New York, would bring him referrals. He reasoned: What really keeps me tied to Burlington? Does my life belong there—now and for always? Isn't it time, perhaps, for a change, a new environment? I'm not married to Three Counties Hospital, nor am I indispensable. There are things I'd miss, it's true; the sense of building and creation, and the people I've worked with. But I've accomplished a great deal; no one can ever deny that. And New York means Denise. Wouldn't it be worth it—all?

At the twentieth floor Denise used her own key to let them in; there was no sign of the manservant O'Donnell had seen earlier.

As if by consent they moved to the terrace. Denise asked, "Kent, would you like a drink?"

"Perhaps later," he said, and reached out toward her. She came to him easily and their lips met. It was a lingering kiss. His arms tightened around her and he felt her body respond to his own. Then gently she disengaged herself.

Half turned away, she said, "There are so many things to think of." Her voice was troubled.

"Are there?" The tone of voice was disbelieving.

"There's a great deal you don't know about me," Denise said. "For one thing, I'm terribly possessive. Did you know that?"

He answered, "It doesn't sound very terrible."

"If we were married," she said, "I'd have to have all of you, not just a part. I couldn't help myself. And I couldn't share you—not even with a hospital."

He laughed. "I imagine we could work out a compromise. Other people do."

She turned back toward him. "When you say it like that I almost believe you." Denise paused. "Will you come back to New York again—soon?"

"Yes."

"How soon?"

He answered, "Whenever you call me."

As if by instinct, she moved toward him and they kissed again, this time with growing passion. Then there was a sound behind them and a shaft of light from a door opening to the living room. Denise pushed herself gently away and a moment later a small figure in pajamas came onto the terrace. A voice said, "I thought I heard someone talking."

"I imagined you were sleeping," Denise said. "This is Dr. O'Donnell." Then to O'Donnell, "This is my daughter Philippa." She added affectionately, "One half of my impossible twins."

The girl looked at O'Donnell with frank curiosity. "Hullo," she said, "I've heard about you."

O'Donnell remembered Denise telling him that both her children were seventeen. The girl seemed small for her age, her body only just beginning to fill out. But she moved with a grace and posture uncannily similar to her mother.

"Hullo, Philippa," he said. "I'm sorry if we disturbed you."

"I couldn't sleep, so I was reading." The girl glanced down at a book in her hand. "It's Herrick. Did you ever read it?"

"I don't think so," O'Donnell said. "As a matter of fact, there wasn't much time for poetry in medical school and I've never really got around to it since."

Philippa picked up the book and opened it. "There's something here for you, Mother." She read attractively with a feeling for words and balance and with a touch of lightness.

> *"That age is best, which is the first,*
> *When youth and blood are warmer;*
> *But being spent, the worse, and worst*
> *Time, still succeed the former.*

> *Then be not coy, but use your time;*
> *And while ye may, go marry:*
> *For having lost but once your prime,*
> *You may for ever tarry."*

"I get the point," Denise said. She turned to O'Donnell. "I may tell you, Kent, that my children are perennially pressing me to remarry."

"We simply think it's the best thing for you," Philippa interjected. She put down the book.

"They do it under the guise of practicality," Denise went on. "Actually they're both revoltingly sentimental." She turned to Philippa. "How would you feel if I married Dr. O'Donnell?"

"Has he asked you?" Philippa's interest was prompt. Without waiting for an answer she exclaimed, "You're going to, of course."

"It will depend, dear," Denise said. "There is, of course, the trifling matter of a divorce to be arranged."

"Oh, that! Daddy was always so unreasonable about *you* doing it. Besides, why do you have to wait?" She faced O'Donnell. "Why don't you just live together? Then you'd have the evidence already arranged and Mother wouldn't have to go away to one of those awful places like Reno."

"There are moments," Denise said, "when I have grave doubts about the value of progressive education. That, I think, will be all." She stepped lightly to Philippa. "Good night, dear."

"Oh, Mother!" the girl said. "Sometimes you're so antediluvian."

"Good night, dear." Denise repeated it firmly.

Philippa turned to O'Donnell. "I guess I have to go."

He said, "It's been a pleasure, Philippa."

The girl came to him. She said artlessly, "If you're going to be my stepfather, I suppose it's all right to kiss you."

He answered, "Why don't we chance it?—whichever way it goes."

He leaned toward her and she kissed him on the lips, then stood back. There was a slight smile, then she said, "You're cute." She warned Denise, "Mother, whatever you do, don't lose this one."

"Philippa!" This time the note of discipline was unmistakable.

Philippa laughed and kissed her mother. Waving airily, she picked up her book of poems and went out.

O'Donnell leaned back against the terrace wall and laughed. At this moment his bachelorhood at Burlington seemed incredibly empty and dull, the prospect of life with Denise in New York more glowingly attractive by the second.

Eighteen

The amputation of Vivian's left leg began at 8:30 A.M. precisely. Punctuality in the operating rooms was something that Dr. O'Donnell had insisted on when he first became chief of surgery at Three Counties, and most surgeons complied with the rule.

The procedure was not complicated, and Lucy Grainger anticipated no problems other than routine. She had already planned to amputate the limb fairly high, well above the knee and in the upper part of the femur. At one point she had considered disarticulating at the hip in the belief that this might give a better chance of getting ahead of the spreading malignancy from the knee. But the disadvantage here would be extreme difficulty later on in fitting an artificial limb to the inadequate stump. That was why she had compromised in planning to leave intact a portion of the thigh.

She had also planned where to cut her flaps so that the flesh would cover the stump adequately. In fact, she had done this last night, sketching out the necessary incisions in her mind, while allowing Vivian to believe that she was making another routine examination.

That had been after she had broken the news to Vivian, of course—a sad, strained session in which the girl at first had been dry-eyed and composed and then, breaking down, had clung to Lucy, her despairing sobs acknowledging that the last barriers of hope had gone. Lucy, although accustomed by training and habit to be clinical and unemotional at such moments, had found herself unusually moved.

The session with the parents subsequently, and later when young Dr. Seddons had come to see her, had been less personal but still troubling. Lucy supposed she would never insulate entirely her own feelings for patients the way some people did, and sometimes she had had to admit to herself that her surface detachment was only a pose, though a necessary one. There was no pose, though, about detachment here in the operating room; that was one place it became essential, and she found herself now, coolly and without personal feelings, assessing the immediate surgical requirements.

The anesthetist, at the head of the operating table, had already given his clearance to proceed. For some minutes now Lucy's assistant—today, one of the hospital interns—had been holding up the leg which was to be removed, so as to allow the blood to drain out as far as possible. Now Lucy began to arrange a pneumatic tourniquet high on the thigh, leaving it, for the moment, loosely in position.

Without being asked the scrub nurse handed scissors across the table, and Lucy began to snip off the bandages which had covered the leg since it had been shaved, then prepped with hexachlorophene, the night before. The bandages fell away and the circulating nurse removed them from the floor.

Lucy glanced at the clock. The leg had been held up, close to vertical, for five minutes and the flesh appeared pale. The intern changed hands and she asked him, "Arms getting tired?"

He grinned behind his face mask. "I wouldn't want to do it for an hour."

The anesthetist had moved to the tourniquet and was looking at Lucy inquiringly. She nodded and said, "Yes, please." The anesthetist began to pump air into the rubber tourniquet, cutting off circulation to the leg, and when he had finished the intern lowered the limb until it rested horizontally on the operating table. Together the intern and scrub nurse draped the patient with a sterile green sheet until only the operative portion of the leg remained exposed. Lucy then began the final prepping, painting the surgical area with alcoholic zephiran.

There was an audience in the O.R. today—two medical students from the university, and Lucy beckoned them closer. The scrub nurse passed a knife, and Lucy began to scrape the tip of the blade against the exposed flesh of the thigh, talking as she worked.

"You'll notice that I'm marking the level of the flaps by scratching them on first. That's to give us our landmarks." Now she began to cut more deeply, exposing the fascia immediately below the skin, with its layer of yellow fatty tissue. "It's important always to make the front flap longer than the back one, so that afterward the suture line comes a little posterially. In that way the patient won't have a scar right at the end of the stump. If we did leave a scar in that position it could be extremely sore when any weight was put upon it."

Now the flesh was cut deeply, the lines of both flaps defined by the blood which had begun to seep out. The effect, front and rear, was rather like two shirttails—one long, one short—which eventually would be brought together and sewn neatly at their edges.

Using a scalpel and working with short, sharp movements, Lucy began to strip back the flesh, upward, exposing the bloody red mass of underlying tissue.

"Rake, please!" The scrub nurse passed the instrument and Lucy positioned it, holding back the loose, cut flesh, clear of the next layer below. She signaled to the intern to hold the rake in place, which he did, and she applied herself to cutting deeper, through the first layer of quadriceps muscle.

"In a moment we shall expose the main arteries. Yes, here we are—first the femoral vessel." As Lucy located it the two medical students leaned forward intently. She went on calmly, matching her action to the words. "We'll try to free the vessels as high up as possible, then pull them down and tie off so that they retract well clear of the stump." The needle which the scrub nurse had passed danced in and out. Lucy tied the big vessels twice to be sure they were secure and would remain so; any later hemorrhage in this area could be catastrophic for the patient. Then, holding her hand for scissors, she took them and severed the main artery leading to the lower limb. The first irrevocable step to amputation had now been taken.

The same procedure followed quickly for the other arteries and veins. Then, cutting again through muscle, Lucy reached and exposed the nerve running parallel downward. As her gloved hands ran over it exploringly, Vivian's body stirred suddenly on the table and all eyes switched quickly to the anesthetist at its head. He nodded reassuringly. "The patient's doing fine; no problems." One of his hands was against Vivian's cheek; it was pale, but her breathing was deep and regular. Her eyes were open but unseeing; with her head fully back, untilted to one side or the other, the pockets of her eyes were deep with water—her own tears, shed in unconsciousness.

"We follow the same procedure with the nerve, as with the arteries and veins—pull it down, tie it off as high as possible, then cut and allow it to retract." Lucy was talking almost automatically, the words following her hands, the habit of teaching strong. She went on calmly, "There's always been a lot of discussion among surgeons on the best way to treat nerve ends during amputation. The object, naturally, is to avoid pain afterward at the stump." She deftly tied a knot and nodded to the intern, who snipped off the spare ends of suture. "Quite a few methods have been tried—injection of alcohol; burning the nerve end with an electric cautery; but the method we're following today is still the simplest and most widely used."

Lucy glanced up at the clock on the O.R. wall. It showed 9:15—forty-five minutes so far since they had begun. She returned her eyes by way of the anesthetist.

"Still all right?"

The anesthetist nodded. "Couldn't be better, Lucy. She's a real healthy girl." Facetiously he asked, "You sure you're taking the leg off the right patient?"

"I'm sure."

Lucy had never enjoyed operating-room jokes about patients on the table, though she had known some surgeons who wisecracked their way from first incision to closure. She supposed it was all in your point of view. Perhaps with some people levity was a means to cover up deeper feelings, perhaps not. At any rate she preferred to change the subject. Beginning to cut the muscles at the back of the leg, she asked the anesthetist, "How's your family?" Lucy paused to use a second rake to hold back the flesh from the new incision.

"They're fine. We're moving into a new house next week."

"Oh, really. Whereabouts?" To the intern she said, "A little higher, please. Try to hold it back right out of the way."

"Somerset Heights. It's a new subdivision in the north end."

The back leg muscles were almost severed. She said, "I think I've heard of it. I expect your wife is pleased."

Now the bone was visible, the whole incision big, red, gaping. The anesthetist answered, "She's in seventh heaven—buying rugs, choosing draperies, all the other things. There's only one problem."

Lucy's fingers went around the leg bone, working up and freeing the surrounding muscles. Speaking for the students' benefit, she said, "You'll notice that I'm pushing the muscles as far out of the way as I can. Then we can sever the bone quite high so that afterward it will be entirely covered with muscle."

The intern was having trouble holding back the overlapping muscles with his two rakes. She helped him position them and he gumbled, "Next time I do this I'll bring my third hand."

"Saw, please."

Again the scrub nurse was ready, placing the handle of the bone saw in Lucy's outstretched palm. To the anesthetist Lucy said, "What problem is that?"

Positioning the saw blade as high as she could, Lucy began to move it in short, even strokes. There was the dull, penetrating sound of bone scrunching as the saw teeth bit inward. The anesthetist said, "Paying for it all."

Lucy laughed. "We'll have to keep you busier—schedule more surgery." She had sawed halfway through the bone now; it was proving tougher than some, but of course young bones were naturally hard. Suddenly the thought occurred to her: this is a moment of tragedy, and yet here we are, casually talking, even jesting, about commonplace things. In a second or two, no more, this leg would be severed and a young girl—little more than a child—would have lost, for always, a part of her life. Never again would she run freely, wholly like other people, or dance, or swim, or ride horseback, or, uninhibited, make love. Some of these things she would eventually do, and others with effort and mechanical aid; but nothing again could ever be quite the same—never so gay or free or careless as with the fullness of youth and the body whole. This was the nub of the tragedy: it had happened too soon.

Lucy paused. Her sensitive fingers told her that the saw cut was almost complete. Then, abruptly, there was a crunching sound, followed by a sharp crack; at the last moment, under the weight of the almost separated limb, the final fragment of bone had snapped. The limb was free and it fell to the table. For the first time raising her voice, Lucy said, "Catch it! Quickly!"

But the warning was too late. As the intern grabbed and missed, the leg slipped from the operating table and thudded to the floor.

"Leave it there!" Lucy spoke sharply as, forgetful of the fact that he would render himself unsterile, the intern bent to retrieve the limb. Embarrassed, he straightened up.

The circulating nurse moved in, collected the leg, and began to wrap it in gauze and paper. Later, along with more packages containing other surgical specimens, it would be collected by a messenger and taken to Pathology.

"Hold the stump clear of the table, please." Lucy gestured to the intern, and he moved around her to comply. The scrub nurse had a rasp ready, and Lucy took it, feeling for the rough edges of bone that the break had left and applying the rasp to them. Again for the students she said, "Always remember to get the bone end clean, making sure that no little spikes stick out, because if they do, they're likely to overgrow and become extremely painful." Without looking up, she asked, "How are we doing for time?"

The anesthetist answered, "It's been seventy minutes."

Lucy returned the rasp. "All right," she said; "now we can begin to sew up." With the end in sight she found herself thinking gratefully of the coffee which would be waiting in the surgeons' room down the hall.

Mike Seddons had, quite literally, sweated out the period while Vivian was undergoing surgery. With the Loburtons—Vivian's parents had remained in Burlington and planned to stay on for the time being—he had gone to one of the small waiting rooms reserved for relatives of surgical patients. Before that, in the early morning and with the hospital only just beginning to come awake, he had met them at the main doorway and taken them to visit Vivian in her hospital room. But there had seemed little to say, and Vivian, already drowsy from sedation, appeared hardly aware that they were with her. Then, a few minutes after they had come, she was wheeled away to the surgical floor.

Now, in the uneasy backwater of the sparsely furnished room with its uncomfortable leatherette chairs and varnished tables, the three of them had run out of even the most perfunctory conversation. Henry Loburton, tall and

heavily built, his thinning hair iron gray, his face creased and
weathered from years spent in the open air, stood by a window, looking down at the street below. Mike Seddons could
predict that in a moment or two Vivian's father would turn
from the window, go back to one of the leatherette chairs,
then after a while get up and cross to the window again. It
was a sequence the older man had been following for more
than an hour, a slow-fire nervousness that caused Seddons
to wish desperately that he would vary it a little—either
move more quickly or, once in a while, change the interval
of time between the two positions.

In contrast, Vivian's mother had remained still—almost, it
seemed, unmoving since they had come here. She had chosen
a straight-backed chair in preference to some of the others
which appeared more comfortable and held herself upright
in a way that suggested a habit of conscious self-discipline.
As she had for some time now, Angela Loburton was looking directly ahead, her eyes, it seemed, on infinity, her hands
crossed delicately in her lap. Today her color was paler than
usual, but the high cheekbones, which accented a natural
dignity and poise, were as noticeable as ever. At one and the
same time she seemed a woman fragile but indestructible.

Since their first meeting a few days before Mike Seddons
had wondered several times about Mrs. Loburton. Her emotion, her fears about Vivian, had been much less transparent than those of her husband; and yet, as the days went by,
Seddons sensed that they were as deep, perhaps deeper. He
also suspected that, despite the apparent masculinity of Vivian's father, her mother possessed by far the stronger character of the two and that she was the rock on which, over
the years of their marriage, her husband had come to depend.

Seddons found himself wondering how it would be between himself and Vivian in the time ahead. Which of them
would prove, in the end, more resolute and more enduring?
He knew that no two people were ever quite equal, either in
strength of character or in leadership, or even in the capacity
to love. He knew, too, that difference in sex had little to do
with it, that women were often stouter than men in mind and
heart, and that apparent masculinity was sometimes a hollow
pose designed to camouflage internal weakness.

Was Vivian stronger than himself, her character finer, her
courage higher? The question had come to him last night

and had remained with him since. He had gone to see her, knowing the decision had been made to amputate and aware that Vivian knew it too. He had found her, not in tears, but smiling. "Come in, Mike darling," she had said, "and please don't look so glum. Dr. Grainger's told me, and I've done my crying, and it's over now—or at least it will be in the morning."

At the words he had felt his love for her deepen, and he had held her and kissed her passionately. Afterward she had twisted his hair affectionately and, holding his head back, had looked directly into his eyes.

"I'm going to have just one leg, Mike," she had said, "for all the rest of my life. I won't be the girl you met—not as you met me, and not as you know me now. If you want out, I'll understand."

He had answered emphatically, "Don't talk like that!"

"Why?" she had said. "Are you afraid to talk about it?"

"No!" It was a loud, firm protest, but even as he made it he had known it to be a lie. He *was* afraid, just as he sensed that Vivian was not—not now, not any more.

It was a reflection of Vivian, he realized, that he could see now in her mother—or, he supposed, the other way around. The sense of strength was there, unmistakable, in both. Could he match it with his own? For the first time a feeling of uneasy doubt assailed him.

Mr. Loburton had broken his routine. He had stopped halfway between the window and the chair. "Michael," he said, "it's been an hour and a half. Can they be very much longer?"

Seddons found Vivian's mother looking at him too. He shook his head. "I don't believe so. Dr. Grainger said she'd come here . . . immediately after." He paused, then added, "We should all know something—very soon."

Nineteen

Reaching into the incubator through the two porthole-like apertures in its side, Dr. Dornberger carefully examined the Alexander baby. Three and a half days had gone by since birth, a fact which, of itself, might normally be taken as a hopeful sign. But there were other symptoms, increasingly apparent, which Dornberger knew must be looked on with disquiet.

He took his time about completing the examination, then stood back thoughtfully, weighing the available evidence in his mind, filtering it through his long years of experience and the countless other cases now behind him. At the end his reasoning confirmed what instinct had already told him; the prognosis was extremely poor. "You know," he said, "I thought for a while he was going to make it."

The young nurse in charge of the premature nursery—the same nurse whom John Alexander had seen a few days before—had been looking at Dornberger expectantly. She said, "His breathing was quite steady until an hour ago, then it became weak. That was when I called you."

A student nurse around the other side of the incubator was following the conversation closely, her eyes above her gauze mask darting from Dornberger to the charge nurse and back again.

"No, he's not breathing well," Dornberger said slowly. He went on, thinking out loud, trying to be sure there was nothing he had missed, "There's more jaundice than there should be, and the feet seem swollen. Tell me again—what was the blood count?"

The charge nurse consulted her clip board. "R.B.C. four point nine million. Seven nucleated red cells per hundred white."

There was another pause, the two nurses watching while Dornberger digested the information. He was thinking: There's altogether too much anemia, though of course it might be an exaggerated normal-type reaction. Aloud he said, "You know, if it weren't for that sensitivity report I'd suspect this child had erythroblastosis."

The charge nurse looked surprised. She said, "But surely, Doctor," then checked herself.

"I know—it couldn't happen." He motioned to the clip board. "All the same, let me see that lab report—the original one on the mother's blood."

Turning over several sheets, the charge nurse found the form and extracted it. It was the report which Dr. Pearson had signed following the altercation with David Coleman. Dornberger studied it carefully, then handed it back. "Well, that's definite enough—negative sensitivity."

It should be definite, of course; but at the back of his mind was a nagging thought: Could the report be wrong? Impossible, he told himself; the pathology department would never make a mistake like that. All the same, he decided, he would drop in and talk with Joe Pearson after rounds.

To the charge nurse Dornberger said, "There's nothing more we can do at the moment. Call me again, please, if there's any change."

"Yes, Doctor."

When Dornberger had gone the student nurse asked, "What was it the doctor said—erythro . . . ?" She stumbled on the word.

"Erythroblastosis—it's a blood disease in babies. It happens sometimes when the mother's blood is Rh negative and the father's Rh positive." The young charge nurse with the red hair answered the question carefully but confidently, as she always did. The students liked being assigned to her; as well as having a reputation for being one of the most able nurses on staff, she was little more than twelve months away from her own student days, having graduated at the top of the senior class the year before. Knowing this, the student had no hesitation in extending her questioning.

"I thought when that happened they changed the baby's blood at birth."

"You mean by an exchange transfusion?"

"Yes."

"That only happens in some cases." The charge nurse went on patiently, "It may depend on the sensitization report on the mother's blood. If the report is positive, it usually means the baby will be born with erythroblastosis and must be given an exchange transfusion immediately after birth. In this case the lab report was negative, so an exchange transfusion wasn't necessary." The charge nurse stopped. Then she added, thoughtfully, half to herself, "It's strange, though, about those symptoms."

Since their argument of several days ago on the subject of laboratory checks the senior pathologist had made no reference to David Coleman's activities in the serology lab. Coleman had no idea what this silence implied—whether he had achieved his point and was to have direct charge of Serology, or if Pearson intended to return to the attack later. Meanwhile, though, the younger pathologist had fallen into the habit of dropping into the lab regularly and reviewing the work being done. As a result he had already formulated several ideas for changes in procedure, and some of the minor ones had been put into effect during the last day or two.

Between himself and Carl Bannister, the elderly lab technician, there was something with might be considered close to an armed truce. John Alexander, on the other hand, had made it plain that he welcomed Coleman's attention to the lab and in the last two days already had made a few suggestions which Coleman had approved.

Alexander had returned to work the day after his wife had been brought to the hospital, despite a gruff but kindly suggestion from Pearson that he could take time off if he wished. Coleman had heard Alexander tell the old pathologist, "Thank you all the same, Doctor; but if I don't work I'll think too much, and it wouldn't help." Pearson had nodded and said that Alexander could do as he pleased and leave the lab to go upstairs and see his wife and baby whenever he wished.

Now David Coleman opened the door of the serology lab and went in.

He found John Alexander at the center lab bench, looking up from a microscope, and, facing him, a white-coated woman with extremely large breasts whom Coleman recalled vaguely having seen around the hospital several times since his own arrival.

As he entered Alexander was saying, "I think perhaps you should ask Dr. Pearson or Dr. Coleman. I'll be making my report to them."

"What report is that?" As Coleman asked casually, the heads of the other two turned toward him.

The woman spoke first. "Oh, Doctor!" She looked at him inquiringly. "You *are* Dr. Coleman?"

"That's right."

"I'm Hilda Straughan." She offered him her hand and added, "Chief dietitian."

"How do you do." As she shook his hand he noticed, fascinated, that her magnificent breasts moved with her arm —an undulant, whalelike rolling motion. Checking his thoughts, he asked, "Is there some sort of problem we can help you with?" He knew from his own experience that pathologists and dietitians usually worked closely in matters of food hygiene.

"There's been a lot of intestinal flu these past few weeks," the dietitian said. She added, "Mostly among the hospital staff."

Coleman laughed. "Tell me a hospital where it doesn't happen now and again."

"Oh, I know." Mrs. Straughan gave the faintest hint of disapproval at the flippancy. "But if food is the reason—and it usually is—I like to pin down the cause if it's possible. Then one can try to prevent the same thing occurring again."

There was an earnestness about this woman which David Coleman found himself respecting. He asked politely, "Do you have any ideas?"

"Very definitely. I suspect my dishwashing machines, Dr. C."

For a moment Coleman was startled at the form of address. Then, recovering, he asked, "Oh, why?" Out of the corner of his eye he saw Bannister enter the room. Now both lab technicians were listening to the conversation.

The dietitian said, "My hot-water booster system is quite inadequate."

The phraseology tempted him to smile, but he resisted it and asked instead, "Has anyone ever pointed that out?"

"I certainly have, Dr. C." Obviously this was a subject on which Mrs. Straughan had strong feelings. She went on, "I've talked to the administrator, Mr. Tomaselli, on several occasions. It was my last talk with Mr. T., in fact, which caused him to ask Dr. Pearson for new lab tests on the dishwashers."

"I see." Coleman turned to John Alexander. "Did you run some tests?"

"Yes, Doctor."

"What did you find?"

"The water temperature *isn't* high enough." Alexander consulted a clip board holding several pages of notes. "I did three tests on each dishwasher, each at a different time of day, and the temperature range was 110 to 130 degrees."

"You see?" The dietitian held up her hands expressively.

"Oh yes." Coleman nodded. "That's much too low."

"That isn't all, Doctor." John Alexander had put the clip

board down and taken a slide from the lab bench. "I'm afraid I've found gas formers of the fecal group. On the plates—*after* they've been through the dishwashers."

"Let me see." Coleman took the slide and moved to the microscope. When he had adjusted the eyepiece the charateristic worm-like bacteria were visible at once. He straightened up.

Mrs. Straughan asked, "What is it? What does it mean?"

Coleman said thoughtfully, "The slide shows gas-forming bacteria. Normally the hot water should destroy them, but as it is they're getting through the dishwashers onto your clean plates."

"Is that serious?"

He considered carefully before answering. "Yes and no. It probably accounts for some of the intestinal flu you spoke of, but that's not too serious in itself. The way in which it might become dangerous is if we happened to get a disease carrier in the hospital."

"A disease carrier?"

Coleman went on to explain. "It's someone who carries disease germs in their body without having the clinical disease themselves. A carrier can be an apparently normal, healthy person. It happens more frequently than you'd think."

"Yes, I see what you mean," Mrs. Straughan said thoughtfully.

Coleman had turned to the two technicians. He asked, "I suppose we *are* doing regular lab checks on all food handlers in the hospital?"

Bannister answered, self-importantly, "Oh yes. Dr. Pearson's very fussy about that."

"Are we right up to date?"

"Yeah." The senior technician thought, then added, "Don't think we've had any for quite a while."

"When was the last?" Coleman asked the question casually, as a matter of routine.

"Just a minute. I'll look at the book." Bannister crossed to the opposite side of the lab.

In his mind David Coleman was weighing the factors involved. If the dishwashers were inefficient—and they appeared to be—something needed to be done promptly; there was no question about that. On the other hand, as long as a careful check was being kept on food handlers—and, according to Bannister, it was—there was no real reason for alarm.

Indifference, though, was something else again. He told John Alexander, "You'd better get your report to Dr. Pearson as soon as you can."

"Yes, Doctor." Alexander went back to his clip board of notes.

Across the room Bannister looked up from a ruled ledger he had spread open on a file cabinet. He called out, "February the twenty-fourth."

Surprised, Coleman asked, "Did you say February?"

"That's right."

"That's almost six months ago." To the dietitian he observed, "You don't appear to have much of a turnover in kitchen staff."

"Oh yes, we do—unfortunately." Mrs. Straughan shook her head emphatically. "We've taken on a lot of new people since February, Dr. C."

Still not understanding, Coleman asked Bannister, "Are you sure about that date?"

"That's the last one." Bannister was cockily sure of himself. It was a pleasing change to be able to tell something to this know-all young doctor. He added, "See for yourself if you like."

Ignoring the suggestion, Coleman said, "But what about the new employees—those who've been taken on since then?"

"There's nothing else here." Bannister shrugged. "If the health office doesn't send us specimens for test, we've no way of knowing about new food handlers." His attitude was one of complete indifference, almost contempt.

A slow burn was rising in Coleman. Controlling it, he said evenly to the dietitian, "I think this is a matter you should look into." For the first time he had begun to realize that something, somewhere, was seriously wrong.

Mrs. Straughan appeared to have had the same thought. She said, "I will—immediately. Thank you, Dr. C." Her breasts bouncing with each step, she went out of the lab.

There was a moment's silence. For the first time Coleman sensed a feeling of unease in Bannister. As their eyes met he asked the technician icily, "Had it occurred to you to wonder *why* no tests for food handlers were coming in?"

"Well . . ." Bannister fidgeted, his earlier confidence evaporated. "I guess I would have—sooner or later."

Coleman surveyed the other with disgust. He said angrily, "I'd say later, wouldn't you?—especially in it meant that you

would have had to do some thinking." At the door he turned.
"I'll be with Dr. Pearson."

The color drained from his face, the older technician still
stood, looking at the door through which Coleman had gone.
His lips framed words—bitter and defeated. "He knows it
all, don't he? Everything in the book. Every perishing thing."

At this moment around Bannister was an aura of failure
and downfall. His own familiar world—the world he had believed inviolate and therefore had done nothing to protect—
was crumbling. A new order was emerging, and in the new
order, through his own shortcoming, there was no room
for himself. Crestfallen, out of place, he appeared only a
weak, pathetic figure whom time was passing by.

Joe Pearson looked up from his desk as Coleman came in.

Without preliminary the younger pathologist announced,
"John Alexander has found gas-forming bacteria—on clean
plates which have been through the dishwasher."

Pearson seemed unsurprised. He said dourly, "It's the hot-
water system."

"I know." David Coleman tried, but failed, to keep sarcasm from his voice. "Has anyone ever tried to do something
about it?"

The old man was looking at him quizzically. He said, with
surprising quietness, "I suppose you think things are run
pretty poorly around here."

"Since you ask me—yes." Coleman's own lips were tight.
He wondered how long the two of them could continue
working together in this kind of atmosphere.

Pearson had flung open a lower drawer of his desk, fumbling among files and papers, talking as he searched. He
seemed to be speaking with a strange mixture of anger and
sorrow. "You're so young and green and full of lofty ideas.
You come here, and it happens to be a time when there's a
new administration, when money is freer than it has been in
years. So you figure that whatever's wrong is because nobody has thought of changing it. Nobody's tried!" He had
found what he wanted and flung a bulging file of papers on
the desk.

"I didn't say that." The words were snapped out, almost
defensively.

Pearson pushed the file toward him. "This is a record of
correspondence about the kitchen hot-water supply. If you'll

take the trouble to read it, you'll find I've been pleading for a new system for years." Pearson's voice rose. He said challengingly, "Go ahead—take a look!"

Opening the file, Coleman read the top memo. He turned a page, then another, then skimmed the other pages beneath. At once he realized how much in error he had been. The memos contained a damning condemnation by Pearson of hospital kitchen hygiene, couched in even stronger terms than he would have used himself. The correspondence appeared to go back several years.

"Well?" Pearson had been watching as he read.

Without hesitation Coleman said, "I'm sorry. I owe you an apology—about that anyway."

"Never mind." Pearson waved his hand irritably, then as the words sank in, "You mean there's something else?"

Coleman said evenly, "In finding out about the dishwashers I also discovered there haven't been any lab tests of food handlers for more than six months."

"Why?" The question rapped out like a sharp explosion.

"Apparently none were sent down from the health office. The chief dietitian is checking on that now."

"And you mean we didn't query it? Nobody in Pathology asked why none were coming?"

"Apparently not."

"That fool Bannister! This is serious." Pearson was genuinely concerned, his earlier hostility to Coleman forgotten.

Coleman said quietly, "I thought you'd want to know."

Pearson had picked up the telephone. After a pause he said, "Get me the administrator."

The conversation which followed was brief and to the point. At the end Pearson replaced the phone and stood up. To Coleman he said, "Tomaselli is on his way down. Let's meet him in the lab."

It took only a few minutes in the lab to run over, for a second time, what David Coleman had already learned. With Pearson and Harry Tomaselli listening, John Alexander recapped his notes and Pearson inspected the slides. As he straightened up from the microscope the chief dietitian entered the lab. The administrator turned to her. "What did you find out?"

"It's incredible but true." Mrs. Straughan shook her head in a gesture of unbelief. She addressed Pearson. "Earlier this

year the health office hired a new clerk. Dr. P. Nobody told
her about lab tests on food handlers. That's the reason none
were sent down."

Tomaselli said, "So there have been no tests now for—
how long?"

"Approximately six and a half months."

Coleman noticed Carl Bannister standing dourly away from
the group, apparently occupied, but he sensed the senior
technician was missing nothing of what was going on.

The administrator asked Pearson, "What do you suggest?"

"There should be a checkup first on all the new employees—as quickly as possible." This time the elder pathologist was incisive and brisk. "After that there will have to
be re-examination of all the others. That means stool culture,
chest X-ray, and a physical. And it should include all the
kitchen workers and anyone else who has anything to do
with food at all."

"Will you arrange that, Mrs. Straughan?" Tomaselli said.
"Work with the health office; they'll handle most of the detail."

"Yes, Mr. T. I'll get onto it right away." She undulated
out of the lab.

"Is there anything else?" Tomaselli had returned his attention to Pearson.

"We need a new steam booster system for those dishwashers—either that or rip them right out and put new
ones in." Pearson's voice rose heatedly. "I've been telling
everybody that for years."

"I know." Tomaselli nodded. "I inherited the file, and it's
on our list. The trouble is, we've had so many capital expenditures." He mused. "I wonder what the comparative cost
would be."

Unreasonably, irritably, Pearson said, "How should I
know? I'm not the plumber."

"I know a little about plumbing; perhaps I can help." At
the softly spoken words the others turned their heads. It
was Dr. Dornberger, his hands, inevitably, busy with his
pipe. He had come into the lab quietly and unnoticed.
Seeing Harry Tomaselli, he asked, "Am I interrupting something?"

Pearson said gruffly, "No. It's all right."

Dornberger saw John Alexander watching him. He said,

"I was with your baby awhile ago, son. I'm afraid he's not doing too well."

"Is there any hope, Doctor?" Alexander asked the question quietly. The others had turned, their expressions softening. Bannister put down a glass pipette and moved closer.

"Not very much, I'm afraid," Dornberger said slowly. There was a silence, then, as if remembering something, he turned to Pearson. "I suppose, Joe, there couldn't be any doubt about that blood-sensitization test on Mrs. Alexander?"

"Doubt?"

"I mean, that it could be wrong."

Pearson shook his head. "No doubt at all, Charlie. Matter of fact, I did it myself—very carefully." He added curiously, "Why did you ask?"

"Just checking." Dornberger puffed at his pipe. "For a while this morning I suspected the child might have had erythroblastosis. It was only a long shot though."

"Be highly unlikely." Pearson was emphatic.

Dornberger said, "Yes, that's what I thought."

Again the silence, their eyes turning to Alexander. David Coleman felt he wanted to say something—anything to divert attention, to make things easier for the young technologist. He told Dornberger, almost without thinking, "There used to be some doubt about sensitization tests—when labs were using just the saline and high-protein methods. Sometimes then a few positive cases would get recorded as negative. Nowadays, though, with an indirect Coombs test as well, it's pretty well foolproof." As he finished speaking, he realized that this lab had only made the change since his own arrival. He had not meant to take a dig at Pearson; at this moment he found himself hoping the old man would not notice. There had been enough quarreling between them without adding to it needlessly.

"But, Dr. Coleman . . ." Alexander's mouth was gaping, his eyes alarmed.

"Yes? What is it?" Coleman was puzzled. Nothing he had said was enough to produce this reaction.

"We didn't do an indirect Coombs test."

Despite his concern for Alexander, Coleman found himself becoming annoyed. Because of Pearson he had wanted to avoid pursuing this subject. Now he was being given no choice. "Oh yes, you did," he said offhandedly. "I remember signing the requisition for Coombs serum."

Alexander was looking at him despairingly, his eyes pleading. He said, "But Dr. Pearson said it wasn't necessary. The test was done just in saline and high protein."

It took Coleman several seconds to absorb what had been said. He saw that Harry Tomaselli, not understanding, was watching the scene curiously. Dornberger's attention had suddenly perked up.

Pearson appeared uncomfortable. He said to Coleman, with a trace of unease, "I meant to tell you at the time. It slipped my mind."

David Coleman's brain was now ice-clear. But before going further he wanted to establish one fact. "Do I understand correctly," he asked Alexander, "that there was no indirect Coombs test whatever?"

As Alexander nodded Dr. Dornberger cut in abruptly. "Wait a minute! Let me get this straight. You mean the mother—Mrs. Alexander—may have sensitized blood after all?"

"Of course she may!" Not caring, Coleman lashed out, his voice rising in pitch. "The saline and high-protein tests are good in a lot of cases but not in all. Anybody who's kept reasonably up to date in hematology should be aware of that." He glanced sideways at Pearson, who appeared not to have stirred. To Dornberger he went on, "That's why I ordered an indirect Coombs."

The administrator was still trying to grasp the medical significance. "This test you're talking about; if you ordered it, why wasn't it done?"

Coleman wheeled on Bannister. His eyes merciless, he asked, "What happened to the requisition I signed—the requisition for Coombs serum?" As the technician hesitated, "Well?"

Bannister was shaking. Barely audible, he mumbled, "I tore it up."

Dornberger said incredulously, "You tore up a doctor's requisition—and without telling him?"

Relentlessly Coleman said, "On whose instructions did you tear it up?"

Bannister was looking at the floor. He said reluctantly, "On Dr. Pearson's instructions."

Dornberger was thinking quickly now. To Coleman he said, "This means the child may have erythroblastosis; everything points to it, in fact."

"Then you'll do an exchange transfusion?"

Dornberger said bitterly, "If it was necessary at all, it should have been done at birth. But there may be a chance, even this late." He looked at the young pathologist as if, by implication, only Coleman's opinion could be trusted. "But I want to be sure. The child hasn't any strength to spare."

"We need a direct Coombs test of the baby's blood." Coleman's reaction was fast and competent. This scene was between himself and Dornberger now; Pearson was standing still, as if dazed by the swiftness of what had happened. To Bannister, Coleman rapped out, "Is there any Coombs serum in the hospital?"

The technician swallowed. "No."

This was something within the administrator's orbit. He asked tersely, "Where do we get it then?"

"There isn't time." Coleman shook his head. "We'll have to get the test done somewhere else—where they've facilities."

"University will do it; they've a bigger lab than ours anyway." Harry Tomaselli had crossed to the telephone. He told the operator, "Get me University Hospital, please." To the others he said, "Who's in charge of pathology there?"

Dornberger said, "Dr. Franz."

"Dr. Franz, please." Tomaselli asked, "Who'll talk with him?"

"I will." Coleman took the phone. The others heard him say, "Dr. Franz? This is Dr. Coleman—assistant pathologist at Three Counties. Could you handle an emergency Coombs test for us?" There was a pause, Coleman listening. Then he said, "Yes, we'll send the sample immediately. Thank you, Doctor. Good-by." He turned back to the room. "We'll need the blood sample quickly."

"I'll help you, Doctor." It was Bannister, a tray of equipment in his hands.

About to reject the offer, Coleman saw the mute appeal in the other man's eyes. He hesitated, then said, "Very well. Come with me."

As they left the administrator called after them. "I'll get a police cruiser. They'll get the sample over there faster."

"Please! I'd like to take it—to go with them." It was John Alexander.

"All right." The administrator had the telephone to his ear. Into it he snapped, "Get me the City Police." To Alexander he said, "Go with the others, then bring the blood sample to the emergency entrance. I'll have the cruiser waiting there."

"Yes, sir." Alexander went out quickly.

"This is the administrator, Three Counties Hospital." Tomaselli was talking into the phone again. "We'd like a police car to deliver an urgent blood sample." He listened briefly. "Yes; our people will be waiting at the emergency entrance. Right." Hanging up the phone, he said, "I'd better make sure they all get together." He went out, leaving Pearson and Dornberger alone.

Within the past few moments a ferment of thoughts had been seething in the elderly obstetrician's mind. Inevitably, in his long years of medical practice, Charles Dornberger had had patients die. Sometimes about their deaths there had seemed almost a predestination. But always he had fought for their lives, at times savagely, and never giving up until the end. And in all occasions—successes as well as failures —he could tell himself truthfully that he had behaved with honor, his standards high, nothing left to chance, the utmost of his skill expended always. There were other physicians, he knew, who were sometimes less exacting. But never, to the best of his own knowledge and belief, had Charles Dornberger failed a patient through inadequacy or neglect.

Until this moment.

Now, it seemed, near the close of his own career, he was to share the sad and bitter harvest of another man's incompetence; and worse—a man who was a friend.

"Joe," he said, "there's something I'd like you to know."

Pearson had lowered himself to a lab stool, his face drained of color, his eyes unfocused. Now he looked up slowly.

"This was a premature baby, Joe; but it was normal, and we could have done an exchange transfusion right after birth." Dornberger paused, and when he went on the turmoil of his own emotions was in his voice. "Joe, we've been friends a long time, and sometimes I've covered up for you, and I've helped you fight your battles. But this time, if this baby dies, so help me God!—I'll take you before the medical board and I'll break you in two."

Twenty

"For Christ sake, what are they doing over there? Why haven't we heard yet?"

Dr. Joseph Pearson's fingers drummed a nervous tattoo
upon his office desk. It was an hour and a quarter since the
blood sample had been taken from the Alexander baby and
promptly dispatched to University Hospital. Now the elder
pathologist and David Coleman were alone in the office.

Coleman said quietly, "I called Dr. Franz a second time.
He said he'll phone the moment they have a result."

Pearson nodded dully. He asked, "Where's the boy—Alexander?"

"The police drove him back. He's with his wife." Coleman hesitated. "While we're waiting—do you think we
should check with the health office about the kitchen situation, make sure the foodhandler checks are being started?"

Pearson shook his head. "Later—when all this is over." He
said intensely, "I can't think of anything else until this thing
is settled."

For the first time since this morning's events, which had
erupted so explosively in the lab, David Coleman found himself wondering about Pearson and what the older man was
feeling. There had been no argument about the validity of
Coleman's statements concerning the sensitization test, and
Pearson's silence on the subject seemed a tacit admission
that his younger colleague was better informed than himself, at any rate in this area. Coleman thought: It must be a
bitter thing to face; and for the first time he felt a stirring of
sympathy for the other man.

Pearson stopped drumming and slammed his hand hard
on the table. "For Pete's sake," he said, "why don't they
call?"

"Is there any news from Pathology?"

Dr. Charles Dornberger, scrubbed and waiting in a small
operating room which adjoined Obstetrics, asked the question of the charge nurse who had entered.

The girl shook her head. "No, Doctor."

"How close are we to being ready?"

The nurse filled two rubber hot-water bottles and placed them beneath a blanket on the tiny operating table that was used for infants. She answered, "Just a few minutes more."

An intern had joined Dornberger. The intern asked, "Do you intend to go ahead with an exchange transfusion—even if you don't have the Coombs test result?"

"Yes," Dornberger answered. "We've lost enough time already and I don't want to add to it." He considered, then went on, "In any case, the anemia in the child now is sufficiently marked to justify a blood exchange even without the test."

The nurse said, "By the way, Doctor, the baby's umbilical cord has been cut short. I wondered if you knew that."

"Yes, thank you, I did." To the intern Dornberger explained, "When we know in advance that an exchange transfusion will be necessary, we leave the umbilical cord long at birth. It makes a convenient point of connection. Unfortunately in this case we didn't know, so the cord was cut."

"How will you proceed?" the intern asked.

"I'll use a local anesthetic and cut down just above the umbilical vein." Turning back to the nurse, Dornberger asked, "Is the blood being warmed?"

She nodded. "Yes, Doctor."

Dornberger told the intern, "It's important to make sure the new blood is close to body temperature. Otherwise it increases the danger of shock."

In a separate compartment of his mind Dornberger was aware that he was talking as much for his own benefit as for the instruction of the intern. Talking at least prevented him from thinking too deeply, and for the moment deep thinking was something Charles Dornberger wanted to avoid. Since he had left Pearson after the showdown in the lab his own mind had been engaged in a torment of anxiety and recrimination. The fact that, technically, he himself was not to blame for what had happened seemed unimportant. It was *his* patient who was in jeopardy, his patient that might die because of the worst kind of medical negligence, and the ultimate responsibility was his alone.

About to continue talking, Dornberger checked himself abruptly. Something was wrong; he had a feeling of dizziness; his head was throbbing, the room swirling. Momentarily he closed his eyes, then opened them. It was all right; things were back in focus, the dizziness almost gone. But when he looked down at his hands he saw they were trembling. He tried to control the movement and failed.

The incubator containing the Alexander baby was being wheeled in. At the same moment he heard the intern ask, "Dr. Dornberger—are you all right?"

It was on the edge of his tongue to answer "yes." He knew that if he did he could carry on, concealing what had happened, with no one but himself aware of it. And then perhaps, even at this late moment, by exercise of skill and judgment he could save this child, salving, at least in some measure, his conscience and integrity.

Then, in the same moment, he remembered all that he had said and believed over the years—about old men clinging to power too long; the boast that when his own time came he would know it and make way; his conviction that he would never handle a case with his own facilities impaired. He thought of these things, then looked down at his shaking hands.

"No," he said, "I don't think I am all right." He paused, and aware for the first time of a deep emotion which made it hard to control his voice, he asked, "Will someone please call Dr. O'Donnell? Tell him I'm unable to go on. I'd like him to take over."

At that moment, in fact and in heart, Dr. Charles Dornberger retired from the practice of medicine.

As the telephone bell rang Pearson snatched the instrument from its cradle.

"Yes?" A pause. "This is Dr. Pearson." He listened. "Very well. Thanks."

Without putting the receiver back he flashed the exchange and asked for an extension number. There was a click, then an answer, and Pearson said, "Get me Dr. Dornberger. It's Dr. Pearson calling."

A voice spoke briefly, then Pearson said, "All right, then give him a message. Tell him I've just heard from the university. The blood test on the Alexander baby is positive. The child has erythroblastosis."

Pearson replaced the phone. Then he looked up, to find David Coleman's eyes upon him.

Dr. Kent O'Donnell was striding through the hospital's main floor on his way to Neurology. He had arranged a consultation there to discuss a partial paralysis condition in one of his own patients.

It was O'Donnell's first day back at Three Counties after his return from New York the evening before. He still felt a sense of exhilaration and freshness from his trip; a change of scene, he told himself, was what every physician needed now and then. Sometimes the daily contact with medicine and sickness could become a depressive, wearing you down after a while without your own awareness of its happening. In the larger sense, too, a change was invigorating and broadening for the mind. And akin to this, more and more since his New York meeting with Denise, the question of ending his own tenure at Three Counties, and of leaving Burlington for good, had kept coming back, to be assessed and weighed in mind, and each time the arguments in favor of a move had seemed more convincing. He knew, of course, that he was strongly motivated by his feelings for Denise and that even until their latest meeting the thought of leaving Burlington had not occurred to him. But he asked himself: was there anything wrong with an individual making a professional choice which weighed in favor of personal happiness? It was not as if he would be quitting medicine; he would merely be changing his base of operations and giving of his best elsewhere. After all, any man's life was the sum of all its parts; without love, if once he found it, the rest of him might wither and be worthless. With love he could be a better man—zealous and devoted—because his life was whole. Again he thought of Denise with a rising sense of excitement and anticipation.

"Dr. O'Donnell. Dr. O'Donnell."

The sound of his own name on the hospital P.A. system brought him back to reality. He stopped, looking around him for a telephone on which to acknowledge the call. He saw one in a glass-enclosed accounting office a few yards away. Going in to use it, he reported to the telephone exchange and a moment later was given Dornberger's message. Responding promptly, he changed direction and headed for the elevators which would take him to the fourth floor and Obstetrics.

While Kent O'Donnell scrubbed, Dornberger, standing alongside, described what had happened in the case and his own reason for calling in the chief of surgery. Dornberger neither dramatized nor held anything back; he related the scene in the pathology lab, as well as the events leading up to it, accurately and without emotion. Only at two points did O'Donnell stop him to interject sharp questions; the remainder of the time he listened carefully, his expression growing grimmer as Dornberger's account proceeded.

O'Donnell's mood of elation was gone now, shattered suddenly and incredibly by what he had learned, by the knowledge that negligence and ignorance—for which, in a very real sense, he himself was responsible—might snuff out the life of a patient in this hospital. He thought bitterly: I could have fired Joe Pearson; there was plenty of reason to. But no! I dallied and procrastinated, playing politics, convincing myself I was behaving reasonably, while all the time I was selling medicine short. He took a sterile towel and dried his hands, then plunged them into gloves which a nurse held out. "All right," he told Dornberger. "Let's go in."

Entering the small operating room, O'Donnell ran his eye over the equipment which had been made ready. He was familiar with exchange-transfusion technique—a fact which Dornberger had known in calling for the chief of surgery—having worked with the heads of Pediatrics and Obstetrics in establishing a standard procedure at Three Counties, based on experience in other hospitals.

The tiny, frail Alexander baby had been taken from its incubator and placed on the warm operating table. Now the assisting nurse, with the intern helping her, was securing the infant in place, using diapers—one around each arm and leg —folded in long narrow strips and fastened with safety pins to the cover of the table. O'Donnell noticed the baby lay very still, making only the slightest of responses to what was being done. In a child so small it was not a hopeful sign.

The nurse unfolded a sterile sheet and draped it over the infant, leaving exposed only the head and navel, the latter area still in process of healing where the umbilical cord had been severed at birth. A local anesthetic had already been administered. Now the girl passed forceps to O'Donnell and, taking them, he picked up a gauze pad and began to prep the operative area. The intern had taken up a clip board and pencil. O'Donnell asked him, "You're going to keep score?"

"Yes, sir."

O'Donnell noticed the tone of respect and in other circum-

stances would have smiled inwardly. Interns and residents—
the hospital's house staff—were a notoriously independent
breed, quick to observe shortcomings in the more senior attending physicians, and to be addressed as "sir" by any of
their number was something of an accolade.

A few minutes ago two student nurses had slipped into the
room and now, following a habit of instruction, O'Donnell
began to describe procedure as he worked.

"An exchange transfusion, as perhaps you know"—O'Donnell glanced toward the student nurses—"is actually a flush-
ing-out process. First we remove some blood from the child,
then replace it with an equivalent amount of donor blood.
After that we do the same thing again and keep doing it
until most of the original, unhealthy blood is gone."

The assisting nurse was inverting a pint bottle of blood on
a stand above the table. O'Donnell said, "The blood bank has
already crossmatched the patient's blood with that of the
donor to ensure that both are compatible. What we must be
sure of also is that we replace exactly the amount of blood
we remove. That's the reason we keep a score sheet." He indicated the intern's clip board.

"Temperature ninety-six," the assisting nurse announced.

O'Donnell said, "Knife, please," and held out his hand.

Using the knife gently, he cut off the dry portion of the
umbilical vein, exposing moist tissue. He put down the knife
and said softly, "Hemostat."

The intern was craning over, watching. O'Donnell said,
"We've isolated the umbilical vein. I'll go into it now and
remove the clot." He held out his hand and the nurse passed
forceps. The blood clot was miniscule, scarcely visible, and
he drew it out, painstakingly and gently. Handling a child
this small was like working with a tiny doll. What were the
chances of success, O'Donnell wondered—of the child's survival. Ordinarily they might have been fair, even good. But
now, with this procedure days late, the hope of success
had been lessened drastically. He glanced at the child's face.
Strangely it was not an ugly face, as the faces of premature children so often were; it was even a little handsome,
with a firm jaw line and a hint of latent strength. For a moment, uncharacteristically allowing his mind to wander, he
thought: What a shame this all is!—to be born with so
much stacked against you.

The assisting nurse was holding a plastic catheter with a needle attached; it was through this that the blood would be drawn off and replaced. O'Donnell took the catheter and with utmost gentleness eased the needle into the umbilical vein. He said, "Check the venous pressure, please."

As he held the catheter vertical, the nurse used a ruler to measure the height of the column of blood. She announced, "Sixty millimeters." The intern wrote it down.

A second plastic tube led to the bottle of blood above them; a third ran to one of the two Monel-metal basins at the foot of the table. Bringing the three tubes together, O'Donnell connected them to a twenty-milliliter syringe with a three-way stopcock at one end. He turned one of the stopcocks through ninety degrees. "Now," he said, "we'll begin withdrawing blood."

His fingers sensitive, he eased the plunger of the syringe toward him gently. This was always a critical moment in an exchange transfusion; if the blood failed to flow freely it would be necessary to remove the catheter and begin the early preparation all over again. Behind him, O'Donnell was conscious of Dornberger leaning forward. Then, smoothly and easily, the blood began to flow, flooding the catheter tube and entering the syringe.

O'Donnell said, "You'll notice that I'm suctioning very slowly and carefully. We'll also remove very little at any one time in this case—because of the smallness of the infant. Normally, with a term baby, we would probably take twenty milliliters at once, but in this instance I shall take only ten, so as to avoid too much fluctuation of the venous pressure."

On his score sheet the intern wrote, 10 ml. out."

Once more O'Donnell turned one of the stopcocks on the syringe, then pressed hard on the plunger. As he did, the blood withdrawn from the child was expelled into one of the metal basins.

Turning the stopcock again, he withdrew donor blood into the syringe, then, tenderly and slowly, injected it into the child.

On his score sheet the intern wrote, 10 ml. in.

Painstakingly O'Donnell went on. Each withdrawal and replacement, accomplished gradually and carefully, took five full minutes. There was a temptation to hurry, particularly in a critical case like this, but O'Donnell was conscious that

speed was something to be shunned. The little body on the
table had small enough resistance already; any effect of
shock could be immediate and fatal.

Then, twenty-five minutes after they had started, the baby
stirred and cried.

It was a frail, thready cry—a weak and feeble protest that
ended almost as soon as it began. But it was a signal of
life, and above the masks of those in the room eyes were
smiling, and somehow hope seemed a trifle closer.

O'Donnell knew better than to jump to hasty conclusions.
Nevertheless, over his shoulder to Dornberger, he said,
"Sounds like he's mad at us. Could be a good sign."

Dornberger too had reacted. He leaned over to read the
intern's score card, then, conscious that he himself was not
in charge, he ventured tentatively, "A little calcium gluco-
nate, do you think?"

"Yes." O'Donnell unscrewed the syringe from the double
stopcock and substituted a ten-cc. syringe of calcium glu-
conate which the nurse had given him. He injected one cc.,
then handed it back. The nurse returned the original syringe
which, in the meantime, she had rinsed in the second metal
bowl.

O'Donnell was conscious of a lessening of tension in the
room. He began to wonder if, after everything, this baby
would pull through. He had seen stranger things happen,
had learned long ago that nothing was impossible, that in
medicine the unexpected was just as often on your side as
against you.

"All right," he said, "let's keep going."

He withdrew ten milliliters, then replaced it. He withdrew
another ten and replaced that. Then another ten—in and out.
And another.

Then, fifty minutes after they had begun, the nurse announced quietly, "The patient's temperature is falling, Doctor. It's ninety-four point three."

He said quickly, "Check the venous pressure."

It was thirty-five—much too low.

"He's not breathing well," the intern said. "Color isn't
good."

O'Donnell told him, "Check the pulse." To the nurse he
said, "Oxygen."

She reached for a rubber mask and held it over the infant's face. A moment later there was a hiss as the oxygen went on.

"Pulse very slow," the intern said.

The nurse said, "Temperature's down to ninety-three."

The intern was listening with a stethoscope. He looked up. "Respiration's failing." Then, a moment later, "He's stopped breathing."

O'Donnell took the stethoscope and listened. He could hear a heartbeat, but it was very faint. He said sharply, "Coramine—one cc."

As the intern turned from the table O'Donnell ripped off the covering sheets and began artificial respiration. In a moment the intern was back. He had wasted no time; in his hand was a hypodermic, poised.

"Straight in the heart," O'Donnell said. "It's our only chance."

In the pathology office Dr. David Coleman was growing restless. He had remained, waiting with Pearson, ever since the telephone message had come announcing the blood-test result. Between them they had disposed of some accumulated surgical reports, but the work had gone slowly, both men knowing that their thoughts were elsewhere. Now close to an hour had gone by and there was still no word.

Fifteen minutes ago Coleman had got up and said tentatively, "Perhaps I should see if there's anything in the lab . . ."

The old man had looked at him, his eyes doglike. Then, almost pleadingly, he had asked, "Would you mind staying?"

Surprised, Coleman had answered, "No; not if you wish," and after that they had gone back to their task of time filling.

For David Coleman, too, the waiting was hard. He knew himself to be almost as tense as Pearson, although at this moment the older man was showing his anxiety more. For the first time Coleman realized how mentally involved he had become in this case. He took no satisfaction from the fact that he had been right and Pearson wrong about the blood test. All he wanted, desperately now, for the sake of the Alexanders, was for their child to live. The force of his own feeling startled him; it was unusual for anything to affect him so deeply. He recalled, though, that he had liked

John Alexander right from the beginning at Three Counties; then later, meeting his wife, knowing that all three of them had had their origins in the same small town, there had seemed to spring up a sense of kinship, unspoken but real.

The time was going slowly, each successive minute of waiting seeming longer than the last. He tried to think of a problem to keep his mind busy; that always helped when you had time to kill. He decided to concentrate on some of the aspects of the Alexander case. Point one, he thought: The fact that the baby's Coombs test now shows positive means that the mother has Rh-sensitized blood also. He speculated on how this might have come about.

The mother, Elizabeth Alexander, could, of course, have become sensitized during her first pregnancy. David Coleman reasoned: It need not have affected their first child; that was the one who had died of—what was it they had told him?— oh yes, bronchitis. It was much more common to find the effect of Rh sensitization during a second pregnancy.

Another possibility, of course, was that Elizabeth might have been given a transfusion of Rh-positive blood at some time or other. He stopped; at the back of his mind was a nagging, unformed thought, an uneasy feeling that he was close to something but could not quite reach it. He concentrated, frowning. Then suddenly the pieces were in place; what he had been groping for was there—vivid and sharply in focus. His mind registered: Transfusions! The accident at New Richmond! The railroad crossing at which Elizabeth's father had been killed, where she herself had been injured but had survived.

Once more Coleman concentrated. He was trying to remember what it was John Alexander had said about Elizabeth that day. The words came back to him: *Elizabeth almost died. But they gave her blood transfusions and she made it. I think that was the first time I was ever in a hospital. I almost lived there for a week.*

It could never be proved, of course, not after all this time; but he was willing to wager everything he had that that was the way it happened. He thought: Existence of the Rh factor only became known to medicine in the 1940s; after that it took another ten years before Rh testing was generally adopted by all hospitals and doctors. In the meantime, there were plenty of places where blood transfusions were given without an Rh cross match; New Richmond was probably one. The time fitted. The accident involving Elizabeth would have been in 1949; he remembered his father telling him about it afterward.

His father! A new thought came to him: it was his own father—Dr. Byron Coleman—who had taken care of the Alexander family, who would have ordered the transfusions Elizabeth Alexander had received. If she had had several transfusions they would have come from more than one donor; the chance of at least some of the blood being Rh positive was almost inevitable. That was the occasion, then, when Elizabeth had become sensitized; he was sure of it now. At the time, of course, there would have been no apparent effect. None, that is, except that her own blood would be building antibodies—antibodies to lurk hidden and unsuspected until, nine years later, they rose in anger, virulent and strong, to destroy her child.

Naturally David Coleman's father could not be blamed, even if the hypothesis were true. He would have prescribed in good faith, using the medical standards of his day. It was true that at the time the Rh factor had been known and in some places Rh cross matching was already in effect. But a busy country G.P. could scarcely be expected to keep up with everything that was new. Or could he? Some physicians of the time—G.P.'s included—were aware of the new horizons opened up by modern blood grouping. *They* had acted promptly to enforce the latest standards. But possibly, David Coleman reasoned, these were younger men. His father at that time was growing old; he worked too hard and long to do much reading. But was that an adequate excuse? Was it an excuse that he himself—David Coleman—would accept from others? Or was there perhaps a double standard—a more lenient set of rules when it came to judging your own kin, even a father who was dead? The thought troubled him. He sensed uneasily that a feeling of personal loyalty was obtruding across some of his own most cherished views. David Coleman wished he had not thought of this. It gave him an uneasy feeling of doubt, of not being absolutely sure . . . of anything at all.

Pearson was looking across at him. He asked, "How long is it now?"

Coleman checked his watch, then answered, "Just over an hour."

"I'm going to call them." Impetuously Pearson reached for

the telephone. Then he hesitated and drew his hand away. "No," he said, "I suppose I'd better not."

In the serology lab John Alexander, too, was conscious of the time. An hour ago he had come back from visiting Elizabeth, and since then he had made several halfhearted attempts to work. But it was obvious to himself that his mind was far removed from what he was doing and he had desisted, rather than risk mistakes. Now, taking up a test tube, he prepared to begin again, but Bannister came over and took it from him.

Looking at the requisition sheet, the older technician said kindly, "I'll do that."

He protested halfheartedly, then Bannister said, "Go on, kid; leave it to me. Why don't you go up with your wife?"

"Thanks all the same, but I think I'll stay. Dr. Coleman said as soon as he heard . . . he'd come and tell me." Alexander's eyes turned to the wall clock again. He said, his voice strained, "They can't be much longer now."

Bannister turned away. "No," he said slowly, "I guess not."

Elizabeth Alexander was in her hospital room alone. She was lying still, head back on the pillows, her eyes open, when Nurse Wilding came in. Elizabeth asked, "Is there any news?"

The elderly, gray-haired nurse shook her head. "I'll tell you just as soon as we hear." Putting down the glass of orange juice she had brought, she said, "I can stay with you for a few minutes if you like."

"Yes, please." Elizabeth smiled faintly, and the nurse pulled a chair near the bed and sat down. Wilding felt relieved to rest her feet; just lately they had been giving her a good deal of pain, and she suspected they would probably force her to quit nursing soon, whether she wanted to or not. Well, she had a feeling she was pretty close to being ready to go.

Wilding wished, though, that she could do something for these two young people. She had taken a fancy to them from the beginning; to her the two of them—husband and wife—seemed almost children. In a way, taking care of this girl, who, it seemed now, was likely to lose her baby, had been almost like caring for the daughter that long ago Wilding had wanted but never had. Wasn't that silly now?—she, with all her years of nursing, getting sentimental at this late day. She asked Elizabeth, "What were you thinking about—when I came in just then?"

"I was thinking about children—fat, roly-poly children scrambling on green grass in afternoon sunshine." Elizabeth's voice had a dreamlike quality. "It was like that in Indiana when I was a little girl—in the summers. Even then I used to think that someday I would have children and that I would sit beside them while they rolled on the grass in the sunshine, just as I had."

"It's a funny thing about children," Wilding said. "Sometimes things turn out so different from the way you thought they would. I had a son, you know. He's a man now."

"No," Elizabeth said, "I didn't know."

"Don't misunderstand me," Wilding said. "He's a fine man —a naval officer. He got married a month or two ago; I had a letter from him telling me."

Elizabeth found herself wondering—what it would be like to bear a son and then have a letter, telling about his getting married.

"I never did feel we got to know one another very well," Wilding was saying. "I expect that was my fault in a way— getting divorced and never giving him a real home."

"But you'll go and see him sometimes?" Elizabeth said. "And there'll be grandchildren, I expect."

"I've thought a lot about that," Wilding said. "I used to think it would be fun. You know—having grandchildren, living somewhere near, then going in the evenings to babysit, and all the rest."

Elizabeth asked, "But won't you—now?"

Wilding shook her head. "I have a feeling that when I go it'll be like visiting strangers. And it won't be often either. You see, my son is stationed in Hawaii; they left last week." She added with a touch of defiant loyalty, "He was coming to see me and bring his wife. Then something came up at the last minute, so they couldn't make it."

There was a silence, then Wilding said, "Well, I'll have to be getting on now." She eased to her feet, then added from the doorway, "Drink your juice, Mrs. Alexander. I'll come and tell you—just as soon as we hear anything at all."

Kent O'Donnell was sweating, and the assisting nurse leaned forward to mop his forehead. Five minutes had passed since artificial respiration had begun, and still there was no response from the tiny body under his hands. His thumbs were on the chest cavity, the remainder of his fingers crossed around the back. The child was so small, O'Donnell's two hands overlapped; he had to use them carefully, aware that with too much pressure the fragile bones would sunder like twigs. Gently, once more, he squeezed and relaxed, the oxygen hissing, trying to induce breath, to coax the tired, tiny lungs back into life with movement of their own.

O'Donnell wanted this baby to live. He knew, if it died, it would mean that Three Counties—his hospital—had failed abjectly in its most basic function: to give proper care to the sick and the weak. This child had not had proper care; it had been given the poorest when it needed the best, and dereliction had edged out skill. He found himself trying to communicate, to transmit his own burning fervor through his finger tips to the faltering heart lying beneath them. *You needed us and we failed you; you probed our weakness and you found us wanting. But please let us try—again, together. Sometimes we do better than this; don't judge us for always by just one failure. There's ignorance and folly in this world, and prejudice and blindness—we've shown you that already. But there are other things, too; good, warm things to live for. So breathe! It's such a simple thing, but so important.* O'Donnell's hands moved back and forth . . . compressing . . . releasing . . . compressing . . . releasing . . . compressing . . .

Another five minutes had passed and the intern was using his stethoscope, listening carefully. Now he straightened up. He caught O'Donnell's eye and shook his head. O'Donnell stopped; he knew it was useless to go on.

Turning to Dornberger, he said quietly, "I'm afraid he's gone."

Their eyes met, and both men knew their feelings were the same.

O'Donnell felt himself gripped by a white-hot fury. Fiercely he ripped off the mask and cap; he tore at the rubber gloves and flung them savagely to the floor.

He felt the others' eyes upon him. His lips in a thin, grim line, he told Dornberger, "All right. Let's go." Then, harshly, to the intern, "If anyone should want me, I'll be with Dr. Pearson."

Twenty-one

In the pathology office the telephone bell jangled sharply and Pearson reached out for the receiver. Then, his face pale, nervousness showing, he stopped. He said to Coleman, "You take it."

As David Coleman crossed the room there was a second impatient ring. A moment later he was saying, "Dr. Coleman speaking." He listened, expressionless, then said, "Thank you," and hung up.

His eyes met Pearson's. He said quietly, "The baby just died."

The other man said nothing. His eyes dropped. Slouched in the office chair, the lined, craggy face half in shadow, his body motionless, he seemed aged and defeated.

Coleman said softly, "I think I'll go to the lab. Someone should talk with John."

There was no answer. As Coleman left the pathology office, Pearson was still sitting, silent and unmoving, his eyes unseeing, his thoughts known only to himself.

Carl Bannister had gone out of the lab when David Coleman came in. John Alexander was there alone, seated on a stool before one of the wall benches, the lab clock immediately above his head. He made no attempt to turn around as Coleman approached, his footsteps slow, the leather of his shoes creaking as he crossed the floor.

There was a silence, then, still without turning, Alexander asked softly, "It's . . . over?"

Without answering Coleman reached out his hand. He let it rest on the other's shoulder.

His voice low, Alexander said, "He died, didn't he?"

"Yes, John," Coleman said gently, "he died. I'm sorry."

He withdrew his hand as Alexander turned slowly. The younger man's face was strained, the tears streaming. He said, softly but intensely, "Why, Dr. Coleman? Why?"

Groping for words, he tried to answer. "Your baby was

premature, John. His chances were not good—even if . . . the other . . . hadn't happened."

Looking him directly in the eyes, Alexander said, "But he *might* have lived."

This was a moment of truth in which evasion had no place. "Yes," Coleman said. "He might have lived."

John Alexander had risen to his feet. His face was close to Coleman's, his eyes imploring, questioning. "How could it happen . . . in a hospital . . . with doctors?"

"John," Coleman said, "at this moment I haven't any answer for you." He added softly, "At this moment I haven't any answer for myself."

Alexander nodded dumbly. He took out a handkerchief and wiped his eyes. Then he said quietly, "Thank you for coming to tell me. I think I'll go to Elizabeth now."

Kent O'Donnell had not spoken during his progress through the hospital with Dr. Dornberger; the intense anger and frustration, which had engulfed him like a wave as he had looked down at the dead child, kept him tight-lipped and silent. As they swept through corridors and pattered down stairways, eschewing the slow-moving elevators, bitterly once more O'Donnell reviled himself for his own inaction about Joe Pearson and the pathology department of Three Counties. God knows, he thought, there had been plenty of danger signs: Rufus and Reubens had warned him, and he had had the evidence of his own eyes to tell him Pearson was failing with his years, his responsibilities growing beyond him in the busy, expanded hospital. But no! He, Kent O'Donnell, M.D., F.R.C.S. (Eng.), F.A.C.S., chief of surgery, medical-board president—off with your hats for a fine, big man! "Send him victorious, happy and glorious, long to reign over us, God save O'Donnell!"—he had been too preoccupied to bestir himself, to use the toughness his job demanded, to face the unpleasantness which was bound to follow action. So, instead, he had looked the other way, pretended all was well, when experience and instinct had told him deep inside he was only hoping that it would be. And where had he been all this time—he, the great man of medicine? Wallowing in hospital politics; supping with Orden Brown; fawning on Eustace Swayne, hoping that by inaction, by permitting a status quo, by leaving Swayne's friend Joe Pearson severely alone, the old tycoon would graciously come through with money for the fancy new hospital buildings—O'Donnell's dream of empire, with himself as king. Well, the hospital might receive the money now, and again it might not. But whether it did or didn't, one price, at least, had already been paid. He thought: You'll find the receipt upstairs—a small dead body in an O.R. on the fourth floor. Then, as they came to Pearson's door, he felt his anger lessen and sorrow take its place. He knocked, and Dornberger followed him in.

Joe Pearson was still sitting, exactly as Coleman had left him. He looked up but made no attempt to rise.

Dornberger spoke first. He spoke quietly, without antagonism, as if wanting to set the mood of this meeting as a service to an old friend. He said, "The baby died, Joe. I suppose you heard."

Pearson said slowly, "Yes. I heard."

"I've told Dr. O'Donnell everything that happened." Dornberger's voice was unsteady. "I'm sorry, Joe. There wasn't much else I could do."

Pearson made a small, helpless gesture with his hands. There was no trace of his old aggressiveness. He said expressionlessly, "It's all right."

Matching his tone to Dornberger's, O'Donnell asked, "Is there anything you want to say, Joe?"

Twice, slowly, Pearson shook his head.

"Joe, if it were just this one thing . . ." O'Donnell found himself searching for the right words, knowing they did not exist. "We all make mistakes. Maybe I could . . ." This was not what he had intended to say. He steadied his voice and went on more firmly. "But it's a long list. Joe, if I have to bring this before the medical board, I think you know how they'll feel. You could make it less painful for yourself, and for all of us, if your resignation were in the administrator's office by ten o'clock tomorrow morning."

Pearson looked at O'Donnell. "Ten o'clock," he said. "You shall have it."

There was a pause. O'Donnell turned away, then back. "Joe," he said, "I'm sorry. But I guess you know, I don't have any choice."

"Yeah." The word was a whisper as Person nodded dully.

"Of course, you'll be eligible for pension. It's only fair after thirty-two years." O'Donnell knew, as he said them, the words had a hollow ring.

For the first time since they had come in Pearson's expression changed. He looked at O'Donnell with a slight, sardonic smile. "Thanks."

Thirty-two years! O'Donnell thought: My God! It was most of any man's working life. And to have it end like this! He wanted to say something more: to try to make it easier for them all; to find phrases in which to speak of the good things Joe Pearson had done—there must be many of them. He was still debating how when Harry Tomaselli came in.

The administrator had entered hurriedly, not waiting to knock. He looked first at Pearson, then his glance took in Dornberger and O'Donnell. "Kent," he said quickly, "I'm glad you're here."

Before O'Donnell could speak Tomaselli had swung back to Pearson. "Joe," he said, "can you come to my office immediately? There's an emergency staff meeting in an hour. I'd like to talk with you first."

O'Donnell said sharply, "An emergency meeting? What for?"

Tomaselli turned. His expression was serious, his eyes troubled. "Typhoid has been discovered in the hospital," he announced. "Dr. Chandler has reported two cases, and there are four more suspected. We've an epidemic on our hands and we have to find the source."

As Elizabeth looked up the door opened and John came in. He closed the door, then stood for a moment with his back against it.

There was nothing said, only with their eyes—grief, entreaty, and an overwhelming love.

She held out her arms and he came into them.

"Johnny! Johnny, darling." It was all she could murmur before she began to cry softly.

After a while, when he had held her tightly, he moved back, then dried her tears with the same handkerchief he had used for his own.

Later still he said, "Elizabeth, honey, if you're still willing, there's something I'd like to do."

"Whatever it is," she answered, "it's 'yes.'"

"I guess you always wanted it," he said. "Now I want it too. I'll write for the papers tomorrow. I'm going to try for medical school."

Mike Seddons got up from the chair and paced around the

small hospital room. "But it's ridiculous," he said heatedly. "It's absurd; it isn't necessary, and I won't do it."

"For my sake, darling. Please!" From the bed Vivian eased herself around so that her face was toward him.

"But it isn't for your sake, Vivian. It's just some damn silly, stupid idea you might have got out of a fourth-rate sentimental novel."

"Mike darling, I love you so much when you get mad. It goes with your beautiful red hair." She smiled at him fondly as, for the first time, her mind moved away from immediate things. "Promise me something."

"What?" He was still angry, the answer curt.

"Promise me that when we're married sometimes you'll get mad—really mad—so we can have fights, then afterward enjoy the fun of making up."

He said indignantly, "That's just about as daft a suggestion as the other one. And anyway, what's the point of talking about getting married when you want me to stay away from you?"

"Only for a week, Mike dear. Just one week; that's all."

"No!"

"Listen to me, darling." She urged, "Please come and sit down. And listen to me—please!"

He hesitated, then returned reluctantly to the chair at the side of the bed. Vivian let her head fall back on the pillows, her face turned sideways toward him. She smiled and reached out her hand. He took it gently, his anger dissolving. Only a vague, disquieting sense of doubt remained.

It was the fourth day since Vivian had returned from surgery, and in the meanwhile her progress had been good. The stump of her thigh was healing well; there was still some localized pain and inevitable soreness, but the big and overwhelming agony of the first two days of recovery had eased, and yesterday Dr. Grainger, with Vivian's knowledge and agreement, had withdrawn the order for injections of demerol which had helped dim the pain over the worst period, now behind. Only one thing Vivian found distressing—a surprising thing that she had not anticipated. The foot of her amputated leg—a foot that was no longer there—itched frequently with a malicious, recurring torment; it was anguish not to be able to scratch it. At first when the feeling came she had groped with her remaining foot for the sole of the other. Then for a while, lightheadedly, she had begun to believe that there had been no amputation after all. It was only when Dr. Grainger had assured her that the sensation was entirely normal and something experienced by most people who had any limb removed that she realized her belief was illusory. Nevertheless, it was an uncanny feeling which Vivian hoped would disappear soon.

Psychologically, too, her progress appeared to be good. From the moment when, the day before surgery, Vivian had accepted the inevitable with the simple courage that had so impressed itself on Mike Seddons the mood had continued and upheld her. There were still moments of blackness and despair; they came to her when she was alone, and twice, waking at night, with the hospital around her quiet and eerie, she had lain crying silently for what had been lost. But mostly she banished the moods, using her innate strength to rise above them.

Lucy Grainger was aware of this and was grateful; it made easier her own task of supervising the healing process. Nonetheless, Lucy knew that for Vivian the real test of her emotions and spirit lay somewhere still ahead. That test would come after the initial shock had passed, when the real significance of events had had time to develop more gradually in Vivian's mind and when the implications for the future were closer and more real. Perhaps the moment might not come for six months or even a year; but sooner or later it would, and Lucy knew that at that time Vivian would pass through the deep darkness of despair to some permanent attitude of mind beyond, whatever that might be. But that was for the future; for the present the short-term prognosis seemed reasonably bright.

Lucy knew, of course—and was aware that Vivian knew it too—that the possibility remained that the osteogenic sarcoma which Dr. Pearson had diagnosed might have metastasized ahead of the amputation, spreading its creeping malignancy elsewhere in Vivian's body. In that case there would be little more that Three Counties Hospital, or medicine generally, could do for Vivian beyond temporary, palliative relief. But later would be time enough to learn if that were true. For the patient's sake it seemed best and wisest at this moment to assume that for Vivian the future stretched indefinitely ahead and to help her adapt to it actively.

Today, also, Vivian's beginning of recovery was reflected in her appearance. For the first time since her return from surgery she had put on make-up, bringing color to her face. Earlier her mother had come in to help arrange her hair, and now, wearing the same nightgown which on a previous occasion had come close to stirring Mike to indiscretion, much of her youthful loveliness was back on view.

Now, as Mike took her hand, she said, "Don't you understand, darling, I want to be sure—sure for my own sake as much as for yours."

"But sure of what?" On Mike Seddons' cheeks there were two points of high color.

She said levelly, "Sure that you really love me."

"Of course I love you." He asked vehemently, "Haven't I been telling you that for the past half-hour? Haven't I said that I want us to marry—as we arranged to before"—he hesitated—"before this happened? Even your mother and father are in favor of it. They've accepted me; why can't you?"

"Oh, but I do accept you, Mike. Gratefully and gladly. Whatever happens between us, I don't believe there could ever be anything quite the same again; at any rate"—for an instant her voice faltered—"not for me."

"Then why . . . ?"

She pleaded, "Please, Mike. Hear me out. You said you would."

Impatiently he said, "Go on."

"Whatever you may say, Mike, I'm not the same girl you met that first time we saw each other. I can't be, ever again." She went on softly, intensely, "That's why I have to be sure —sure that you love me for what I am and not for what I was. Don't you see, darling, if we're going to spend the rest of our lives together, I couldn't bear to think—not later on, not ever—that you married me . . . out of pity. No, don't stop me; just listen. I know you think it isn't true, and perhaps it isn't; and I hope it isn't—with all my heart. But, Mike, you're kind and generous, and you might even be doing this—for that reason—without admitting it to yourself."

He snapped back, "Are you suggesting I don't know my own motives?"

Vivian answered softly, "Do any of us really know?"

"I know mine." He took her hands gently, their faces close. "I know that I love you—whole or in part, yesterday, today, or tomorrow. And I know that I want to marry you—without doubts, without pity, without waiting one day longer than we have to."

"Then do this one thing for me—*because* you love me. Go away from me now, and even though you're in the hospital, don't come back to see me for one week—seven whole days." Vivian looked at him levelly. She went on quietly, "In that time think of everything—of me, what our life would be like together; how it would be for you—living with a cripple; the things we couldn't share and those we could; our children—how it would affect them, and through them, you; everything, Mike—everything there is. Then when you've done that, come back and tell me, and if you're still sure, I promise that I'll never question you again. It's just seven days, darling—seven days out of both our lives. It isn't very much."

"Goddam," he said, "you're obstinate."

"I know." She smiled. "You'll do it then?"

"I'll do it for four days—no more."

Vivian shook her head. "Six—no less."

"Make it five," he said, "and you've got a deal."

She hesitated and Mike said, "It's positively my best offer."

Vivian laughed; it was the first time she had. "All right. Five days from this moment."

"Like hell from this moment!" Mike said. "Maybe ten minutes from now. First I've got a little storing up to do. For a young fellow with my hot blood five days is a long time."

He moved the bedside chair closer, then reached out. It was a long kiss, alternately passionate and tender.

At the end Vivian made a grimace and broke away. She sighed and eased herself to a new position in the bed.

Mike inquired anxiously, "Is something wrong?"

Vivian shook her head. "Not really." Then she asked him, "Mike, where have they got my leg—the gone one, I mean?"

He seemed startled, then told her, "In Pathology—in a refrigerator, I expect."

Vivian drew in a long breath, then expelled it slowly. "Mike darling," she said, "please go downstairs and scratch the foot."

The hospital's board room was crowded. News of the emergency meeting had gone swiftly around the hospital, and physicians not attending Three Counties that day had been notified in their downtown offices and at home. Rumors of Joe Pearson's downfall and his impending departure had also traveled with equal speed and had been the subject of a buzz of discussion which had quieted as Pearson entered, the administrator and David Coleman with him.

Kent O'Donnell was already at the head of the long walnut table. Glancing around, he could see most of the familiar faces. Gil Bartlett, his beard wagging rapidly, was chatting with Roger Hilton, the young surgeon who had joined Three Counties' staff a month or two ago. John McEwan, the e.n.t. specialist, was in what appeared to be a heated discussion with Ding Dong Bell and fat Lewis Toynbee, the internist. Bill Rufus, a tie of brilliant green and yellow marking him out from the crowd, was about to seat himself in the second row of chairs. Immediately in front, looking over a page of handwritten notes, was Dr. Harvey Chandler, chief of medicine. There were several members of the house staff, and among them O'Donnell noticed McNeil, the pathology resident. Alongside the administrator, attending the meeting by special request, was Mrs. Straughan, the chief dietitian. Nearby was Ernie Reubens, who appeared to be quizzically appraising the dietitian's quivering, voluptuous breasts. Absent from the meeting was the familiar figure of Charlie Dornberger, who had already made known his intention to retire immediately.

Looking toward the door, O'Donnell saw Lucy Grainger come in; she caught his eye and smiled slightly. Seeing Lucy was a reminder of the personal decision about his own future which, when all this was settled and done, he had still to face. Then suddenly he realized that since this morning he had not once thought of Denise. The hospital activity had driven all awareness of her from his mind, and he knew that for the next day or two, anyway, there would be other occasions when the same thing would be true. O'Donnell wondered how Denise herself would react about taking second place to medical affairs. Would she be understanding? As understanding, say, as Lucy would be? Fleeting as the thought was, it made him uncomfortable, as if by the mental comparison he had been disloyal. For the moment he preferred to think of present things. Now, he decided, it was time the meeting began.

O'Donnell rapped for silence, then waited until the talk stilled and those who had been standing had slipped into their seats. He began quietly. "Ladies and gentlemen, I think all of us are aware that epidemics in hospitals are not unique and, in fact, are a good deal more frequent than most members of the public realize. In a way, I suppose, one might say that epidemics are a hazard of our existence. When one considers how many diseases we harbor inside these walls, it's surprising, really, there are not more." All eyes in the room were upon him. He paused for a moment, then continued. "I have no wish to minimize what has happened, but I want us to keep a sense of proportion. Dr. Chandler, perhaps you'd be kind enough to lead off."

As O'Donnell sat down the chief of medicine rose to his feet.

"To begin with, let's summarize." Harvey Chandler was holding his page of notes, and his glance moved theatrically around the room. Harvey's enjoying this, O'Donnell thought; but then he always does enjoy attention. The medical chieftain went on, "The picture so far is that we have two definite cases of typhoid and four suspected. All of the cases are hospital employees, and we may count ourselves fortunate that no patients are affected—yet. Because of the number of cases I'm sure it's evident to you, as it is to me, that we have a typhoid carrier somewhere in the hospital. Now, I may say I'm as shocked as everyone else must have been to learn that examination of food handlers here hasn't been done for . . ."

At the mention of food handlers O'Donnell had jolted to attention. Now he cut in, quietly, as politely as he could.

"Excuse me, Doctor."

"Yes?" Chandler's tone made it plain the interruption was not appreciated.

Gently O'Donnell said, "We're going to be dealing with that phase very shortly, Harvey. I wonder if, for the moment, you would outline the clinical aspects."

He could sense the other man's resentment. Harvey Chandler, who was virtually equal to O'Donnell in the hospital hierarchy, did not like this at all. Moreover, Dr. Chandler enjoyed talking at length; he had a reputation for never employing one word where it was possible to use two or three. Now he grumbled, "Well, if you wish, but . . ."

Suavely, but firmly, O'Donnell put in, "Thank you."

Chandler shot him a glance which said: We'll discuss this later in private. Then, after a barely perceptible pause, he went on, "For the benefit of those of you who are not familiar with typhoid—and I realize there will be some, because there isn't too much of it around nowadays—I'll run over the principal early-stage symptoms. Generally speaking, there's a rising fever, chills, and a slow pulse. There's also a low blood count and, naturally, the characteristic rose spots. In addition to all that a patient will probably complain of a dull headache, no appetite, and general aching. Some patients may say they're drowsy in the daytime and that they're restless at night. One thing to look out for also is bronchitis; that's quite common with typhoid, and you may encounter nosebleed too. And, of course, a tender, swollen spleen."

The chief of medicine sat down. O'Donnell asked, "Any questions?"

Lucy Grainger asked, "I take it that typhoid shots are being arranged."

"Yes," Chandler said, "for all employees and staff, also patients who are well enough to have them."

"What about kitchen arrangements?" The question was from Bill Rufus.

O'Donnell said, "If you don't mind, we'll come to that shortly. At this point is there anything more medically?" He looked around; there was a shaking of heads. "Very well, then. We'll hear from Pathology." He announced quietly, "Dr. Pearson."

Until this moment there had been background noises in the room—fidgeting, the movement of chairs, murmurs of conversation aside from the main discussion. But now there was a hush as eyes turned curiously to where, halfway down the long table, Joe Pearson sat. Since entering he had not spoken but had remained quite still, his eyes fixed directly ahead. For once he had no cigar lighted, and the effect was like the absence of a familiar trade-mark. Even now, as his name was called, he made no move.

O'Donnell waited. He was about to repeat the announcement when Pearson stirred. As his chair went back the old pathologist rose to his feet.

Slowly his eyes swept the board room. They went the length of the table, then returned to its head. Looking directly at O'Donnell, Pearson said, "This epidemic should not have happened. Nor would it, if Pathology had been alert to a breakdown in hygiene precautions. It is the responsibility of my department, and therefore my own responsibility, that this neglect occurred."

Again a silence. It was as if history had been made. In this room so many times Joe Pearson had charged others with error and misjudgment. Now he stood himself—accuser and accused.

O'Donnell wondered if he should interrupt. He decided not. Again Pearson looked around him. Then he said slowly, "Having allocated some of the blame, we must now prevent the outbreak going further." He glanced across the table at Harry Tomaselli. "The administrator, the heads of departments, and I have formulated certain procedures to be carried out at once. I will tell you what they are."

Now Pearson paused, and when he resumed there was a stronger note to his voice. It was almost, O'Donnell thought, as if in this single moment the old man were throwing off some of his years, as if providing a glimpse of what he had been like long ago as a younger practitioner—intense, earnest, and competent. The old sardonic humor, the air of borderline contempt, which all of them in this room had come to know so well, were gone. In their place were authority and know-how and the forthright frankness of one who accepts without question the fact that he is speaking with equals.

"The immediate problem," Pearson said, "is to locate the source of infection. Because of the failure to check food handlers properly over the past six months it is logical that we should suspect food as a means of contamination and should begin our search there. For this reason there must be a medical inspection of all food handlers before the next hospital meal is served." From his frayed woolen vest he extracted a watch and placed it on the table. "The time is now 2:15 P.M. That gives us two and three-quarter hours. In that time every employee who has any part in the preparation and serving of hospital food is to be given a thorough physical check. Facilities are being set up now in the outpatient clinics. I understand that all the internists and house staff were notified before this meeting." He glanced around and there was a nodding of heads. "Very well. As soon as we are finished here Dr. Coleman"—Pearson glanced down at David Coleman beside him—"will give you your assignment to a specific room."

Gesturing toward the chief dietitian, Pearson said, "Mrs. Straughan is arranging to assemble all the people concerned, and they will be reporting to Outpatients in batches of twelve. That means ninety-five people to be examined within the time we have.

"When you make these examinations, by the way, remember that the typhoid carrier—and we are assuming there is a carrier—probably has none of the symptoms Dr. Chandler described. What you should look for particularly is any lack of personal cleanliness. And anyone you have doubts about should be suspended from duty for the time being."

Pearson stopped as if thinking. So far he had consulted no notes. Now he went on again. "Of course, we are all aware that physical checkups will not give us the whole story. We may be lucky and find the individual we're looking for that way, but the chances are we won't. Most likely the major work will come in the labs as soon as the medicals are completed. All the people you examine are to be told that stool cultures are required and stool samples must be in the hospital by tomorrow morning." There was the ghost of a smile. "Constipation will not be taken as an excuse; and if anyone can come through with a sample today we will, of course, accept it gratefully.

"The labs are being set up now to cope with all the cultures we shall be doing. Of course, it will take us a few days—two or three at least—to handle all those stool samples."

A voice—O'Donnell thought it was Gil Bartlett's—said quietly, "Ninety-five people! That's a lot of shit." A ripple of laughter ran around the table.

Pearson turned. "Yes," he said, "it is a lot. But we shall do our best."

With that he sat down.

Lucy signaled with her hand, and O'Donnell nodded for her to speak. She asked, "If the source of infection is not found immediately, will we continue to use the hospital kitchens—to serve food here?"

"For the moment—yes," O'Donnell answered.

The administrator added, "My office is checking now to see if there's any outside caterer who could handle food supply if that were felt necessary. I doubt, though, if there's anyone in town who has facilities—at short notice like this—to do it."

Bill Rufus asked, "What's our policy to be on admissions?"

"I'm sorry," O'Donnell said. "I should have mentioned that. As of this moment we've stopped admissions. The admitting department has already been notified. But, of course, we're hoping pathology can track down the source of infection quickly, and then we'll review our admissions policy again. Anything else?"

There were no more questions. Looking down the table, O'Donnell asked, "Dr. Coleman, do you have anything to add?"

David Coleman shook his head. "No."

O'Donnell closed the file which had been open in front of him. "Very well, ladies and gentlemen, I suggest we get started." Then, as chairs scraped back and conversation began, he asked Pearson, "Joe, could I have a word with you?"

Together they crossed to a window, away from the others who were filing out through the door. O'Donnell said quietly, making sure his voice did not carry, "Joe, naturally you'll remain in charge of Pathology during this outbreak. But I think I must make clear to you that, concerning other things, nothing has changed."

Pearson nodded slowly. "Yes," he said, "I'd already figured that."

Twenty-two

Like a general appraising his forces ahead of battle, Dr. Joseph Pearson surveyed the pathology lab.

With him were David Coleman, the pathology resident Dr. McNeil, Carl Bannister, and John Alexander. Pearson, Coleman, and McNeil had come directly from the emergency staff meeting in the board room. The other two, acting on earlier instructions, had cleared the lab of all but immediate, essential work.

When Pearson had completed his inspection he addressed the other four. "Our problem," he announced, "is one of detection. Out of a field of approximately ninety-five people—the food handlers—it is our business to track down a single individual whom we believe to be spreading typhoid germs within this hospital. It is also a problem of speed; the longer we take, the worse the epidemic will be. Our means of detection will be the stool specimens which will start coming in today, with the bulk of them arriving tomorrow."

He addressed Roger McNeil. "Dr. McNeil, your job for the next few days will be to keep the lab clear of non-essential work. Check all routine requisitions coming in and decide how many of them should have priority and which can be postponed, at least for a day or two. The lab items which in your opinion are urgent can be handled by Carl Bannister. Work with him as much as you can, but don't load him with any more than is essential; the rest of the time we'll use him on our major project." Pearson continued as McNeil nodded. "You yourself will have to take care of all surgical reports. Process those which appear urgent and accumulate anything that can wait. If there's any diagnosis about which you're not absolutely sure, call Dr. Coleman or myself."

"Right. I'll check with the office now." McNeil went out.

To the others Pearson said, "We shall use a separate plate for each single stool culture. I don't want to take the risk of putting several cultures together, then having one overgrow the others; it would mean we'd lose time and have to start again." He asked Alexander, "Do we have sufficient MacConkey's medium ready to handle close to a hundred cultures?"

John Alexander was pale and his eyes red-rimmed. He had returned from Elizabeth only a half-hour before. Nevertheless he responded promptly, "No," he said, "I doubt if we've more than a couple of dozen. Normally that's several days' supply."

When he had spoken, realizing that his reaction to a question about the lab had sprung from habit, John Alexander wondered what his own feelings were toward Dr. Pearson. He found he could not define them. He supposed he should hate this old man whose negligence had caused his own son's death, and perhaps later on he would. But for now there was only a dull, deep aching and a sense of melancholy. Maybe it was as well for the time being that a great deal of work appeared to be facing them all. At least he could try to lose himself in some of it.

"I understand," Pearson said. "Well, then, will you work

in the media kitchen and stay with it until all the plates are ready for use? We must have them all by the end of today."

"I'll get started." Alexander followed McNeil out.

Now Pearson was thinking aloud. "We shall have ninety-five cultures, say a hundred. Assume that 50 per cent will be lactose positive, leaving the other 50 per cent to be investigated further; it shouldn't be more than that." He glanced at Coleman for confirmation.

"I'd agree." Coleman nodded.

"All right then; we shall need ten sugar tubes to a culture. Fifty cultures—that means five hundred subcultures." Turning to Bannister, Pearson asked, "How many sugar tubes are ready—clean and sterilized?"

Bannister considered. "Probably two hundred."

"Are you sure?" Pearson looked at him searchingly.

Bannister colored. Then he said, "A hundred and fifty anyway."

"Then order three hundred and fifty more. Call the supply house and say we want them delivered today, and no excuses. Tell them we'll take care of the paper work later." Pearson went on. "When you've done that, begin preparing the tubes in sets of ten. Use those on hand first, then the others when they come. Check your sugar supplies too. Remember you'll need glucose, lactose, dulcitol, sucrose, mannitol, maltose, xylose, arabinose, rhamnose, and one tube for indole production."

Pearson had rattled off the names without hesitation. With the ghost of a smile he said to Bannister, "You'll find the list and table of reactions for Salmonella typhi on page sixty-six of laboratory standing orders. All right, get moving."

Hastily Bannister scurried to the telephone.

Turning to David Coleman, Pearson asked, "Can you think of anything I've forgotten?"

Coleman shook his head. The old man's grasp of the situation, as well as his celerity and thoroughness, had left Coleman both surprised and impressed. "No," he said, "I can't think of a thing."

For a moment Pearson regarded the younger man. Then he said, "In that case, let's go and have coffee. It may be the last chance we'll have for quite a few days."

Now that Mike Seddons had gone, it came to Vivian just how

big a gap his absence left behind and how long-drawn-out
the next few days were going to seem without him. She believed, though, she had been right in asking Mike to remain away for a time. It would give them both a chance to
adjust and to think clearly about the future. Not that Vivian
needed any time to think herself; she was quite sure of her
own feelings, but it was fairer to Mike this way. Or was it?
For the first time it occurred to her that by acting as
she had perhaps she was asking Mike to prove his love for
her, while accepting her own without question.

But that was not what she had intended. Vivian wondered
uneasily, though, if Mike had taken it that way—if she had
appeared to him untrusting and unwilling to accept his devotion at face value. He hadn't seemed to, it was true; but
perhaps after thinking things over, as she herself was doing
at this moment, he might decide that was the way it was.
She speculated on whether she should call him or send a note
explaining what she had really intended—that is, if she were
sure herself. Was she sure though—even now? At times it was
so difficult to think clearly; you started out doing what you
thought was right, then you wondered if someone else might
misinterpret, might look for hidden meanings that you had
never considered yourself. How could you be really sure
what was the best thing to do about anything . . . anywhere
. . . ever . . . ?

There was a light tap on the door and Mrs. Loburton
came in. Seeing her, suddenly Vivian forgot that she was
all of nineteen, adult, able to decide things for herself. She
held out her arms. "Oh, Mother," she said, "I'm so terribly
mixed up."

The physical checkups on food handlers were proceeding
briskly. In a small consulting room—the first of a row of
similar rooms in the outpatients' department—Dr. Harvey
Chandler was concluding his examination of one of the male
cooks. "All right," he said, "you may get dressed."

At first the chief of medicine had not been sure whether it
would be dignified for him to handle some of the physicals
himself or not. But eventually he had decided to, his attitude being somewhat that of a commanding officer who
feels morally bound to position himself at the head of his
troops during a beach-head assault.

Actually Dr. Chandler had been inclined to resent the

dominance of the situation up to this point by Drs. O'Donnell and Pearson. O'Donnell was, of course, the medical-board president and entitled to be concerned with the over-all welfare of the hospital. All the same, Chandler reasoned, he *was* merely a surgeon and typhoid was essentially a matter for internal medicine.

In a sense the chief of medicine felt deprived of a starring role in the present crisis. In some of his more intimate thoughts Dr. Chandler sometimes pictured himself as a man of destiny, but opportunities to prove the point were all too rare. Now, with an opportunity at hand, he was being relegated, if not to a minor role, at least to a secondary one. He had to admit, however, that the arrangements made by O'Donnell and Pearson appeared to be working well, and at least they all had the common aim of ending this deplorable outbreak of typhoid. Frowning slightly, he told the cook who had now dressed, "Remember to be especially careful about hygiene. And practice absolute cleanliness when you're working in the kitchen."

"Yes, Doctor."

As the man went out Kent O'Donnell came in. "Hi," he said. "How's it going?"

Chandler's first inclination was to reply huffily. Then, he decided, perhaps there was not really that much to be concerned about. And apart from the minor fault of O'Donnell's being—in Chandler's opinion—a little too democratic at times, he was a good man to have at the head of the board and certainly a big improvement over his predecessor. Therefore, amiably enough, he answered, "I lost count some time ago. I suppose we're getting through them. But there's nothing to show so far."

"What's the news of the typhoid patients?" O'Donnell asked. "And the four suspected cases?"

"You can make it four definite now," Chandler said, "and scratch two of the suspects."

"Anyone in danger?"

"I don't think so. Thank God for antibiotics! Fifteen years ago we'd have been in a lot more trouble than we are."

"Yes, I suppose so." O'Donnell knew better than to inquire about isolation procedure. For all his pompousness Chandler could always be relied on to do the correct thing medically.

"Two of the patients are nurses," Chandler said. "One's

from Psychiatry, the other from Urology. The other two are men—a generator-room worker and a clerk from the records office."

"All from widely separated parts of the hospital," O'Donnell said thoughtfully.

"Exactly! There's no common denominator except hospital food. All four took their meals in the hospital cafeteria. I don't think there's any question that we're on the right track."

"Then I won't hold you up," O'Donnell said. "You've two more people waiting outside, but some of the other men have more, and we're shifting them around."

"Very well," Chandler said. "I'll just keep going until we're clear; nothing must stop us—no matter how long it takes." He sat in his chair a little straighter. He had the feeling that there was a touch of deering-do and a ring of Old Glory to his own forthright words.

"Right you are," O'Donnell said. "I'll leave you to it."

A little piqued by the casual reaction, the chief of medicine said stiffly, "You might ask the nurse to send in the next one, will you?"

"Sure."

O'Donnell went out, and a moment later a girl kitchen worker entered. She was holding a card.

Chandler said, "I'll take that. Sit down, please." He put the card in front of him and selected a blank case-history sheet.

"Yes, sir," the girl said.

"Now, first I want your medical history—yourself and your family—as far back as we can go. Let's start with your parents."

With the girl responding to his careful questioning, Chandler's rapidly written notes began to fill the sheet in front of him. As always, when he was finished the result would be a model of good case-history reporting, suitable for inclusion in any medical textbook. One of the reasons Dr. Chandler was chief of medicine at Three Counties was because he was an extremely precise and conscientious clinician.

Walking away from the commandeered outpatients' department, Kent O'Donnell permitted himself to think, for the first time with any degree of perspective, of some of the day's events so far. It was now midafternoon, and since this morning so much had happened that it had been impossible to grasp the implications of it all.

In swift and unexpected succession had come, first, the incident of the mis-diagnosed child and, shortly afterward, its death. Then there had followed: Pearson's firing, Charlie Dornberger's retirement, the discovery that an elementary hygiene precaution had been neglected in the hospital for more than six months, and now the occurrence of typhoid, with the threat of an even graver epidemic hanging over Three Counties like an avenging sword.

So much, it seemed, had broken loose at once. Why? How had it happened? Was it a sudden symptom of a malaise that, undetected until now, had gripped the hospital? Was there more to come perhaps? Was this the signal of a general disintegration soon to follow? Had they all been guilty of a sense of complacency—of which O'Donnell himself might be the instigator?

He thought: We were all sure, so sure, that this regime was better than the last. We worked to make it so. We believed we were creating and progressing, building a temple of healing, a place where good medicine would be learned and practiced. But have we failed—ignominiously and blindly—through the very goodness of our own intentions? Have we been stupid and unseeing—our eyes on the cloud tops, uplifted by the glister of ideals, yet ignoring the plain earthy warning of everyday events? What have we built here? O'Donnell searched his mind. Is it, in truth, a place of healing? Or have we raised, in folly, a whited sepulcher —an empty, antiseptic shrine?

Preoccupied, his thoughts burning and intense, O'Donnell had strode through the hospital instinctively, unconscious of his surroundings. Now he came to his office and went inside.

He crossed to the window and stood looking down at the hospital forecourt. As always, there was a movement of people, coming and going. He saw a man limping, a woman holding his arm; they passed beneath and out of sight. A car drew up; a man jumped out and helped a woman into it. A nurse appeared, handing the woman a baby. The doors slammed; the car moved on. A boy on crutches came into view; he moved quickly, swinging his body with the ease of practice. He was stopped by an old man in a raincoat; the old man seemed uncertain where to go. The boy pointed. They moved together toward the hospital doors.

O'Donnell thought: They come to us in supplication, holding faith. Are we worthy of it? Do our successes mitigate our failures? Can we, in time, by devotion atone for error? Shall we ever know?

More practically, he reasoned: After today there must be many changes. They must plug gaps—not only those already exposed, but others they would uncover by diligent searching. They must probe for weaknesses—among themselves and in the hospital fabric. There must be greater self-criticism, more self-examination. Let today, he thought, stand as a bright and shining beacon—a cross of sorrow, a signal for a new beginning.

There was much to do, a great deal of work ahead. They would begin with Pathology—the weak spot where tribulation had begun. After that there must be reorganization elsewhere—there were several departments which he suspected were in need of it. It was definite now that work on the new buildings would begin in the spring, and the two programs could merge together. O'Donnell began to plan, his brain functioning swiftly.

The telephone rang sharply.

The operator announced, "Dr. O'Donnell, long distance is calling."

It was Denise. Her voice had the same soft huskiness that had attracted him before. When they had exchanged greetings she said, "Kent darling, I want you to come to New York this next weekend. I've invited some people for Friday night and I intend to show you off."

He hesitated only a moment. Then he said, "I'm terribly sorry, Denise—I won't be able to make it."

"But you *must* come." Her voice was insistent. "I've sent out the invitations and I can't possibly cancel them."

"I'm afraid you don't understand." He felt himself struggling awkwardly to find the right words. "We have an epidemic here. I have to stay until it's cleared up, then for a while at least there'll be other things that must be done."

"But you said you'd come, dearest—whenever I called you." There was the slightest hint of petulance. He found himself wishing he were with Denise. He was sure then that he could make her understand. Or could he?

He answered, "Unfortunately I didn't know that this would happen."

"But you're in charge of the hospital. Surely, just for a day or two, you can make someone else responsible." It was obvious that Denise had no intention of understanding.

He said quietly, "I'm afraid not."

There was a silence at the other end of the line. Then Denise said lightly, "I did warn you, Kent—I'm a very possessive person."

He started to say, "Denise dear, please——" then stopped.

"Is that really your final answer?" The voice on the phone was still soft, almost caressing.

"It has to be," he said. "I'm sorry." He added, "I'll call you, Denise—just as soon as I can get away."

"Yes," she said, "do that, Kent. Good-by."

"Good-by," he answered, then thoughtfully replaced the phone.

It was midmorning—the second day of the typhoid outbreak.

As Dr. Pearson had predicted, while a few stool samples had reached the lab yesterday afternoon, the bulk had arrived within the past hour.

The samples, contained in small cardboard cups with lids, were set out in rows on the center table of the pathology lab. Each was identified as to source, and Pearson, seated on a wooden chair at one end of the table, was adding a lab serial number and preparing report sheets on which the culture results would be recorded later.

As Pearson completed the preliminary paper work, he passed each specimen behind him to where David Coleman and John Alexander, working side by side, were preparing the culture plates.

Bannister, alone at a side table, was handling other orders on the lab which McNeil—now enthroned in the pathology office—had decided could not be delayed.

The lab stank.

With the exception of David Coleman all in the room were smoking, Pearson sending forth great clouds of cigar smoke to combat the odor as lids were lifted from the stool-specimen cups. Earlier Pearson had silently offered Coleman a cigar and the younger pathologist had lighted it for a while.

But he had found the cigar almost as unpleasant as the undiluted air and had allowed it to go out.

The youthful hospital messenger who was Bannister's avowed enemy had derived great satisfaction from bringing the specimens in, and with each new batch he had a fresh line of banter to accompany it. On his first trip he had looked at Bannister and announced, "They certainly found the right place to send this stuff." Later he had told Coleman, "Got six new flavors for you, Doctor." Now, setting a series of cartons in front of Pearson, he had asked, "You like cream and sugar in yours, sir?" Pearson grunted and went on writing.

John Alexander was working methodically, his mind concentrated on the work in hand. With the same fluidity of movement which David Coleman had noted at their first meeting he reached for a specimen cup and removed the cardboard lid. He pulled a petri dish toward him and, using a crayon pencil, copied the number from the lid onto the dish. Now he took a small platinum loop fixed to the end of a wooden handle and sterilized it in a burner flame. Next he passed the loop through the stool specimen, transferring a small portion of it to a tube of sterile saline. He repeated the process, then, using the platinum loop again, planted some of the solution on the culture plate, moving the loop in even, steady strokes.

Now he labeled the saline tube and placed it in a rack. The petri dish, with its culture plate, he carried across the lab to an incubator. There it would remain until the following day when subcultures, if necessary, could be begun. The process was one which could not be hurried.

He turned away to find David Coleman close behind him. On impulse Alexander said quietly, conscious of Pearson across the room, "Doctor, there's something I wanted to tell you."

"What is it?" Coleman added a petri dish himself to the incubator and closed the door.

"I . . . that is, we . . . have decided to take your advice. I'm going to apply for medical school."

"I'm glad." Coleman spoke with genuine feeling. "I'm sure it will turn out well."

"What will turn out well?" It was Pearson, his head lifted, watching.

Coleman went back to his work position, seated himself, and opened a new specimen. He said matter-of-factly, "John's just told me he's decided to apply for medical school. I advised him some time ago that he should."

"Oh." Pearson looked at Alexander sharply. He asked, "How will you afford it?"

"My wife can work, for one thing, Doctor. And then I thought I might get some lab work out of school hours; a lot of medical students do." Alexander paused, then, glancing at Coleman, he added, "I don't imagine it will be easy. But we think it will be worth it."

"I see." Pearson had blown out smoke; now he put down his cigar. He seemed about to say something else, then hesitated. Finally he asked, "How is your wife?"

Quietly Alexander answered, "She'll be all right. Thank you."

For a moment there was silence. Then Pearson said slowly, "I wish there was something I could say to you." He paused. "But I don't suppose words would do very much good."

Alexander met the old man's eyes. "No, Dr. Pearson," he said, "I don't believe they would."

Alone in her hospital room, Vivian had been trying to read a novel which her mother had brought, but her mind would not register the words. She sighed and put the book down. At this moment she wished desperately that she had not forced Mike into promising to stay away. She wondered: should she send for him? Her eyes went to the telephone; if she called he would come, probably within minutes. Did it really matter—this silly idea of hers of a few days' separation for them both to think things over? After all, they were in love; wasn't that enough? Should she call? Her hand wavered. She was on the point of picking up the receiver when her sense of purpose won out. No! She would wait. This was already the second day. The other three would go quickly, then she would have Mike to herself—for good and all.

In the house-staff common room, off duty for half an hour, Mike Seddons lay back in one of the deep leather armchairs. He was doing exactly what Vivian had told him—thinking of what it would be like living with a wife who had only one leg.

Twenty-three

It was early afternoon. Four days had gone by since the initial cases of typhoid in Three Counties Hospital had been reported.

Now, in the administrator's office, serious-faced and silent, Orden Brown, the board chairman, and Kent O'Donnell were listening to Harry Tomaselli speaking on the telephone.

"Yes," the administrator said, "I understand." There was a pause, then he continued, "If that becomes necessary we shall be ready with all arrangements. At five o'clock then. Good-by." He replaced the phone.

"Well?" Orden Brown asked impatiently.

"The City Health Department is giving us until this evening," Tomaselli said quietly. "If we've failed to locate the typhoid carrier by then we shall be required to close the kitchens."

"But do they realize what that means?" O'Donnell had risen to his feet, his voice agitated. "Don't they know it will practically have the same effect as closing the hospital. You've told them, haven't you, that we can't get outside catering for more than a handful of patients?"

Still quietly, Tomaselli said, "I've told them, but it doesn't make any difference. The trouble is, the public-health people are afraid of an outbreak in the city."

Orden Brown asked, "Is there any news at all from Pathology?"

"No." O'Donnell shook his head. "They're still working. I was in there half an hour ago."

"I can't understand it!" The board chairman was more disturbed than O'Donnell had ever seen him before. "Four days and ten typhoid cases right here in the hospital—four of them patients—and we still haven't come up with the source!"

"There's no question it's a big job for the lab," O'Donnell said, "and I'm sure they haven't wasted any time."

"No one's blaming anyone," Orden Brown snapped; "not at this stage anyway. But we're got to show some results."

"Joe Pearson told me they expect to be through with all

their cultures by midmorning tomorrow. If the typhoid carrier is among the food handlers, they'll have to have traced him by then." O'Donnell appealed to Tomaselli. "Can't you persuade the public-health people to hold off—at least until midday tomorrow?"

The administrator shook his head negatively. "I tried earlier. But they've given us four days already; they won't wait any longer. The city health officer was here again this morning, and he's returning at five o'clock. If there's nothing to report by then I'm afraid we'll have to accept their ruling."

"And meanwhile," Orden Brown asked, "what do you propose?"

"My department is already at work." Harry Tomaselli's voice held the sense of shock and unbelief that gripped them all. "We're proceeding on the assumption that we shall have to close down."

There was a silence, then the administrator asked, "Kent, could you come back here at five—to meet the health officer with me?"

"Yes," O'Donnell said glumly. "I suppose I should be here."

The tension in the lab was equaled only by the tiredness of the three men working there.

Dr. Joseph Pearson was haggard, his eye red-rimmed, and weariness written in the slowness of his movements. For the past four days and three nights he had remained at the hospital, snatching only a few hours of sleep on a cot which he had had moved into the pathology office. It was two days since he had shaved; his clothes were rumpled and his hair wild. Only for one period of several hours on the second day had he been missing from Pathology, with no one knowing where he had gone and Coleman unable to locate him despite several inquiries from the administrator and Kent O'Donnell. Subsequently Pearson had reappeared, offering no explanation for his absence, and had continued his supervision of the cultures and subcultures which occupied them still.

Now Pearson asked, "How many have we done?"

Dr. Coleman checked a list. "Eighty-nine," he said. "That leaves another five in incubation which we'll have tomorrow morning."

David Coleman, though appearing fresher than the senior pathologist, and with none of the outward signs of personal neglect which Pearson exhibited, was conscious of an oppressive weariness which made him wonder if his own endurance would last as long as the older man's. Unlike Pearson, Coleman had slept at his own apartment on each of the three nights, going there from the lab well after midnight and returning to the hospital around six the following morning.

Early as he had been, though, in arriving, only on one occasion had he preceded John Alexander, and then by a mere few minutes. The other times the young technologist had already been occupied at one of the lab benches, working—as he had since the beginning—like a precisely geared machine, his movements accurate and economic, his written record of each test stage painstakingly recorded in neat and legible lettering. Nor had it been necessary—after the initial start—to issue more instructions. Alexander was so obviuolsy competent and aware of what he was doing that Dr. Pearson, after inspecting his progress briefly, had nodded approval and from that point had left him entirely alone.

Turning from Coleman to Alexander, Pearson asked now, "What are your figures on the subcultures?"

Reading from notes, Alexander answered, "Of the eighty-nine plates checked, forty-two have been separated for subculturing, and two hundred and eighty subcultures planted."

Pearson calculated mentally. Half to himself he said, "That means another hundred and ten subcultures still to check, including tomorrow's batch."

Glancing across at John Alexander, David Coleman wondered what the younger man was feeling at this moment and whether the act of throwing himself so intensely into this endeavor was proving an outlet for at least some of his personal grief. It had been four days since the Alexander baby's death. In that time the original sense of shock and desolation which the young technologist had shown had disappeared, at any rate superficially. Coleman suspected, though, that John Alexander's emotions were still not far below the surface, and he had sensed something of their presence in Alexander's announced intention to enroll in medical school. It was a subject which David Coleman had not pursued so far, but he had resolved, as soon as this present crisis was over, to have a long talk with Alexander. There was a good deal of advice and guidance which Coleman could offer the younger man, based on his own experiences. Certainly, as Alexander had said, it would not be easy for him—particular-

ly financially—to give up a salaried job and become a student
once more, but there were certain guideposts Coleman could
point to and pitfalls which he might help Alexander to avoid.

The fourth member of the original lab team, Carl Bannister, was temporarily disqualified. The senior technician had
worked through three days and most of the nights, handling
routine lab work alone and assisting the others whenever he
could. This morning, however, his speech had been slurred
and he was so obviously near exhaustion that David Coleman, without consulting Pearson, had ordered him home.
Bannister had departed gratefully and without argument.

The preparatory work on the stool samples arriving in the
lab had gone on continuously. By the second day, however,
those samples which had been dealt with first had been in
incubation long enough for investigation. Once again Dr.
Pearson had divided his forces in order to keep the work
flowing, John Alexander and himself handling the new stage,
while David Coleman continued to deal with the remaining
stool samples still coming in.

Removed from the incubator, the pink-tinged surface of
the prepared petri dishes showed small, moist bacteria colonies where the tiny amounts of human feces had been added
the previous day. With every individual stool containing mil-
lions of bacteria, the next task was to separate those colonies
which were obviously harmless from those which must be
investigated further.

Pink-tinged colonies of bacteria were eliminated at once
as harboring no typhoid. Pale colonies, where typhoid
bacilli might conceivably lurk, had samples taken from them
for subculture in sugar tubes with liquid media. There were
ten sugar tubes to each original culture, each tube containing a different reagent. It was these reagents which, after
further incubation, would finally show which stool sample,
if any, contained the marauding and infectious typhoid germs.

Now, on the fourth day, all the stool samples were finally
in. They had been obtained from everyone on the hospital
staff involved in any way with the receiving, preparation, or
distribution of food, and the task of processing them would
continue until well into tomorrow. At the moment the 280
subcultures which John Alexander had referred to were dis-
tributed in racks around the lab and in incubators. But although on many of these the final checks were complete,

none so far had revealed the individual—the suspected typhoid carrier—whom, anxiously and diligently, they had been seeking day and night.

The telephone bell rang and Pearson, nearest to the lab wall phone, answered it. "Yes?" He listened, then said, "No; nothing yet. I keep telling you—I'll call as soon as we find anything." He replaced the instrument.

John Alexander, succumbing to a sudden tiredness, completed an entry on a data sheet, then dropped into a straight-back lab chair. Momentarily he closed his eyes with relief at his own sudden inactivity.

From alongside David Coleman said, "Why don't you take an hour or two off, John—maybe go upstairs and stay with your wife for a while?"

Alexander got to his feet again. He knew that if he remained seated too long he could easily fall asleep. "I'll do one more series," he said, "then I think I will."

Taking a rack of subcultures from the incubator, he collected a fresh data sheet and began to line up the ten sugar tubes he was about to check. Glancing at the lab wall clock, he noted with surprise that another day was running out. The time was ten minutes to five.

Kent O'Donnell replaced the telephone. Answering Harry Tomaselli's unspoken question, he said, "Joe Pearson says there's nothing new."

In the administrator's birch-paneled office there was a silence, both men bleakly aware of the implications of this latest lack of news. Both knew, too, that around them, outside the administration suite, the work of the hospital was grinding to a halt.

Since early afternoon the plan for contraction of patient service, devised by Harry Tomaselli several days earlier and now made necessary by the impending shutdown of the hospital kitchens, had been going steadily into effect. Commencing with breakfast tomorrow, one hundred meals for patients on regular diet would be prepared by two local restaurants, combining forces for the occasion, and would be delivered to the hospital for seriously ill patients who could not be moved. Of the remaining patients, as many as possible were being discharged to their homes, while others, for whom hospital care was still essential, were being transferred

to other institutions in and around Burlington, now mobiliz-
ing their own facilities to meet the emergency influx from
Three Counties.

An hour ago, knowing that the process of transfer would
have to continue far into the night, Harry Tomaselli had given
the order for evacuation to begin. Now a line of ambulances,
summoned by telephone from all available points, had begun
to assemble outside the emergency entrance. Meanwhile, in
the wards and private pavilion, nurses and doctors were
working briskly, moving patients from beds to stretchers and
wheel chairs in readiness for their unexpected journey. For
those with time for thinking it was a sad and somber moment. For the first time in its forty-year history Three Counties Hospital was turning the sick and the injured away from
its doors.

There was a light tap, and Orden Brown entered the administrator's office. He listened attentively while Harry
Tomaselli reported what had been done since their meeting
four hours earlier. At the end the board chairman asked,
"The city health authorities—have they been here again?"

"Not yet," Tomaselli answered. "We're expecting them
now."

Orden Brown said quietly, "Then if you don't mind, I'll
wait with you."

After a pause the board chairman turned to O'Donnell.
"Kent, this isn't important now, but I'll tell you while I think
of it. I've had a call from Eustace Swayne. When all this is
over he would like you to go and see him."

For an instant the effrontery of the request left O'Donnell
speechless. It was obvious why Eustace Swayne wanted to
talk with him; there could be only one reason—despite everything the old man intended to use his money and influence
in an attempt to intercede for his friend, Dr. Joseph Pearson.
After all that had happened over the past few days it seemed
unbelievable that such blindness and presumption could exist.
A boiling fury seethed within O'Donnell. He said explosively,
"To hell with Eustace Swayne and all his works!"

"May I remind you," Orden Brown said icily, "that you
happen to be speaking of a member of the hospital board.
Whatever your disagreements, he at least is entitled to be
treated with courtesy."

O'Donnell faced Orden Brown, his eyes blazing. Very
well, he thought, if this is the showdown, then let's have it.

I've finished with hospital politics—for good and as of now.

At the same moment a buzzer sounded on the administrator's desk. "Mr. Tomaselli," a girl's voice said on the intercom, "the public-health officers have just arrived."

It was three minutes to five.

As they had on a morning six weeks earlier—the day on which, as he realized now, Kent O'Donnell had received his first warning of impending disruption in the hospital—the chimes of the Church of the Redeemer announced the hour as the small group threaded its way through the corridors of Three Counties. Led by O'Donnell, it included Orden Brown, Harry Tomaselli, and Dr. Norbert Ford, city health officer of Burlington. Behind them were Mrs. Straughan, the chief dietitian, who had arrived at the administration suite as they were leaving, and a young assistant health officer whose name O'Donnell had missed in the flurry of introductions.

Now that his initial anger was over, the chief of surgery was relieved that the interruption of a few minutes ago had prevented what could have become a major quarrel between himself and Orden Brown. He realized that all of them, himself included, had become unnaturally tense over the past few days, and the board chairman had, after all, done no more than relay a message. O'Donnell's real quarrel was with Eustace Swayne, and he had already resolved to meet the old tycoon face to face as soon as this present business was over. Then, whatever overtures Swayne chose to make, O'Donnell planned to respond with plain, blunt words, no matter what the consequences might be.

It had been Kent O'Donnell's suggestion that the group should visit the pathology department. He had told the city health officer, "At least you'll see we're doing everything possible to trace the source of infection."

Dr. Ford had at first demurred. "There's been no suggestion that you're not, and I doubt if I could add anything to what your pathologists are doing," he had said. But at O'Donnell's insistence he had agreed to go, and now they were en route to the basement pathology lab.

John Alexander glanced up as the group entered, then continued with the sugar test he was carrying out. Pearson, on seeing O'Donnell and Orden Brown, moved forward to meet them, wiping both hands on his already soiled lab coat. At a signal from Harry Tomaselli, David Coleman followed him.

O'Donnell handled the introductions. As Pearson and Dr. Norbert Ford shook hands the health officer asked, "Have you come up with anything?"

"Not yet." Pearson gestured around the lab. "As you can see, we're still working."

O'Donnell said, "Joe, I thought you should know. Dr. Ford has ordered the closing of our kitchens."

"Today?" There was disbelief in Pearson's voice.

The health officer nodded gravely. "I'm afraid so."

"But you can't do that! It's ridiculous!" This was the old aggressive Pearson, his voice belligerent, eyes flashing behind the mask of tiredness. He stormed on, "Why, man alive, we'll be working all night, and every subculture will be finished by midday tomorrow. If there's a carrier, all the chances are we'll have learned who it is."

"I'm sorry." The health officer shook his head. "We can't take that chance."

"But closing the kitchens means closing the hospital." Pearson fumed. "Surely you can wait until morning—at least until then."

"I'm afraid not." Dr. Ford was polite but firm. "In any case, the decision is not entirely mine. The city simply cannot afford the possibility of a wider epidemic. At the moment your outbreak is within these walls, but at any point it could spread outside. It's that we're thinking of."

Harry Tomaselli put in, "We're serving the evening meal, Joe, and that will be the last. We're sending home all the patients we can and transferring most of the others."

There was silence. Pearson's face muscles were working. His deep-set, red-rimmed eyes seemed close to tears. His voice near a whisper, he said, "I never thought I'd see the day . . ."

As the group turned away O'Donnell added quietly, "To tell the truth, Joe, neither did I."

They had reached the door when John Alexander announced, "I have it."

As a unit the group turned. Pearson asked sharply, "You have what?"

"A definite typhoid." Alexander pointed to the row of sugar tubes on which he had been working.

"Let me see!" Almost at a run, Pearson crossed the lab. The others had turned back into the room.

Pearson looked at the row of tubes. Nervously his tongue touched his lips. If Alexander were right, this was the moment they had worked for. "Call off the list," he said.

John Alexander picked up a textbook open at a double page. It was a tabulated chart of biochemical reactions of bacteria in sugar tubes. Putting a finger on the column headed "Salmonella typhi," he prepared to read down.

Pearson picked up the first of the ten tubes. He called out, "Glucose."

Checking the list, Alexander answered, "Acid formation, but no gas."

Pearson nodded. He replaced the tube and selected a second. "Lactose."

"No acid, no gas," Alexander read.

"Right." A pause. "Dulcitol."

Again Alexander read, "No acid, no gas."

"Sucrose."

"No acid, no gas." Once more the correct reaction for typhoid bacilli. The tension in the room was mounting.

Pearson took another tube. "Mannitol."

"Acid formation, but no gas."

"Correct." Another. "Maltose."

"Acid, but no gas."

Pearson nodded. Six down, four to go. Now he said, "Xylose."

Once more Alexander read, "Acid, but no gas."

Seven.

"Arabinose."

John Alexander said, "Either acid but no gas or no reaction at all."

Pearson announced, "No reaction."

Eight. Two more.

"Rhamnose?"

"No reaction."

Pearson looked at the tube. He said softly, "No reaction." One to go.

From the last tube Pearson read, "Indole production."

"Negative," Alexander said, and replaced the book.

Pearson turned to the others. He said, "There's no question. This is the typhoid carrier."

"Who is it?" The administrator was first to ask.

Pearson turned over a petri dish. He read off, Number seventy-two."

David Coleman had already reached for a ledger. There was a list with entries in his own handwriting. He announced, "Charlotte Burgess."

"I know her!" Mrs. Straughan said quickly. "She works on the serving counter."

As if by instinct, all eyes swung to the clock. It was seven minutes after five.

Mrs. Straughan said urgently, "The dinner! They're beginning to serve the evening meal!"

"Let's get to the dining room fast!" As he spoke, Harry Tomaselli was already at the door.

On the hospital's second floor the nursing supervisor entered Vivian's room with a harassed air, glancing at the door number as she came in.

"Oh yes, you're Miss Loburton." She consulted a clip board and made a penciled notation. "You'll be transferred to the West Burlington Clinic."

Vivian asked, "When will it be, please?" She had already learned, earlier in the afternoon, of the impending move and the reason for it.

"The ambulances are very busy now," the supervisor said. "I expect it will be several hours—probably about nine o'clock tonight. Your own nurse will be in to help you with your things in plenty of time."

"Thank you," Vivian said.

Her mind back with the clip board, the supervisor nodded and went out.

This was the time, Vivian decided, to call Mike. Their five days of separation were not due to end until tomorrow, but neither of them had contemplated anything like this. Besides, she had already come to regret the whole idea of having a period of time apart; she saw it now as a stupid and unnecessary notion which she wished had never occurred to her.

Her hand went out for the bedside telephone, and this time there was no hesitation. When the operator answered Vivian said, "Dr. Michael Seddons, please."

"One moment."

There was a wait of several minutes, then the operator came on the line. "Dr. Seddons is away from the hospital with one of the transfer ambulances. Can someone else help?"

"No, thank you," Vivian said. "I'd like to leave a message though."

The operator asked, "Is this a medical matter?"

She hesitated. "Well, not really."

"We can only take urgent medical messages now. Will you make your call later, please." There was a click as the line went dead. Slowly Vivian replaced the telephone.

Outside in the hallway she could hear commotion and raised voices. She sensed an undercurrent of excitement; there was a sharp order given, then a clatter as an object fell to the floor, and someone laughed. It all sounded commonplace, and yet at this moment her mind clamored to share in it, to be a part of whatever was going on. Then her eyes fell to the bedclothes, to where the coverlet went flat at the point where her left leg ended. Suddenly, for the first time, Vivian felt fearfully and desperately alone.

"Oh, Mike!" she whispered. "Mike darling—wherever you are, please come to me soon!"

Nurse Penfield was about to enter the cafeteria when she saw the group bearing down toward her. She recognized the administrator and the chief of surgery. Behind them, her big breasts bouncing with the effort of keeping up, was Mrs. Straughan, the chief dietitian.

Passing through the cafeteria entrance, Harry Tomaselli slowed his pace. He told Mrs. Straughan, "I want this done quickly and quietly."

The dietitian nodded, and together they entered the kitchens through a service doorway.

O'Donnell beckoned Nurse Penfield. "Come with me, please. I'd like you to help us."

What happened next was done with swiftness and precision. One moment a middle-aged woman was serving at the cafeteria counter. The next, Mrs. Straughan had taken her arm and had steered her into the diet office at the rear. O'Donnell told the bewildered woman, "One moment, please," and motioned Nurse Penfield to remain with her.

"Take the food she was serving and incinerate it," he instructed Mrs. Straughan. "Get back any you can that's already been served. Remove any dishes she may have touched and boil them."

The chief dietitian went out to the serving counter. In a few minutes O'Donnell's instructions had been followed and the cafeteria line was moving once more. Only a few individuals closest to the scene were aware of what had occurred.

In the office at the rear O'Donnell told the woman kitchen worker, "Mrs. Burgess, I must ask you to regard yourself as a patient in the hospital." He added kindly, "Try not to be alarmed; everything will be explained to you."

To Nurse Penfield he said, "Take this patient to the isolation ward. She's to have contact with no one. I'll call Dr. Chandler and he'll issue instructions."

Gently Elaine Penfield led the frightened woman away.

Afterward Mrs. Straughan asked curiously, "What happens to her now, Dr. O.?"

"She'll be well looked after," O'Donnell said. "She'll stay in isolation, and the internists will study her for a while. Sometimes, you know, a typhoid carrier may have an infected gall bladder, and if that's the case she'll probably be operated on." He added, "There'll be follow-up checks, of course, on all the other people who have been affected. Harvey Chandler will see to that."

On the diet-office telephone Harry Tomaselli was telling an assistant, "That's what I said: cancel everything—transfers, discharges other than normal, catered meals, the whole works. And when you've done that you can call the admitting office." The administrator grinned across the desk at O'Donnell. "Tell them that Three Counties Hospital is back in business."

Tomaselli hung up the phone and accepted the cup of coffee which the chief dietitian had poured him from her private percolator.

"By the way, Mrs. Straughan," he said, "there hasn't been time to tell you before, but you're getting your new dishwashers. The board has approved the expenditure and the contract has been let. I expect the work will begin next week."

The dietitian nodded; obviously the information was something she had anticipated. Now her mind had moved ahead to other things. "There's something else I'd like to show you while you're here, Mr. T. I need my refrigerator enlarged."

She eyed the administrator sternly. "I hope this time it won't require an epidemic to prove my point."

The administrator sighed and rose to his feet. He asked O'Donnell, "Do *you* have any more problems today?"

"Not today," O'Donnell answered. "Tomorrow, though, there's one item of business I intend to deal with personally."

He was thinking of Eustace Swayne.

Twenty-four

David Coleman had not slept well. Through the night his thoughts had kept returning to Three Counties Hospital, its pathology department, and Dr. Joseph Pearson.

None of the events of the past few days had changed in the slightest degree Dr. Pearson's culpability in the death of the Alexander baby. Whatever his responsibility a week ago, it still remained the same. Nor had Coleman revised his own opinion that pathology at Three Counties was an administrative mess, bogged down by outdated concepts and handicapped by antiquated methods and equipment which should have been shaken loose long since.

And yet, uneasily over the past four days, David Coleman had found his feelings toward Pearson changing and moderating. Why? A week ago he had looked on Pearson as a near-senile incompetent, clinging to power beyond his time. Since then nothing tangible had happened to change that conviction. What reason was there, then, for his own uneasiness about it now?

It was true, of course, that the old man had handled the typhoid outbreak and its aftermath with a decision and competence that was perhaps a good deal better than Coleman could have managed himself. But was that so surprising? After all, experience counted for something; and the situation being what it was, it was understandable that Pearson should want to rise to it well.

But it was his own total view of Pearson that was less clear-cut, less firm. A week ago he had classified the old pathologist—whatever his achievements of the past—among the intellectual "havenots." Now David Coleman was no longer sure. He suspected that in time to come he would be unsure about a good deal more.

The sleeplessness had brought him early to the hospital, and it was a little after 8 A.M. when he entered the pathology office. Roger McNeil, the resident, was at Pearson's desk.

"Good morning," McNeil said. "You're the first. I guess the others are sleeping in."

David Coleman asked, "Did we get very far behind—with other work?"

"It isn't too bad," McNeil said. "There's quite a bit of non-urgent stuff, but I kept pace with all the rest." He added, "Seddons helped a lot. I've told him he should stick with pathology instead of going back to surgery."

Another thought had been troubling Coleman. He asked the resident, "That student nurse—the one who had the amputation. Has the leg been dissected yet?" He was remembering that this was the diagnosis on which Pearson and himself had differed.

"No." McNeil selected a case file from several on the desk. "Vivian Loburton," he read out, "that's the girl's name. It wasn't urgent, so I left it. The leg is still in the refrigerator. Do you want to do it yourself?"

"Yes," Coleman said. "I think I will."

He took the file and went to the autopsy-room annex. From the morgue refrigerator he obtained the leg and began to remove the gauze wrappings. Exposed, the flesh was cold and white, the blood coagulated where the limb had been severed halfway up the thigh. He felt for the area of tumor and encountered it at once—a hard lumpish mass on the medial side, just below the knee. Taking a knife, he cut down deeply, his interest mounting at what he saw.

The manservant took Kent O'Donnell's topcoat and hat, hanging them in a closet of the gloomy, lofty hallway. Looking about him, O'Donnell wondered why anyone—wealthy or not—would choose to live in such surroundings. Then he reflected that perhaps to someone like Eustace Swayne the gaunt spaciousness, the beamed and paneled opulence, the walls of cold chiseled stone, conveyed a feudal sense of power, linked through history to older days and places. O'Donnell speculated on what would happen to this house when the old man died. More than likely it would become a museum or an art gallery or perhaps merely stand empty and decay as so many of these places had. The notion that someone else would take it as a home seemed inconceivable. This was a place which, logic said, should close its doors at five until next morning. Then he remembered that within these austere walls Denise must have spent her childhood. He wondered if she had been happy here.

"Mr. Swayne is a little tired today, sir," the manservant said. "He asked if you would mind if he received you in his bedroom."

"I don't mind," O'Donnell said. It occurred to him that perhaps the bedroom might be an appropriate place for what he had to say. If Eustace Swayne had apoplexy as a result, at least there would be a handy place to lie him down. He followed the manservant up the wide, curved stairway, then down a corridor, their footsteps silenced by deep broadloom. At a heavy, studded door the man tapped lightly and lifted a wrought-iron latch. He ushered O'Donnell into the spacious room beyond.

At first O'Donnell failed to see Eustace Swayne. Instead his eyes were caught by a massive fireplace framing a roaring log fire. The heat from the fire was like an impact, the room almost unbearably hot on the already mild late-August morning. Then he saw Swayne, propped up by pillows in a huge four-poster bed, a monogrammed robe draped around his shoulders. As he approached O'Donnell noticed with shock how frail the old man had become since their last meeting—the night of the dinner with Orden Brown and Denise.

"Thank you for coming," Swayne said. His voice, too, was weaker than before. He motioned his visitor to a chair beside the bed.

As he seated himself O'Donnell said, "I heard you wanted to see me." In his own mind he was already revising some of the forthright statements which earlier he had planned to make. Nothing would change his own stand, of course, concerning Joe Pearson, but at least he could be gentle. O'Donnell had no wish now to tangle with this ailing old man; any contest between them would be too uneven.

"Joe Pearson has been to see me," Swayne said. "Three days ago, I think it was."

So that was where Pearson had been those missing hours when they were trying to locate him. "Yes," O'Donnell answered, "I imagined he would."

"He told me that he's leaving the hospital." The old man's voice sounded weary; there was no hint so far of the denunciation of O'Donnell which the chief of surgery had expected.

Curious about what was coming next, he answered, "Yes, that's true."

The old man was silent. Then he said, "I suppose there are some things no one can control." There was a trace of bitterness now. Or was it resignation? It was hard to be sure.

"I think there are," O'Donnell answered gently.

"When Joe Pearson came to see me," Eustace Swayne said, "he made two requests. The first was that my donation to the hospital building fund should have no stipulations attached. I have agreed."

There was a pause, O'Donnell silent, as the significance of the words sank in. The old man went on, "The second request was a personal one. You have an employee at the hospital—his name is Alexander, I believe."

"Yes," O'Donnell said wonderingly. "John Alexander—he's a laboratory technologist."

"They lost a child?"

O'Donnell nodded.

"Joe Pearson asked that I pay the boy's way through medical school. I can do it, of course—quite easily. Money at least has a few remaining uses." Swayne reached for a thick manila envelope which had been lying on the quilt. "I have already instructed my lawyers. There will be a fund—enough to take care of fees and for him and his wife to live comfortably. Afterward, if he chooses to specialize, there will be money for that too." The old man paused, as if tired by speaking. Then he continued, "What I have in mind now is something more permanent. Later there will be others—I suppose equally deserving. I would like the fund to continue and to be administered by the Three Counties' medical board. I shall insist on only one condition."

Eustace Swayne looked squarely at O'Donnell. He said defiantly, "The fund will be named the Joseph Pearson Medical Endowment. Do you object?"

Moved and ashamed, O'Donnell answered, "Sir, far from objecting, in my opinion it will be one of the finest things you have ever done."

"Please tell me the truth, Mike," Vivian said. "I want to know."

They faced each other—Vivian in the hospital bed, Mike Seddons standing, apprehensively, beside it.

It was their first meeting following their time apart. Last night, after cancellation of Vivian's transfer order, she had tried a second time to reach Mike by telephone, but without success. This morning he had come, without her calling, as they had arranged six days ago. Now her eyes searched his face, fear nudging her, instinct telling what her mind refused to know.

"Vivian," Mike said, and she could see him trembling, "I've got to talk to you."

There was no answer, only Vivian's steady gaze meeting his own. His lips were dry; he moistened them with his tongue. He knew that his face was flushed, felt his heart pounding. His instinct was to turn and run. Instead he stood, hesitating, groping for words which refused to come.

"I think I know what you want to say, Mike." Vivian's voice was flat; it seemed drained of emotion. "You don't want to marry me. I'd be a burden to you—now, like this."

"Oh, Vivian darling——"

"Don't, Mike!" she said. "Please don't!"

He said urgently, imploringly, "Please listen to me, Vivian —hear me out! It isn't that simple . . ." Again his speech faltered.

For three days he had sought the right words and phrases to meet this moment, yet knowing whatever form they took the effect would be the same. In the interval between their last meeting Mike Seddons had probed the inner chasms of his soul and conscience. What he had found there had left him with disgust and self-contempt, but he had emerged with truth. He knew with certainty that a marriage between himself and Vivian would never succeed—not because of her inadequacy, but through his own.

In moments of searching self-examination he had forced himself to consider situations the two of them might meet together. In a flood light of imagination he had seen them entering a crowded room—himself young, virile, unimpaired; but Vivian on his arm, moving slowly, awkwardly, perhaps with a cane, and only as an artificial limb allowed. He had seen himself dive through surf, or lie on a beach near-naked in the sun, but with Vivian dressed decorously, sharing none of it because a prothesis was ugly when exposed and, if removed, she would become a grotesque, immobile freak—an object for pitying or averted eyes.

And more than this.

Overcoming every reluctance and instinctive decency, he had let himself consider sex. He had pictured the scene at night, before bed. Would Vivian unstrap her synthetic leg alone, or would he help her? Could there be intimacies of undressing, knowing what lay beneath? And how would they make love—with the leg on or off? If on, how would it be— the hard, unyielding plastic pressing against his own urgent body? If off, how would the stump feel beneath him? Would there be fulfillment—in intercourse with a body no longer whole?

Mike Seddons sweated. He had plumbed the depths and found his own reflection.

Vivian said, "You needn't explain, Mike." This time her voice was choked.

"But I want to! I've got to! There are so many things we both have to think of." Now the words came quickly, tumbling out in an eager effort to make Vivian understand, to know the agony of mind he had suffered before coming here. Even at this moment he needed her understanding.

He started to say, "Look, Vivian. I've thought about it and you'll be better off . . ."

He found her eyes regarding him. He had never noticed before how steady and direct they were. "Please don't lie, Mike," she said. "I think you'd better go."

He knew it was no good. All that he wanted now was to get away from here, not to have to meet Vivian's eyes. But still he hesitated. He asked, "What will you do?"

"I really don't know. To tell you the truth, I haven't thought much about it." Vivian's voice was steady, but it betrayed the effort she was making. "Perhaps I'll go on in nursing, if they'll have me. Of course, I really don't know if I'm cured, and if I'm not, how long I've got. That's so, isn't it, Mike?"

He had the grace to lower his eyes.

At the doorway he looked back for the last time. "Goodby, Vivian," he said.

She tried to answer, but her self-control had been taxed too long.

From the second floor Mike Seddons used the stairway to reach Pathology. He entered the autopsy room and in the annex found David Coleman dissecting a leg. Seddons looked at the limb and saw it white and lifeless, the dark blood seeping out from Coleman's knife cuts. For an instant of horror he pictured it nylon-sheathed, a high-heeled sandal upon the foot. Then, with an awful fascination, he crossed the room and read the name in the open case file.

When he had done so, Mike Seddons went into the corridor and vomited against the wall.

"Oh, Dr. Coleman! Do come in."

Kent O'Donnell got up courteously from his office desk as the young pathologist entered the room. David Coleman had been cleaning up after the dissection when the message from the chief of surgery had reached him.

"Sit down, won't you?" O'Donnell held out an engraved gold case. "Cigarette?"

"Thank you." Coleman took a cigarette and accepted the light O'Donnell offered. He leaned back, relaxed, in one of the leather armchairs. An instinct told him that what was to follow would be a turning point in his life.

O'Donnell moved behind the desk to the office window. He stood with his back to it, the morning sun behind him. "I imagine you've heard," he said, "that Dr. Pearson has resigned."

"Yes, I'd heard." Coleman answered quietly, then to his own surprise he heard himself saying, "You know, of course, these past few days he hasn't spared himself. He's been here day and night."

"Yes, I know." O'Donnell regarded the glowing tip of his cigarette. "But it doesn't change anything. You realize that?"

Coleman knew that the chief of surgery was right. "No," he said, "I don't suppose it does."

"Joe has expressed a wish to leave at once," O'Donnell continued. "It means there will be an immediate vacancy here for a director of pathology. Shall you accept?"

For a second David Coleman hesitated. This was the thing he had coveted—a department of his own; freedom to reorganize, to mobilize the new aids of science, to practice good medicine, and to make pathology count as he knew it truly could. This was the cup he had sought. Kent O'Donnell had lifted it to his lips.

Then fear struck him. Suddenly he was appalled at the awesome responsibility he would have to hold. It occurred to him there would be no one senior to relieve him of decisions; the ultimate choice—the final diagnosis—would be his alone. Could he face it? Was he yet ready? He was still young; if he chose, he could continue as a second-in-command for several years more. After that there would be other openings—plenty of time to move ahead. Then he knew that there was no escaping, that this moment had been moving toward him since his own first arrival at Three Counties Hospital.

"Yes," he said. "If it's offered to me, I shall accept."

"I can tell you that it will be offered." O'Donnell smiled. He asked, "Would you tell me something?"

"If I can."

The chief of surgery paused. In his mind he was choosing the right phrases for the question he wanted to put. He sensed that what was to be said next would be important to them both. Finally he asked, "Will you tell me what your attitude is—to medicine and to this hospital?"

"It's hard to put into words," Coleman said.

"Will you try?"

David Coleman considered. It was true there were things he believed, but even to himself he had seldom expressed them. Now, perhaps, was a time for definition.

"I suppose the real thing," he said slowly, "is that all of us—physicians, the hospital, medical technology—exist only for one thing: for patients, for healing of the sick. I believe we forget this sometimes. I think we become absorbed in medicine, science, better hospitals; and we forget that all these things have only one reason for existence—people. People who need us, who come to medicine for help." He stopped. "I've put it clumsily."

"No," O'Donnell said. "You've put it very well." He had a sense of triumph and of hope. Instinct had not belied him; he had chosen well. He foresaw that the two of them—as chief of surgery and director of pathology—would be good together. They would go on and build and, with them, Three Counties would progress. Not all that they wrought would be perfect; it never was. There would be flaws and failures, but at least their aims were the same, their feelings shared. They would have to remain close; Coleman was younger than himself, and there were areas in which O'Donnell's greater experience could be of help. In these past few weeks the chief of surgery himself had learned a good deal. He had learned that zeal could lead to complacency as surely as indifference, and that disaster could be reached by many routes. But from now on he would fight complacency on every front, and Pathology, with young Dr. Coleman at its head, could be a stout right arm.

A thought occurred to him. He asked, "One more thing. How do you feel about Joe Pearson and the way he's leaving?"

"I'm not sure," David Coleman said. "I've been wishing I knew."

"It's not such a bad thing to be unsure sometimes. It takes us away from rigid thinking." O'Donnell smiled. "There are some things I think you should know though. I've been talking with some of the older men on staff; they've told me incidents, things I didn't know about." He paused. "Joe Pearson has done a great deal for this hospital in thirty-two years —things that are mostly forgotten now or that people like you and me don't always get to hear about. He started the blood bank, you know. It's strange to think of it, but there was a lot of opposition at the time. Then he worked for the formation of a tissue committee; I'm told a good many staff men fought him bitterly on that. But he got the committee and it did a lot to raise the standard of surgery here. Joe did some investigative work, too—on the cause and incidence of thyroid cancer. Most of it's generally accepted now, but few people remember that it came from Joe Pearson."

"I didn't know," Coleman said. "Thank you for telling me."

"Well, these things get forgotten. Joe brought a lot of new things into the lab, too—new tests, new equipment. Unfortunately there came a time when he didn't do new things any more. He let himself vegetate and get in a rut. It happens sometimes."

Suddenly Coleman thought of his own father, his strong suspicion that the sensitized blood which killed the Alexanders' child had stemmed from a transfusion his father had given years before—given without Rh typing, even though the dangers were already known to medicine.

"Yes," he said. "I suppose it does."

Both men had risen and moved to the door. As they went out O'Donnell said softly, "It's a good thing for all of us to have compassion. You see, you never know whether someday you'll need it yourself."

Lucy Grainger said, "Kent, you look tired."

It was early afternoon, and O'Donnell had paused in a main-floor corridor. Unnoticed, she had stopped beside him.

Dear Lucy, he thought—unchanged, warm and tender. Was it really less than a week ago that he had considered leaving Burlington and marrying Denise? At the moment it all seemed far away—a nostalgic interlude that now was nothing more. Here was where he belonged; in this place, for good or ill, was where his destiny lay.

He took her arm. "Lucy," he said, "let's meet soon. There's a lot we have to talk about."

"All right." She smiled with affection. "You may take me to dinner tomorrow."

Side by side, they moved on down the hallway, and it was somehow reassuring to have her beside him. He glanced sideways at her profile, and there came to him a sense of certainty that for both of them there was much that was good ahead. Perhaps it would take time to adjust, but in the end he knew they would find their future together.

Lucy was thinking: Dreams do come true; perhaps mine will—someday soon.

Dusk came early to Pathology. It was a price they paid for working in the hospital basement. Snapping lights on, David Coleman decided that one of his early projects would be to move the department to a better location. The day when pathologists were automatically relegated to the bowels of the hospital was over; light and air were as much requisites for them as for any other branch of medicine.

He entered the pathology office and found Pearson at his desk. The old man was emptying the contents of the drawers. He looked up as Coleman came in.

"It's a funny thing," he said, "how much junk you can accumulate in thirty-two years."

For a moment David Coleman watched. Then he said, "I'm sorry."

"Nothing to be sorry about." Pearson answered gruffly. He closed the last drawer and put papers in a case. "I hear you're getting a new job. Congratulations."

Coleman said, and meant it, "I wish it could have been some other way."

"Too late to worry now." He snapped the locks on the case and looked around. "Well, I guess that's everything. If you find anything else you can send it with my pension check."

"There's something I want to tell you," Coleman said.

"What's that?"

Coleman spoke carefully. "The student nurse—the one who had her leg amputated. I dissected the limb this morning. You were right. I was wrong. It was malignant. Osteogenic sarcoma without a doubt."

The old man paused. He gave the impression that his thoughts were far away. "I'm glad I didn't make a mistake," he said slowly, "about that anyway."

He picked up a topcoat and moved to the door. He seemed about to go, then turned back. Almost diffidently he asked, "Do you mind if I give you some advice?"

Coleman shook his head. "Please do."

"You're young," Pearson said. "You're full of spice and vinegar—that's good. You know your stuff too. You're up to date—you know things that I never did, never will now. Take my advice and try to keep it that way. It'll be tough to do; make no mistake about it." He waved toward the desk he had just vacated. "You'll sit in that chair and the phone will ring, and it'll be the administrator—talking about budgets. Next minute one of the lab staff will want to quit; and you'll have to smooth that out. And the doctors will come in, and they'll want this bit of information and that." The old man smiled thinly. "Then you'll get the salesman—the man with the unbreakable test tube and the burner that never goes out. And when you're through seeing him there'll be another and another and another. Until at the end of a day you'll wonder what happened to it and what you've accomplished, what you've achieved."

Pearson stopped and Coleman waited. He sensed that in his words the old pathologist was reliving a part of his own past. He went on, "That's the way the next day can go, and the next, and the one after that. Until you find a year has slipped by, and another, and another. And while you're doing all this you'll send other people on courses to hear about the new things in medicine—because you can't take time out to go yourself. And you'll quit investigation and research; and because you work so hard, you'll be tired at night, and you won't feel like reading textbooks. And then suddenly, one day, you'll find everything you knew is out of date. That's when it's too late to change."

Emotion-charged, the voice faltered. Pearson put a hand

on Coleman's arm. He said imploringly, "Listen to an old man who's been through it all, who made the mistake of falling behind. Don't let it happen to you! Lock yourself in a closet if you have to! Get away from the phone and the files and paper, and read and learn and listen and keep up to date! Then they can never touch you, never say, 'He's finished, all washed up; he belongs to yesterday.' Because you'll know as much as they do—and more. Because you'll have experience to go with it . . ."

The voice trailed off and Pearson turned away.

"I shall try to remember," Coleman said. He added gently, "I'll come with you to the door."

They climbed the stairs from Pathology, and on the hospital's main floor the bustle of early-evening activity was just beginning. A nurse passed them hurriedly; she carried a diet tray, her starched uniform swishing. They moved aside to let a wheel chair by; in it was a middle-aged man, one leg in a cast, holding a pair of crutches like oars withdrawn into a boat. A trio of student nurses went past laughing. A Women's Auxiliary worker propelled a cart with magazines. A man clutching a bouquet of flowers headed for the elevators. Somewhere out of sight a child was crying. It was the hospital world: a living organism, a mirror of the greater world outside.

Pearson was looking around him. Coleman thought: Thirty-two years, and he's seeing it all, perhaps for the last time. He wondered: How will it be when my own time comes? Shall I remember this moment thirty years from now? Will I understand it better then?

On the public-address system a voice announced, "Dr. David Coleman. Dr. Coleman to the surgical floor."

"It's started," Pearson said. "It'll be a frozen section—you'd better go." He held out his hand. "Good luck."

Coleman found it hard to speak. "Thank you," he said.

The old man nodded and turned away.

"Good night, Dr. Pearson." It was one of the senior nurses.

"Good night," Pearson said. Then, on the way out, he stopped under a "No Smoking" sign to light a cigar.